# Also by Elle Kennedy

**Prep**

*Misfit*

*Rogue*

**Briar U**

*The Chase*

*The Risk*

*The Play*

*The Dare*

**Off-Campus**

*The Deal*

*The Mistake*

*The Score*

*The Goal*

*The Legacy*

**Campus Diaries**

*The Graham Effect*

*The Dixon Rule*

*The Charlie Method*

ELLE
KENNEDY

Bloom books

Please note: Content warnings for this book may contain spoilers. Flip to the back of the book or visit ellekennedy.com/love-song to learn more.


Cover design by Hannah DiPietro/Sourcebooks
Cover art © Katie Smith
Internal design by Cat at TRC Designs
Internal images © alexdndz/Shutterstock, Kaleo/Shutterstock, 1Arts/Shutterstock, Sntpzh/Depositphotos, collsebastian@hotmail.com/Depositphotos, JavidH/Depositphotos, thipftisland/Depositphotos, stockgiu/Depositphotos, vovan13/Depositphotos



Published by Bloom Books, an imprint of Sourcebooks
1935 Brookdale RD, Naperville, IL 60563-2773
(630) 961-3900
sourcebooks.com

Cataloging-in-Publication Data is on file with the Library of Congress.

Printed and bound in the United States of America.
POD

*To everyone who feels a little lost in life—your song isn't over.*

# Prologue

## BLAKE

*Fuckboy till he dies*

**TWO YEARS AGO**

WYATT GRAHAM IS STARING AT me.

It's taken my brain and me several twists and turns to reach this conclusion.

At first, we were convinced he was staring at the oil painting above my head, the weird one depicting his father playing hockey on a rink of lava. Wyatt's twin, Gigi, said it was a gift from their eccentric elderly neighbor, and their dad felt too guilty not hanging it up.

Next, we decided I must have something stuck in my teeth (I don't. I checked), chocolate all over my face from dessert (I don't, also checked), or a huge zit that sprang up after I applied my makeup before dinner (no zits, only obnoxious freckles).

Until finally, we came around to the idea that the hottest man to ever walk this earth is indeed staring at me.

Which raises the question—*why*?

Considering Wyatt views a romantic connection between us as tragically hysterical, I'm genuinely stumped as to why his eyes are following my every move tonight.

As we've done every year since I was born, we're spending Christmas Eve with the Grahams in their beautiful house just outside Boston. It's a tradition. My dad and the twins' dad have been best friends since college and are obsessed with each other, so our families spend most holidays together.

The game room smells like cinnamon from the gingerbread cookies Gigi's mom was baking all day and is lit only by the glow of the fixture over the pool table, which Gigi and Luke Ryder are currently circling. Wyatt leans against the wall, his hand curled lazily around a beer bottle. When he chuckles at the taunt Gigi tosses her husband's way, a little shiver rolls up my spine. Even his laughter gives off a dangerous energy. Wyatt Graham has always been hazardous to my heart rate.

If I wasn't still riding the buzz from the red wine my dad had been too distracted to cut off, I probably wouldn't be openly ogling the guy. But it's impossible not to stare at those veiled green eyes and perfectly chiseled features, just a hint of scruff on his strong jaw. His shirt is unbuttoned to reveal a tight white tank that emphasizes his broad chest, and when he rakes a hand through his messy brown hair, the silver ring on his middle finger catches the light. He wears a few other rings too, including a chunky black one that sort of looks like a wedding band. Hilarious, because Wyatt's never getting married. *Fuckboy till he dies*, Gigi always says.

"Speaking of playing hard to get," Gigi calls, glancing my way.

I snap out of my thoughts, clueless about their conversation and how it got to me.

"What?" I say.

"Diana told me Isaac asked you to be his girlfriend, and you told him you'd—" She snorts, air quoting me. "'Take it under consideration.'"

Ryder gives a soft chuckle while Wyatt sips his beer and watches us.

"Yeah." I shrug. "I still don't know how I feel about it."

"You've been dating for two months," she reminds me, her gray eyes twinkling. "Seems like you should know by now if you like the guy."

She's not wrong. I *should* know. And it's not that I don't like Isaac. He's been pursuing me hard all semester. Or, if you listen to my father, "love bombing" me. Isaac comes on strong, no doubt, but I don't believe he's a walking red flag the way my father has declared.

The problem is I'm not sure I can picture us long-term. Isaac is outgoing, goofy, and attention-seeking. I'm sarcastic, a lot more chill, and not looking for the spotlight. I'm good spending the whole day listening to a podcast or reading a book; he's wired to constantly be doing something exciting. Not to mention he's going to the NFL the moment he graduates from Briar University. I know how flashy the NFL lifestyle can be. The money, the women, the attention. That's not me.

Still, the phrase *opposites attract* didn't materialize out of nowhere. Might be a cliché, sure, but it's statistically proven that opposites do attract. Sometimes they complement each other. Other times, those relationships explode in a spectacular fashion.

I don't know yet which kind of opposites Isaac and I are.

"You're taking way too long to respond," Gigi informs me, grinning. "This poor guy."

"Is this the football player?" Ryder asks as he leans over the table to line up his shot.

"Yeah," Gigi answers for me. "Isaac Grant. He was the resident campus man-whore before our Blakey brought him to his knees." She's the only one I let get away with calling me *Blakey*. Anyone else would get murdered.

"I do have that effect on men," I say, more joking than serious, but I don't miss the way Wyatt's gaze rests on me again. Every time I glance his way, he's already watching.

Why is he staring? My brain and I are now revisiting the idea that there's broccoli jammed between my teeth. Except that would mean he has a broccoli kink, because the way he's looking at me says *turn-on* and not *gross*. Which is inconceivable to me given what happened on New Year's Eve two years ago.

My mind suddenly flashes back to that god-awful night. The living nightmare I experienced, a tomato-faced, trembling sixteen-year-old, drunk on one glass of champagne, blurting out to Wyatt that I had a crush on him.

And...

He laughed.

I confessed to my crush, and he *laughed.*

Granted, it wasn't in a *ha ha, everyone point at Blake Logan and laugh at how pathetic she is* way. There was no cruelty in his tone. It was more of a nervous laugh, yet it was a hot, sharp knife to the heart. To add insult to injury, he ruffled my hair as he rose from the couch.

He ruffled.

My hair.

And then? The final stab to my mangled, bloody, shredded-to-ribbons heart?

"Probably best to get over that, kid," he said.

*Kid.*

Part of me died from embarrassment that night. I never brought it up again. Neither did Wyatt.

And now here we are. I'm eighteen, certainly not a kid anymore. And certainly not imagining the heat in his gaze.

I hastily sip my wine and watch Gigi and Ryder finish out their billiards battle. Wyatt doesn't say a single word to me. He spends most of the game mocking Ryder.

"Eight ball, corner pocket," Ryder says.

"Well, that's ambitious of you, Bill," Wyatt remarks.

"Confident," Ryder returns, then executes the shot to perfection. He lifts his head to smirk at Wyatt. "Anything else to add, Bill?"

"Bill?" I echo blankly, and Wyatt's head finally shifts toward me.

Gigi answers for the boys. "BIL as in brother-in-law. It's their nickname for each other. They think they're being cute."

Ryder racks the balls, and we play another game, this time girls against boys. I blow nearly every shot, because it turns out it's hard to shoot pool when a tall, sexy, intense musician is hyperfixated on you.

Hours later, the house is dead silent, everyone asleep but me. I lie on my bed in the guest room, my restless thoughts drifting back to Wyatt and Isaac and men in general. Whenever I close my eyes, I see Wyatt's deep green eyes tracking me like I'm the only person in the house.

Eventually, I give up on sleep and go downstairs to the kitchen, not bothering to look decent. I'm barefoot and in my underwear and an oversize sweater that barely covers my upper thighs.

I've just finished pouring a glass of water at the fridge when I hear his voice.

"Can't sleep?"

I jump, nearly dropping my glass. Water sloshes over the rim and spills onto my knuckles. "Jesus. You scared me."

I turn to find him standing in the shadows, leaning against the doorframe. A bottle of beer dangles from his fingers, and his hair is even messier than it was two hours ago. He's definitely feeling the alcohol, his gaze more than a little hazy. He looks...dangerous. Tired, drunk, and beautiful.

"Sorry," he says, then takes a swig of beer.

"You can't sleep either?" I sip my water, watching him. "Is your mind also racing?"

Wyatt shrugs. "I never sleep."

"Vampire?"

"Obviously."

With a hint of a smile, he steps into the kitchen, his face illuminated by only the strip of lights running beneath the cabinets. Then he tips his head back and drinks more beer.

"Drinking alone, are we?" I try to sound casual despite my thundering pulse.

"Just a nightcap." He takes another sip, his gaze flicking down my legs and back up again, so blatant it triggers a ripple of heat up my neck.

I set my water glass on the counter, determined not to let him see me blush.

"Why's your mind racing?" he asks.

"I don't know," I lie.

"You thinking about that guy? The football player who asked you to be his girlfriend?"

I hesitate. "Yeah."

He moves closer, propping a hip against the counter. "You don't want to say yes."

"I… He's really into me. And he's sweet."

"Sweet," Wyatt echoes, like the word bores him. "That's not an answer."

I'm utterly aware of how close he's standing. How his voice has dropped just enough to feel like it's sliding under my skin.

"I don't know if I want a relationship with Isaac," I confess. "He's not… I don't know…serious, I guess. Everything's kind of surface level with him."

Wyatt's mouth curves in an infuriating little smirk. "How's the sex?"

My cheeks are burning. "It's... We haven't..." I'm flustered. Ugh. I never get flustered. I hate that Wyatt Graham brings out that side of me. "We haven't slept together yet. But we've done other stuff."

"Okay. How's the other stuff?" He laughs suddenly. "You know what? Don't bother answering. If you were satisfied with the football player, you wouldn't have been eye-fucking me all night."

My mouth drops open. "Excuse me?"

"What?" He grins, swallowing another swig. "Am I wrong?"

"I was *not* doing that."

"Yes. You were." He licks a drop of beer off his bottom lip, raking that hot gaze over me. Slow and deliberate.

I hate how my heart races just from him looking at me like that. "*You're* the one who was staring at me all night." I lift my chin in challenge. "Why?"

He goes quiet. I assume he's not going to answer or that he'll throw out a dismissive response, but he surprises me by saying, "I don't know."

My heart flips.

"But I can't seem to stop," he finishes, his voice dropping another octave.

He moves toward me, his hip trailing over the counter as he gets nearer.

I swallow, only to find that my throat is a desert.

"Blake," he mutters.

"Hmm?" I tilt my face up to his, my pulse skittering.

His eyes lower to my mouth. The tension between us is palpable. I'm practically inhaling it. How is this happening? Since when does Wyatt Graham look at me like he wants to kiss me?

And since when does he reach out and cup my cheek?

And lower his head?

And—

Without warning, his lips brush the side of my neck.

It's a featherlight caress, a whisper of a graze, but I can scarcely breathe. I don't want to make a sound or move a muscle for fear that he'll stop.

His hand slides up, long fingers skimming my waist over my sweater. As I stand there frozen with desire, he kisses his way up to my ear, unleashing goose bumps everywhere his mouth touches. His breath is hot over the lobe as my name once again breaks on his lips.

"Blake..."

I force myself to speak, even if it means breaking the spell. "What are you doing?"

"Don't fucking know," he mumbles against my cheek. "Want me to stop?"

"No," I whisper.

The stubble on his chin tickles my jaw, and I tilt my face, desperate for a real kiss, but he denies me. Instead, those hungry lips find my neck again, and I gasp when he suddenly lifts me up on the counter. My ass collides with granite, and then I'm locked in by both his arms, his biceps straining as he hovers over me.

Slowly...achingly slowly...he starts to lower me backward.

My hands instinctively loop around his neck, and heat flares in his eyes when my nails dig into his skin.

He smells so good. I don't know what that scent is, but I'm desperate to breathe it in. Something a bit spicy, a little smoky, and entirely masculine. His lips are mere inches away. God, I want to kiss him more than I want my next breath.

"This..." He buries his face in the crook of my neck again. "Is a fucking bad idea."

He's right. We're on the kitchen counter in his parents' house. At any moment, someone could come downstairs and catch us.

But I couldn't stop this if I tried.

His tongue travels up my neck at the same time as he parts my thighs and steps between them. He presses himself against me, and I whimper at the feel of his long, thick erection straining inside his jeans.

"Are you turned on?" His voice is a low tease at my ear, and his hands are gripping my waist now, slowly dragging my lower body toward his.

"Mm-hmm," I manage to get out.

"You wet for me?" Breathing hard, Wyatt rolls his hips and grinds against my throbbing core.

I'm shocked by how fast the pleasure builds. How natural it feels to wrap my legs around him and rock my hips to meet his thrusts. And yes, I *am* wet for him. I'm soaked. Desperate to tear off my underwear, rip off his jeans, and pull him inside my body. As I claw at his zipper, he grinds harder, and I'm momentarily distracted by the jolt of pleasure that ripples through my clit.

Oh fuck, I'm close to coming.

I tighten my legs around him, straining for deeper contact, for relief, for anything that will ease the relentless ache between my legs.

When his thick erection slides over my clit again, a desperate, throaty moan slips out, loud enough to wake a person or six.

And to finally break the spell.

He abruptly lifts his head, and now he's peering down at me, eyes wild and hazy. As if realizing what he's doing, he stumbles backward.

I instantly grieve the loss of his body heat, the wisps of impending orgasm dissipating like a cloud of steam.

"Jesus," he mutters. "Go to bed, Blake. Please."

My lips are still tingling, aching for the kiss that almost happened.

My body continues to tremble from his chest caging me on the counter and his hard dick pressed up on me.

I stare at him, my heart pounding so hard it hurts. "I don't want to go to bed."

Wyatt's eyelids close for a second, then blink open as he drags a hand through his hair. "Then I will."

Disappointment crashes down on me as I watch him disappear up the stairs. He doesn't look back. Not even once.

I don't sleep a wink. I'm too riled up. Too turned on. Too angry. Too confused.

Too everything.

I'm not the kind of girl who likes drama. If I was, I would've already agreed to be Isaac's girlfriend; he's as melodramatic and over-the-top as they come. Me, I've made it a point in my life to be as drama-free as possible, which is why Wyatt's erratic and unpredictable behavior last night grates so much.

Why the hell did he mess with my head like that?

Although I'm up at dawn, I force myself to remain in bed until a less obscene time, finally heading downstairs around 6:45. Everyone else is still asleep. I don't hear any whispered voices. No soft footsteps. So I'm startled when I enter the kitchen to find Wyatt drinking a coffee at the counter.

The same counter where he dry humped me into oblivion last night.

"Morning," he says.

His tone is...normal. No awkwardness. Not a trace of tension.

"Morning," I reply.

"Coffee's fresh." Wyatt nods toward the counter.

I hide my frown as I walk to the coffee maker. "Did you sleep at all?"

"Not really." He watches me, casually sipping his coffee like he hadn't set me on fire a mere six hours ago.

Silence descends over the kitchen. I grab a mug from the cupboard. Wyatt says nothing as I pour, as I observe him over the rim of the mug.

Seconds tick by. The silence drags on.

Finally, I can't take it anymore.

"Are we not going to talk about last night?"

A wrinkle appears in his brow. "What do you mean?"

I stare at him. "Do you not remember what happened?"

Wyatt gives me a blank look that makes my stomach sink. "I was pretty gone," he admits, scratching the back of his neck. "Did I do something stupid?"

I search his face for even a flicker of memory, but all I see is blank curiosity. "You don't remember *anything*?"

"No. I was wasted." He studies my expression. "Shit. Was I an asshole to you? What did I say?"

The knot in my chest tightens. He really doesn't remember.

"No," I say, forcing a shrug. "You weren't a total ass. Just made a couple comments about Isaac and our relationship."

He smiles faintly. "Sorry. I was probably just looking out for you."

Then, in that maddeningly big-brother way he'd done two years ago, he reaches out and ruffles my hair.

"Don't listen to me, kid. I don't know shit about love." Wyatt shrugs. "You should give your football player a chance. Seems like he genuinely likes you."

My cheeks are scorching. I don't know whether to be mortified or furious. "Yeah. Sure. Thanks, Wyatt. Maybe I will."

# Chapter 1

## BLAKE

*Bitten by a gator in a sandpit*

**PRESENT DAY**

AIRPORTS WERE CREATED BY THE devil to test humanity.

Truly, I cannot think of a more dehumanizing experience. Doesn't even matter if you're arriving or departing—you're herded into lines like the vile cattle you are, crammed into holding pens disguised as gates, and forced to beg for scraps of seating and water that doesn't cost twenty-six dollars.

All this is to say: I'm ready to murder someone by the time a staticky voice over the PA announces that after an unfortunate *forty-two-minute* delay, our bags are finally being unloaded from the plane. So please be patient, folks. The conveyer belt will belch out those bags any minute now. We promise.

It's official. I live in Logan Airport now. I'm never leaving.

When I was a kid, my dad told me this airport was named after him. Even worse, he kept the lie going for so long that I used this fraudulent information as a "fun fact" about myself during a sixth-grade presentation. "Logan Airport is named after my dad, the famous hockey player," I bragged to the class, at which point my teacher chided, "This is untrue. We don't tell lies in this classroom, Blake," and I went home crying.

Speaking of my father, he calls while I'm waiting at baggage claim with the rest of the cattle.

"Hey, Dad." I scan the carousel, which is finally spitting out the first few bags. I flew business class, so my suitcase should be coming out first. Theoretically. This airport has already fucked me once tonight.

"Hey, sweet pea. You still at the airport?"

"Yep." I already texted him the second we landed, but I knew that wouldn't be enough to satisfy him. He needs to hear my voice. Otherwise he assumes the plane crashed in the Atlantic and my "just landed!" message was a prescheduled text or a glitch in the phone matrix.

Did I mention my father is a wee bit overprotective?

"I wish you let me pick you up," Dad grumbles.

"My car's at the airport. Long-term parking, remember?"

A man steps forward and jostles me hard as he tries to find his bag. I glare at his back because he's, like, eight feet tall, and now I can't see the carousel at all.

"Do you want to come home for dinner tomorrow night?"

"Maybe," I say absently. "I'll see what Isaac's thinking."

There's a pause.

There's always a pause.

That's what happens when your father can't stand your boyfriend.

"I mean, if he's busy, *you* can still come," Dad says in a hopeful tone.

"Don't sound too excited about the prospect of me coming alone."

"Look, kiddo, it's not that I don't like him—"

"You hate him," I cut in.

"I don't hate him. I just don't like him."

I choke on my laughter and sidestep the giant in front of me. Peering at the emerging suitcases and duffels, I finally catch a glimpse of red. I always tie a bright hair scrunchie around the handle of my black suitcase.

"Dad, I see my bag. I'm hanging up now."

I disconnect before he can argue and elbow my way through the waiting travelers. I might be small, but dating a football player has taught me some tricks. I don't even apologize to the guy who squawks in outrage when my arm connects with his ribs. His fault for not moving when I said, "'Scuse me."

I grab my suitcase, and from there it's a short trip to the parking level. Five minutes later, I'm leaving the airport garage behind the wheel of my Land Rover. Well, Isaac's. He has two cars, so he lets me drive the SUV while he always takes the Porsche.

My father, of course, thinks Isaac's passion for cars is super fucked up and a sign of psychopathy. This coming from a mechanic's son who can rebuild an engine without batting an eye. Because when *he's* into cars, it's a totally normal, healthy hobby.

But when Isaac Grant likes cars? I'm about to be the subject of a true-crime documentary.

A least my mother doesn't overtly hate the man I'm living with. *Overtly* being the operative word. I sense she doesn't love him either, but she'll never say it out loud. Mom has way more tact than that.

Still no text from Isaac, I realize. That's unusual. My dad and his little man gang refer to Isaac as the "Love Bomber." Even now, after we've been together for two and a half years, living together for one, they refuse to give him a chance. At this point, I think Dad and his hockey buddies just hate Isaac because he plays football. With that said—and I'm *not* conceding that my boyfriend is a love bomber—Isaac does blow up my phone constantly. I've been in Paris for the past two weeks, and even with the time difference, he was texting me all the time.

Tonight, he ignored my just-landed text *and* the on-my-way-home one I just sent.

A prickly sensation tightens my stomach as I glance at my phone. It lights up the moment I check, but my burst of relief fades into annoyance when I see it's my dad.

Shocking.

"You need help," I say in lieu of hello. I turn onto the highway ramp. "Like, serious help. We need to get you in therapy."

"You hung up on me," he accuses.

"Yes, because I'm busy."

"Are you on your way to that fancy building of yours?"

"It's not that fancy," I object.

To be fair, it is. Isaac wasted no time spending his NFL signing bonus. I'm proud of him, though, and I have no doubt he'll have a hell of a rookie season this fall. At Briar, he was the star of the team, helping them win three national championships, and he was named MVP three years in a row.

"It's just you're not a building person," Dad is saying. "You love houses. And porches. Nice, big, wraparound porches where you can sit on a wicker chair and read. Where do you even read, Blake? Is he depriving you of reading?"

"Oh my God, stop. And guess what, Dad? I love houses, but I'm also fine with condos. And even if I wasn't, sometimes you need to make compromises in relationships, right?"

"Oh really? Did *he* compromise? You still have a year left of college. He couldn't even be bothered to find something in the middle? When I played for Providence and your mom was still at Briar, we found a place between Hastings and Boston. Meanwhile, the love bomber makes you commute an hour and a half to school?" Dad grumbles in displeasure.

Truth be told, that did irk a little. Since Isaac was able to graduate a semester early, he convinced me to break our Hastings lease and move to Boston where he could be closer to his new team and have access to better training facilities. He starts training camp in a few months, and he's determined to excel. And he was *so* excited about this condo. It's difficult to say no to Isaac when he's looking at you with those pleading little-boy eyes.

Still, I refuse to give my dad the satisfaction of being right.

"It's fine. I don't mind the commute, actually. I got some of my textbooks on audio, so I'm able to study as I drive."

"You will always defend this potato, won't you?"

I choke out a laugh. "He's not a potato!"

"Good point. I like potatoes."

"Dad," I warn.

"Fine. I'm gonna let this go."

"No, you won't. You'll just bitch about him the next time we talk. Anyway, I'm going now. Tell Mom I said hi and I'll text her later."

The rest of the drive is blessedly quiet. Except, damn it, it's back. The uneasy churning in my gut. A humming noise in my body urging me to turn around, have dinner with my parents, don't go to the fancy high-rise near Beacon Hill.

I once read about a lady down in Florida who ignored her sixth sense. She wrote a whole memoir about it. She claims that on a regular old Sunday morning, every cell in her body was telling her not to take her kids to the playground that day, but she ignored the humming, prickling, buzzing sensations in her stomach.

Moral of the story? If you don't listen to your internal warning system, you're going to get bitten by a gator in a sandpit.

But that probably won't happen to me tonight.

I scan my key to get into the underground of our building, then ride the elevator up to the twenty-third floor, juggling my purse and carting my luggage behind me. As I walk down the carpeted hallway toward my front door, the little hairs on the back of my neck are standing on edge. Something feels off, but I can't for the life of me figure out what.

I've never been insecure about our relationship. Yes, Isaac attracts attention wherever he goes and is about to be an NFL star, but I never worried he might get bored of me. He's infatuated with me, and he's been a good boyfriend. It didn't even occur to me that he might stray.

And yet as I approach my door, with my phone too silent from Isaac's lack of texts, I'm envisioning a trail of clothing from the front hall to our bedroom.

A discarded bra, a thong, his boxers…

*You're acting crazy*, a voice informs me.

I totally am. If he was cheating on me, there's no way he would have someone in there right now. I'm not surprising him by coming home early. He *knew* I was due home tonight. He told me to have a safe flight eight hours ago, then chided me when I told him that's sort of up to the pilot and beyond my control. Isaac isn't exactly in love with my dry humor, though I suspect that's mostly because it usually goes over his head.

I turn the key in the lock and enter the condo. Despite myself, my gaze drops to the polished floor. No underwear trail. That's a good sign.

"Babe?" I call.

No response. But his shoes are in the hall. His keys and his wallet are on the kitchen counter. I wander deeper into the apartment toward our bedroom, still battling that anxious feeling. I feel crazy.

The door is ajar. Slowly, I nudge it open.

He's on his side, one long leg thrust out from the twisted sheet. I focus briefly on his muscular thigh before my gaze trails upward to his sculpted bicep. His arm is slung around his pillow, which he's holding tight to his chest, the way he usually holds me when we fall asleep together.

Relief hits me, a smile tugging on my lips.

He's sound asleep in our bed.

Alone.

Did I mention he's alone?

Now I feel like a total asshole for even thinking he might not be.

I pause in the doorway, admiring him. The sunlight streaming in through the blinds is casting a golden glow over the golden god in my bed. Make that *ginger* god. Isaac vehemently denies it when you point out he has red hair, but insisting your hair is "blond with a splash of strawberry" doesn't make it so.

A soft groan comes from the bed. He shifts slightly. I hate interrupting his nap, but I've been gone for two weeks, and I missed him.

I sit at the edge of the bed and gently run my fingers over his reddish-brown beard. He hasn't shaved in several days.

"Hey," I say softly. I bend down, brushing my lips over his forehead.

He stirs, eyelids fluttering. He twitches for a second, and then his eyes slowly slide open. A happy smile curves his lips. "Babe," he says. "You're here."

My heart skips a beat at his jubilant tone. "I'm here."

He blinks a couple times. "Oh shit. Sorry. I was asleep. I wanted to get in a quick nap after dinner so I could stay up late and worship you."

I grin. "Conserving your strength for the worshipping. I approve."

"How was the flight?"

"It was good."

He tugs me toward him and wraps his arms around me, then starts planting kisses all over my neck and face until I'm laughing.

"Really missed you," Isaac mumbles against my cheek.

"I missed you too."

Our lips find each other at the same time as my phone vibrates in my pocket. He feels it against his thigh and snickers.

"Babe, let's save the sex toys for after dinner?"

With a snort, I pull out my phone, not to check it but to put it on silent. It won't stop buzzing, and it's annoying me.

"Let me guess," Isaac says, sighing. "Daddy?"

"No, he already called earlier. Twice."

My boyfriend's face becomes stricken. "Shit, you didn't tell him I didn't pick you up from the airport, did you?"

"Yes. Why?"

Isaac groans in response. "Blake!"

"What? It's not a big deal. Made more sense for me to park."

"Yeah, but *he* won't see it that way. Fucking hell, babe, now he has another thing to hold against me."

I swallow my own groan. Isaac's desperate need to win my father's approval has been a point of contention throughout our entire relationship. Not just Dad's approval but anyone's, really. Isaac isn't happy unless he's being adored by the masses. Not the most attractive quality in a man, and it would probably bother me a lot more if it weren't for the fact that Isaac adores as hard as he craves adoration.

"My dad is just grumpy because you play football and not hockey," I reassure him. "It has nothing to do with your personality. Deep down, he knows you're amazing."

"Fine," Isaac huffs, then reaches for me again. "But now you owe me a make-out session to lift my spirits."

When my phone vibrates again, I lean forward to put it away, but as

I'm setting it on the nightstand, I catch a glimpse of the notification on the screen. It's a message from Gigi, but I can only see the beginning of it.

GIGI

I'm so sorry, Blakey. Are—

I frown. She's sorry? About what?

"Wait," I say when Isaac presses his lips to my neck again. "Hold on, sorry. This actually looks important."

I swipe to open the notification and discover not just one message but a bunch of them.

GIGI

Have you seen this?? Alex just sent it to me.

Maybe it's a deep fake or something?

OK did some digging. It's legit. The girl says it's real. She just released an official statement.

I'm so sorry, Blakey. Are you okay?

"What is it?" Isaac asks, an impatient note in his voice.

This time, I can't ignore the fluttery sensation in my stomach. Or the chill that sweeps through my body. Slowly, I ease away from him.

"Babe?" he presses.

I click the link Gigi included in her first message. When it pops up, I don't bother to hit Play.

The title is bad enough.

**Leaked SEX Tape: Pats prospect and cheerleader CAUGHT in explicit viral video!**

## DAD CHAT

JOHN LOGAN

*Hypothetically.* If one were to "remove" the cheating potato who broke their daughter's heart, how could one do it without leaving a trace? Asking for a friend.

DEAN DI LAURENTIS

Is the friend named John?

JOHN LOGAN

Yes.

JOHN TUCKER

I am not the friend.

My daughters are capable of murdering their own cheating exes. I'd confess and serve the jail time for them, though.

JOHN LOGAN

So if we wanted to disappear somebody, what's the first step?

GARRETT GRAHAM

The logistics on this are tricky. Also against the law.

JOHN LOGAN

There's gotta be a way to get rid of him without breaking any laws. Poison in his protein shakes?

GARRETT GRAHAM

You'd fuck up the dosages. We need something more efficient.

COLIN FITZGERALD

What if we send him to a remote cabin and "accidentally" lock him inside for a weekend? Give him some time to think about his bad decisions?

DEAN DI LAURENTIS

How are you my brother-in-law? That's such a pussy idea.

COLIN FITZGERALD

I'm excusing myself from this conversation.

JOHN TUCKER

Just looked this up. It's illegal to lock someone in a cabin.

DEAN DI LAURENTIS

To recap: murder = illegal. Forced confinement = illegal. Who would've thought.

JOHN LOGAN

Fine. New goal. MTAC.

JOHN TUCKER

??

DEAN DI LAURENTIS

Why are you like this

JAKE CONNELLY

MTAC?

GARRETT GRAHAM

Make the asshole cry.

JOHN LOGAN

I love you so much, man.

DEAN DI LAURENTIS

Send him a strongly worded letter.

GARRETT GRAHAM

I know the NFL commissioner. I could try to get his rookie contract canceled.

JAKE CONNELLY

That is diabolical, G.

JOHN LOGAN

Don't call him G. He's MY best friend.

JAKE CONNELLY

I'm excusing myself from this conversation.

# Chapter 2

## BLAKE

*Bruised but not broken*

IT'S BEEN SIX WEEKS, AND I still haven't cried.

My friends don't think it's normal. Gigi even called me a robot the other day, which was a joke, I know, but it got to me. When your boyfriend of nearly three years cheats on you, it's customary to cry, isn't it?

Historically, I'm not a big crier. Crying invites attention, and that's the one thing I've shied away from for most of my life. But it's not like I *never* cry. A sad movie with a lost puppy or a broken relationship? I cry like a baby. Watching Gigi walk down the aisle at her wedding? Sobs.

Ergo, I know I'm *capable* of tears.

So where the fuck are they?

The first few days following our breakup, when I realized my eyes were bone-dry and that wasn't changing, I wondered if perhaps I was never actually in love with Isaac. But that doesn't feel right. I *did* love him, and I'm grieving this loss. Every time I think about him, it feels like someone is stabbing my heart with a thousand knives.

*Isaac* cried. When I packed up all my stuff, he was in tears. Hysterical. He begged me to stay, promising it would never happen again.

But there's no coming back from what he did. If it was just about a sex tape? Fine. I mean, not "fine." I still wouldn't have forgiven him—I hold a grudge till the day I die. But it might've been an easier pill to swallow. One crazy night, drank too much, gave in to temptation, and decided to film it like some sleazy amateur porn star.

But it wasn't one night.

It was many, many nights.

For a *year*.

All those times he told me he was going out with the boys, when we were still living in Hastings near campus, he'd been hooking up with Heather the cheerleader. Apparently, they met when the Pats were still wooing Isaac during his junior year. He claims it didn't mean anything, that there were zero emotions involved. It was just a "sexual thing." As if that makes it better. Nothing about this is *better*.

And I still haven't fucking cried.

For the second time in six weeks, I'm getting off another plane and taking another parental call, this time from my mom. I've been staying with them since I moved out, and although I love my parents dearly, I'm looking forward to not having someone ask me if I'm okay every five seconds.

To his credit, after the cheating was exposed, my father didn't organize a vigilante squad to help him murder Isaac. Though I heard that in their group chat, Dad and his friends were trying to decide if there was a way to claim insanity. It's sweet he cares this much, but I can't wait to taste some freedom.

"How're you doing, sweetie?" Mom asks as I exit the airport and search the pickup lane for my ride.

"Good. Just trying to find my driver."

I finally spot the silver sedan and wave at the driver, who slides out to help me with my bag. As he loads it into the trunk, I breathe in the night air, letting it wash over me like a soothing balm.

It's nice to be back in Lake Tahoe. My family co-owns a house here with the Grahams. It used to be a rental, but when the property came up for sale last year, we couldn't pass it up. The lake house is going to be my home for the next three months, and I've never been more excited for an escape. The usual faces will start showing up the third week of July—we have a big family blowout here every year—but for the most part, it will just be me and my thoughts.

But not my tears.

Because I still haven't cried.

Which is normal. Totally normal. The online therapist said so.

"Is the alarm code still the same?" I slide into the back seat, balancing the phone on my shoulder as I buckle my seat belt.

"Yep, I texted it to you," Mom says. "Oh, and we asked the houseman to go in and prep everything for you, make sure the house is nice and clean."

"Do you think this will be the year we finally meet him?"

"Oh my God, honey. *Imagine*?"

I swallow a laugh. As my father likes to say, Houseman Henry is an urban legend around these parts. For the past five years, he's been our property manager/housekeeper/deliveryman/handyman, and yet not a single one of us has met him in person. He always manages to get his tasks done when nobody is around. Uncle Dean swears he saw him once—at dawn, wearing plaid, dropping off spare gas cans in the boathouse—but nobody believes him.

"He can't deliver groceries until tomorrow," she continues, "but—"

"I don't want Henry buying my groceries," I protest. "I already told you I'm planning to get a job this summer."

"And I already told you we don't expect that of you. You've had a summer job every year since you were fourteen, honey. You're allowed to take one summer off. In fact, your father and I would prefer it."

I wrinkle my forehead. "You would?"

"Yes. This is your last summer before you graduate. I want you to spend it getting to know yourself, not distracting yourself with a job you don't need. I know you have some money saved up, and your dad and I are happy to spoil you this summer with groceries." Her tone grows gentle. "You told me you were worried about the future, and I don't want you worrying, my girl. I'd rather you take this time to figure out what you want to do."

Emotion squeezes my chest. Part of me wishes I never confessed those fears; there's nothing I hate more than pointing out my own inadequacies. But I should've known my mom wouldn't judge me for the talk we had last week when I admitted it scares me that I'm going into my senior year this fall but am no closer to figuring out what I'm going to do afterward.

Truth is I've never felt a deep-seated passion for anything. My best friend and sorority sister, Juliette, has known since middle school that she's interested in nursing. Gigi knew from frickin' *birth* that she wanted to play hockey.

Me, I've switched majors three times, finally landing on broadcasting last year. But what am I going to do with a broadcasting degree? I have no interest in being on television. Radio barely exists anymore. I could get into podcasting, but about what? Who makes a living podcasting anyway? Unless your podcast breaks out and starts raking in the ad money, it'll likely just fade away into obscurity.

Passion aside, there isn't much I'm even *good* at. All my friends are disgustingly good at something. I'm surrounded by prodigies, in fact. Talented athletes like Gigi, supermodels like our friend Alex, high-powered lawyers like Alex's sister Jamie.

There is nothing worse than being ordinary among the extraordinary.

It's embarrassing even.

"I want this to be the summer of Blake," Mom says firmly. "I think it'll be really good for you."

I bite my lip. "Okay," I relent. "But I'm going to research a gazillion postgraduation jobs while I'm here. Deal?"

"Deal. Are you almost at the house?"

I peer out the window. "Yep."

"Good. Make sure you lock up and set the alarm when you get there."

"I will."

"And if a serial killer comes—"

"I'll dive off the dock and swim to the Martin house."

Mom and I have discussed many a contingency plan about how to escape a killer. I'm not too worried about getting murdered in Lake Tahoe, though. Our house is in a gated, affluent neighborhood, a nice perk that comes from having a father with a long and illustrious career in professional hockey alongside my surrogate uncle Garrett. Our families can afford nice things, and while I don't consider myself spoiled, I recognize how fortunate I am and try to never take that for granted.

"Are you sure you're okay?" Mom's voice softens. "On the Isaac front, I mean."

"I'm fine," I assure her, then repeat the motto she recited to me growing up whenever something shitty happened. Like in the fifth grade when my best friend dumped me for no perceivable reason and proceeded to bully me for six torturous months. "Bruised but not broken, right?"

"Exactly. I love you, my girl."

"Love you too."

I slide the phone into my purse and focus out the window, the dark scenery blurring past my vision. The driver doesn't try to make small talk, and I adore him for that. I haven't been good company to anyone since Isaac decided to film himself in a cowboy costume smacking Heather's ass as he fucked her from behind.

Did I mention they made their little tape on Halloween?

Heather was dressed as a sexy astronaut and kept screaming "Yes, Houston!" I don't think she realized Houston isn't a person. They both set women's lib back about a hundred years.

This summer away is going to be good for me. I desperately need it. And not to nurse a broken heart like my parents believe. With every day that passes, Isaac gets smaller in my mental rearview mirror. Six weeks later, my ego is more bruised than my heart, and the more pressing issue weighing me down is what the hell I'm going to do with my life.

I banish the familiar doubts and frustrations, because thanks to my mom, I've been given a reprieve. I don't need to figure it all out right this second. I have three months to come up with a plan.

Three months to get to know myself.

The car's tires crunch over gravel, stopping at the enormous iron gates, where I have to lean halfway out the window to enter the code. A few moments later, the sprawling lake house comes into view.

Our house is a little...extra. Located on the west shore, it's eight thousand square feet and offers panoramic views of the water and the surrounding Sierra Nevada mountains. It's more of a compound if anything, with the main house, various outbuildings, and a gorgeous two-story boathouse boasting its own four-bedroom apartment upstairs.

It was a long journey from Boston, but when the car stops and I glimpse the house, with its massive windows that reflect the lake and sky, every mile feels worth it.

As the driver hops out to get my suitcase, I step into the alpine air and inhale deeply. I love the way it smells here. So crisp and fresh. Like freedom.

"Thank you so much," I tell the dark-haired man, then wait until the sedan disappears down the long drive before I turn toward the wide stone steps.

I input another code at the front entrance, and the huge double doors unlock for me. Another familiar smell fills my happy nostrils. Cedar, leather, and fireplace smoke. Inside is a mix of natural stone and exposed beams. Floor-to-ceiling glass windows overlook the wraparound upper deck, with gorgeous views of the lower deck, dock, and boathouse.

I roll my suitcase toward the grand staircase and leave it at the bottom. I'll lug it up later. Upstairs are twelve bedrooms, most with en suite baths, while three of the rooms have wall-to-wall bunks to accommodate the large family gatherings we hold every summer. When I was younger, the girls would all pile into a room and have monthlong sleepovers. As the co-owning families, the Grahams and I get our own rooms now.

I go into the kitchen and open the fridge, not expecting much since Henry isn't delivering groceries until tomorrow. But I'm startled to find a case of beer and an entire shelf of still and sparkling water. I reach for a bottle, then decide *what the hell* and pry one of the beers from the case instead. It's some artsy IPA, which makes no difference to me because all beer tastes the same no matter where it's from or what it's called.

I wander through the great room toward the french doors and step onto the deck, sipping my beer as I approach the railing. The slight breeze tickles my neck, drawing my attention to the lake. Natural stone steps wind down to the second deck below and then lower still to the dock. We even have our own private beach and a long pier extending from the boathouse.

It's cool out, but I don't mind. I take the stairs down to the dock, the weathered slats creaking slightly beneath my sneakers as I walk to the edge. A sense of peace washes over me as I listen to the low drone of insects and the soft hush of water lapping at the wooden pillars beneath the deck.

The moon sits low in the sky tonight, practically in reach. Its light creates silvery lines across the water. Lake Tahoe is so beautiful. I could see myself living here full-time one day.

"This is going to be a good summer," I murmur to myself.

My voice sounds so quiet in the still night air. I swallow another sip of my beer just as the dock creaks again. I catch a flash of movement and turn my head, and my heart rockets into my throat when I glimpse the shadowy figure only a few feet away.

He stumbles toward me, making a growling sound, thick and menacing.

Holy shit.

He *growled* at me. Like a fucking rottweiler.

"Don't come near me!" I burst out.

As fear and adrenaline spike in my blood, I act on instinct. I am *not* going to be the woman who gets bitten by the alligator in the sandpit. No fucking way.

With a high-pitched scream, I hurl the beer can at my would-be assailant. I'm rewarded by a loud crunch, as if I've hit bone. He lets out an outraged shout, but I'm already leaping forward to kick him in the balls, just the way Master Kato taught us at our mother/daughter self-defense class. That gets me a strangled expletive before the growler promptly doubles over, providing me with precious seconds to escape.

I spin to run, but my heel catches on a plank, and suddenly the dock shifts beneath my feet. I lose my balance and topple over.

For some baffling reason, the serial killer tries to steady me.

The next thing I know, we're both falling headfirst into the lake.

# Chapter 3

## WYATT

*Blake Logan is taking her clothes off*

I WOKE UP FROM A beautiful sleep, and now I'm drowning.

Literally.

Cold water closes over my head. A frigid, glacial kind of cold that bites through your clothes and cuts down to the bone. My breath escapes in a flurry of bubbles as my body seizes against the shock. The freezing water of Lake Tahoe is barely swimmable in May during the day. At night, it feels like my lungs have closed up. Jesus. I actually can't breathe.

Survival instincts kick in as I find myself completely submerged. My hoodie and sweatpants are having the opposite effect—rather than serving as a heat source, they're pulling me deeper into the lake. While little needles stab into any inch of skin that's exposed, I fight the dizzying disorientation and kick up with my bare feet. A few seconds later, I break the surface, gasping. The air I suck into my lungs feels even colder than the water, but at least I'm breathing again.

I hear someone else gasping beside me and look over to find the criminal who did this to me. This chick brazenly walked into my house, cracked open a beer, and meandered down here to admire the lake like she's on fucking vacation. I don't know who she is, but—

"Wyatt?"

I falter at the sound of my name escaping her lips. It takes a second to recognize her.

"Blake?" I spit out a mouthful of lake water. "What the hell are you doing here?"

We're both treading water, arms moving in circles and legs kicking beneath the surface.

"Me? What are *you* doing here? Nobody was supposed to be here!"

She's got me there. I did leave Nashville and come to Tahoe without telling anyone. In my defense, I pull shit like this all the time. Didn't realize I needed to send an itinerary to every family friend whenever I get restless.

"Oh my God, I can actually see my breath," she mutters. "Can we please have this argument on land?"

Without awaiting a response, she starts swimming away. I swim after her, and we're both dripping wet and shaking uncontrollably by the time we heave ourselves up the ladder onto the dock. And my left cheekbone is throbbing. I gingerly touch it and wince.

"You threw a beer at me," I accuse.

She shows no remorse. "Because you snuck up behind me in the dark and growled."

"I didn't growl. I said *hey*."

"It sounded like a growl."

I grit my teeth. "My voice was hoarse because I just woke up. To find a burglar on my dock—"

"Oh my God, you're so dramatic. This is my house too."

"Yeah, a house you're not supposed to be at."

"Neither are you!"

"So that gives you the right to throw a beer can at me?" I challenge.

"You pushed me into the lake!" she huffs.

"No, you tripped and pulled me in with you."

We both glare at each other. We look like drowned rats. Blake's brown hair is matted to her face and cheeks, and her teeth are chattering loud enough for me to hear it.

"I need to get out of these wet clothes," she grumbles, putting an end to the most aggravating argument I've ever had. "I genuinely think I have hypothermia."

"You don't have hypothermia."

"You don't know that," she says over her shoulder, stomping away.

I watch her go, frustration rooting me in place.

Blake Logan.

Fuck.

Of all the people who could've showed up to intrude on my summer, the universe had to send the one girl I've been avoiding for years.

Smothering a groan, I trudge toward the lounge chair where I was peacefully sleeping before Blake decided to ruin my night. My acoustic guitar leans against the neighboring chair, which is covered with paper, all the sheets I'd torn from my notebook strewn across the canvas fabric. I gather the papers, shoving them into the book, then grab the guitar by its neck and climb the stairs to the main deck. Each step is punctuated by the sloshing from my waterlogged clothes.

Rather than enter through the kitchen, Blake goes around the side of the house. I catch up to her as she stumbles into the mudroom, a huge room full of coat hooks, shoe racks, and cabinets with beach towels. Blake approaches the long bench spanning one wall. When she realizes I'm standing in the doorway, she glares at me again.

"Turn around," she orders.

I give her some privacy, but it's impossible not to hear what's happening behind me. The slopping, squishing noises as she removes her soaked clothing, each item hitting the floor with a plop.

Blake Logan is taking her clothes off.

Jesus fucking Christ.

"Okay," she says a minute later. "I'm decent."

I'm relieved to see she's wearing a royal-blue bathrobe now. Except the robe keeps slipping off her shoulder, the collar gaping just enough to tease at the curve of her collarbone and the smooth, pale skin beneath it. I bet her nipples are hard from the cold. I wonder what color they are. Pale pink, I bet. Like little round, pink pearls.

Oh fuck.

I'm getting hard.

"Stop glaring at me," she mutters. "This wasn't my fault."

She thinks I'm glaring. Guess that's cool. Better than her knowing I'm imagining sucking on her nipples.

She shakes out her head, and instead of giving wet dog, it gives wet goddess, the long strands clinging to her pale cheeks like dark ribbons. I wrestle my gaze away and try to distract myself from my semihard dick by pulling off my soaked hoodie. I toss it on the bench, all the while avoiding Blake's stormy gaze and reminding myself that this is what happens when you're not getting laid.

That's all this is. Six months of celibacy taking their toll on me. Nothing to do with the woman in the bathrobe.

"Why is this thing so huge?" She holds up one sleeve and watches it flop over. She really is drowning in that robe.

I give a wry grin. "I'm pretty sure that's Dean's."

"How do you know?"

I gesture to the breast pocket. The initials DDL are stitched on it in white thread. Dean Di Laurentis. The robe I grab for myself says JT. John Tucker.

"They have matching monogrammed robes?" Blake sighs. "Why are they like this?"

"They" refers to my dad and his college friends. They're like brothers, only the way-too-close, always-in-each-other's-business kind of brothers. They talk daily in their multiple group chats. Vacation together. Share obscure inside jokes and running pranks that none of the kids understand or care to try. It's…intense.

"Maybe once you've worn a hockey uniform for most of your life, you need your name on every other piece of clothing you own," I answer. "I'm pretty sure they got these made after Tucker built that sauna out back for Princess Alex."

As Blake heads for the door that leads into the house, I drop my sweatpants and boxers and throw on my own robe. It fits me fine, but I've got almost a foot on Blake in height and at least seventy pounds of muscle. I leave our discarded clothing on the bench. I'll throw 'em in the dryer later. Right now, I need to get warm.

I follow her into the kitchen. She pushes some wet strands away from her face, and a droplet of lake water squeezes out from the bottom of her hair. Just a teeny single drop. I follow it with the intensity of a dog watching his owner's dinner. It slides down her neck to her shoulder and disappears beneath the terry cloth like a taunt. Then the robe slides off her shoulder again, exposing smooth skin.

I bite down a groan and turn away.

This no-sex thing was supposed to help me combat my writer's block. According to Cole Tanner, my former bandmate, celibacy restarts your creative juices. Allows for no distractions, fostering nothing but pure focus. Artistic soul ecstasy over mindless bodily orgasms.

But my buddy clearly didn't account for Blake's naked body beneath that robe.

The last time she and I were alone, it was also in a kitchen.

With a counter.

Which I lifted her onto and then splayed her across like a feast for me to devour.

And I almost did. I still remember how good she smelled, like coconut and strawberries and pure temptation. Fresh and sweet, just like Blake herself. And when I was dragging my tongue over her neck, kissing and sucking on her silky skin, she tasted so fucking good.

I'd like to blame the alcohol for what I did that night, but that would be bullshit. I wasn't that drunk. I *wanted* to taste her. I wanted to spread her legs and let her feel how hard she made me.

In that one reckless moment, I allowed myself to bite into the forbidden fruit that is Blake Logan.

Before that, I'd successfully managed to avoid her for two years, ever since she confessed to having a crush on me. She was sixteen at the time. I was nineteen, turning twenty. If I'm being honest, I never once looked at her in that way before that day. *Really* looked at her. But I'm a guy, and when a girl tells you she wants you, it plants the seed in your mind. Makes you think. So I started paying attention. I started to notice.

And I noticed things I shouldn't.

Like how impossibly blue her eyes are.

The pitch of her laughter, how it sounds like a song.

Her sarcasm.

Her walls. I don't know why they're there, but I've always been attracted to walls.

But she was too damn young, so I shut it down hard. Wouldn't let myself even go there.

Until Christmas Eve, when she showed up at our house looking hotter than she had any right to look, with that dark wavy hair that begs for a man's fingers and those big blue eyes surrounded by sooty lashes. Talking about some douchey football player who wanted to make her his girl, all the while sneaking glances at me, practically broadcasting that I could have her if I made a move.

Like an idiot, I made a move.

And then pretended not to remember.

I'm a fucking prick.

"I need to infuse hot tea into my veins," Blake announces. She walks to the electric kettle on the gleaming counter and goes to fill it up with water.

"That sounds good," I admit. "Can you make me one?"

She glances over her shoulder, waiting. "Please?"

"I'm not saying please to the girl who threw me into the lake."

"You *pushed* me—" She stops, her eyes widening. "Oh no."

"What?"

"So I may have broken your face."

Despite myself, a burst of laughter sputters out. I go to the mirror in the corridor to examine my reflection, sighing when I see my cheek. Blake got me right in the bone, and the skin is already starting to turn purple. Definitely gonna be a bruise tomorrow. Close enough to my eye that it might end up being a shiner too.

"I take no responsibility for the hypothermia," Blake says when I return to the kitchen, "but I will very graciously apologize for the beer can."

"Where'd you learn to throw like that, kid? Did you train with a major-league pitcher?"

"My dad," she says before frowning at me. "And don't call me kid."

"Why not?"

"Because I'm not five years old."

I slide onto one of the stools at the counter. "Whatever you say, kid."

She ignores that. "Let me find something for your face."

As we wait for the kettle to boil, she rummages in the freezer and pulls out an ice pack.

"Get that away from me," I squawk. "I'm still freezing."

She ignores that too, pressing the pack against the left side of my face. "Trust me. You'll thank me in the morning."

My breath hitches, and I hope she doesn't notice. Her face is so close to mine, I can practically make out every freckle. The color is finally returning to her cheeks, giving them a pinkish hue.

"You have a lot of freckles," I mutter.

"Oh wow, really? I never noticed." Leaving me to ice my own cheek, she grabs two mugs from the cabinet. "What are you doing in Tahoe, Wyatt? I had my flight booked four days ago. We even checked with your parents to see if anyone would be here before mid-July, and they said no."

"Yeah, it was sort of an impulsive decision."

"They don't know you're here?"

"Well, I assume they will now." I give her a pointed look.

Blake rolls her eyes. "What, did I ruin it? You were trying to hide from your family?"

"Not hide. Just...regroup."

"Regroup," she echoes.

"Yes."

I don't elaborate. It's hard enough for *me* to make sense of what's in my own head, let alone articulate it to other people. My mind is in a perpetual state of chaos. When I'm writing, I can channel the noise into something beautiful. Something productive. But when I'm blocked, the noise becomes deafening.

It's been a year.

I haven't written anything in a goddamn year. Anything good, that is. I hoped that a change of scenery might help, but Blake just threw a wrench in that.

"How long are you here for?" I ask warily.

"The whole summer."

Shit. That was my plan.

The kettle starts hissing, diverting her attention. She keeps her back to me as she prepares our tea, giving me an opportunity to stare without consequences. Her long hair cascades down the back of her robe in damp waves, curling at the ends. There might be something wrong with me, some dormant hair kink she triggers in me, because I notice Blake's hair every time she's in the same room as me, my mind flooded with images of all the things I could do to it.

Wind it around my fingers.

Tighten my fist in it.

Use it to yank her head back while I'm filling her from behind—

I blink when she slides a mug in front of me.

"Thanks," I say, sounding more irritable than I intend. I hate where my thoughts drift whenever she's around. Yes, I like to fuck, but I'm not some sex-obsessed hound dog who fantasizes about boning every female in my vicinity. It pisses me off that I can't control the lust Blake stirs up in me.

I gulp down the peppermint tea, welcoming the scalding liquid. Maybe a burnt windpipe will distract me from my twitching dick.

"How long are *you* here?" she asks.

"I don't know. Probably the whole summer too."

"Well, we can't both be here."

"Glad we agree on that." I lift a brow. "So when are you leaving?"

Her jaw falls open. "Excuse me?"

Yeah. I'm being an ass. I don't care. I need to focus on songwriting, on getting my music back on track. There's no way I can spend the entire summer in close quarters with this girl. Torturing me with her hotness and reminding me of all the reasons I can't go there.

"We can't both stay, which means one of us has to go, right?" I shrug at her. "I got here first."

"I'm not leaving." She juts her chin, the epitome of obstinate.

"Yeah, you are, kid."

"Please stop calling me that."

Now she sounds tired, and when I study her face, I see it. The fatigue lining her eyes. The way her mouth quivers a little, as if it's a challenge to keep her jaw set in that stubborn line.

"You know what?" she finally says, setting down her tea. "Whatever. I don't need your permission to stay in my own house. So if you'll excuse me, I'm going up to the blue room to unpack my—"

"I'm in the blue room."

Her brow furrows. "But the blue room is my room."

"We don't have assigned rooms here, Logan."

"Yes, we do. Gigi's is the yellow room. Our parents have the two master suites. Mine is the blue room. And yours is the mountain room."

"What can I tell you? I'm crashing in the blue room."

Dead silence falls over the kitchen.

Blake stares at me, not making a single sound. For the first time since we almost drowned, she actually seems distraught.

"Quit staring at me like that," I grumble. "This isn't a big deal. Just take the yellow room. Gigi won't be here for months."

Her bottom lip begins to tremble.

I narrow my eyes. "What's happening right now?"

Her breathing grows choppy.

Oh, I see. "Are you trying to manipulate me?" I say in amusement. "Because that won't work on me." My twin sister used to pull this shit all the time when she was trying to get her way. I'm impervious to a woman's crocodile tears. "I'm not giving up the blue room. I'm already settled in."

The next thing I know, Blake bursts into tears.

Not just tears—sobs. High-pitched, gulping, heaving sobs. And they don't look or sound like the fake variety.

Because I'm not a total dickhead, I tug on her forearm and pull her toward me. "Hey, c'mere. Stop crying, Logan."

Without a word, she buries her face against the front of my robe, her slender body shaking from each uncontrollable sob. A bit stunned, I wrap my arms around her shuddering shoulders, trying to comfort her.

"Fuck's sake, Blake, it's just a room. I'm—Christ, fine. You can have it."

She tries to speak, but another wail flies out instead of words. I rub her shoulders, feeling her chest rise abruptly with every shallow inhale. It's several minutes before she pulls back, wiping her wet face with the oversize sleeves of her robe.

"I'm sorry," she blubbers, eyes glassy and rimmed with red. She moans in misery. "I don't even know why I'm crying."

Tears continue streaming down her cheeks, and although it's not the time to notice, I realize she's a pretty crier. I've seen some messy, snotty, blotchy criers, but Blake pulls it off. I think it's the freckles. They make the tears look cute.

"I'm so sorry," she says again.

"It's fine. I'll pack up my shit—"

"My boyfriend made a sex tape with a New England Patriots

cheerleader," she blurts out.

I blink at the random interjection. "Oh. Yeah. I know. It's been the hot topic on all the family group chats for weeks."

She lets out a strangled laugh. "Of course it has."

Taking a deep breath, she swipes her sleeve over her face again, mopping up the lingering tears. She picks up her tea and gulps down the rest of it, then slams the mug down and snaps her shoulders into a straight line.

"This didn't happen," she says sternly. "You didn't see me cry."

"Who was crying?"

A hint of a smile touches her lips. "Also, as a show of good faith, I'll take the yellow room. But tomorrow we need to hash out the summer ground rules. Because there *will* be ground rules."

Her eyes pin me down, sharp and serious now. Christ. They're so blue. A light and airy blue, like clear daytime skies, yet with so much depth I forget how to breathe for a second.

I could look into those eyes all night long and never get bored.

Instead, I wrest my gaze away, because I have to. As inexplicably drawn as I am to her, it's never going to happen. The truth is I'd fucking wreck her. Because girls like Blake fall hard, and I'm not the man who sticks around to catch them.

# Chapter 4

## BLAKE

*Why does he have to be shirtless?*

SUNLIGHT STREAMS INTO THE BEDROOM and bounces off the yellow walls, pulling me from a surprisingly restful sleep. I assumed I'd have nightmares about drowning in the lake while Wyatt stood on the dock shouting "Hang in there, kid!" but I slept great.

I roll over to find several text messages from Juliette on my phone, all from this morning because I forgot about the time difference when I spammed her phone last night. It wasn't until my fifth message that I remembered she's three hours ahead of me on the East Coast, and it was two in the morning for her.

Curling onto my side, I scroll through her responses to my tirade about Wyatt ruining my summer.

JULIETTE

Ruin his summer right back. Walk around topless 24/7 so he's in a constant state of blue balls.

Grinning to myself, I type a quick reply.

Honestly, he probably wouldn't even notice.

It's eleven a.m. for her, so I'm not surprised to see her typing back immediately.

JULIETTE

Boys always notice tits. Always.

I think you underestimate how invisible I am to this guy.

JULIETTE

You weren't invisible the night he mauled you on the kitchen counter like a horny Santa.

Might as well have been. He doesn't remember it even happened.

A pang of anxiety tugs on my stomach as I play out the rest of the summer in my head. Sharing meals with him. Seeing him on the dock, in the water, sprawled on the couch. This is a big house, but I won't be able to avoid him every second of the day. We'll be practically on top of each other, and not in a sexy way. The word *sexy* isn't in Wyatt's vocabulary where I'm concerned.

I can't spend the summer with him, Jules. And he was SUCH a dick yesterday. Snapping at me and acting all annoyed, like I purposely showed up here to ruin his plans.

JULIETTE

You need to stop giving this asshole so much power over you.

She's right. I care way too much about what Wyatt Graham thinks of me.

But I'm no longer the pathetic teenager with stars in her eyes. I'm turning twenty-one soon. I'm an adult, a grown woman who doesn't need to beg for a man's attention. And if Wyatt wants to be a dick to me, I can be a dick right back. I'm not interested in impressing him anymore. Which is probably a good thing, because breaking down and crying in his arms last night isn't the way to impress anyone.

But hey, at least I finally cried. Guess I'm not a robot after all.

JULIETTE

Oh btw I went to your building yesterday and grabbed that box like you asked. Isaac left it downstairs with the doorman.

I perk up. Finally! I've been messaging the cheater every week for the past month, bugging him to box up some items I'd forgotten at the condo.

Thank you. I love you so much.

Hot Boi's finally back where he belongs!

JULIETTE

So. About that.

I have bad news.

Incoming.

A photo pops up, triggering an outraged gasp.

Oh my God. That *asshole*.

I'm already typing a new message, this one directed at Isaac, as I climb out of bed. I hit Send, then pad into the hallway on bare feet, my bad mood only getting worse. If I was in the *blue* room, I'd have an en suite, but thanks to Wyatt, I'm forced to use the hall bathroom.

Teeth brushed and bladder empty, I grab my phone and go downstairs, walking into the kitchen to the sound of a very pissed-off Wyatt. The french doors sit wide open, letting the cool morning breeze waft inside. Our house faces east, which means we wake up every morning to the Sierras catching the morning light. It's gorgeous.

Wyatt is standing on the deck with his back to me. Shirtless.

God, why does he have to be shirtless?

With the sunlight slanting just the right way to catch the strong lines of his back, I can't help but admire him. Fine, ogle him. Everything about Wyatt's body, every fucking inch of him, is ogle-worthy. Wide shoulders, narrow waist. Defined muscles that ripple beneath his suntanned skin with every move he makes. He wanders closer to the railing, and his hair now catches the sun's rays, making it appear more gold than brown.

The way he's cut, you'd think he was an athlete like his father and not a tortured, chain-smoking musician. Gigi told me he quit smoking, but evidently not. A cigarette dangles from the corner of his mouth, lending him a dangerous air. And his hair is longer from the last time I saw him. It keeps falling onto his forehead, making my fingers itch to sweep it away.

I pass the long dining room table, which is covered with pieces from a newly started jigsaw puzzle. I don't want to eavesdrop on Wyatt's conversation, but I also don't want to interrupt, so I make sure my footsteps are extra loud as I enter the kitchen to pour myself some coffee. Of course, he's barely noticed me my whole life, so why would today be any different?

"Yeah, Dad, I heard you. I'm not a total prick, okay? I'll—" Wyatt stops talking, turning toward the door and spotting me in the kitchen. "All right, Blake's up. I gotta go. You know, make sure she's fed and watered."

My jaw drops. What the fuck?

He stubs out his cigarette in the ashtray, then comes sauntering into the house as if he hadn't just spoken about me in the most dehumanizing way.

"*Fed and watered?*" I demand, throwing his words back at him.

He heads for the coffee maker. "Sorry, that was more for my dad's benefit."

"At my expense," I growl. "I'm not a fucking pet, Wyatt."

"And I'm not a fucking babysitter."

"Good, because I don't need one. I don't care what your dad says—"

"It's not just my dad," he interrupts in annoyance. "It's all of them." He holds up his phone, waving it around. "They pulled me into Dad Chat against my will and warned me that if I don't protect our precious Blake Logan with my life, then I, and I quote, 'sacrifice' *my* life."

"They didn't." I narrow my eyes.

Without a word, Wyatt unlocks the phone and slides it across the counter. I lean in, skimming the last few messages in the chat.

Oh my fucking God. My father *actually* said that.

JOHN LOGAN

If you don't protect her with your life, you sacrifice that life.

GARRETT GRAHAM

You realize you're speaking to my only son, right?

DEAN DI LAURENTIS

Remember when Logan used to be normal?

JOHN TUCKER

You'll still have your son-in-law, G. You can sacrifice one.

WYATT GRAHAM

You're all insane. Please release me from this psych ward.

"Then after I left the group, my dad called me to hammer the point home," Wyatt grumbles as he gets himself a cup of coffee. "I'm under strict orders to not leave your side this summer."

"Really? Well, guess what? You *will* be leaving my side. In fact, you will be as far away from my side as humanly possible."

As he lifts the cup to his lips, I notice the purple bruise shadowing his cheekbone. I feel a prickle of guilt, but not enough to apologize again. He ambushed me like a feral dock dweller last night. I regret nothing.

We're interrupted by the buzzing of my phone as two messages pop up. Isaac responding to my angry text. Awesome.

I chug the rest of my coffee and stomp toward the sink.

"He's in your contacts as 'the cheater'?" Wyatt sounds amused.

I turn to find him peering at my screen. "Stop reading my messages," I order.

"Why haven't you blocked him?"

"Because we have unfinished business."

"You can't possibly be thinking of taking him back."

"I'm not. And even if I was, it's none of your business." I snatch the phone before he can read any more notifications.

My irritation rises to sky-high levels. All I wanted was to have a nice, relaxing summer. Do some soul-searching. Figure out my life plan. Instead, I'm stuck here with the guy who laughed when I told him I liked him and then two years later *forgot* about grinding his dick all over me.

Angling away from Wyatt, I click the chat thread to check what bullshit Isaac wants to feed me this morning.

THE CHEATER

I didn't forget to put him in the box.

I'm keeping Hot Boi.

My jaw drops. I expected an excuse, not a confession. I angrily type a reply.

You CANNOT be serious.

THE CHEATER

Dead serious. He belongs with me.

FFS Isaac. This isn't a custody battle for a human child. I'm the one who bought him.

THE CHEATER

And I'm the one who named him. I bonded with him. You never even respected the heat settings.

OMG How is this happening right now. It's a toaster!!!

THE CHEATER

See this is why you don't deserve him. You underestimate him. He has a croissant mode.

"This is a child." Wyatt's voice echoes over my shoulder, making me jump.

"Stop reading my texts," I say in exasperation.

"You realize that, right, Logan? You dated a child."

"Yes, that is clear now, *Graham*. Thank you so much for pointing it out."

"With that said, and please don't hate me, but…" Wyatt's lips twitch. "His sense of humor is stellar."

"Don't you dare compliment him," I mutter, even as I'm furiously composing another text.

You used croissant mode once and then you whined for an hour because it over-toasted. Hot Boi is mine. I want him back.

THE CHEATER

We all want things in this life.

I swallow a scream of frustration. Why are men so fucking crazy!

"Sort of seems like you're still into this guy," Wyatt says lightly, sipping his coffee. "Otherwise you wouldn't be picking fights about a toaster."

"It's my toaster," I shoot back. "And it's a matter of principle."

"Whatever you say, kid."

A wave of anger slams into me. "No." I jam my finger in the air, because I've had it up to here. I'm done. Fucking *done*. "Call me that one more time and I'll smash your guitar to smithereens."

He simply arches a brow.

"I mean it," I warn. "Don't call me that. And do me a favor? Just leave me the hell alone. I'm not going anywhere, and if you insist on staying here too, fine, go ahead and stay. But I don't need you to babysit me, I don't need you to talk to me, and you know what? Don't even *look* at me—"

"You never used to be this dramatic."

I spit out an incensed curse and turn my back on him, because if I have to see that infuriating smirk for one second longer, I'm liable to punch it off his face. I take a deep breath and try to calm myself.

"That's very mature, Blake. Just turn your back in the middle of a conversation."

"The conversation was over," I say stiffly, then march off before he can say another word.

I spend the rest of the morning avoiding him. I eat breakfast alone on the front porch, then curl up with a thriller about a lady who wakes one morning to discover she has a whole-ass family she doesn't remember. I don't see why she's so scared. I'd love to wake up to an entirely new life. One where my father doesn't constantly butt into my business, my boyfriend doesn't screw cheerleaders, and my former crush doesn't view me as a burdensome toddler.

Eventually, my sulking gets tedious, so I throw on a bathing suit under my clothes and pack a small tote. Sunscreen, towel, earbuds, water bottle. Good to go. All that's left is the keys to the bowrider, the twenty-four-foot speedboat our families purchased last year. It's the only boat I feel confident at the helm of; our cruiser and motor yacht are way too big.

The boat keys aren't hanging from their usual hook, so I head outside, spotting Wyatt below on the dock. He's got his guitar on his lap, but he's not playing it, too busy leaning over to scribble in that notebook of his. A beer bottle sits on the table beside him, and as usual, he's smoking a cigarette, his long fingers flicking a tower of ash into the plastic ashtray next to his beer.

It's only eleven in the morning. I wonder if his parents know that he comes to Tahoe to chain-smoke and day drink.

*I* should be babysitting *him*.

I descend the stone steps that wind down the side of the house. The lake stretches endlessly before me, deep blue water ringed by snowy peaks and pine-covered slopes. God, it's gorgeous here. There isn't a single cloud in the sky today.

As I tip my head up to the sun, it settles in my chest and warms me in a way I haven't felt in weeks. For the first time since I learned of Isaac's betrayal, my shoulders lose some of the tension.

On the sprawling dock, some Adirondack chairs are angled toward the water. Nearby, half a dozen lounge chairs are arranged in a neat line, a couple of them shaded by an enormous red umbrella. My flip-flops slap the wood as I walk up to Wyatt's chair.

"Okay," I announce. "Let's discuss this like adults."

He looks up, smoke curling out the corner of his mouth. He takes one last drag, then snuffs his cigarette in the ashtray.

"Oh, we're speaking now?" His eyes gleam with amusement.

I let out a slow, calming breath. "I'm sorry I lost my temper before. I just don't appreciate being talked about like I'm a houseplant or a damn Chihuahua. With that said, if we're going to be here for the summer, we need rules."

"I don't like rules."

"Shocking. Mr. Tortured Musician doesn't want to follow any rules." I cross my arms over the front of my cropped white hoodie. "I think the only way to handle this is if you stay out of my way and I stay out of your way."

"There's still time for you to go," he drawls, and damned if that doesn't sting.

He doesn't want me here, I get it. But that shouldn't hurt as much as it does.

"What, you're worried I'll cramp your style?" I taunt. "Get in the way of your hookup parade?"

"Hookup parade??" he echoes, rolling his eyes.

"Yes. It's no secret you've screwed half the lake."

I regret the words the moment they slip out. It's the truth, though, as far as I know. Gigi doesn't discuss her brother's sex life—I think she'd prefer to be kept *out* of the loop—but most of the other hockey kids, as we refer to ourselves, have no qualms about gossiping.

According to Alex, Wyatt's penis is a popular Lake Tahoe attraction. An obsession, even, if the rumors about Rosie are true. Apparently, Wyatt hooked up with a local named Rosie, who was so heartbroken after he ended it that her family sold their house and moved to Reno. But I'm not sure I believe that part. No parents would make real estate decisions based on their daughter's love life.

"I wouldn't say half." His green eyes take on a cocky glint. "But I can't promise I won't bring someone home."

That stings too.

Damn it.

It shouldn't sting.

"How scandalous," I say sarcastically.

"Also can't promise we'll stay in my room..."

"My room, you mean. The blue room is mine." I raise a brow when his words register. "So, what, you're saying I can expect to come down to the dock at night and find some random townie blowing you?"

"Maybe. I do enjoy a nice dock blowjob."

I can't stop the unwitting image that enters my head. Wyatt undoing his pants and pulling out his cock. Guiding it inside a warm, willing mouth.

*My* warm, willing mouth.

"If you're good, I might even let you watch," he says blithely.

My mouth goes entirely dry. I try to swallow, but it feels like it's stuffed with cotton balls.

This man is such an annoying contradiction. He can go from veiled and mysterious to an incorrigible flirt in the blink of an eye. And you never, ever know which version of him you're going to get. I've seen him turn up the charm with Gigi's friends, with Alex, with random women on the street. He lures them in with those heavy-lidded, seductive eyes until their clothes melt off, and then—bam. He shuts down. Eyes shuttered, flashing that enigmatic smile. The one that warns you, *don't dig too deep, you won't like what you find.*

I've always been drawn to that careless smile and all the secrets it holds. It calls at something inside me.

I finally find my voice. "If you're trying to scare me away, it won't work. I'm not leaving. This is *my* summer, not yours."

"You can't just claim 'summer.' It belongs to all of us. But if you're determined to stay, then I guess we just do our best to leave each other alone."

"Perfect. You can sit on the dock and write your depressing songs—"

"And you can lick your wounds," he finishes.

"I'm not licking my wounds. I'm regrouping," I say, mimicking his phrase from last night. "Anyway, great. That's settled. Now where are the keys to the bowrider? They're not where they usually are."

"Oh, I've got them here. Why?"

"Because I'm taking the boat out."

"Like hell you are."

"I know how to drive a boat." We've all had our boating licenses since we were twelve. It's the first thing our parents made us do once we started coming to Tahoe.

"Look," he says firmly, "I'm not taking the babysitting duties seriously, no matter how much Logan threatens me. But your parents would actually kill me if I let you drive the boat on your own. What if it capsizes?"

"Why would it capsize?" I sputter.

"I don't know. What if a rogue wave hits?"

"A rogue wave in Lake Tahoe?"

"Or you run out of gas—"

"Then I'll call you. There's a signal on this lake. It's not like I'm going off the grid."

Gritting his teeth, Wyatt slides off the lounge chair, holding his guitar by its neck. "Fucking fine. Whatever. If you insist on taking the boat out, then I'm coming with you."

# Chapter 5

## WYATT

*Is this turning you on or something?*

THE BOWRIDER TEARS ACROSS THE lake, its hull slapping against the water. Blake gives it more gas, and the roar of the engine echoes off the tree-lined shoreline, white sheets of spray exploding on either side of the boat.

Normally, I would love it. The fine mist soaking my face, the blue sky above us and blue water below us. Unfortunately, the person driving the boat is a lunatic.

"Slow down," I shout at Blake.

She looks over at me, her ponytail whipping in the wind, blue eyes gleaming with excitement.

"No," she shouts back.

Oh my God. Maybe her father was right to recruit me. Why didn't I know that Blake Logan was a daredevil? This is the kind of irresponsible shit my buddies and I would pull. And I don't like being made to be the adult in the equation.

I clutch the side rail as the bow bounces from each hard slice through the choppy water.

"Goddamn it, Logan!"

She laughs harder as Lake Tahoe unfurls in a wild blur around us. Just as I'm about to go over there and forcibly yank her out of the pilot seat, she eases up on the throttle, and we begin to slow. The wind dies and I can hear my own thoughts again. Then she cuts the throttle entirely and shifts into neutral. Fucking finally.

"Pleased with yourself?" I ask.

She turns to grin at me. Her hair is a tangled mess, and I watch with fascination I hate feeling as she releases it from the ponytail and finger combs it until it's cascading over one shoulder.

With a happy sigh, she says, "It's so nice driving the boat without my father watching from the dock with a pair of binoculars."

I snicker. Of all my dad's friends, John Logan is the most entertaining, I'll give him that. Tucker is too nice, all sugary sweet. And Dean has that confidence that gets exhausting sometimes. Like, dude, can you stop being so charming? He's not even trying; it's just his personality.

Logan is the hilarious one. A solid, laid-back presence, always there when you need him. If he loves you, he's quick to show it. He wears his heart on his sleeve, unlike his daughter, this wild-haired brunette with the cautious eyes. Growing up, I always wondered what Blake was hiding behind that unreadable gaze. It intrigued me, even as a kid.

As an adult, it's a much headier thought, because not only do I want to know all her secrets, but I also want to make those eyes gleam. I want them raw and unguarded. I want to see how dark and heavy-lidded they get when she's having an orgasm.

Fuck. I bet her eyes look so pretty when she's coming.

"You want to anchor here?" She's already kicking off her sandals.

I cough, snapping out of my inappropriate thoughts. "Sure."

I grab the rope coil and move to the bow to drop the anchor. It hits the water with a satisfying splash, the line hissing through my fingers until finally tugging tight. A sense of peace washes over me as the boat bobs in place while the sun high above us ripples over the water. It's creating a mesmerizing effect. Like gold coins scattered across the lake.

I tuck the image away. It's a nice one. Maybe it belongs in a song.

With the sun beating down on my head, I strip off my shirt and toss it aside. Blake unzips her cropped hoodie, leaving her in a pink bikini top and tiny denim shorts that barely cover her ass.

"I'm gonna sunbathe for a while," she says, popping open the button of her shorts while I pretend not to notice.

I walk barefoot to the back of the boat, where I haphazardly dropped my guitar on the padded seat. Oh, Betty. My old girl. This guitar's been through a lot. She's no longer glossy but a dull brown now. A couple of the tuning pegs are bent, and there's a deep scratch on the side of her neck.

"You sure your precious guitar should be on board?" Blake mocks. "Aren't you worried? You know, when the rogue wave hits."

"Nah. Betty's the boat guitar. She knows the risks."

"Your boat guitar is named Betty? Also, what is a boat guitar?"

"It's a guitar I'm okay losing. If she falls overboard, I'll survive. I got her for twenty bucks at a secondhand shop. What, you think I'd bring one of my real guitars out here?"

"I'm not versed in your guitar transporting habits, Wyatt."

She's wiggling out of her shorts now. I avert my eyes. Then I unavert them, because I'm a man and I have no willpower when it comes to this girl. Her body is so fucking tight. Perky ass, long legs, cute tits. And those freckles. They're everywhere. I want to map them out with my tongue.

I shove my sunglasses off my forehead and onto the bridge of my nose. It's my only defense against the feral look I'm sure I'm sporting. It also lets me watch her apply sunscreen without coming off like I'm openly ogling her as she rubs the cream all over her arms, her collarbone, her stomach, between her tits—

*Stop looking.*

Right. Gulping, I unzip my backpack and rummage inside for my songbook until my fingers collide with the worn leather cover. I need to focus on something other than Blake's tits. She's too young for me.

*She's twenty*, reminds a voice in my head.

True. And turning twenty-one soon—her birthday is in July. So no matter how much I want to keep viewing her that way, she really isn't a kid anymore.

Neither am I for that matter. I'll be twenty-five this fall. Which raises the question: What the hell is up with *time*? I feel like only yesterday, I was eighteen, telling my parents I didn't want to go to college and that I was moving to Nashville to launch my music career. Then I blinked and it's six years later, with no career in sight. Sure, I make a living gigging. I get a decent number of streams on the music platforms and tons of hits on my video channel. But I'm not playing sold-out stadiums or winning Grammys, now am I?

My mom won her first Grammy when she was twenty-five.

I hate that my brain always harps on that fact. I always have to remind myself that Mom's musical journey isn't the typical one. Most people don't land a job with a huge producer right out of college. They don't get the opportunity to work on an up-and-coming hip-hop artist's album. To write and produce the hit song that would go on to sweep every awards show that year.

My mother is talented beyond belief, but she also got lucky. Other songwriters don't have such an easy time of it. Case in point—me.

The irony is I *could* have it easy. But the one thing I'll never do is use my mother's connections to advance my career, even as everyone around me insists I'm a fucking moron not to.

Our boat starts rocking a bit harder. I hear an engine, followed by a wolf whistle that skitters across the water toward us.

"Is that you, Wyatt?" chirps a female voice.

The sleek white speedboat gets closer, revealing three older women in big sunglasses and floppy hats. They're all wearing skimpy bikinis and all displaying some impressive curves.

Squinting behind my Ray-Bans, I hide a grin when I recognize Liz Brown. She owns a house nearby.

"Hey, Mrs. Brown," I call out.

"Honey, what did I tell you about calling me Mrs. Brown? It's Liz." She lifts her sunglasses to her forehead and peers into our boat. "That's not Gigi, is it?"

"No, it's me," Blake tells our neighbor, waving awkwardly. "Blake. Hi, Mrs. Brown."

"Blakey? Oh my God. Look how gorgeous you are." Turning back to me, Liz offers an impish smile. "We're up here for the week. Girls' trip—"

"Girls' trip!" her friends whoop, waving around their plastic wine goblets. It's obvious they've been drinking for...a while.

"But you know you're welcome anytime, Wyatt," Liz finishes. "Stop by for a glass of wine."

"Thanks," I say noncommittally. "I might take you up on that."

"You do that, honey."

I'm grinning as they speed away, their wake sending a sheet of mist into our boat.

"You're welcome anytime," Blake mimics.

I glance over. "Jealous?"

"Yes, Graham, I'm jealous that you're banging women twice your age in Tahoe."

"Hey, I don't think she's even forty."

"Didn't deny the banging part..."

"One time. Ages ago."

"But you never forget your first cougar, right?"

With a laugh, I pick up the tube of sunscreen she left on the chair and flip open the cap. I'm about to squeeze some into my palm when from the corner of my eye, I see her delicate fingers undoing the hot-pink strings at her back.

The two triangles slide loose and—

*Plop.*

"That's a lot of sunscreen," she remarks.

I stare down at my hand to find I've squirted nearly half the tube into it.

Jesus Christ.

*Don't fucking look*, I tell myself.

Out loud, I direct a sharp order her way, keeping my gaze firmly at eye level. "Put your top back on."

She eyes me like *I'm* the crazy one. "No. I told you I want to tan."

"Do it in your bathing suit."

"I don't want tan lines."

I have no idea how I'm managing to engage in conversation when her bare tits are in my face. Despite my valiant efforts, my gaze dips for a second.

I knew her nipples would be pink.

When I lift my head, she's smirking like a brat.

"I'm not kidding," I warn.

"Oh, I know. Neither am I. The top stays off," Blake says airily. "Deal with it."

"You're impossible," I mutter, staring intently at my feet. I'm worried that if I let myself look one second longer, even just at her eyes, I'll lose every ounce of restraint I've built over the years of pretending I don't see her.

God, I should've just stayed on the dock. Though in my defense, when I insisted on coming along for this boat ride, I didn't factor in that she might decide to take her goddamn top off.

Hearing my phone buzzing, I lunge for it, desperate for a distraction.

MIRA

Paula's mom just saw you on the lake. You didn't tell me you were in Tahoe.

Shit. Bad distraction.

Mira lives on the north side of the lake. We hooked up a few times last summer, but I cut it off after she told me she was falling for me. They always fucking fall for me.

It's a dick move, but I ignore the message. I don't want to start things up again or send the wrong signals.

Then a second message pops up.

MIRA

Hit me up if you feel like it.

And a third message.

It's a nude.

Damn, she has a nice rack…

Nope. Can't have this on my phone. It'll make it too tempting to give in and call her when I'm drunk and horny.

But I don't delete it fast enough, because Blake—a very topless

Blake—manages to sneak a peek as she approaches me.

"Are you looking at porn?" she exclaims.

"No." The picture disappears from the screen as I hit Delete.

"So *my* boobs are a national emergency, but you can leer at phone boobs. Got it."

"Relax, Logan. Someone sent a nude. I was deleting it."

Her jaw drops. "You *deleted* it? Wow. Don't ever tell her or you'll destroy her self-esteem."

"Make up your mind. Do you want me to leer at phone boobs or not?"

Snickering, she stalks past me, and her side boob grazes my arm.

Jesus fucking Christ.

Tits on my phone. Tits on my boat. God help me.

I shift my gaze back to the water, but it flits back to Blake as if drawn by a magnet. She saunters to the open bow and spreads a red-and-white-striped towel across the padded sundeck. Boobs out for the entire lake to see.

"Seriously, put those away."

"You're being ridiculous" is her response.

I can't tell if she's doing this on purpose. If she's *trying* to get a reaction out of me. But she's not even acknowledging my presence anymore. She lies down on the towel, stretches out on her back, and plops her sunglasses on her freckled nose.

"Your father's gonna kill me," I moan.

"Only if you tell him."

Stifling a curse, I pick up her top and stalk to the bow. "Here," I say, trying to hand her the bikini.

She rises on her elbows and peers up at me, blue eyes peeking out from the top of her shades. Her nipples are glistening. It's the sunscreen, I know, but it makes them look wet. Like they've just been licked and sucked and—

"Take it," I growl when she bats my hand away.

"What the hell is wrong with you? Is this turning you on or something?"

Frustration has me spitting out a retort I instantly regret. "Hardly. You think I haven't seen a pair of tits before? Yours aren't anything special."

Blake stiffens for a moment before spitting back a curt, "Oh, fuck you."

I don't know why I said that. Her breasts are perfect.

Focusing on the water as if my life depends on it, I try to get my body under control by fishing for the coldest beer in the small cooler I brought with us.

"So who sent the nude?" Her tone is grudging, as if she doesn't want to ask but can't help herself. "Mrs. Brown?"

"No." I don't elaborate.

"Then who?" she pushes.

"Someone who heard I was in town."

"One of your other Tahoe groupies?"

"Obviously." I pull the tab of the can, and it opens with a sharp hiss.

"Can you toss me one of those?"

"Nope. You're underage."

"I'm turning twenty-one in six weeks," she reminds me.

"Great, then I'll toss you a beer in six weeks."

"If you don't get me a beer, I'm taking my bottoms off too."

Jesus.

Christ.

With a groan jammed in my throat, I grab another beer and slam the can down beside her.

"Thank you," she says sweetly.

Annoyed, I march back to my guitar. Because enough. I refuse to play these games with her. If she wants to flash her tits to every passing boater, let her. I have bigger concerns at the moment.

I need to write something.

Anything.

Balancing Betty in my lap, I grab my notebook and pencil and turn to a fresh page. Everything I wrote yesterday was so bad, it's not even worth revising. Let's start new.

I focus on the blank page, trying to clear my head. To let the warm rays and soft breeze guide me to inspiration. That gold coin line. It was nice, right? Poetic?

Gold coins scattered on the water.
Wind tangled in your hair.

My pencil stops moving.

Keep going, I order myself. Write something.

Fucking anything.

I scrawl another line, then stare in disgust at what I wrote.

The sky knows me today.

What the hell does that even mean? The sky knows me today? Knows me how? And did it not know me yesterday? What changed for the sky?

I squeeze the pencil between my fingers, hard enough that it starts to bend. This is pathetic. Why can't I write anything good anymore?

My phone vibrates again. A wave of relief rushes through me. Oh thank God. Someone to put me out of my uncreative misery.

It's a message from Cole, who's taken three days to respond to the lyrics I sent him. I haven't been taking it personally, since he's not only prepping for a global tour, but this week he's collaborating with a talented young singer in Nashville. Aimee Faye is poised to be a superstar, though her style runs more toward sexy pop country in contrast to Cole's old-school country. I can't wait to hear what they come up with.

COLE

Could be better.

Not exactly a ringing endorsement.

The feedback doesn't surprise me, though. Everything I've sent him this year belongs in a landfill. And I appreciate my buddy's honesty. This is why we vibed so well when we were in the band. Me, Cole, and Gus, one of the most talented drummers I've ever met.

Gus plays in the house band for me when I'm in the studio, but Cole, well, he's levels above us now. A bona fide star. The band broke up after we all realized we were each better suited for solo shit, but Cole's the only one who's actually made it. He fucking deserves it too. It's inspiring to see a Black artist finding success in a genre that hasn't always been welcoming to anyone without pasty skin and a scraggly mullet. I'm proud of him.

I know. It's ass.

COLE

Not total ass. Maybe just one ass cheek.

All right, critique me.

COLE

The lyrics don't make sense, bro. And your last 3 tracks have been about the sky. You got a sky fetish or something?

Yeah, I fuck clouds for fun.

COLE

I'm screenshotting that.

Okay. Real talk. This song is just a bunch of metaphors that don't mean anything. No idea what you're trying to say. No depth. Doesn't feel like it's coming from your heart, or any part of your body for that matter. Hell, at this point, drop the metaphors and write a song about wanting to bone. Even that would be more real than whatever you're sending me lately.

I don't write about sex. It's overdone.

COLE

Because people dig it. It excites them. This duet I'm recording with Aimee right now? "We Ride at Dawn." What do you think it's about, bro? A duel? Driving her around in my pickup? Fuck no. It's about how badly I want to ride her pussy and how much she enjoys depriving me of it and making me wait till morning.

Not my style.

COLE

Make it your style. Sex sells, G. Always has, always will.

The strains of a familiar melody jolt me from Cole's lecture. Blake is playing a pop song on her phone.

Speaking of sex sells.

"Turn that off," I tell her.

She rolls onto her stomach with zero shame, rising on her forearms so I have a perfect view of the top swells of her breasts. She has no idea what she's doing to me. Or maybe she does.

"Can I ask you something?" Her tone is worrisomely polite.

"What?"

"Do you think you're the captain of this boat? Because you're barking orders like you are." Blake puts on a stern voice. "*Put your top on. Don't drink that. Turn off that music.*"

"This isn't music."

"It's Mollie May! She's the biggest pop star in the world."

"Doesn't make her music good."

"Oh my God. You fucking snob."

"Oh, and yes, I *am* the captain of this boat. Because I'm older."

"Yeah, well, you're about to have a mutiny on your hands, Cap, if you don't stop this power trip." She flops back down and rests her cheek on her crossed arms. "If I can't listen to my music, at least play something on Betty. I like listening to music while I'm dozing."

It's a fair compromise. And since every line I've written thus far is utter shit, I give up on lyrics and start strumming the guitar. I don't play anything in particular, just a slow, airy melody that matches this current vibe of bobbing on the waves in the sunshine.

"That's pretty," Blake says, twisting her head toward me. "Is that a real song?"

I shake my head. "Nah. Just making it up on the spot."

"Oh."

I can't see her expression behind her sunglasses, but something about her wistful tone amuses me.

"Why do you sound sad about that?"

"I'm not sad. I'm...jealous," she admits. "I envy you."

"Yeah? Why?"

"Because you're so talented. You play, like, five instruments—"

"Three."

"—your voice is incredible, and your lyrics are beautiful. Of course I'm envious. I wish I had a talent like yours. I'm not good at anything."

"You're good at annoying me," I say helpfully.

"Awesome. I'll wear it as a badge of honor."

"And you *are* talented, Logan. Don't you have, like, a perfect

GPA?"

She brushes that off. "How is that a talent?"

"It means you're really smart," I point out.

"Lots of people are smart. Doesn't make me special."

A frown surfaces. She can't possibly believe she's not special. Just looking at her, you know she is. Her mere energy screams *special.*

Before I can argue, she asks, "Any new developments in Nashville?"

Instantly, my relaxed mood fades.

"Not really. I gig every weekend. I write, I record, I post shit online. But it's like... Success hinges on more than just talent, you know? It always involves a bit of luck too. The right song in front of the right audience at the right time." I absently strum a few chords. "I need to write it. That song. *The* song."

"I mean, not to state the obvious, but isn't your mother an award-winning songwriter?"

Frustration clamps around my throat. "Yes, she is. That's the problem."

"How is that a problem? Seriously, Wyatt, think about the opportunity you have here that other people don't. You want *the song*. Why not team up with Hannah and—"

"I don't want to write a song with my mom. I don't want her help."

"So stubborn," Blake chides.

My hand clenches around the guitar's neck. "You don't get it. I want to feel like I succeeded on my own. On my own merits. Without help."

"Everybody needs help." Her voice grows gentle. "You're lucky you have two parents who are supportive and willing to help you out."

“Maybe,” I say vaguely. “But that doesn’t change the fact that I want to do this alone.” When I feel her gaze on me, I shift awkwardly in my seat. “What?”

“Look at you,” she teases. “Not being a dick for ten whole minutes.”

“You know me. I like to keep people on their toes.”

Blake gives me a solemn nod. “Of course. Gotta make them guess which Wyatt Graham they’ll get that day. Will he be a raging asshole? A creative genius? A lake fuckboy?”

“Hey, lake fuckboy is a great gig,” I say, and she responds with a smile that almost knocks me on my ass.

I’m frozen for a second. I’ve seen her smile before, but not like this, and I suddenly feel like someone seeing color for the first time. *This* smile is unguarded. It’s soft and alive and shining brighter than the sun. It traps my breath halfway in my chest.

For a moment, the entire world simply…stops.

I blink, the lyric floating through my mind.

*Your smile stops the world.*

As Blake resumes her sunbathing, I grab my notebook and scribble the line down before it slips into the ether.

Fuck.

I don’t know what just happened, but I know I’ll be chasing that smile in songs for a long time.

# Chapter 6

## BLAKE

*A victim of the lake*

THE MOOD IS LIGHTER WHEN we tie off the bowrider a few hours later. Despite the rocky start to the day, Wyatt finally calmed his grouchy ass down, scribbling up a storm on the boat while I napped. I'm not sure what inspired him, but I much prefer a chill Wyatt to the one who was snapping at me for daring to sunbathe.

At the house, we discover that like the urban legend he is, Houseman Henry paid us a visit when we were gone. The fridge and freezer are overflowing with food, including the juiciest-looking steaks from the butcher in town. Part of me still feels like a spoiled brat who's taking advantage of her parents, but I keep reminding myself it's what they want. *Summer of Blake*, Mom had encouraged. So I'm giving myself permission to be spoiled.

I go upstairs to take a shower and wash off the sunscreen and sweat from the day. When I come down to prep dinner, I stop halfway to the fridge, momentarily derailed by the sight of Wyatt in the dining room.

He's at the table, shirtless, leaning over the puzzle that I noticed this morning. For some reason, I assumed someone else had started it, but I realize now how dumb that is. He's the only other person here, unless Houseman Henry secretly shows up when we're out to work on a jigsaw puzzle. Actually… I wouldn't put it past him.

I wander over to pick up the box. It depicts a lake scene at night, with a huge moon reflected in the black water and a family of swans congregating beneath a willow tree with dark, dangling branches that look like skeleton fingers. Other than the red canoe in the center of the lake, the puzzle is an obnoxious expanse of black and white in different gradients.

Wyatt is scowling at a piece like it murdered his family in a past life, but I'm too busy ogling his bare chest and wondering how he could make an activity this nerdy look pornographic. My eyes rest on the V of his hips. I love man vees. They're so lickable.

I wonder what he'd do if I dropped to my knees and licked his man vee.

The thought makes me snort out loud.

Wyatt glances at me. "Can I help you?" he says politely.

I snap out of it. "Are you doing a puzzle?"

"No, I'm just putting these pieces in place for no reason. They don't form an image at all."

"Wyatt Graham is doing a puzzle."

"Yeah, so?"

"Fuckboys don't puzzle."

"I'm not a boy. I'm a man."

"Got it. So you're a fuckman."

With a sigh, he leans forward again, abs tightening. I gulp down a flood of saliva. Oh my God. His abs are lickable too. So are his pecs. They're just defined enough to be sexy but not bulky enough to look like gym boobs.

I can't handle him like this. Bare-chested, hair messed, sweatpants low. It should be illegal for someone to be this hot while doing a *puzzle.*

"Why aren't you putting together the frame first?" I ask him.

"That's not how I roll."

"That's the only way to puzzle," I argue.

"I have a system, okay? The Graham system."

"It's inefficient."

"Can you please go away? This is my activity. Go find your own."

I pluck a few edge pieces out of the box and start making a pile.

"No," Wyatt growls. "I told you, I don't go by edges. I go by colors."

"It's all black and white!"

"And red," he says smugly, pointing to the canoe.

"You know what? Fine. Do your stupid puzzle without my help. It's only, what..." I check the box. "Four thousand pieces? I'm sure your system will have you finishing this in no time. Fucking asshole."

His snort tickles my shoulder blades as I go to prep dinner.

I soon discover that Wyatt is a kitchen nuisance. Abandoning his puzzle, he wanders over and gets in the way constantly. Bumping into me. Jostling me with his elbow. Swiping a cherry tomato from the bowl when I'm in the middle of tossing the salad. When I open the fridge, he's randomly standing there, even though he's not getting anything.

"You need to get out of here," I blurt out. "You're in my way! Go prep the grill."

"The grill is heating up."

"I don't care. You're being intrusive."

"*You're* being intrusive. You intruded on my summer."

"Oh my God, just go and stand silently outside and wait for the barbecue to heat up and get out of my life."

"You're very bossy," he says, smiling faintly. "Has anyone ever told you that?"

"Yes."

"I'm digging it."

"Oh really. You enjoy being bossed around."

"Outside the bedroom? Sure," he says, then saunters off and leaves me battling a jolt of desire.

The idea of Wyatt being commanding in the bedroom sends a tiny thrill down my spine and—

Nope.

I'm not allowed to think about what he enjoys in bed.

Through the glass doors, I watch him pull on a long-sleeved shirt. His sweatpants ride lower on his hips as he lifts his arms, and I gulp because I don't think he's wearing anything underneath those pants. My eyes instinctively focus on his ass. I sort of want him to turn around so I can search for the outline of his dick, and oh my God, that is the perviest thing I've ever thought, and I should be ashamed of myself.

I force my gaze away and focus on the salad and roasted potatoes.

By the time I step onto the deck, he's set the table, and the smell of grilled sirloin fills my nostrils. My stomach rumbles in response. I got a lot of sun today and didn't eat much, so I'm ravenous.

"Can we talk about the puzzle now?" I ask as I cut off a piece of steak. "I have some constructive criticism."

"No."

"I checked out your sorting trays, and you're putting pieces that belong to the moon into the tray with the swans."

"Logan," he says. "Go find your own puzzle."

"You know what? Maybe I will. Then you can watch me puzzle circles around your sorry ass."

"Oh wow. I keep forgetting how competitive you are."

"I'm not competitive," I object.

"Remember when you were a kid and used to challenge Gigi to foot races and then cried each time she beat you?"

"I didn't cry. I just teared up."

"That's crying."

"Crying occurs when the tears exit your eyes. If they're still contained, it doesn't count."

"It totally counts."

We spend the rest of dinner bickering about literally everything. Whether ketchup belongs on steak. If humans could ever live on the moon. The correct orientation of the toilet paper roll. At first, I think maybe he's picking the wrong answers just to annoy me.

But then I realize what's happening.

"The dynamic is off," I announce, cutting him off midsentence as he tries to explain why I'm wrong about mosquitoes. Mr. Naive over here *actually* believes we can eradicate them without it affecting the food chain. I can't even.

"What do you mean?" Wyatt says. "What dynamic?"

"That's why we keep arguing. Because we've never spent any time alone together, and it's a shock to the system. Like, I don't know what your personality is without your sister here."

"Well, I don't know what your personality is without your dad standing there glaring at anyone who talks to you."

I snicker. "Not anyone. Just the Golden Boys."

The Golden Boys refers to three of the more entertaining hockey kids in our circle—Beau, AJ, and Gray. A year younger than I am, they're a hell-raising, heartbreaking trio of budding hockey stars. I've never met a straight woman who didn't fall over backward for one of the Golden Boys.

I finish my prosecco, which I'm surprised Wyatt didn't try to confiscate. But he didn't say a word when I pulled the bottle out of the wine fridge. I'm on my second glass now, and it's loosening my tongue.

"God, imagine if he knew I lost my virginity to one of them?" I giggle as I picture my dad's reaction.

Wyatt's surprised gaze flies to mine. "Which one?"

"Beau," I confess.

"Ah, the goldenest of the Golden Boys."

He's not wrong. Beau Di Laurentis is the definition of golden. I'm talking blond hair, bright green eyes, dazzling smile. The worst part? He's also a genuinely good guy. The all-American sweetheart.

"How was it?" Intrigue flickers in Wyatt's eyes. And I swear I see a spark of heat too.

But that's probably wishful thinking. I don't make Wyatt hot. For a moment there, when we were on the boat today, I thought maybe I was actually affecting him. He seemed so flustered at the sight of my boobs that it gave me a little ego boost. But then he informed me they "weren't anything special," so who the fuck knows. He's too difficult to pin down.

"I'm not telling you that," I reply.

"Why not?"

"Do you want to tell me about the night you lost *your* virginity?"

"I mean, it wasn't that eventful. I lasted about ten strokes before blowing my load."

"Was it to Mrs. Brown?"

He grins. "No. It was to an age-appropriate girl."

"How old were you?"

"Fifteen. How old were you with Golden Boy?"

"Seventeen."

He sips his beer, and my gaze is drawn to his mouth. Ugh. It isn't fair. Even almost three years later, I can clearly remember how those lips felt trailing up my neck, when his body was pressed up against me and I wanted him so badly it made me dizzy.

He never kissed me.

He kissed my neck, my jaw, that sensitive spot beneath my ear. But not my lips.

Sometimes I wonder if he did that on purpose. Maybe he knew that if our lips touched, I'd never forget it.

Catching me staring, Wyatt lifts a brow. "What?"

"Nothing." I quickly avert my eyes, feeling a blush rising in my cheeks.

His tone is casual when he speaks again. "How did that happen anyway? You and Beau? Where was it?"

"Their place in Connecticut. My parents and I were spending the weekend, and I stayed home when everyone went out for dinner. Beau had plans that night. Otherwise, I doubt Dad would've left us alone. But his plans fell through."

"And the rest is virginity history," Wyatt finishes.

"Yep."

"What was his move?"

"Pretty sure it was *my* move. I didn't want to go to college a virgin."

"So you lost it just for the sake of losing it?" He makes a tsking noise. "You're better than that, freckles."

"Don't call me that."

"I can go back to *kid*," he offers.

I give him a dirty look. "Don't you dare."

Wyatt leans back in his chair. "Was it his first time?"

"Ugh. No. Guy's a year younger than me and he was already a

sex pro."

"Did he go down on you?"

My face burns hotter. "I'm not answering that."

He chuckles. "You're blushing. That means yes."

I get to my feet, eager to end this conversation before my cheeks literally burst into flames. "Come on, let's clean up. I still need to get ready."

Just like that, the lighthearted mood dies.

"For what?" he demands.

"I'm going into town tonight."

"For what purpose?"

I stare at him. "For the purpose of fun."

His expression darkens. He pauses, as if thinking it over. Then he shakes his head. "No. You're not going."

I start to stack our dishes. "Hey, Wyatt, guess what? You have no say in how I spend my time."

"Maybe not, but one message to Man Chat, and I know someone who'll be *very* interested in your plans."

"Oh no!" I roll my eyes. "You realize my dad is across the country, right? He can tell me not to go to a bar tonight until he's blue in the face. But guess who's still going to the bar?"

"Oh, so now it's a bar?"

"It was always a bar," I say in exasperation. "I want to go out. Meet people."

"Guys?"

"I don't know. Maybe. What do you care?"

*It's not like you're interested in me*, I almost snap, but I'm not opening that can of worms. Best to leave our past encounters where they belong—inside the small dungeon in my gut labeled HUMILIATION. Bringing up his lack of interest won't lead to anything but an uncomfortable conversation.

I'm about to carry the plates inside when a flood of light suddenly illuminates the deck.

Wyatt and I both swivel our heads in alarm. I can't see it, but there's a boat down below, its lights slicing through the dark water. And since everything carries on this lake, we can hear them perfectly.

"Darlie?" someone says in a loud hiss. Sounds like a man.

We exchange a look.

"Are you Darlie?" I murmur.

He chokes out a laugh. "No, I'm not Darlie."

"Darlie." Another voice now. A higher pitch but also male. "Show yourself."

What the hell is happening?

My eyes widen when Wyatt heads for the stairs. I swiftly reach for his arm and tug him backward.

"Stop that," I whisper. "Don't go *toward* the crazy people in the lake. What if they have a gun?"

"Why would they have a gun?"

"Maybe they're trying to kill Darlie."

He ponders that for a moment, then shrugs. "I think we'll be fine."

Ignoring my hushed protests, he bounds down the stairs, and because I can't let him die alone, I hurry after him.

"Darlie! We heard you the other night. You were crying out. You want someone to see you. *We* see you."

The boat is almost directly at our dock now.

"Hey, bro?" Wyatt calls out.

"Who's there?" one of the voices shouts back.

"The owner of this house" is Wyatt's wry response.

I sidle up to him, squinting at the boat. A midsize motorboat, carrying two men in their early to mid-twenties. The moon is bright tonight, offering a good view of them. One is muscular and broad-shouldered with bushy brown hair and a thick beard. The other is wiry and blond, wearing a tank top from Mollie May's latest world tour. So obviously I like him on the spot.

They cut the engine, their boat drifting closer to the dock. "This is your place?" the big one says. "Excellent! You would've heard Darlie last night then."

"Who's Darlie?" I ask curiously.

"She's a victim of the lake."

Okay.

I regret asking.

The smaller guy pokes the big one in the ribs. "Stop. You're being creepy, Spence." To us, he offers a reassuring smile. "Hold on, let me explain. I swear he's not crazy. We're paranormal podcasters."

Oh, so they're *both* crazy.

Wyatt nods at the men. "All right."

All right? That's all he's got to say about...whatever this is?

"I promise you we're totally normal dudes." The small one quickly introduces himself. "I'm Spencer."

"And I'm Spencer," says the bigger one.

Wyatt and I share another look.

"Both of you?" I finally say.

"Yup," confirms the bigger Spencer. "Spelled the same and everything."

"College roommates too," the smaller Spencer adds. "It's like the universe knew."

"Our middle names are different, though," Big Spencer says. "Which is a shame. Imagine if we were both Spencer James Hands? How cosmic would that be?"

"I'm sorry, did you say Hands?" Wyatt shifts his gaze between them. I suspect his head is spinning in perfect sync with mine.

"Hanz. With a Z." Little Spencer hooks a thumb at his partner. "Blame this beautiful asshole. I took his last name."

That's sweet. "How long have you been married?" I ask.

"Oh, we're not married yet. I preemptively took it."

Wow.

"So, um, about this lake victim?" I prompt. "Do you mean like a ghost?"

"Yes. One of many," Big Spencer reveals. "This lake is teeming with ghosts."

Now I'm intrigued. "Is it really?"

"Oh yeah. Tahoe is steeped in the supernatural. Have you never heard of the Tahoe Biltmore?"

"The hotel?" I say blankly.

"Try the most haunted hotel in the area," Little Spencer retorts. He seems like the more dramatic one, speaking with extravagant hand gestures. "The paranormal activity there is off the charts. Doors opening, slamming. Unintelligible whispers. Creepy knocks. Guests are constantly spotting Mary hanging out in the stairwells."

"Mary?" I echo, while Wyatt gives me a look that says *please don't indulge this*.

"The showgirl who haunts the hotel. She wears a miniskirt and go-go boots," Little Spencer says.

"And has no face," Big Spencer pipes up.

"But we're not here to rehash the same old nonsense that every other paranormal expert investigates," Little Spencer informs me. "Like the Biltmore or the mansion on Fannette Island." He adopts a jeering tone. "Ooooh, I smell cinnamon toast. Soooo cool."

"What?" I've never been more confused in my life.

"The Fannette Island ghost was something of a breakfast connoisseur," Big Spencer explains. "Her favorite breakfast was cinnamon toast, and all the park rangers claim they can smell cinnamon when they're out there."

I nod solemnly. "Got it. But you're not here to chase dead showgirls or cinnamon ghosts."

"Correct. We're not interested in all the cases that have been done to death—no pun intended." Little Spencer chortles before going gravely serious again. No pun intended. "One of the lesser-known sightings is of a woman named Darlie Gallagher. She drowned herself in the lake after her fiancé left her for her younger sister. Happened about fifty years ago."

"But don't worry," Big Spencer assures us. "She's not evil."

"Well, that's a relief," Wyatt says, and I hope they don't realize he's fucking with them.

"If anything, you're lucky to have her," Little Spencer confirms. "As far as ghosts go, Darlie is kind and generous. And she *loves* love. Which, frankly, shows a deep emotional maturity on her part that most humans can only dream of having. I mean, here she is, her heart shattered to pieces by her lover and her sister, yet she still believes in the power of love. Still desperate for others to experience it."

Oh my God. I don't think I'm drunk enough for this conversation.

"We've been here about a week. You know, checking out the sites, hitting up the local library," Big Spencer tells us. "According to our research, Darlie usually appears during a full moon."

"Is she a werewolf?" Wyatt asks, and I can see him trying not to laugh.

"No. But there was a full moon the night she drowned. And there was a full moon last night when we were cruising the lake."

"We *heard* her," Little Spencer says triumphantly. "And, oh my wow, you guys. It was like...these screams were coming from deep beneath the water. High-pitched. Ringing with such anguish. Calling out for love."

"Real longing," Big Spencer agrees, nodding.

I bite my lip. Hard. Oh boy.

"Um, so... I hate to disappoint you," I tell the Spencers. "But... I think that was me."

Their expressions collapse. "What do you mean it was you?" Little Spencer demands.

"Yeah, so we"—I gesture between me and Wyatt—"sort of fell in the lake last night by accident—"

"By accident?" Wyatt cuts in.

"Well, he pushed me in," I say sweetly. "And, well, I remember screaming pretty loudly, out of shock and because the water was stupidly cold, and then I got hypothermia—"

"She didn't get hypothermia," interjects Wyatt.

"Anyway, I'm sorry," I finish. "No Darlie sighting last night. That was just me."

"Well, shit," Big Spencer says.

They sit there wallowing in their disappointment for a moment until Little Spencer brightens.

"You know what?" he says. "It's cool. Totally fine. Just because it wasn't her last night doesn't mean she won't show up tonight, right? Look how big the moon is. Totally still big enough for her to want to haunt people and infect them with her love bug."

"I mean, I'd prefer she didn't," Wyatt hedges in.

The Spencers ignore him and fix their pleading gazes on me. I think they've clocked me as the more receptive one.

"Do you mind if we sit out here by your dock for a while and listen?" Big Spencer asks.

"Sure, knock yourself out," I say, shrugging. "We're just…going to go back inside."

"We'll catch you guys on the lake tomorrow!" Little Spencer calls after us.

"That's what I'm afraid of," Wyatt mumbles under his breath.

We leave the two boat weirdos to their own devices and quickly ascend the steps back up to the house. Not a word passes between us. It isn't until the french doors are firmly closed, providing a sound barrier to the lake, that we look at each other and burst out laughing.

I double over, wheezing from the giggles. Wyatt rubs tears from his eyes, pushing hair away from his face as he laughs his ass off.

"Jesus Christ," he croaks.

"Okay," I say when my laughter finally subsides. "They were nuts, yes. But they were kind of adorable."

"They were not adorable, Logan."

"Also, and I'm not joking, but I'm really intrigued about this Darlie case. And all the supernatural Tahoe stories?" I glance at him on my way to the staircase. "Do you need the Jeep tomorrow, or can I take it?"

"Take it where?" he asks suspiciously.

"You realize I'm allowed to drive to town by myself without telling you what it's for, right?"

"Take it where?" he repeats.

"Oh my God. If you must know, I want to hit up the library." I head up the stairs, over my shoulder adding, "I'm getting changed now."

"Right, into your pajamas. I approve."

I stop halfway on the staircase and peer down at him. "I told you I'm going out. That hasn't changed."

"You're not going out."

"Oh, I am. And guess what else? You're not invited."

He glares at me from the bottom of the stairs. "Like hell I'm not."

"Sorry, Graham. I'm just gonna order a car and be on my way."

"I'll drive you," Wyatt says through clenched teeth. I can see his jaw ticking from the strain.

"Nope," I answer cheerfully. "Because you're not coming."

"Oh, I insist."

He stomps off, and I'm grinning to myself as I climb the rest of the stairs. Reverse psychology. Works every time.

# Chapter 7

## WYATT

*Everyone gets jealous*

THE BAR IS ONE OF those lake-town dives with string lights and wooden tables with sticky tops. We find a seat in the back near a jukebox that's cranking out classic rock my dad would drool over. Speaking of drooling, our waiter can't stop checking out Blake, though I don't blame him because I'm doing the same damn thing. The infuriating woman changed into a sundress designed to get a man hard. Short, white, and innocent in the kind of way that isn't innocent at all.

Kill me.

I'd much rather be back at the house with my guitar, but she was determined to go out tonight, with or without me. And, well, the latter wasn't an option, so…here I am. Nursing a whiskey I don't even want, trying not to notice the way her dress rides up as she settles on a stool. At least she's drinking a virgin cocktail. That's reassuring, I suppose.

Fuck. How did I let everyone get in my head like this? I need to be keeping my distance from Blake, and instead I'm sticking to her like glue because the entire family keeps reminding me she's fresh off a breakup and needs someone to watch out for her.

That someone should *not* be me.

Like, I'm the worst person for the job.

Whatever she sees in my expression has Blake rolling her eyes. "Jeez, Graham. Your brooding is off the charts, even by your high standards of brooding."

"Stop flirting with the waiter," I say flatly.

She gapes at me. "I'm sorry, what? What the hell is wrong with you?"

"Nothing. But don't think I didn't see that hand action when he gave you your drink."

"*Hand action*?"

"You touched his hand. And your smile was too friendly. He thought you were hitting on him."

"Oh my God. My hand *grazed* his when I was accepting my drink, and I gave him a polite thank-you smile." She bends her head to wrap her lips around her straw, taking a long sip. "Why are you suddenly so concerned about everything I do? You're not my dad."

She's right. I'm not her dad. I'm the selfish prick who has no right to want her this badly. But I do. Every time she laughs, I want to inject that sound directly into my soul. Every time she rolls her eyes at me, I want to shove her against the wall and show her exactly what I've been holding back.

I've always been attracted to her, but until now, it was *just* attraction. Which made it easy to draw a line and follow a self-imposed hands-off rule. I can get sex anywhere. I don't need to risk hurting a close family friend for it.

But today, it's felt like a lot more than lust. It's felt like goddamn obsession. Because today, she's been living inside my head. Even now,

I keep replaying every conversation we had, every time she smiled, every dumb joke she made. And that strange ache I've felt in my chest since she got here is the worst part, because it reminds me too much of being a preteen with my first crush.

This isn't a fucking crush. I'm not that guy. And I've known this girl most of my life. Why the hell am I obsessing *now*?

It's the celibacy vow. That's got to be it. Combined with the fact that I can't seem to get away from her. Close quarters, hot girl, no sex. Clearly that's a recipe for *fuck with Wyatt's head*.

I set my glass down too hard, jolting the tabletop. "I'm just trying to look out for you."

"Well, don't. I don't need it," she says irritably, planting both hands on the table before wincing. "Ew! Why is this so sticky?" She lifts her palms and grimaces at them. Then, with a grumble, she slides off the stool. "Awesome. Now I need to wash my hands."

Every man in a fifty-foot radius watches her go.

Once she disappears into the restroom corridor, I reach for my phone and text the dude who put me in this position. Cole swore this celibacy plan would help. He did it himself last year, a full sex cleanse after years of fuckboying his way through life. And I've heard his celibacy tracks. His new album slays, and he's going on a world tour this fall, which means there's obviously some method to this madness.

So why isn't it working for *me*?

This no-sex thing is messing with my head.

COLE

Told you it wouldn't be easy. Chin up, little buddy. Just avoid temptation.

How am I supposed to do that when temptation literally showed up at my door?

COLE

What does that mean?

It means the girl who's the definition of forbidden fruit is spending the summer with me.

COLE

Fuck's sake. Only you have this sort of luck, Graham. I swear you were born with a horseshoe up your ass.

Oh, and she likes to tan topless.

COLE

Nice. Channel it into a sexy track.

I'm not selling sex.

COLE

You're such a stubborn asshole, G.

When Blake returns to the table, I do my best to de-scowl and paste on a pleasant expression. Truth is we had a pretty good day. I even wrote something that wasn't garbage, thanks to Blake. She inspired one line that spawned an entire verse. If she wants to have fun tonight, maybe I should stop getting in her way.

"Any update on the toaster situation?" I ask her.

She eyes me distrustfully.

"What?"

"Is this how the summer is going to play out?" She twirls her straw, making the ice cubes clack against her glass. "One second you're cool, and then you're snapping at me and insulting my boobs. Then you're totally normal, talking about music and swapping virginity stories, and then boom—forbidding me from leaving the house. And now you're pretending to care about my custody battle for Hot Boi? I want off this ride, Graham."

I let out a rueful breath. "I'm sorry for insulting your boobs earlier."

"And my taste in music."

"Well, no. Your taste in music sucks."

"Mollie May is catchy!"

"She's surface level," I shoot back.

"Right, and you're an endless abyss of deep. Sooooo deep." Blake presents me with the dramatic rolling of her eyes.

I toy with my condensation-drenched beer label, slowly peeling it off the bottle. "I mean, I'm trying to be. But it's not working. I've had writer's block for almost a year now."

She falters. "Oh shit. I'm sorry. Why didn't you say something earlier? I didn't realize you were blocked."

"It's fine. It happens."

"It's not 'fine.' Music is your whole life. And it's how you make a living. Do you have any, like, strategies to combat writer's block? Have you had it before?"

"Never like this," I find myself admitting.

"That's awful."

The sympathy that flashes in her eyes prickles at me, mostly because I have a tough time separating sympathy from pity. I fucking *hate* pity.

I rip a piece of the label, and the narrow strip curls into itself. "It's fine," I repeat, firmer this time, because I don't want to talk about this anymore. "I'll get over it. I have a plan."

"Okay. What's the plan?"

"No sex."

Blake looks confused. "What?"

I rub the back of my neck, feeling sheepish. "I'm off sex for a while."

"What's a while?" she demands.

"Haven't gotten laid in six months."

"Bullshit."

"It's true." I tip back the bottle and gulp down a mouthful of beer.

"How are you still alive?"

I laugh mid-sip, coughing. "Funny."

"No, seriously. I can't believe you're not having sex. This must be torture for you."

"How often do you think I fuck, freckles?"

The moment the question pops out, I grit my teeth, reminding myself I'm not supposed to say shit like that around her. It's bad enough that I allowed the virginity conversation earlier.

*Allowed?*

Fine. Initiated.

I regret that now, because the only thing it achieved was planting visions in my head of Blake having sex with Beau of all people. I certainly didn't expect the hot rush of jealousy I felt at the knowledge that she'd given it up to him.

It's so fucking wrong, but I wish I was her first.

"So you're forsaking sex for music?" Blake muses, oblivious to my inner turmoil.

"Sort of." I grudgingly continue. "I was talking to Cole, my old bandmate—"

"Cole Tanner? Oh my God, he's so hot."

I roll my eyes at her. "How is that relevant to anything?"

"It's not. Just stating a fact."

"Anyway, supposedly celibacy is a creative reset. Helps clear your head. You know, channel the frustration and pent-up..." I search for the right word.

"Semen?" she offers, and I huff out a laugh.

"Lust," I correct. "Cole swears it'll get me back in touch with my work."

"So basically, you've been acting like a cranky asshole because you haven't had sex?" She curiously seeks out my gaze. "Do you jerk off?"

Oh, hell. Why did I open this door?

"That's none of your business."

"No, tell me. Are you abstaining from orgasms in general or just sex with another person?"

"I jerk off," I answer against my will. My vocal cords are working of their own volition without input from my brain.

Blake pops her straw back in her mouth, realizing her glass is empty when she sucks in nothing but air. "I'm gonna grab another," she says. "Want me to get you another beer?"

I narrow my eyes on her. "With what ID?"

"Definitely not a fake one," she says innocently.

I sigh as she darts off. This girl will be the death of me.

My phone buzzes, a much-needed distraction. Or not. Because it's my sister asking how Blake's doing. I swear this entire family network is obsessed with Blake Logan's well-being.

She's fine. We went out on the boat today.

GIGI

Are you being nice to her?

Sometimes.

GIGI

LMAO You're such a dick.

This was supposed to be my writing summer, Stan.

GIGI

Well, now it's your be-a-nice-human summer where you get to show some compassion for the girl whose heart got broken.

Trust me, she's doing fine.

More than fine, in fact. My shoulders go rigid when I notice Blake chatting with the bartender. She leans against the counter to hear him better over the music. He's leaning toward her too.

There's an unsettling amount of leaning happening right now.

Are they flirting? And does he have a mullet?

Who has a mullet this day and age?

Absentmindedly, I type a text while monitoring the situation unfolding across the room. The guy is young, early twenties, but something about the way he's leering at Blake gives him a creepy old man vibe.

Thoughts on mullets?

GIGI

Your subject changing skills never fail to amaze me.

I don't like them.

Exactly. Nobody fucking likes them.

At the bar, Blake laughs at something the Mullet says, then touches his arm. It's light, casual. But intentional. I know that move. I do it all the time. Laugh, lean in, touch the arm.

My hand curls around my empty beer bottle, my grip so tight I'm surprised the glass doesn't shatter in my palm. I have to remind myself that only twenty minutes ago, I had decided to let her have fun. If she wants to flirt with a guy whose barber should be executed, then fine, I won't get in her way.

I shift on the stool and force myself to focus on the music. A live trio is playing on the small stage, blasting out an old grunge song. It's not half bad.

But all I can hear is Blake's melodic laughter rising over the crashing cymbals.

My gaze unwittingly returns to the bar. The Mullet is even closer now, practically draped over the damn counter. He has way too much confidence for someone wearing that many bracelets. Like, they're taking up half his arm. One bracelet, cool. That's punk rock. Some rings, okay. This is extreme. And sad.

When my jaw tightens to the point of pain, I have to forcibly unclench it. Christ. I don't know why this bothers me so much. This girl is off-limits. I won't fucking touch her.

But here I am, sitting at a sticky high-top table contemplating murder while Blake smiles at some asshole who doesn't deserve to be breathing the same air as her.

Not that I do either. She's too damn good for me. She's clever and funny and fearless, and she deserves someone who can make her feel...safe. Cherished.

That's not me. I break women without trying. Without meaning to. They always fall for me, no matter how clear I make it at the beginning that it won't lead to forever. I'm not built for forever. I can't commit to one girl, and I certainly can't be tied down, not when all I desire from this life is to be on the road, touring and making music.

But women always think they'll be the exception, the ones to make me fall—and they always get hurt. I don't want to hurt Blake.

And maybe...maybe I'm also resisting opening that door because she looks at me sometimes in a way that makes me uncomfortable. Like she sees straight through the chaos inside me.

Her laughter travels in my direction again. I hate the gleam in the

Mullet's eyes every time Blake laughs. I'm a man, so I know what he's thinking: What are my odds of going home with her?

*Zero, pal.*

Maybe I should just fuck her.

I let the idea percolate. Sex always has a way of squashing a crush. For me at least. I know from experience that all it takes is one night for me to get my endorphin rush and be on my way.

Who knows? The sex might not even be that good, right? Maybe these past few years of lusting from afar have built this up into something that can never live up to my jerk-off fantasies. Hell, and it's presumptuous to think she'd even let me in her pants. She's got better taste than that.

At the bar, the Mullet makes her giggle by tugging on a strand of her hair.

He's touching her goddamn hair now?

Oh hell no.

This isn't jealousy, I assure myself. It's responsibility. She's fresh out of a relationship and she's vulnerable. She doesn't know what she wants right now. But I guarantee it's not the douchebag with the mullet.

I cross the bar in three long strides, sliding in beside her.

Blake turns in surprise. "Hey."

"It's late," I say coldly. "We're leaving."

The Mullet interjects. "We're in the middle of a conversation."

I spare him a look. "She's done talking."

Frowning, the guy glances at Blake. "Is this your boyfriend or your bodyguard?"

She huffs out a laugh. "Neither."

"Let's go," I tell her.

Our gazes lock, and whatever she sees on my face has her

capitulating.

"Sorry," she tells the Mullet. "I guess we're leaving."

Without another word, she grabs her purse off the stool and follows me out of the bar. It isn't until we're halfway across the parking lot that she stops in her tracks.

"What happened back there, Wyatt?"

I continue walking toward the Jeep. "Nothing. I wanted to go."

"Were you jealous?"

The accusation stings my back. I stop, waiting for her to catch up to me. "I don't get jealous."

"Everyone gets jealous," Blake says irritably. "And honestly, you're kind of acting like it right now."

"I have no reason to be jealous of anyone tonight, Logan."

"Right. Silly me." Her lips curl. "I guess this is just your celibacy plan making you act like a dickhead again?"

"Yes," I say lightly. "That's all it is, freckles."

I pretend not to see the hurt that clouds her expression. Same way I pretended not to see it when she was sixteen, confessing her crush, and I patted her head like she was a toddler. Or the way I pretended not to see it the morning after I almost fucked her on Christmas Eve and played dumb.

I still believe I was doing the right thing in both instances, but the pain in her eyes has stayed with me. Haunted me.

For a second, I almost tell her how goddamn often I think about her. But keeping her at arm's length is what I'm skilled at, so I keep talking like an asshole.

"I'm just annoyed, okay? I didn't want to spend the rest of my night watching you fake laugh with some bartender."

"Who says it was fake laughter?"

"That kid has never told a funny joke in his life, Blake."

"Oh, because you're hilarious? Cracking jokes left and right? You've been a jerk fifty percent of the day."

"And you've been a distraction," I shoot back. "Flirting. Teasing. Showing off your tits. I'm trying to write."

"Oh my God, you are such an arrogant asshole. Did you ever think that what I do has nothing to do with you? Maybe I actually don't want tan lines? Maybe I want to talk to the cute bartender? And I was barely even flirting with him! I was just being friendly."

"Friendly," I repeat mockingly. "Is that what we're calling it now?"

"What the hell is your problem?" Blake demands.

*I don't know*, I want to groan.

Instead, I double down.

"My problem is that you're desperate for attention from any guy who'll give you five seconds. And now that your boyfriend finally did what everyone saw coming, you're flirting with everyone to make yourself feel better."

Her jaw drops. "Excuse me?"

I plow on, because I'm too reckless and riled up to stop. "You're not trying to be friendly. You're trying to be wanted."

Blake doesn't say anything for several beats. But behind her look of disbelief, I glimpse that familiar darkness. A storm of hurt.

Finally, she marches to the passenger side of the Jeep. "Unlock it," she snaps at me.

The ride home is fraught with tension. Blake's arms are crossed tight to her chest, her body language advising me to keep my mouth shut. For once, I do.

I focus on the curve of the road winding around the lake while Blake fixes her gaze out the window and gives me the silent treatment. By the time we get back to the house, the silence is suffocating, closing around my windpipe. She jumps out of the Jeep, her sundress swirling around her legs.

I follow her to the porch and pretend I'm not watching the way her hair catches in the moonlight. I might be obsessed with her hair. Not sure when it happened, but here we are.

"Good night," she mutters in the front hall and heads for the stairs.

I go to the kitchen, wondering whether to grab a beer and my guitar and sit outside or just punch myself in the face for how badly I've screwed up today.

I choose option number three: go upstairs and try to sleep for once in my life.

I step into the second-floor hallway just as Blake emerges from the hall bathroom, because like an asshole, I stole her room with the en suite.

She's in her pajamas, though I use the term loosely. It's nothing but a tiny pair of shorts and a white tank top that I can see right through. Her face is scrubbed clean, pink and shiny with her freckles on full display. Her hair is loose and cascading down her back.

Somehow, she's even more dangerous like this. Without the sexy, slutty sundress or the mascara and lip gloss. Bare and effortless. The kind of beautiful that makes you forget how to breathe.

"Shouldn't you put on something warmer?" I ask like an idiot. "It gets cold at night."

"Always telling me what to wear, huh, Wyatt?" Her voice is surly.

"No, that's not what I mean. You'll just get…cold." Jesus. *Shut the hell up*, I tell myself.

"I'm fine," she mutters, then turns on her heel.

She's done with the conversation.

I let her be done. Because if I open my mouth again, I'm not sure I'd be able to keep lying.

Since I've decided to battle my insomnia tonight by actually attempting to sleep, I strip off my clothes and slide into bed naked, trying to make myself comfortable. But there's no comfortable sleeping position to be had when your dick is rock-hard.

I'm too primed from tonight. Too pent-up from these past six months. Celibacy is not a natural state for me. I like to fuck. I *need* to fuck.

I roll over, and my erection stabs the mattress. I'm so hard it hurts.

After several minutes of ignoring my aching balls, I think, *screw it*. Might as well take care of this. Leaning over, I grab my phone from the nightstand, prepared to find some porn.

Instead, I pull up Blake's IG account.

This is so wrong. On so many levels. I recognize this. Not proud of it either. But knowing all this doesn't stop me from scrolling through her feed until I find a photo that shows some skin.

It's a selfie she took last summer at the Di Laurentis place in St. Barts. She's sprawled on a lounge chair, wearing a skimpy red bikini. Her hair is twisted up into a messy bun, wavy strands framing her face to emphasize sun-kissed cheeks and an array of freckles. She's got one knee propped up in a pose that draws the eye—*my* eye, at least—right between her legs.

I imagine nudging aside the thin strip of fabric and exposing her pussy—and holy hell, my dick practically leaps into my hand. I bite my lip to stifle a groan, gripping the base tight before I come too fast. But then I realize, why prolong it? The faster I release this tension, the faster I can go back to looking at Blake Logan in an unpornographic way.

My strokes are fast, fueled by pure, helpless, inappropriate lust. I jerk off to the sight of Blake in that slutty bikini, thrusting into my fist while pretending it's her greedy mouth. Her perfect face gazes up at me from my phone, and I imagine those pink, pouty lips wrapped tight around me, sucking me dry.

The climax hits me like a train, unleashing a rush of pleasure through my body. I grunt, coming all over my stomach and squeezing my tip to get every last drop out. Breathing hard, I grab some tissues from the bed table and clean myself up. After that release, I should be relaxed. Drowsy. Ready to finally, *finally*, sleep.

But it has the opposite effect. I'm more awake than ever now. With a sigh, I kick the covers off my legs and climb out of bed in search of my clothes.

Guess I'm writing on the dock again tonight.

## GOLDEN BOYS

WYATT

Mullets. Not hot, right?

BEAU

Fuck no.

AJ

Not in the slightest.

GRAY

They're hot if you're a bassist in a country-metal band called Moonshine Possum.

BEAU

Name of your next band, Wyatt.

OK, but we're in agreement? Like a mullet is on the same level as that mustache Gray grew last year, right?

GRAY

wtf don't drag me into this. That stache was elite.

AJ

You looked like a gym teacher mid-divorce.

Or the narc on a cop procedural.

Or one of those pervs on the predator catching shows.

BEAU

Bahahahahahahah

GRAY

Dude, that stache got me laid three times in one week, and one of the times was in a hammock.

BEAU

Wait that's actually impressive.

AJ

idk did she call you sir or detective, tho?

Forget I brought it up.

# Chapter 8

## BLAKE

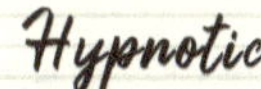


GIGI CALLS THE NEXT MORNING while I'm getting dressed. It's a workday for her, but she has a home office in the Dallas house she shares with her husband, who also happens to be her biggest client. When she didn't make the Olympics women's hockey team in college, Gigi pivoted to a career as a sports agent. Because she was able to bring in Luke Ryder, the best player to come out of college hockey in a decade, she landed a junior agenting role at one of the top agencies in the country.

"Is my brother driving you insane yet?"

I pull my denim shorts up my legs and zip them. "Oh yeah."

Gigi laughs. "Figured. He's a handful."

He's a moody asshole, more like it. Which is something I never knew about Wyatt. I've spent time with him on family vacations but never just the two of us and not when I'm hyperaware of everything he's doing. Or not doing. For example, looking at me. When I came downstairs in my pajamas earlier and told him my plans for the day, he didn't look my way even once as he made himself some coffee.

*I* looked, though, and what I saw was a cause for concern. Eyes heavy with fatigue. Days-old stubble on his face.

"I don't think he sleeps," I tell Gigi. "Should I be worried about that?"

"Oh, that's nothing new. He's had insomnia most of his life."

"He has? I didn't know that."

"He doesn't really talk about it. But you can usually tell it's getting worse when he acts like a bigger dickhead than normal."

"Then he must be suffering from it big-time." I'm unable to stop the sarcasm. "He acted like a total jerk last night."

Her tone sharpens. "What did he do?"

Deciding it's not a can of worms I want to open right now, I backpedal. "Nothing heinous or anything. He just snapped at me a few times."

*You're desperate for attention from any guy who'll give you five seconds.*

*You're not trying to be friendly. You're trying to be wanted.*

My chest tightens with embarrassment as Wyatt's accusations echo through my mind.

Fuck him for saying that. And fuck him for mocking me about how everyone knew Isaac would cheat on me. If they all knew, why didn't they warn me then? Why did they let me play house with the man and plan a future with him?

"He hurt my feelings." The words slip out before I can curb them. "It wasn't cool."

"Aw, Blakey." Gigi's heavy sigh fills my ear. "Listen, Wyatt can be a dick, yes, but he's also a secret softie. If you tell him he hurt your feelings, I promise you he'll take it to heart and never do it again. He's kind of a sap when he's trying to make things up to someone."

I don't know if I want to experience sappy Wyatt. I can't soften to him, because every time I do, he turns around and obliterates my pride.

"It's fine," I say lightly. "I'm letting it go."

"What are you up to today?" she asks.

"Going to the library."

"You know school's out for summer, right?"

"I know. But we met these paranormal podcasters last night—"

"I'm sorry, what?"

Laughing, I catch her up on the Spencers. "They claim that Lake Tahoe has a supernatural history, and you know me—now I must research it."

"You're such a nerd. But have fun, I guess?"

After we say goodbye, I go downstairs and find Wyatt waiting for me in the kitchen.

"You ready to go?" he says brusquely.

"No," I retort. "You're not coming with me. I don't need an escort to the *library*."

For the first time all morning, his gaze finds mine. "I'm not going to the library. I have something to do in town, so I need the Jeep. I'll drop you off."

I relax. "Oh. Okay. I'll allow it. Let me grab a travel mug."

Wyatt doesn't say another word as we climb into the Jeep and make the drive to Tahoe City. The silence makes me antsy, so I fill it by scrolling on my phone, cycling past mindless photos from friends and influencers and a few posts from the Delta Pi account announcing our summer charity events. I never envisioned myself being part of a sorority, but Mom encouraged me to pledge because she said it would be a built-in friend group. Turns out? Not at all. Other than my mentor, Charlie, who graduated a few years ago, the only Delta Pi I'm close with is Juliette, and neither of us even live in the sorority house.

I'm about to keep scrolling when something catches my eye—a photo posted on Tyrell's account. Ty is one of Isaac's teammates at Briar.

My stomach drops as I register what I'm seeing. It's a group shot taken at a party in the backyard of one of the off-campus football houses. I see Ty's smiling face. A couple other teammates. Two girls I don't recognize.

And Isaac and Heather.

The cheater and the cheerleader, in the flesh.

Tears sting my eyes. Lovely. Six tearless weeks and now they're pouring out willy-nilly at the most inconvenient times.

I shouldn't care that Isaac is seeing Heather now. He was already seeing her while he was with me. But the fact that they're attending a Briar party together like an actual couple makes me question Isaac's vehement there-were-no-emotions-involved defense. You don't start dating someone you're not emotionally attached to, right?

Unless they're fuck buddies. I suppose that could be it.

But… They were holding hands in that picture. Fuck buddies don't hold hands.

Ugh.

Maybe *I* need a fuck buddy. Or a hookup at least. Juliette insists it will be good for my flailing confidence. Make me feel desirable again. But the only guy who was even remotely cute at the bar last night was Landon the bartender. I could've even disregarded the mullet if I'd been attracted to him. Unfortunately, it's impossible to feel an attraction for anyone else when Wyatt Graham is breathing the same air as them. If Wyatt's in the room, my traitorous nervous system refuses to acknowledge pheromones that emanate from someone other than him.

Wyatt slows down when we enter the busy mountain town. I shift my gaze out the window and take in the familiar sights of North Lake Boulevard, with its little cafés and restaurants, quaint boutiques, and several gear shops. There are hanging flower baskets on all the patios, providing a splash of color that succeeds in bolstering my mood a little.

We turn off the main boulevard, driving a few blocks west of the lake before pulling into the parking lot of the newly built community center, a complex comprising a library, fitness center, and sports arena.

I assumed he would drop me out front and then go off to day drink or something, but he pulls the Jeep into an actual space and shuts off the engine.

"I thought you had to do something in town," I say.

"I do. I'm just parking here."

"And walking to the boulevard?" I'm confused. "It's, like, two miles away."

He reaches for the door handle. "It'll be a nice stroll."

Hopping out of the Jeep, I sling my messenger bag over my shoulder. I brought an oversize one in case I decide to check out any books.

"Why are you being weird?" I ask Wyatt.

"I'm not being weird. You're the weird one. Just go to the library."

"Jeez, Graham. Is someone on their period?"

"Shut it, Logan." He confuses me further by locking the Jeep and then casually leaning against the driver's door.

"What, you're not embarking on your epic walk yet?"

"No, I'm gonna have a cigarette first. Is that allowed?" With a surly look, he fishes his smokes out of his pocket, then shoves one in the corner of his mouth while he searches for a lighter.

"Whatever." I hike up my bag. "All right. I'll see you in two hours."

"Sounds good."

I saunter toward the library, but for some reason, everything about…whatever *that* was…has triggered my suspicions. He was definitely acting strange. Wyatt's way cooler than that. I swear he was even fidgeting when he was putting the cigarette in his mouth.

On a hunch, I enter the library but stop in the small vestibule at the doors. Then I twist around to peer at the parking lot.

Oh yeah. Wyatt's up to something.

He stamps the barely smoked cigarette with his sneaker before walking to the trunk. I narrow my eyes when he hauls out a large black duffel bag. It's a very familiar bag.

Bag over his shoulder, he stalks across the lot toward the enormous, boxy building with metal siding and a slate-gray roof. At the sports arena's entrance, the glass doors are cloudy with condensation from the air inside.

I dart out of the library and hurry after Wyatt. He has earbuds in, so he doesn't hear me coming. I catch up to him just as he slides through the doors.

He jolts when I grab his arm, spinning around. His expression darkens with displeasure when he sees me. Very deliberately, he presses a button on his phone, I assume to shut his music off.

"You're playing hockey!" I accuse.

"Go away," Wyatt grumbles.

"Does your father know?"

"No. And I don't want him to. Now if you'll excuse me…"

"I don't understand. You hate hockey."

"I don't hate hockey. I like hitting the ice and shooting some pucks. Or playing for fun like the Boxing Day Beatdown or our family shootouts. I just never wanted to play professionally."

"Why are you hiding it?"

"Because I know my dad. He'll get way too excited about this.

Read more into it than it actually means."

"Oh, God forbid we please our parents."

He gives me a dirty look. "Blake."

"Wyatt," I mimic.

Sighing, he takes off walking again while I trail after him like an eager puppy wanting to play ball with its owner.

"Go away," he says over his shoulder.

"No, I want to watch you play."

"Since when? You're the one who hates hockey."

"I don't hate it either. I'm indifferent," I say. "But now I'm invested. It's not every day I get to see *the* Wyatt Graham on the ice."

We reach the men's locker room, where he stops to glare at me again. "What? You gonna follow me into the lockers too?"

I think it over. "If I wait out here, are you going to try to sneak out the back so I don't witness you playing hockey?"

"It's a risk."

My gaze shifts back to the door, bringing a grin to Wyatt's face.

"You're not coming in there," he warns.

"Why? Because I might see your dick?"

He simply sighs again, but I can see him trying not to laugh. "Oh my God. Just fuck off."

At that, he ducks into the locker room, and because I do have some etiquette and wasn't raised by wolves, I head to the rink instead. It seems to be some sort of free hour, because there's nobody out on the ice save for a fair-haired man teaching his son how to skate. The boy can't be older than four, and he's literally the cutest thing I've ever seen in his puffy blue coat and tiny black skates.

Sometimes I wonder if my dad wishes he'd had a son he could share his hockey love with. Instead, he got me, a stubborn girl who only wanted to read books or watch football. To Dad's credit, if he ever did resent it, he never once showed it. In fact, he went above and beyond to bond with me. The man who doesn't love reading read *all* the books for my freshman literature class so he could discuss them with me and help me study.

My dad's pretty great.

Rather than sit in the stands, I find a spot in front of the plexiglass and stand there. Hugging my arms against the chill, I watch my breath puff out in the cold air. I've spent my whole life in ice rinks, but I'll never love it the way my father does.

Not long after, Wyatt enters the arena. He's not in full padding, but he does wear a helmet, a black practice jersey, and hockey pants. And he's enormous on skates, I realize. The blades add a couple inches to his already commanding height.

Eyeing me in irritation, he snaps his helmet into place, then pushes the low wooden door that opens onto the ice. A minute later, he's joined by another man, this one in full pads. Goalie gear.

I walk along the plexi, trailing the two guys toward one end of the rink where a net is already set up. The newcomer drops a bucket of pucks on center ice before skating with a very reluctant Wyatt in my direction.

"Blake," Wyatt says gruffly, his voice a tad muffled behind the glass. "This is Miguel. He plays for the local men's league. Miguel, this is Blake. Family friend."

"Nice to meet you," I say, smiling at Miguel.

"Likewise!" Unlike Wyatt, this guy actually smiles back, flashing his dimples before gliding toward the net and dropping into a slutty butterfly stretch.

"Can you please go to the library?" Wyatt grumbles at me.

"I could. Or..." I lift my phone and snap a picture of his unhappy face. "I can do this."

Mumbling under his breath—something not very nice, I suspect—he skates to the blue line and spills a handful of pucks from the bucket onto the ice.

As unimpressed as I've always been with hockey (and hockey *players*), I can't take my eyes off Wyatt. Watching him skate, I can see why Garrett wanted so desperately for his son to follow in his footsteps. Wyatt is deceptively slow. He moves with a lazy grace, almost seductive as he allows the goalie to grow accustomed to the insolent tempo, to grow complacent...before suddenly kicking into another gear, catching Miguel off guard by firing a dizzyingly fast bullet at the net.

Score.

For the next ten minutes, Miguel doesn't make a single save. Sure, could be he's the worst goalie on the planet, but I've been watching hockey my entire life. Miguel has skills. He's got a fast glove. It's just that Wyatt's glove shots are faster. Miguel is quick with the pads, but Wyatt is quicker to find a slot and squeeze that puck in.

The rink echoes with the familiar sounds I grew up with. The sharp thwack of Wyatt's stick striking the puck, followed by the dull *thunk* of it hitting the goalie's pads. It's hypnotic.

No, *he's* hypnotic.

He moves with purpose. Fluid. Powerful. Every shot is deliberate, but he isn't showing off. He's just...focused. Sweat beads along his brow, and as always, I feel the urge to lick it off. This guy has triggered some sort of licking fetish in me. I'm always imagining dragging my tongue over his skin.

I track him through the plexiglass. For the first time since they hit the ice, Miguel stops the puck, knocking it away. Wyatt grins, and it's boyish and light and tugs at my chest. It's rare to see him smile like that. I've spent the past few days watching him brooding on the dock, his forehead furrowed as he tries to battle his writer's block. Here, he actually appears to be having fun.

Although he'd probably yell at me for it, I start snapping pictures of him on the ice. I'm tempted to send them to Gigi, but I curb the impulse. It's obvious he doesn't want his family to know about this.

Which is wild to me. He should be proud of how good he is. At hockey, at music. I would *kill* to be that good at something. Instead, I'm just a passionless, talentless college chick who's probably going to end up working a boring, soul-sucking nine-to-five after graduation while everyone around me shines in their chosen field.

When the chill in the air finally gets to me and the boredom sets in, I tuck my phone in my pocket and wave at Wyatt. He glides backward before pivoting, his skates scraping across the ice as he comes toward me.

"You taking off?" he calls.

"Yeah, I'm going to the library now."

Nodding, he removes his glove and shoves his sweat-dampened hair away from his forehead. He is inconceivably attractive.

"All right," he says. "I'll meet you at the car."

He's about to skate away when my brain decides to hijack my mouth.

"You hurt my feelings."

He stops, pivoting again on his blades. A deep crease appears in his brow. "What?"

"You hurt my feelings," I repeat, shifting my feet in discomfort. "Yesterday. You made me feel...small. And pathetic." *Shut the hell up, Blake*, I scream at myself. But my emotions have taken the reins. "Like there's something wrong with wanting to wear a pretty dress and go out."

Wyatt visibly swallows.

"You made me feel like maybe I deserved to be cheated on," I mutter, now staring at my sneakers. "Because I was so stupid and apparently didn't see it coming."

The silence from him drags, eliciting a rush of frustration. I find the courage to lift my gaze, only to be met with...nothing. His expression reveals absolutely nothing.

"Anyway." I shrug. "That's all I wanted to say."

Still, he doesn't speak.

Clenching my teeth, I step away from the plexiglass. Okay then. Screw you, asshole.

"Blake."

I stop at the sound of my name, turning toward the glass.

"What?" I mutter.

Our eyes lock. When he speaks, his voice is low and husky.

"It won't happen again."

# Chapter 9

## BLAKE

*Want to know what I'm good for?*

WE BARELY SPEAK FOR THE rest of the day.

So much for Wyatt wanting to make it up to people whose feelings he hurt. Or maybe he only does that with his sister. Either way, Gigi was wrong. Telling him he hurt me only resulted in his ignoring me.

Now it's nearly dinnertime, and I don't know if I should cook enough stir-fry for two or fend for myself tonight. Wyatt's been hanging out on the dock since we got back from our library excursion/ top secret hockey practice.

I watch him from the window. He's shirtless, hair damp as if he'd just had a swim. His guitar is balanced across his lap, and he's writing in that worn notebook he always has on him.

From up here, he could be mistaken for peaceful. Relaxed. But he keeps shaking his head in disgust, which tells the real story. I saw him constantly do that on the boat yesterday, when he was unhappy with the words on the page.

Something inside me softens. I want to be pissed at him. To hate him for the way he mocks me and makes light of my feelings, accuses me of wanting attention. But it's difficult to hold on to anger when he's sitting there like that, clearly battling something inside himself. And because being a bleeding heart is one of my fatal flaws, I suddenly feel bad about calling him a moody asshole.

I don't think his problem is mood swings. I think...he's stuck. Beyond writer's block. Beyond insomnia. Looking at him now, I don't see a guy who lashes out because he's a dick. I see one who's unhappy with his life and can't find his way forward.

Before I can stop myself, I go outside and descend the steps to the dock.

He must hear the snapping of my flip-flops, but he doesn't look up. His pencil sits loosely between his fingers. In the distance, the sun is starting to drop behind the trees, creating a golden aura around his head.

"Hey." I pause a short distance away.

"Hey."

I move closer, my curiosity getting the better of me as I glance at the page in front of him. I see scratches and smudges, circles around words, and entire phrases crossed out with aggressive strokes.

"Wanted to check if you're coming up for dinner," I say. "Should I make extra?"

"Yeah, sure. Sounds great." He sounds distracted.

"How's the song going?"

"It's not." His profile is tight, revealing his frustration.

"I'm sorry." I watch him shove the leather cover closed and set it beside him. "I love that you write in a notebook. So old school of you," I remark, trying to lighten the mood.

He finally glances at me, only briefly, before looking at his pencil, twisting it between his fingers. "Yeah. I like seeing the words on the page."

"Does it make a difference?" I ask curiously.

"Sort of. I don't know." He spins the pencil again. "Writing it down feels...messier. More authentic. When I type shit out on my phone or on a laptop, it doesn't feel real. It becomes too polished before I know what I'm actually trying to say."

I nod slowly. "That makes sense."

"Does it?"

"Yeah. Writing it by hand is like...like you're physically connected to the page. I get that."

He gives a noncommittal grunt.

"So what's the song about?" I ask.

"It's not working."

"That's not what I asked."

"It doesn't matter, Blake. It's a shit song. I've been sitting out here for days trying to force something that isn't there."

"I think you're being too hard on yourself."

"Christ," he mutters.

A frown touches my lips. "What?"

"Nothing. It's just... I haven't written anything decent in a year. It all feels forced. Repetitive. Generic."

I hear the shame that drips from that last word. I suppose every musician dreads being viewed as generic.

"I'm turning twenty-five this year, and I don't even have a backup plan. If I can't make a living making music, what the hell else am I supposed to do?"

I know exactly how he feels. I've felt the same crippling anxiety about my future for most of my life. But unlike me, Wyatt has *talent*. How does he not realize this gives him an edge? A real shot at greatness.

"Look, I know you said you don't want to use your mom's connections," I hedge, but I don't even get to finish that thought.

"Drop it, Blake." He rubs the bridge of his nose, his features creasing with frustration. "Do you think it's easy being Hannah Graham's son? One of the best songwriters of her generation? You think it's easy being *Garrett* Graham's son? Mr. Perfect? It's so much damn pressure. And the only way I'm going to rise above that pressure is if I do this on my own. Otherwise it won't feel earned. I *need* to write a song this summer. A fucking good one."

I'm startled by how forthcoming he's being. Usually getting Wyatt to open up is like pulling teeth.

Worried I'll scare him off by pushing too hard, I put on a careful tone. "Is this really about a song?"

I regret the question, as his expression instantly clouds over. "Don't psychoanalyze me. It's a waste of time."

"I'm not. I'm just trying to—"

"Distract me," he cuts in. "That's what you're always doing. Fucking distracting me."

I'm taken aback by his sharp tone. "Wyatt—"

"Whatever." He abruptly gets to his feet. "I'm not having dinner. I think I'll go out instead."

"Where?"

He doesn't answer. He just grabs his guitar and heads for the stairs, leaving me alone on the dock.

Wyatt's gone for hours. Even though he doesn't drive, ordering a car instead, I still almost call Gigi a dozen times to ask if I should worry.

Just past eleven, the rumble of an engine and the slam of a car door break the silence of the night. A burst of relief flickers through me. He's back.

Downstairs, the alarm beeps as it's disengaged, then beeps again as he arms it. When I hear his heavy footsteps climbing the staircase, I debate staying in my room, but I want to make sure he's okay. He seemed really upset before he left earlier.

I step into the dark hallway just as he emerges onto the second-floor landing.

"Hey," I say tentatively. "You okay?"

"Fine," he mumbles.

And then he trips on the floor runner and catches himself against the wall, bumping into a photograph of Dumpy and Bergeron, the Graham family dogs. Luckily, the frame doesn't fall.

I eye him in disapproval. "Are you drunk?"

"No," he says belligerently. He takes a couple more steps and stumbles again. "Maybe a little."

He starts to laugh, but I'm not amused. I flick on the light and stalk toward him, and we nearly collide in the middle of the hallway. He's noticeably swaying on his feet.

"Jesus," I say. "How much did you drink? What the hell is wrong with you?"

"How much time do you have?"

I don't even crack a smile. "Wyatt."

Ignoring me, he staggers forward, trying to make it to his room. He's beyond wasted. Eyes unfocused. Hair messy as he drags one hand through it. And even still, there's something obnoxiously magnetic about him. With his black T-shirt, ripped jeans, and those rings winking in the hall light, he's the epitome of bad boy.

"Here's the thing, *Blake*." He drunkenly overemphasizes my name. "You show up here, and my head stops working."

My heart stutters in my chest. "What?"

"You heard me. My head. Stops. Working. You smile and you

talk and you ask questions, and suddenly I'm in my own goddamn way."

I gape at him. "Are you blaming me for your writer's block?"

"No." He curses under his breath, sounding tormented. "You're... just you. You're there."

"Where?" I'm so confused.

"Everywhere."

Drawing a breath, I search his expression, needing to make sense of his nonsensical words. Now he's raking both hands through his unruly hair, as if he wants to tear it out by the roots.

"I hurt your feelings," he grinds out.

I blink. "What?"

"You said I hurt you." His voice is sandpaper-rough, hazy green eyes trying to focus on my face. "I'm a prick, Blake. Don't you get that?"

A frown wrinkles my brow. "Wyatt..." I start.

"No. You need to stop."

"Stop what?"

"Always looking at me like I'm worth a damn. I'm not fucking special." He sways on his feet again, scrubbing his palm over his jaw. "Remember that night you said you were into me? Know what I wanted to ask you? *What the hell are you thinking?* Because I'm not worth your time. Wasn't worth it back then. Not worth it now."

Alarm settles in my chest. I've never heard him talk like this before. Every word is dripping with disgust. And something else... Something raw and shameful. A darkness I've sensed in him before but haven't glimpsed until now.

"Want to know what I'm good for?" Wyatt says roughly.

"W-what?" My dry throat is making me stammer.

"I'm good for one thing. My dick." He laughs, a harsh, raspy sound that sends a shiver up my spine. "I have a really good dick."

Damned if that doesn't turn me on.

"I'm a great lay." He licks his bottom lip, a feral glint in his eyes. "I can fuck you so good."

*Do it*, I want to beg. Right here. Right now. I want him to spin me around, yank my pajama shorts off, and drive his cock inside me. I want it so badly I can scarcely breathe.

"They all love my dick," he says, still laughing. "They fucking love it. And then they always want more." His laughter dissolves in a sputtering expletive. "See, though, that's the part I can't do. There's no such thing as more. Not with me. There's only what I give you in the moment."

He's making my head spin, not only with his words but with his drunken swaying. I reach out to try to steady him, but he pushes my hand away.

"No," he mutters. "Don't waste your time on me. You're better off without this fantasy you've built in your head."

The last threads of my patience officially snap. "I don't fantasize about you. Not anymore. You think I want this version of you? This drunk asshole who can't even be bothered to apologize for hurting my feelings? Hard pass, Wyatt."

With a bitter laugh of my own, I shake my head and stomp toward my room.

He doesn't come after me.

I hear him stumble into the blue room, followed by a loud thump that elicits a pang of concern. Despite myself, I walk back to make sure he didn't fall and smash his head open. I peek at the open doorway and realize the thump was Wyatt collapsing on his mattress. He's face down and spread-eagled, one cheek pressed against the pillow.

I linger for a moment, my heart squeezing painfully.

He looks so…lost.

Swallowing the lump in my throat, I quietly close his door and head back to my room.

I hate that I'm always finding compassion for him. I hate how weak it makes me, this exhausting instinct to keep showing up emotionally even when he constantly slams the door in my face. Telling me not to waste my time on him. Whether he meant romantically or as a friend, I don't know, but I can't fight the feeling that he's purposely trying to push me away. Donning this fuckboy asshole mask so I don't try to peer too close. So nobody does.

I slide into bed and force myself not to replay our entire conversation. I try to forget how anguished he sounded. How defeated he looked. The way his voice cracked when he uttered the words that are now running on a loop in my mind.

*I'm not fucking special.*

# Chapter 10

## BLAKE

*It's okay to be a raging nerd*

I'M EATING A BOWL OF cereal at the counter when Wyatt enters the kitchen. I'm startled by his appearance, which is a drastic change from last night. He shaved this morning, and without the scruff I've grown accustomed to, he's lost some of that dangerous edge. In his white T-shirt and khaki shorts, with his hair pushed away from his forehead, he looks more like one of the Golden Boys than his bad boy musician self.

*I have a really good dick.*

Heat suffuses my cheeks. I can still hear his low, seductive voice uttering those words. Promising how good he could fuck me.

"I don't sleep much."

I put down my spoon. "What?"

"It started around the beginning of high school," he says gruffly. "The insomnia. Not sure why. Nothing really helps, not even sleeping pills."

I wait for him to continue.

"I can usually get by with a few hours a night, but sometimes it turns me into a cranky asshole. That's usually when I resort to alcohol to knock myself out." His teeth work his bottom lip. "I don't use it as a sleep crutch often—the booze, I mean. Only if it's been, like, three or four days without sleep."

"Three or four days without sleep?" I echo in disbelief. "Jesus, Wyatt. Have you seen a doctor for it?"

He nods. "A few. They're the ones who prescribed the pills. But like I said, they don't work. And I refuse to take anything stronger. I don't want to rely on fucking tranquilizers."

"No, I don't blame you," I say quietly. "I wouldn't want to either."

"I got drunk last night and was a total ass to you," he says with visible regret. "And I'm sorry. I'm not making excuses for my behavior, I promise, but… I just wanted to sleep."

Damn it. The vulnerability swimming in his gaze makes it so hard to stay pissed at him.

"Anyway," he says, letting out a breath. "I feel like I'm constantly biting your head off, and I want you to know that's going to stop. I'm sorry for what I said the other night about you wanting attention. I'm sorry I made you feel like there's something wrong with you putting on a dress and going out."

I slowly meet his eyes. They're so earnest. "Apology accepted."

He hesitates for a beat. "We're friends, right?"

"Of course."

"Okay. I'm going to start acting like it then."

"No more snapping at me and dictating what to wear?"

"No, because you're right. I'm not your dad or your babysitter. You should spend your summer however you want to spend it."

"Thank you." A smile tickles my lips. "But you don't need to worry. Right now, my big plans for the summer mostly involve the library. I'm heading there soon." I get up and carry my bowl to the sink. "That is, if I can take the Jeep without you having a nervous breakdown?"

"I'll do my best," he says with a wink, and just like that, all the tension of the last few days melts away.

I'm in high spirits as I drive to the library, which I'm finding to be a treasure trove of information. The Spencers were right. Lake Tahoe has an interesting history, especially all the hauntings. I don't believe in ghosts—I'm a *need to see it to believe it* kind of girl—but I'm having a blast with the research. God, and the digital file I'm compiling on Darlie Gallagher and the mystery surrounding her death? It's spectacular. Easy-to-find tabs, subject headings, an index, even a glossary. I impress myself sometimes.

I spend the next several days in the library, reading old articles and digging into the lake's history. Today, Wyatt joins me again, disappearing into the arena while I do my research next door, and on the drive home, I regale him with everything I learned.

"Okay, so there's actually no evidence that Darlie drowned. No news articles about a drowning. No death certificate for her. Or at least I haven't found one yet. I put in a request with the county records office for it—"

"Seriously?" he interrupts, grinning at me. "You're going to a lot of trouble here."

"Not really. It was just one email," I protest.

Except now I feel sheepish. This Darlie case is turning into an obsession, I fully recognize that. I should be researching jobs like I insisted to Mom I would. But this is what always happens when I find a topic that fascinates me. I tumble down rabbit holes and never want to come out.

Wyatt senses my embarrassment, and his smile widens. "It's okay to be a raging nerd, Logan."

"Not everyone can be a cool rocker like you, Graham."

"Exactly." He flicks the turn signal and makes a left turn. "So there's no evidence that Darlie Gallagher even existed?"

"Oh no, she existed. I found her birth certificate, and there was an engagement announcement for her and Raymond Loughlin in the *Tahoe Tribune.*"

"Wait. Loughlin? The same Loughlins who own that mansion on the cliff?"

"Yep," I say triumphantly. "Darlie and Raymond knew each other their whole lives, but they didn't start dating until they were nineteen. Her family was well-off but nowhere near as wealthy as the Loughlins. They're the old-money kind of rich. And from what I've read, Raymond was one of those polished yacht-club dudes who was going to be a big-shot banker. Never had a job in his life. Darlie worked as a waitress in town, and they fell in love. She used to sneak out at midnight, paddle a boat across the lake, and meet Raymond under this huge tree on the Loughlin property."

"So far, this sounds like a rom-com."

"For all we know, maybe it is. I can't find much else about these people," I say glumly. "I think it'll be easier to track down what happened to Raymond, because his family is still around, but Darlie basically dropped off the face of the earth."

"Or dropped into the bottom of the lake. If we believe the boat weirdos."

"And every true-crime forum. They all insist that Raymond left Darlie for her younger sister Dolly—"

"Darlie and Dolly? Really?"

"Hey, I didn't name them." I grin. "And their mom's name was Dotty. According to the internet, Raymond and Dolly started sneaking off together. They would meet at the lighthouse on Fannette island to hook up."

"So basically this dude was turning every place in Tahoe into some kind of sex landmark."

"And may or may not have caused a woman to drown herself."

"Stand-up guy."

"Right?"

We develop a routine over the next week. Wyatt writes or lounges during the day while I research Darlie and the Loughlin family. We have lunch. We swim. He strums his guitar while I tan on the dock. And after dinner, without fail, we sit at the dining table and work on the puzzle.

We don't speak other than to trash-talk or argue whether a piece belongs to the dark sky or the dark water or the dark trees. The only fun part of this puzzle is the red canoe, over which Wyatt and I valiantly battle for domination.

"Why is this four thousand pieces?" he growls on a Monday night. "Aren't puzzles supposed to be a thousand pieces or less? What kind of sadist decides to pick four thousand?"

"Maybe it's an ex of yours who wants to torture you." I pause, something occurring to me. "Wait. Do you even have any exes? Like a real ex?" I strain my mind, trying to remember his girlfriends.

"Natalie in high school," he supplies. "That lasted almost a year. And six months with Rhett a couple years ago."

"What a great name," I say enviously. "I wish my name was Rhett."

"No, you don't. She was nuts."

"That's what all fuckmen say about their exes."

"She slashed my tires after I broke up with her."

My jaw drops. "I take it back."

"But at least she isn't holding my toaster hostage."

The reminder makes me frown. "Oh, I already have a plan about how to get Hot Boi back. I'm gonna bribe Joseph to let me upstairs when I'm back in Boston."

"And Joseph is?"

"The doorman. He loves me."

Wyatt snorts. "Oh, by the way, I forgot. My mom texted earlier. She wants us to send Henry a grocery list for the week."

"Nope," I say stubbornly. "I already told my mom I don't want Henry getting all our food. I'm buying my own groceries from now on."

"All right, then let's go to the supermarket tomorrow," he says, and the following morning, we pile into the Jeep for a grocery shopping adventure.

We start in the cereal aisle. I trail after him while he pushes our cart. When he reaches for a box on the top shelf, I admire his bare arms. The golden tan. Sinewy muscles. Dark hair falling onto his forehead. I'm not the only one checking him out—every woman in our vicinity is mentally undressing him. In those faded, threadbare jeans and sleeveless Bruins T-shirt representing his dad, he's the hottest guy in the store and probably the planet.

I stop to grab my favorite cereal, eliciting a stern reprimand from Wyatt.

"Seriously? No way. That's not the cereal we're buying."

"But it's nutritious."

"Cereal should not be nutritious. It should be delicious." He puts my healthy granola and oats cereal back on the shelf and grabs a horrific sugary concoction instead. Dropping it in the cart, he rolls away, whistling to himself.

I stare at him in disbelief. "I didn't agree to that!"

"Don't care," he says without turning around.

"You guys are a cute couple," an amused voice remarks from behind me.

It belongs to a young woman around my age with dark skin and black hair arranged in two braids, a baseball cap atop her head. She looks familiar, but I can't place her.

"Do I know you from somewhere?" I ask at the same time as she says, "I know you."

We both laugh.

"Are you local?" she asks.

I shake my head. "No, but my family's been coming here every summer since I was a kid. We just bought a place on the west shore a couple years ago. Blue boathouse with white trim?"

She brightens. "Oh, the Grahams."

"Logans, actually. I'm Blake. My dad was teammates with Garrett Graham." I keep studying her. "Why do you look so familiar to me? Are *you* local?"

"I'm Annaliese Jackson. I live over in Dollar Point, but my brother Eddie spends a lot of time at your place in the summers. He's friends with Beau."

"Oh, shit. Yes. I know your family. Your parents are like *the* real estate agents of Lake Tahoe."

She grins, flashing a pair of deep dimples. "Just my mom. That's her gorgeous face on all the signs. My dad is a developer. He builds most of the houses around here."

We hear a wave of raucous laughter in the next aisle, and then a trio of young men round the corner.

"Liese!" one of them whines. "What the hell? Why's it taking you so long to get a box of—" He stops when he notices me. "Oh, I see. Yes. I would also stop for her." He flashes me a lopsided smile. "I would stop for you."

I have to laugh. "Thanks."

"These are my friends from college," Annaliese says, quickly making the introductions.

The one who can't stop checking me out is Clay. Preston is the tall, lanky one in the red 49ers cap. And the one pulling up the rear is Kuri, whose stunning face could stop traffic.

"We all just graduated," Annaliese tells me. "So the boys came up for the week. Sort of like a graduation celebration." She glances at her friends. "Blake is here for the summer."

"Nice! We should chill," Clay says immediately.

I shrug. "Sure."

"You should see her house," Annaliese says to the guys. "It's sick. Remember that huge boathouse we saw when we were cruising yesterday? With the blue doors and the rooftop deck?"

"Holy shit, that's your property?" Preston exclaims. "The hockey house?"

"Wait, your dad's Garrett Graham?" Kuri blurts out.

"John Logan," I correct. "But we co-own the house with the Grahams."

Preston shivers. "Oh my God. That is incredible."

"You guys are welcome to come by," I tell them. "I mean, I'll have to check with my handler first, but I'm sure it's fine."

"You mean your boyfriend?" Annaliese says in amusement.

"He's not my boyfriend."

"She's single," Kuri says happily, and I can't stop a chuckle. He seems like the goofball of the group.

"What's your number?" Annaliese slides her phone out of the pocket of her cutoffs. She keys in the digits I recite. "Perfect. I'll text you later. We can figure something out."

"Sounds good," I say. She seems cool, and her friends are entertaining.

As the group wanders off, I track Wyatt down to the dairy aisle.

"Where have you been?" he says absently. "Crying in the cereal aisle?"

"No, just ran into some locals. I invited them over."

His gaze sharpens. "What locals?"

"Don't you dare snap into babysitter mode," I scold. "I'm an adult and I can invite friends over if I want. Anyway, it's Annaliese. The Golden Boys can vouch for her."

"Oh, I remember her. Yeah, she's cool. What kind of ice cream should we get?" He's holding up two different containers. "Choc-shock cherry explosion or praline fudge-mallow?"

I gawk at him. "Do you realize how much sugar is in those?"

He ponders that, then says, "You're right. We should get both." He deposits both tubs in the cart and pushes it forward.

As we get into the checkout line, I spot Annaliese and her friends loading items onto the neighboring conveyor belt. She grins when she notices me and Wyatt, and a minute later, my phone buzzes in my pocket.

ANNALIESE

You should hit that. He's so hot.

He refers to me as "kid."

ANNALIESE

Ouch.

Yeah.

In the parking lot, I admire Wyatt's arms again as he bends into the trunk, stacking paper bags inside it. Why do his muscles flex so much?

"Wyatt?" a female voice says. Bright and overly eager.

I glance over to see a woman in the next row of cars. She's in her early twenties, with long brown hair, a tiny sundress, and oversize sunglasses.

Wyatt straightens only to offer a polite nod. "Hey, Rosie. How's it going?"

Rosie. Why does that name sound so familiar...

Oh my God.

The canoe girl.

It takes some effort to keep my jaw closed. This is the girl who was so devastated when Wyatt moved on to his next hookup that she showed up in the middle of the night in a canoe, crying her eyes out and screaming for him to come down to the dock and talk to her. I wasn't present for the theatrics, but Beau was, and he swears it happened. And then right after that, her family sold their house, though I still maintain that part is a coincidence.

The brunette approaches us with a nervous laugh, the sound pitched just a tad too high. "It's so weird running into you. I was *just* thinking about you the other day."

"Yeah?" His tone suggests he doesn't need any more details than that.

But Rosie keeps talking. "Yeah. I'm in town visiting Harriet, and we were talking about the night we all went cliff jumping on the island. Do you remember that?"

He nods absently. "Fun times."

Her smile wavers for a second. "So fun."

Wyatt's not even looking at her as he finishes loading the groceries, and I feel a pang of sympathy for the woman.

"How've you been?" Rosie pushes.

"Good. You?"

"Great. Busy. But not too busy for, um, you know, seeing friends or whatever." She stops, regrouping. "You know, if you wanted to hang out while I'm in town."

Oh God. This is mortifying. It's like watching a slow-motion train wreck. I edge toward the side of the Jeep, wishing I could melt into the pavement.

"Glad you're doing well" is Wyatt's response. He might as well have picked up a crossbow and shot an arrow into her heart.

Getting the message, Rosie flattens her lips and steps away. She flicks a frown in my direction, then stalks off, her sandals striking the asphalt with each quick step.

I wait until we're inside the Jeep before glaring at him. "Did you have to be so cold?"

"Not cold," he corrects. "Polite."

"Dude, that was cold. She was crushed. Was that the same Rosie who...you know...the canoe crier?"

"Yup." He starts the engine. "Trust me, I learned the hard way what happens when you encourage her. Even a friendly smile has her envisioning weddings and babies. So...boundaries."

I suppose that makes sense, but I still feel awful for the girl. That rejection *sucked.*

And I can't help putting myself in Rosie's shoes, imagining what would've happened if I'd hooked up with Wyatt on Christmas Eve, only to have him look right through me the next day. The way he just looked at her.

I honestly don't know if I would've survived that.

So maybe it's better that I've never experienced...whatever it is that Wyatt gives these women. This magic dick he speaks of like it's a curse.

Maybe it's better if I never open that door.

# Chapter 11

## WYATT

*Go easy on the LMD*

IT'S ANOTHER GORGEOUS AFTERNOON. I sit on the dock, my phone resting on my shoulder as I listen to my manager drone on and on about a producer who's supposedly desperate to get into the studio with me.

"Matt," I interrupt, "I get you're trying to sell me on him, but I checked out his stuff, and his style is completely different from mine. He works with boy bands."

"Yeah, well, maybe you need to pivot."

"I'm not joining a boy band." The thought makes me chuckle as I envision myself dancing in sync with four other guys in matching denim overalls with no shirt or some shit.

"I wouldn't even dream of suggesting it," Matt says with a laugh of his own. "All I'm saying is… Maybe consider going the pop route."

Why is everyone trying to turn me into a goddamn pop star?

"I'm not a pop artist."

"But you could be," he says.

"But I don't want to be."

"Wyatt."

His tone tells me I'm about to be lectured about "the reality of the music biz."

"The reality of the music biz," he continues, "is that those who don't adapt die. So you can toil away for years, chasing your artistic vision and trying to stay pure to it, or you can make a sacrifice to get your foot in the door. Write a song you know will be popular, something that appeals to the masses, and then for your second album? Do whatever tickles your creative fancy."

"Or I get pigeonholed into whatever sellout nonsense I put in the first album," I counter. "Then *that* becomes my style, and I blow up and get stuck churning out pop songs for the rest of my life."

"Oh no," he says sarcastically. "You blow up and become a big star."

Frustration tightens my throat. He doesn't get it. Nobody does. They think I'm just being a fucking diva. That I'm too stubborn to "adapt" or too pretentious to write pop music.

But that isn't it. It's not that I don't *want* to write it—it's that I *can't* write it. The last time I tried writing a bubblegum pop song, I stared at a blank page for days. Sure, I know a few songwriters in Nashville who could probably write me some killer pop tracks, but... I guess this is where my diva side crops up. Because I don't want to sing prepackaged songs that someone else hands me. I want to compose my own music.

"Look, Wyatt, I love the whole angsty, folksy-rock, singer-songwriter vibe you've got going on. But it's clearly not working for us. If you consider singing something more mainstream, there'd be no shortage of producers willing to team up with you. Tobey Dodson, to name one. He'd work with you in a heartbeat—"

"Why in a heartbeat?" I cut in suspiciously.

"Well, he was talking to your mother—"

"No."

"Wyatt—"

"I said no."

"Why not, damn it? Christ, kid. I've never seen anybody fight the nepo baby label as hard as you."

Aggravation sizzles through me. "Because I'm not a nepo baby. I want to create my own opportunities and make it on my own. Otherwise it just feels like it's been handed to me."

"Let it get handed to you. Jesus fucking Christ."

"I'll talk to you later, okay? I'll think on it."

I hit End before he can argue. I stare at the phone for a second, then grit my teeth and call my mom.

"Hey, honey!" Mom says, sounding happy to hear from me. "How's Tahoe?"

"It's good. How's Boston?"

"Wonderful. Your sister and Luke just got here. They're spending the weekend."

"BIL's there? Nice." I love my brother-in-law, even if I still can't get over the fact that I actually have one of those.

My twin sister getting married at twenty-one wasn't exactly on my bingo card for that year, yet somehow, their marriage has lasted way longer than I thought it would. I assumed the quickie marriage in Vegas would result in a quickie divorce wherever you get quickie divorces. But three years later, they still act like newlyweds, and now I can't imagine our lives without my grumpy, allergic-to-talking, stupidly talented BIL.

"So to what do I owe this call?" Mom's tone is wry. I'm not a big caller, as my family can attest. I try to check in with my folks once a week, but I'm not great at sticking to that schedule, and it's usually much longer stretches between calls.

"I just got off the phone with Matt." I pause. "He said you and Tobey Dodson were talking about me."

Mom's laughter fills my ear. "Oh, don't start with that," she chides. "Tobey and I weren't talking about you in the way you think we were talking about you."

"Really?" I challenge.

"Really. I ran into him at the studio in New York last week. He asked how my kids were. I said you two were great. And then he mentioned he'd been listening to 'Silver' on repeat and asked if you were working on anything new."

I falter. "Silver" is one of my most streamed songs—and it's not pop, not in the slightest. It's intimate and reflective, with a focus on the vocals. But not the typical breathy, voice-cracking, singer-songwriter delivery where vocalists in the genre tend to gravitate. It's warmer and has a folk edge.

When Matt said Tobey Dodson wanted to work with me, I assumed that meant pivoting genres. So why was Dodson raving about "Silver"?

"*He* asked you?" My head is spinning. "Unprompted?"

"Unprompted," Mom confirms, and I believe her, because my mother isn't a liar. She always tells it like it is. "And then he asked me for your contact info..." She trails off enticingly.

"Bullshit."

"Swear to God."

"Did you give it to him?"

"Yes, but don't worry. I consulted the rule book first."

I chuckle sheepishly. Yeah, I'm a dick. I've given my mom a set of rules regarding what she's allowed and not allowed to do in terms of professional conduct. Not allowed: pimping me out to any of her contacts, sending them links to my songs, hyping me up at industry functions.

But if someone approaches *her*...

"So he genuinely wants to work with me?" I feel a stir of excitement in my chest. "On songs in the same vein as 'Silver'?"

"Well, he wants to listen to your new stuff before he decides if it's something he's interested in producing. I'm sure he'll reach out sometime soon."

"Shit."

"That's a good thing, honey," she says, and I can practically see her smiling. "Take the fucking win."

I'd love to.

If I had any new stuff.

But I don't. What I *do* have is a notebook full of overly flowery, poorly metaphored garbage.

Which means I need to get to work. ASAP. Looks like today is going to be a full-steam-ahead writing marathon.

"How's Blake doing?" Mom asks, changing the subject.

The sound of her name conjures her like a genie from a lamp, as I suddenly become aware of Blake stepping onto the upper deck. I'm not even facing in that direction, but I *feel* her. For some annoying reason, my body is highly attuned to her presence.

I twist my head, and sure enough, there she is, standing at the railing. In her trademark cutoff shorts and bikini top, sunglasses on and a towel hanging off her arm. Her hair is arranged in a side braid, making my fingers tingle. Each time she wears a braid, I just want to undo it. To run my fingers through her hair, spread it out, and watch those luscious waves fall down her delicate back.

"Wyatt?"

I snap out of it. "Oh. Sorry. Yeah, Mom, she's fine."

"Has she spoken to you about the breakup at all?"

"No." Other than bursting into spontaneous tears the first night, Blake barely mentions Isaac outside the context of the toaster she's determined to get back.

"Aw. Well, that's not good," Mom clucks. "Grace is worried because Blake is such a private person. She rarely let her emotions out. Hides behind that sarcastic exterior. But sometimes you need to let it out, you know?"

"Mom," I warn. "I'm already her babysitter. I don't need to be her therapist too."

"I'm not asking you to be. Just saying be gentle with her. Listen to her if she brings it up instead of brushing it off."

"Fine. I gotta go. Blake's here."

Her footsteps thud on the stairs, and she appears on the dock at the same time as I hear the rumble of a boat engine. Blake struts to the edge and raises her hand to wave at the approaching vessel.

"Annaliese and her friends are spending the day," she tells me over her shoulder. "And before you throw a grumpy Graham fit, I told you about this two days ago, and you didn't object."

I watch as she jogs down to the pier and catches the rope that one of the dudes on board tosses her. Awesome. So much for a quiet writing day.

The new arrivals are annoying, but they bring some damn good weed. I split a joint with Kuri, who tells me he's an engineering major at the University of Nevada and *not* a male model like I expect. Kid's half Japanese and half Black and one of the best-looking dudes I've ever seen in my life.

Once I'm good and stoned, I stretch out in my usual lounge chair, sunglasses shielding my eyes. I doze in the sun while Kuri and the other two guys have a cannonball competition, repeatedly hurling themselves off the dock into the water.

Blake and Annaliese disappear into the house for what feels like forever, finally returning with a pitcher full of some fruity cocktail. They sip from hot-pink straws that my dad got Uncle Dean last year when they came up here to celebrate his birthday. For some inexplicable reason, they always buy Dean pink things. It's an inside joke I don't get or frankly need to be part of. That entire friend group is beyond help.

As I lie there, snippets of conversation keep wafting in my direction. Kuri seems cool, but his buddies are beyond sex-obsessed. Clay and Preston, because of course their names are Clay and Preston. Those are, like, the requisite pervy frat boy names.

Somehow, they manage to turn everything into a sex joke or double entendre. Annaliese and Blake just laugh it off. Kudos to them for being able to do that. I grew up around hockey players and have heard every type of locker room talk imaginable, but this Clay guy is starting to grate on me.

"So, like, she says she can't come from penetration. Fine, whatever. But guess what, babe? There ain't always time to go down on you for forty fucking minutes before we go to pound town."

My fingers tighten around my beer.

"Dude, if *your* dick can't make her come? Like that huge hog? There's no hope for the rest of us."

"Yours isn't that bad," Clay graciously tells Preston. "It's above the national average."

Why do these dudes know so much about each other's dicks? It's weird.

"But yeah, I've got a winning hog." Clay snorts. "Liese can vouch for that."

Annaliese gives him a shove, which has him jostling Blake mid-sip, spilling pinkish-orange slush on her chest.

She mops up her collarbone with the corner of her towel, then stands. "Does anyone want a refill of LMD?" It's what she's been calling the cocktail, which looks more like a slushie than an actual drink.

"Hey, freckles," I call toward her. "Maybe go easy on the LMD?"

"Don't," she warns.

"Just saying. I'm the responsible adult here and—"

"You are not the adult, and you're the furthest thing from responsible. Aren't you the one who led the charge on the boathouse roof jumping contest last summer?"

"Wait, you guys can jump off that thing?" Preston shifts his gaze to the boathouse.

I nod absently. "Yeah. You don't even need a running start."

"New fun level unlocked," Kuri says happily.

Even Annaliese brightens. "Oh, right! Eddie was telling me about that. He and the Golden Boys were trying to see who could jump closest to the swim platform."

"Hundred bucks says it's me," Clay declares, shooting to his feet.

The others follow suit, but Annaliese hesitates then, glancing toward me. "You sure it's cool?" she asks. At least *someone* is recognizing my authority here.

I sit up and scrutinize the group to gauge their level of intoxication. But I've only seen the guys consume one beer each, and Annaliese and Blake have barely finished their first round of Blake's slushy monstrosity.

"Yeah, it's fine," I say, and the four of them waste no time sprinting off the dock toward the boathouse.

Blake lingers, distracting me for a moment when she starts undoing her braid. At first, I think it's for my benefit, until I realize she's just rebraiding it to make it tighter.

"So let me get this straight," she says. "You'll let us jump off the boathouse, but you won't let me have a second cup of Logan Mouth Delight?"

"Jesus, is that what LMD stands for? Also, it's not a real drink."

"It's a Logan original."

"It has a dumb name."

"I'll pass your feedback along to my dad," she says sweetly.

She flips the braid so it hangs down her back, and I notice she hasn't completely wiped the drink that spilled on her. A pink rivulet has joined forces with a bead of sweat to roll off her collarbone, lazily travelling down before disappearing into the floral-print triangle covering her left breast. I have a vision of pulling her toward me, licking that sticky pink line until I reach her tit, pushing the bathing suit aside, and—

"Wyatt."

I jolt out of it. Shit. It's the weed. Weed makes some people lethargic, but it has the opposite effect on me. I get horny when I'm stoned.

"Are you doing the boathouse jump with us?"

"What do you mean *us*?" I say with a snort. "We both know you're not making that jump."

"Yes, I am."

"Logan. Have you forgotten I've known you your entire life? You can't even step onto a second-floor balcony without panicking."

It's no secret that Blake inherited her mother's fear of heights. She and Aunt Grace were the ones holding everyone's purses and packs whenever we went to theme parks as kids. One time, I suggested Grace ride a roller coaster with me, and she asked if I was on drugs.

"It's not that high," Blake objects, but her wary blue eyes shift toward the boathouse. Her friends are already on the roof, surveying the water below.

"Logan!" Annaliese shouts. "Come on!"

Fortitude hardens Blake's expression as she refocuses it on me. "Stop getting in my head," she chides.

"I didn't get in your head. I simply reminded you of your phobia."

"It's not a phobia. And I go up on that roof all the time. It doesn't count as a height."

"I've never seen you get within six feet of the edge."

"I stand at the edge all the time."

I lift a brow. "Really?"

"Well, *near* the edge," she amends. "Ugh. Oh my God. Whatever. Get out of my head!"

With an outraged noise, she shoves her feet into her flip-flops and stalks off. I watch in amusement as she ascends the wooden staircase on the side of the boathouse to join her new friends. Then I get distracted by the way the sun gleams off her hair. The light brown appears almost blond in this light.

Blake approaches the edge of the roof. Her steps are extra careful, as if she's afraid she might forget how to walk and accidentally topple off the boathouse. I don't mean to laugh, but a chuckle slips out. It's impossible for her to have heard it from this far away, yet her head swivels my way. I don't miss the flash of misery on her face before she glares at me.

I take another sip of beer and give her a little wave.

She peers over the edge for a moment, then turns to exchange a few words with Annaliese. I swallow my laughter as I watch Blake stride back to the stairs and stomp down them.

"Everything okay?" I call out with an innocent smile.

She stops to scowl at me. "Someone needs to be in the water to judge who jumps the farthest."

"Uh-huh. Sure."

I'm still grinning as she marches to the end of the pier and dives into the lake.

# Chapter 12

## BLAKE

*Fucking Beautiful*

ANNALIESE AND THE BOYS STAY well into the night. When it gets colder, we move the party from the dock to the great room, where we play drunk charades and a game of "never have I ever" that devolves so fast that Annaliese and I immediately say we're done. Her friends are horndogs. Coming from the enchanting Kuri, it's not that bad, but the other two are very broey. Every time Clay says something flirtatious, it just sounds gross. And Preston reminds me too much of Isaac. He has his red hair and the same bulky build.

Speaking of my ex, he just texted, determined to stand his ground on the escalating Hot Boi situation.

THE CHEATER

Just buy a new one. I don't see the big fucking deal.

I want the one I already bought.

THE CHEATER

Like it was even your money. Daddy bought it for his princess.

The accusation has me fuming. Low blow. I could easily buy a new toaster, but *that's not the point.*

"I still can't believe you broke up with an NFL player," Annaliese remarks as she watches me rage text my ex.

"Maybe he'll get cut in training camp," I say hopefully.

"With that monster rookie contract they gave him? No way." Clay drops his empty bottle on the coffee table and gets to his feet. "Need another beer."

On the other end of the couch, Preston rolls his eyes at me. "I don't get why you ended it. All professional athletes cheat."

Annaliese stares at him in shock. "That doesn't make it okay, Pres."

"Just saying, it's part of the lifestyle. You think all their wives and girlfriends aren't aware of it? They just turn the other cheek because they want their flashy diamonds and their cars and mansions."

"Yeah, well, I don't want any of that," I retort. "I want someone who doesn't cheat on me."

"Honestly, I'm surprised you were even interested in being part of that lifestyle," Annaliese tells me, sounding bemused. "You don't seem like the type who enjoys the spotlight."

"I mean, I don't love it," I admit. "But I was never really in the spotlight with Isaac. I don't think that would've changed once he started in the NFL." I offer a little shrug. "I was his plus-one. The woman behind the man. Nobody ever paid much attention to me when I was with him..." I trail off, suddenly disturbed by my own words.

But it's true, I realize. I was Isaac's arm candy, for lack of a better word. The cute, unassuming sorority girl he could bring to events, who looked good in a dress and could chat with the other girlfriends but never hog his spotlight.

Fuck.

Is that what drew him to me? For some reason, that notion

bothers me.

Annaliese snorts loudly. "I'd rather die than be some man's plus-one. This day and age, it's time for the man to be behind the woman."

"Oh, I'd *love* to be behind you, Liese," Preston declares, and she flicks up her middle finger.

I catch a blur of motion from the kitchen. Clay is grabbing a beer from the fridge. But rather than rejoin us, he leaves the bottle on the counter and wanders toward the stairs.

That instantly raises my hackles. I made it clear they can't go roaming around the house, and while I'd like to say I trust these guys by virtue of them being friends with Annaliese, I don't. Sadly, it's not unheard of for guests to try to steal memorabilia from my dad and Garrett's study. It's happened before. And we have valuable photographs and a few framed jerseys hanging on the walls upstairs.

"I'll be right back," I say, cutting Annaliese off midsentence. "I don't want Clay wandering around the house by himself. I'm gonna go get him."

"Yeah, go get him, tiger," Preston drawls.

I track Clay to the top of the stairs, which elicits a rush of annoyance. "What are you doing?"

He offers a sheepish look. "Sorry. I was following the trail of pictures. I wanted to see this last one." He gestures to a frame.

I relax slightly. Heading up the stairs, I join him on the spacious landing where he's admiring a photograph of my father and Garrett Graham in their Bruins jerseys, arms thrust up in victory as their teammates celebrate on the ice all around them. This was the first time they won the Stanley Cup together.

"It's so sick that you're from, like, hockey royalty," Clay tells me, stars in his eyes.

"Honestly, I'm not much of a hockey fan," I admit.

"Bullshit."

"It's true. I know everything about the game, but it's not something I'd put on in my spare time."

He cocks his head. "So what *do* you put on in your spare time?"

I shrug. "Sappy movies that make me cry or those reality TV competition shows. And I listen to a lot of podcasts."

"Do you watch porn?"

Ew. Who asks somebody that?

"Not really," I say.

He grins. "That's not a no."

I grit my teeth and take a step away. "We should go back downstairs."

He reaches for my hand. "Wait."

I stifle a sigh. "What?"

"You're saying you don't feel this thing between us? We've been flirting all day."

"I mean, *you've* been flirting all day."

His eyes flash. "So it was one-sided?"

*Yes*, I want to snap. My parents encouraged me to always be blunt and clear about my intentions. Don't leave it up to the other person to guess, my dad always says. If you're not interested, you're not interested.

But my father is a man, and he's never had to deal with drunk dudes whose egos get all bent out of shape when you reject them. It's a very delicate line you have to walk as a woman.

"Let's go downstairs," I repeat.

I blink and both his hands are on my waist, trying to tug me closer. "I think you're beautiful, Blake."

"Thank you," I mutter while swiftly stepping out of his grasp.

"Come on, one kiss."

"No."

"Just one—"

He's suddenly hauled backward, releasing a startled yelp like a puppy that just got kicked.

"She said no."

I turn to find Wyatt on the landing, his green eyes burning with anger and disgust.

Clay recovers quickly, putting on a careless smirk. "How about you don't speak for the girl?"

"How about you don't touch the woman when she tells you she doesn't want you to touch her?"

"Oh, fuck off. Like you haven't been touching her when it's only the two of you here," Clay sneers. "So *you* can hook up with her, but no one else can—"

Before he can finish, Wyatt slams him against the wall. I dart out of the way, panic flying up my throat as Clay's back collides with the picture he was admiring. The frame slides off the wall and clatters down the staircase, stopping halfway. Wyatt doesn't pay it any attention. He's busy restraining Clay by the collar, his forearm pressed on the guy's throat.

Speaking in a cold, deadly voice I've never heard from him, he says, "It's time for you to get the hell out of my house."

When Clay struggles against the hold, Wyatt jams his arm deeper into his windpipe.

"I'm sorry, what was that? You were agreeing with me that it's time for you to go?"

Clay's eyes start watering as he gasps for air.

"Wyatt," I murmur, and he releases Clay in a heartbeat, as if controlled by that one soft syllable.

The other guy coughs, clutching his throat. "You're a fucking psycho, dude."

Macho man that he is, Clay elbows Wyatt as he stomps toward the stairs. Then he doubles down on douchery by kicking the fallen photograph and sending it skittering. The frame hadn't broken during the initial fall. Now it does, shattering to pieces at the bottom of the staircase.

I press my lips together, then glance at Wyatt. "Let me talk to Annaliese. You stay up here and calm down."

Jaw tight, he stalks toward the bedrooms.

Downstairs, I find the three guys loitering near the back doors while Annaliese gathers the empty bottles from the table.

"You don't have to do that," I tell her.

At the sound of my voice, she abandons the bottles. "Clay said Wyatt attacked him?" she exclaims.

"No. Wyatt was defending me," I say stiffly, shooting a glare in Clay's direction. He glares back, unrepentant.

Her eyes widen. "Defending you?" Now *she* turns to glare at him. "What the hell did you do, Clayton?"

"Nothing," says the surly-faced guy. "Just didn't realize we were hanging out with a cocktease."

"Cocktease?" Annaliese roars. "Don't make me smack you upside the head!"

I hide a smile. "It's fine," I assure the angry woman. "Just a little misunderstanding. Clay thought we were vibing, but we weren't." I flick my eyes at him. "Right, Clay?"

After a beat, he mutters, "Right."

The other two boys wear apologetic expressions as they say goodbye to me. Kuri thanks me for a great day, which, honestly, it sort of was before Clay decided to ruin it with his creepiness.

Annaliese waits until the three guys are outside before turning to me with a sigh. "I'm sorry about Clay. He gets a bit aggro when he's drunk."

"Clearly."

"I hope he didn't go too far."

"No. Just went in for a kiss. Wyatt probably overreacted."

Her lips twitch.

"What?" I say.

"He didn't overreact, Logan. He was marking his territory."

My forehead creases. "Who? Wyatt?"

"Oh yeah. That boy has it bad."

A laugh pops out of my mouth. "Trust me, he doesn't."

"Trust me," she mimics. "He was sneaking looks at you all day. Very unplatonic looks, I might add. He's into you. But sure, keep denying it. Anyway." Annaliese flashes an earnest smile. "I loved chilling with you today. Next time we'll go out just you and me, yeah? The boys are leaving on Monday."

"Sounds good."

I lock up after her and watch as the small group heads down to the pier, where their boat is docked. Annaliese only had one drink this entire day, so I trust her to get the three drunks home safely.

Even though it's one a.m. and it could probably wait till morning, I finish gathering the empties and put them in the bin under the sink because I'm a little neurotic when it comes to cleaning. Then I notice the table looks sticky, and so does the counter, and... Fine, I might be a little more than *a little* neurotic. I spend the next fifteen minutes sweeping up the broken picture frame and wiping down every surface on the main floor before finally trudging up the stairs.

Getting to the yellow room requires passing the blue room, and I hesitate in front of Wyatt's door. Then I knock.

"Yeah," he says. It's not exactly a *come in*, but it's not a *go away*.

I open the door and peek in. He's standing at the dormer window, his gaze fixed on the lake, but he turns around when I enter.

"You okay?" he asks.

"I'm fine. He didn't do anything."

"He touched you without your permission."

"And you took care of it. Although choking him was a bit extreme."

That gets me a crooked smile. "I wasn't choking him. He could've gotten out of that hold if he really tried."

I toy with the edge of my braid, and those heavy-lidded eyes fixate on *me* now. Following the small motions of my hand as I twist the braid. Unlike Annaliese, I did have more than one drink. At least three LMDs. And I feel it in my blood, in the way my body heats under Wyatt's thorough scrutiny.

"Can I do something?" His voice is soft and seductive.

My pulse races. "Do what?"

He slowly closes the distance between us, his bare chest gleaming in the darkness. I don't know why he doesn't have the light on. The moonlight is the only thing illuminating the bedroom, casting shadows over his chiseled features.

*He's into you.*

I suddenly hear Annaliese's voice in my head, insisting that Wyatt has it bad for me. But if he does, he would just make a move. Wyatt's not shy. He doesn't play coy. I've seen him flash that careless smile dozens of times to get a woman into bed.

When he reaches for my braid, his fingers brush mine, and an electric shock travels through me.

"Can I just…undo this?"

The braid, I realize. He means my braid. It's suddenly hard to breathe. I manage to swallow. "Sure?"

Oh God. Maybe this is the move.

Is he making a move?

Time stands still. I don't know what's happening, and the not knowing only adds to the thrill. To the danger. I'm standing in Wyatt Graham's bedroom while his long fingers pull the elastic off and begin to untwine my plaited hair. When those fingers thread through my hair, tugging lightly, a shiver skitters down my spine. I can breathe again, but it's shallow. Strained. The spot between my legs tingles wildly. This is turning me on. He's not even doing anything sexual, and I'm turned on.

He remains focused on my face, but I don't know if he's actually seeing me. It's that faraway gleam Wyatt gets sometimes, like he's caught a glimpse of something godly and mysterious that we mere mortals can never tap into.

Finally, my hair is loose. He captures the long strands in his fist and gently moves it aside so it's cascading over one shoulder.

The silence stretches between us like a live wire.

He stares at my mouth now. I wonder if he's thinking the same thing I am. That all it would take is an inch, maybe two, and there'd be no more pretending this is just friendship.

"Wyatt..."

The sound of his name doesn't pull him out of the trance. I don't think he's drunk, and I only saw him smoke half a joint much earlier in the day. As he steps closer and exhales slightly, all I smell is the mint of his toothpaste and the scent of his shampoo.

My lips feel dry, so I lick them. The quick motion captures his attention. My heart takes off in a wild gallop when he rubs his thumb over my bottom lip before curling his hand around my jaw. He's so much taller that I have to peek up at him.

I don't know what he's seeing, but he whispers, "Fucking beautiful."

Our eyes lock. His rough fingertips stroke my cheek.

And then he jerks and releases me.

"Sorry," he mumbles as my skin weeps from the loss of his touch. "I just... Your hair gave me an idea for a song."

"My hair?" I echo weakly.

Wyatt visibly swallows. "You never know when inspiration will strike." He clears his throat. "You going to bed now?"

"Yeah. I guess."

He grabs his notebook from the desk. "Cool. I'm gonna write on the dock for a while."

"Don't forget to set the alarm when you come back in," I say.

He nods, and then he's gone.

Stop the World

Baby, I was fine before you, I think I was fine
I was grounded, I swear, before you were mine
But now you're here and I'm falling
Should've run
But you're calling

You say my name and I ~~drop~~ forget who I am
You kiss me once and I know that I'm gone
Cause your smile stops the world
And the world is a song

You smile at me
~~and I'll love you forever~~ and I feel like I could love you forever
just for that.
Just for the way you say
"yeah?"
when you're half listening.
~~I didn't even notice you'd become~~
When did you become
~~the thing~~ what I measure time by?

Before you
After you

And now you're here and I'm falling
Losing control
Cause you're calling

You say my name and I ~~drop~~ forget who I am
You kiss me once and I know that I'm gone
Cause your smile stops the world
And the world is a song

And if I lose myself in you
if I fall too far
if the world stops
every time you smile,
I'll stay right here
until it starts again

# Chapter 13

## BLAKE

### The sex tree

WYATT

Come to the playing field.

THE TEXT APPEARS AS I'M pouring a cup of coffee at the counter. My heart stutters. He wants me to go outside and meet him?

This has to be about last night. The almost kiss.

Because that was totally an almost kiss.

I think.

I still can't make sense of what happened in his bedroom. His fingers in my hair. His eyes boring into me like he was peering into my soul.

My palms are clammy from nerves as I carry my coffee outside and step off the front porch. A minute later, I find Wyatt standing in the grassy clearing on the far side of the house, staring at a net.

This was not what I expected when he texted to come to the playing field.

We call it the playing field because this is where all the dads go when their competitive instincts kick in, propelling them to play volleyball or croquet or lawn bowling or whatever else allows them to either high-five as teammates or shout obscenities as opponents.

Yesterday, there was nothing in the clearing.

Today, there's a net. Not a volleyball regulation net but a couple of feet shorter.

Gripping the handle of my mug, I saunter toward him. "Badminton?"

"Yeah, I think so," he replies, still staring.

"Did you set that up?"

"No. Henry must have done it when we were asleep."

"Okay, I'm about to put forth a hypothesis, and I need you to seriously consider it." I purse my lips for a moment. "Do you think Houseman Henry might be one of the Tahoe ghosts?"

"No," Wyatt says.

"You didn't even consider it!"

"Because it's dumb."

"Here. Hold this." I hand him my cup and pull up my phone. "I'm texting my dad so he can explain the net."

Why is there a badminton net outside?

DAD

Oh, we just decided last night. Badminton tourney this summer when we're all there. Participation mandatory. G's making up the brackets.

I groan in dismay. "They're going to force us to participate in a tournament, and there are brackets."

"Why are there always brackets?" Wyatt sighs.

Did we not learn our lesson from the lawn bowling tournament? You and Dean didn't speak for weeks afterward.

DAD

Because he's a fucking cheater.

I'm going now.

I slide my phone in my pocket and give Wyatt a questioning look. "Is there anything else you wanted to discuss?"

"Nah. That was it." He hooks his thumbs in the waistband of his sweatpants, causing them to dip lower. Oh no. I can see the top of the man vee. It's too distracting.

I force my gaze upward. "Nothing at all?" I prompt.

"Nope."

My frustration mounts. Really? We're just going to ignore it? He defended my honor last night, unbraided my hair like some kind of sexy hairstylist, and almost kissed me. But "nope." Nothing to see here, folks.

Annoyed, I chug the rest of my coffee. "Okay, great. I'm off then."

"Wait. Where are you going?" He scrutinizes my attire—bike shorts, rash guard, and cross-trainers—as if noticing for the first time. "Why do you look like you're about to run a triathlon?"

"I'm going on a hike with the Spencers. They're picking me up on the dock in ten minutes."

"I'm sorry—you're going on a boat ride slash hike with the crazy men in the lake?"

"They're not crazy."

"How are you even in contact with them?" Wyatt demands.

"Oh, Little Spencer slid into my DMs."

"I don't like this."

"Which part?"

"Any of it," he says in exasperation. "Random men DMing you. Luring you onto their boat by inviting you on a very suspicious hike—"

"Why is it suspicious? We're just visiting Darlie and Raymond's tree near the Loughlin place."

"The sex tree?" Wyatt sounds outraged.

"Yeah."

"Let me get this straight. You're letting two grown men whisk you away by boat so you can hike up a cliff to visit a tree where the ghost who haunts our dock used to fuck her lover before he left her for her sister? You are literally *begging* to get murdered."

I lean in to pat him on the arm. "You know, if you and my dad entered an overprotective competition, I honestly don't know who would win. Same goes for who's crazier."

Wyatt clenches his jaw. "Give me five minutes to throw on some real clothes."

"You're not coming with us," I protest.

He's already stalking toward the house. "Yes, I am."

"You said you have to write today—"

"I'll write later," he says over his shoulder.

The Spencers pick us up in their rented speedboat and make no effort to hide the fact that they're checking Wyatt out as he climbs on board. I don't blame them one iota. He's wearing khaki shorts, hiking boots, and a tight white T-shirt that hugs his abs, and with his sunglasses on and a baseball cap shielding his face, he looks like some kind of edible adventure boy.

It's hard to talk over the wind, so I lean back and enjoy the water misting my face as the boat bounces on the waves. Less than fifteen minutes later, Big Spencer slows as we approach a little cove shaded by towering pines. A small dock juts from the rocky shore, and he carefully glides up beside it while Little Spencer hops onto the rickety wooden platform and ties us off.

Wyatt jumps out next and extends his hand to me. I take it, ignoring the jolt of electricity that travels through me. I hate how much he affects me. Stupid pheromones.

"It's just up here," Little Spencer says when we're all on land. He's sporting another Mollie May shirt today, this one sky-blue with fringe around the hem because Mollie May wears fringed costumes at all her shows.

"You've been here before?" I say as we follow them toward the opening of the path.

"A few times. We spent the night last week."

"Really?" I say in surprise.

Big Spencer nods. "Camped right under the tree. We thought maybe she'd want to return to her lover."

"Of course," Wyatt says solemnly. "Who wouldn't."

Little Spencer rolls his eyes. "It's okay, handsome. You don't have to be a believer."

"You camped here? But isn't this private property?" I ask.

"Not the tree," Big Spencer says smugly. "We pulled all the county surveys to check the property lines. Loughlin land ends a half mile east of the tree."

We trek up the path, which is only wide enough for two people to walk side by side. The Spencers prove to be surprisingly athletic, bounding ahead of us. Wyatt and I follow behind, silently navigating overgrown roots and pushing away branches that hang too low on the trail.

It isn't until the Spencers are out of earshot that Wyatt glances over and lowers his voice. "So about last night."

"Oh," I say brightly, "are we finally going to talk about how you almost kissed me?"

"I didn't almost kiss you," he mutters.

"Really? So you didn't fall into some sort of love trance and finger comb my hair and then touch my mouth and lean in for a kiss?"

When I hear an audible snicker from up ahead, I realize the Spencers are not as out of earshot as I thought.

"It wasn't a love trance," he argues. "It was a music trance."

"A music trance," I echo dubiously.

"Yeah. I was hearing music in my head. It was your hair maybe. I don't know. I had an idea for a song and got lost in thought." He gives me a sidelong look. "I wasn't going to kiss you."

"Uh-huh. If you say so."

Grumbling irritably, he walks faster and is soon outpacing the Spencers.

Little Spencer slows, waiting for me to catch up. As we fall into step with each other, he murmurs, "Oh, that boy was absolutely going to kiss you."

I feel vindicated. "Right?"

It's another ten minutes before we reach the top of the bluff and five more before Big Spencer calls out, "Over here."

The tree is more impressive than I expected. It's a lone pine but not some scrawny one. The trunk is massive, gnarled with age, and the high branches stretch wide and uneven, casting pockets of shade all over the tall grass. At the base, wildflowers push up through the dirt, and one of the tree's lower limbs juts out low enough that it creates a natural bench you can actually sit on.

"Wow, this is beautiful," I marvel.

"Right?" Little Spencer beams. "You can totally picture Darlie and Raymond coming out here and boning, can't you?"

"I mean, I wasn't picturing them boning, but...sure."

I approach the tree, breathing in the scent of pine needles and earth. I half expect to find initials carved into the trunk, a romantic heart with DG and RL scratched inside it, but there's nothing but jagged, flaky stretches of bark.

"So Raymond lived up there?" I peer at the slope in the distance, trying to make out the Loughlin house through the pines. You can see the enormous property if you're on the water but not from here.

"Yep," Big Spencer confirms. "And according to legend, he snuck out every night to meet Darlie here."

"To bone," pipes up Little Spencer.

"What legend is this?" Wyatt sounds exasperated. "Like, is there any actual proof they met at this tree? For all you know, this is just a random tree that got dragged into this story against its will."

"We read it in interviews," Little Spencer says defensively. "Members of the Loughlin family have spoken about it over the years."

"Okay, and what proof did they offer?" Wyatt challenges. "Other than hearing it in stories passed from generation to generation?"

"Oh, so you're discounting oral history?" Little Spencer shoots back. "You'd make a terrible historian. Who wants a granola bar?"

I blink at the sudden topic change. "Ah, no thanks. I'm good."

"Same," Wyatt says.

"Suit yourself." Little Spencer digs into his fanny pack, glancing at Big Spencer. "Chocolate chip or chewy oats, babe?"

As the Spencers sit on the branch bench and munch on their granola bars, I wander off, phone in hand. Might as well capture some pictures of the view while we're up here. Wyatt comes up beside me as

I'm framing a shot of the lake.

"You feeling better about this murder hike?" I ask him.

"Yeah," he says grudgingly. "They seem harmless."

"Told you."

I turn around to snap some photos of the sex tree.

"I can't imagine loving someone so much that I'd want to kill myself if they broke my heart," I muse. "Can you?"

"Me personally? Nah. I can't see myself ever catching feelings that run that deep."

"Goes against the fuckboy code?"

He rolls his eyes. "Careful, Blakey… Keep using 'fuckboy' as a slur, and I'll tell everyone you've been slut-shaming me."

"Don't call me Blakey," I grumble. "Only Gigi gets that pass. And we both know you own that label. You go out of your way to make it clear to girls that you're there for a good time, not a long time."

That gets me a shrug. "Nothing wrong with knowing your own limitations."

"But you have been in love, right?"

Wyatt nods. "Plenty of times. But not the kind of love we're talking about." He goes quiet for a beat before continuing thoughtfully. "I think I can imagine it, though. What Darlie felt for Raymond. Love so all-consuming that when it's gone, you don't want to move on. You don't *want* to heal."

I bite my lip, overwhelmed by the sudden intensity.

"It's like…" He trails off again. "You just want to stop existing in a world where you're no longer loved by her. Because erasing yourself hurts a lot less than staying behind without her."

My throat constricts, a strange sensation traveling through my body. For a self-proclaimed good-time guy, he's conveying some very profound thoughts about love.

"Have you ever felt anything like that before?" Wyatt asks gruffly.

Slowly, I shake my head. "No. But I thought maybe with Isaac..." I stop, unsure where I'm going with this. "Isaac acted like he loved me like that. He was so over-the-top about his feelings, especially in public...all the grand gestures and declarations of love..." I swallow through my tight throat. "But I don't think he felt even a fraction of what you just described."

A flicker of discomfort crosses Wyatt's expression, almost as if he's realized how deep we've gone. "Eh," he finally says. "Makes for a great love song, but in real life? It's probably overrated."

GARRETT

Guys, a Graham needs to win the badminton tourney. Let's make it happen.

RYDER

What if Gigi and I win? We're Ryders.

GARRETT

You're a Graham, son. Act like it.

JOHN

I need you to know that I adore you both, you are my entire world, and I will lay my life down for you.

GRACE

But?

JOHN

But when it comes to the Tahoe Games, my partner is Allie. She and I have a good thing going and we're not giving it up.

BLAKE

Mom, how have you not divorced him yet?

## DEAN'S GENES

DEAN

If a Di Laurentis doesn't win this, you will bring shame upon this house. Beau, Ivy—you need to step up. I would try, but I got stuck with Grace.

ALLIE

What about me?

DEAN

You're dead to us. You were exiled from the family when you chose *him* as your partner four years ago.

BEAU

Sorry, Mom, he's right.

ALLIE

We have a good thing going and we're not giving it up. We're undefeated.

IVY

I refuse to participate in this group chat until someone changes the name.

ALLIE

Ivy has a point. My genes are clearly the superior ones.

DEAN

Is someone talking? I feel like I hear someone talking but it might be a traitor and we don't acknowledge traitors here in Dean's Genes.

**TUCKER TIME**

JOHN

Darlins', your mama and I love you very much. But we will be the winning pair even if we have to crush your bones to dust.

ALEX

Love you too, Daddy.

JAMIE

Love you, Dad.

# Chapter 14

## BLAKE

*Prepare to eat my shuttlecock*

"WE SHOULD PLAY," I SUGGEST when we get back to the house. I didn't expect that hike to get so deep, and I'm desperate to lighten the mood. Dissecting the concept of all-consuming love with Wyatt has left me unsettled.

"Play what?" he says blankly.

"Badminton."

"Seriously?"

"Why not? Our crazy fathers will be thrilled to hear we're commencing our training early."

"True." Wyatt twists his baseball cap around. "All right. I'm in."

A quick text to his dad tells us that Houseman Henry stored all the equipment in the boathouse, so while Wyatt retrieves it, I jog into the house to grab a cooler of water bottles. Wyatt's already at the clearing when I return. He's stripped off his shirt, which means all he's wearing now are those slutty khaki shorts and a backward cap. God help me.

It's hot, so I take my shirt off too, leaving me in a padded sports bra and biker shorts. I tighten the laces of my sneakers so I'm not tripping over myself on the court.

Wyatt frowns. "You're wearing a bra."

"Oh no. Is that gonna make you want to kiss me again?"

Rolling his eyes, he passes me a racket while juggling a few badminton birdies in his other hand. "You know how to play, right?"

"Nope," I say cheerfully. "But I assume you smash it over the net as hard as you can?"

"I mean, pretty much, yeah. But once the shuttlecock—"

"Please stop trying to turn me on."

He snorts. "The birdie. Official name is shuttlecock."

"Who named it that? Probably someone with a small penis, right?"

Wyatt laughs harder. "Why does his penis have to be small?"

"Because he's treating it like a space shuttle. Like he wants it to be a rocket. But it's not. So he's projecting via badminton."

"Yes, that's exactly what's happening."

We jog to opposite sides of the net. I adjust my grip on the racket. "Loser does the dishes for the rest of the summer," I call out.

"I'm not taking that bet."

"Scared?"

He spins the racket, showing off. "No, I just know that you can never bet on sports outcomes to go your way. What if I trip on a rock and break my leg? Then you'd win by default."

"You know who wouldn't trip and break their leg?"

"Who?"

"A good badminton player."

"Oh, fuck off. No bet."

"Fine. Winner gets the glory."

Although he's, like, ten feet taller than me, I'm decently athletic, so the match ends up being competitive right off the bat.

Wyatt tosses the shuttlecock into the air, then smacks it with a loud *thwack*, sending it flying toward me with unexpected speed.

I lunge, my sneakers squeaking on the grass. Somehow, I manage to return it with enough force to make him sprint backward. Wow. I'm good at this.

The game escalates fast. Suddenly we're not just volleying anymore. We're going *hard*. Wyatt dives for a save, landing on his side and barely popping the shuttlecock back over the net, and as it hurtles my way, I don't bother playing nice. I smash it down like I'm trying to end his professional badminton career.

"Fuck off! That was a body shot!" he shouts, laughing breathlessly.

"Play better, sweetheart," I tell him, twirling my racket in a dainty spin.

"You're a mean badminton player," he informs me.

"What's a matter, songboy? Can't handle the heat?"

"Songboy? Don't make fun of music."

"I'm not making fun of music. I'm making fun of *you*."

After my next serve, our rally hits ten volleys. We're both panting by the time I miss the eleventh return.

Sweat drips down Wyatt's temple as he raises his racket again. "Prepare to eat my shuttlecock, Logan."

"That sounds so wrong," I reply through a wave of laughter.

We're both starting to glisten. Sweat is dripping between my breasts and coating my face. I call a time-out and jog to the cooler to grab some ice cubes. I rub them over my neck and collarbone, sighing happily at the cooling sensation. It doesn't even occur to me I might be acting seductive until Wyatt eyes me over the bottle of water he's chugging.

"Freckles," he warns, wiping water off the side of his mouth.

"You need to stop."

"Stop what?"

"I don't know. Trying to tempt me."

My jaw drops. "You are so full of yourself."

"Really? So rubbing ice all over your tits is not for my benefit?"

"Is it working?" I challenge.

"So you *are* doing it."

"No, I'm just saying, if you think I'm trying to tempt you and you're being tempted, then maybe the problem is yours."

We stare at each other.

"This fucking dynamic," he mutters.

Yes, it's very strange. I'll give him that. We argue all the time. Constantly goading each other, testing each other. But it's not hostile. He just draws out emotions in me.

That and he's so gorgeous I can't think straight. The sun is making the sheen of sweat on his chest glisten, tracing the delicious cut of his abs. My mouth waters as I watch a bead of sweat drip from the curve of his collarbone and slide down his torso, winding a path through the light dusting of hair that arrows into his waistband.

"I'm not trying to tempt you," I say, finding my voice. "I'm overheated." I pop an ice cube into my mouth and crunch it loudly between my teeth. "Come on. Let's continue the game so I can finish embarrassing you."

We're drenched in sweat by the time we call it quits. Wyatt emerges the victor, but I'm genuinely impressed with myself. I didn't expect to be this good at badminton of all things. Maybe I'll put some real effort into this family tournament the dads are planning.

I flex my right wrist, finding it surprisingly tender. "Jeez. Who would've thought flicking a shuttlecock would make me this sore?"

Wyatt sighs. "Please don't ever use the phrase *flicking a*

*shuttlecock* again."

"Too sexy?"

"Obviously."

Grinning, I set my racket on top of the cooler. "I'm going to take a shower and then fix some lunch. What do you want to eat?"

"Burgers?" he suggests.

"Sure. I'll prep some sides when I'm out of the shower."

"I'm gonna put the equipment away," he says, bending to pluck a birdie off the ground. "It all needs to go back to the boathouse. I'll find you in a bit."

I go inside to wash the layers of sweat off my body, then change into a loose sundress and brush my wet hair into a ponytail. When I check my phone, I find a missed call from Beau Di Laurentis, quickly tapping his name to call him back.

Rather than hello, Beau answers with, "I need you."

"What's wrong?" I ask instantly. "Who do I need to hurt?"

I'm only half kidding. Truth be told, the Golden Boys are my ride or dies, especially Beau. It could've gone sideways real fast after we slept together, but to my relief, there's been no awkwardness between us since that night. Which only affirms that he was the right man for the job. Not only was he gentle and patient, but he also behaved perfectly afterward. Beau's honestly the best guy I know.

"The rest of our family," Beau answers. "We're going to crush them. You and me. The two Bs."

"I'm sorry. Is this about the badminton tournament?"

"Yeah, word just came down the pipe that it's—"

"What pipe?" I interrupt with a snort.

"Man Chat. We were just informed it's mixed pairs. Ergo, I'm claiming you as my partner."

There's a buzz in my ear. "Hold on. I'm getting a text."

"Don't you dare answer it," Beau growls. "It's gonna be AJ."

I tilt the phone to peer at the screen. Sure enough, it's a text from AJ Connelly.

AJ

Hey B. I need you to be my partner for the badminton tourney.

"He's trying to be your partner, isn't he?" demands Beau. "Tell him he's too late."

"I don't know," I tease. "He's got a few pounds of muscle on you."

"Blake Josephine Logan," he warns. "Remember who gave you your first orgasm..."

I burst out laughing. "Don't you dare use that against me in the name of *badminton.*"

His tone takes on a pleading note. "Come on, I asked you first. Say yes."

"Sure, whatever, yes."

"Yes! I love you! Thanks, B."

"You're welcome. All right, I gotta go prep dinner."

"Wait, how's it going in Tahoe? I heard Wyatt's there."

"Yeah, he's up here writing music."

"You guys hanging out a lot?"

"A little. But you know him. He's in his own world when it comes to his music. And I've been researching a lake haunting. We went out today to look at the tree where my ghost met her secret lover before she drowned herself."

There's a beat.

Then Beau sighs. "You are such a raging dork. I can't wait to see you."

"Right back at you."

After we say goodbye, I open AJ's text to respond.

Sorry, I've already been claimed.

AJ

Asshole. Now I'm gonna be stuck with Ivy.

Isn't your girlfriend coming this year?

AJ

Tara doesn't have an athletic bone in her body.

You can try to take Alex.

AJ

She'll be with Wyatt.

Fuck you, Blake Josephine. Always playing favorites.

I love you too, Adam Jensen.

As I'm heading downstairs, I send a message to my family group chat.

Hey guys, this badminton thing is getting way too serious. The Golden Boys are ready to kill each other to partner up with me. This is supposed to be fun.

DAD

This is a blood fight to the death. There is nothing more serious than this.

That's on me. I should've known better than to expect common sense from my father.

In the kitchen, I slice up a tomato and prep other burger fixings. Wyatt isn't on the deck, and I notice the barbecue hasn't even been turned on, so I walk outside to the railing and scan the area in search of him. When my gaze locates him, I almost choke on my tongue.

He's standing under the outdoor shower behind the boathouse.

Naked. Gripping his dick.

Oh.

I guess *his* wrist isn't sore.

I can't breathe, my heart hammering hard against my ribs. Wyatt has one hand pressed against the wooden wall, and with his body slightly bent and angled to the side, I'm provided with a perfect view of not only his gorgeous dick but also his tight ass.

His body is spectacular, just like I knew it would be.

I'm frozen in place, captivated by the sight of his fist moving over his long, thick shaft. I know I should walk away, but I can't make my legs function.

And then it's too late, because his head shifts and our eyes collide.

# Chapter 15

## WYATT

*Sometimes friends pull their dicks out*

I SHOULD STOP.

I mean, obviously I should stop.

I have my hand around my dick and Blake Logan's eyes on it. No way this ends well. Figuratively anyway. Jacking off always ends great for me.

Although I know it's wrong, I can't look away. She's too far to make out all those unique little details of her face that haunt my fantasies. Like the stormy gray flecks swimming among the sky-blue. The freckles peppering her cheeks and the bridge of her nose. She has freckles on her chest too, scattered across her collarbone and the swells of her breasts. I picture her perfect pink nipples, and the memory of them has me thrusting harder into my hand.

Up on the deck, Blake parts her lips, and now I'm picturing them wrapped around me. She's standing at the railing, but in my mind, she's kneeling in front of me, and instead of fucking my hand, I'm fucking her mouth. That sweet little O suctioned tight around the head of my cock.

She watches me, mesmerized. This is wrong on so many levels, but I don't care. Common sense has fled, replaced by the heat coursing through my veins as all the blood in my body sizzles down to my hard dick.

Lukewarm water from the showerhead streams over my chest and down my body. I fight the urge to speed up, because if I finish now, this moment has to end, and I want her to keep watching. This might be the hottest thing I've ever jerked off to, and she's not even naked.

I bite my lip to stifle a groan, but it slips out anyway. With Blake's eyes glued to me, I squeeze my swollen head, and precome spills out. My cock is wet and glistening as I thrust into my fist, gliding it up and down my shaft.

*Look at it, baby*, I silently plead at her. *See what you do to me.*

I feel it building. The arousal, the impending orgasm. Pulling my balls tight to my body. I'm on the verge of coming, but I'm not ready, so I slow my strokes, careful not to push myself over the edge.

My breathing escapes in shorter gasps now. Head spinning. All I can focus on is the pleasure, which is only intensified by the fact that Blake is witnessing this. My balls ache, and I lock my fist tight around me, forcing my wet cock through my fingers, pretending I'm fucking her mouth, her pussy, anything she lets me.

Screw it.

I need to come.

I want her to see.

I quicken my strokes, and within seconds, I'm shuddering with release, waves of pleasure pulsing through my body until I'm heaving for breath. I shoot everywhere. All over my hand, my abs. Ropes of come spill out of my fist onto the ground. I keep stroking through the mind-blowing climax, squeezing every last drop out, while Blake watches with big eyes.

I'm spent by the time the orgasm ebbs. My dick stays hard, though.

He wants to go again. I don't blame him. That was just a tease.

I suck in a ragged breath and push my hair out of my face before turning to shut off the water. When I turn back, the deck is empty. Blake is gone.

We act like nothing happened.

Maybe not the most mature approach, but it seems to suit both of us. I grill burgers and Blake makes potato salad, and we eat on the deck. And while I clear the table and do the dishes, she stays at the table, reading a book she checked out from the library.

"Any Darlie developments?" I ask after I'm done cleaning up.

She looks up, causing her high ponytail to swing over her shoulder. As usual, I'm dying to take her hair down. Even more so now that I've actually touched it. Now that I know how silky it feels between my fingers.

I lied to her this morning. I *was* going to kiss her. I was seconds away from kissing her senseless in fact. It was a miracle that I managed to resist the lure, but I'm glad I did. I stayed up all night writing because of that. There's something to be said for blue balls and bone-deep longing.

Still, I need to stop placing myself in the path of temptation like that. I can't afford any distractions right now, not when Tobey Dodson is going to be calling me any day to discuss my "new stuff." So… I need new stuff. I need to write. To concentrate on the music and not the freckle-faced temptress who decided to crash my summer.

Blake and I can be friends. Friendship is safe. No pressure, no expectations, just sharing the occasional meal together, playing badminton—

*Jerking off in front of her*, mocks an inner voice.

All right. In hindsight, that wasn't the smartest move of mine. But it was just a little slip. Sometimes friends pull their dicks out and come all over themselves while another friend watches.

*Your coping skills are unreal*, that voice informs me.

Fucking fine. I crossed a line, just like on Christmas Eve two years ago. But that ends right now. Friendship commenced.

"This isn't a Darlie book," Blake says absently, flipping to the next page. "I'm reading about the history of jigsaw puzzles."

Of course she is.

"Explain?" Grinning, I flop into the chair across from hers and light a cigarette.

Blake shrugs. "I was curious about how puzzles got popular, so I found a book about it. It's actually supercool."

"Cool and puzzles aren't two words that really go together."

"Says the guy who was doing the puzzle *before* I showed up." She puts the book down. "I just learned that the first puzzles weren't even called puzzles. They were called 'dissected maps' because this cartographer in the 1700s used to mount maps on a wooden board and then cut along the national boundary lines to create geography puzzles. They used them in schools. How cool is that?"

"Again, not using the word cool correctly," I inform her, but I sort of love how excited she gets about these random topics. And truth be told, she does make them sound cooler when she explains them.

Her phone vibrates, and she leans forward to check it. Her face brightens. "Oh, nice. Little Spencer sent me a link to the latest episode of their podcast. I'm getting a sneak peek."

"Is this podcast just the two of them sitting around talking about ghosts?" I pause for a moment. "Honest question—are we sure these dudes won't break into our house in the middle of the night and try to kill us in order to create ghosts?"

"Pretty sure. But if they do, I'll make sure they kill me first to buy you some time," she says graciously.

I snicker. "Thank you. I appreciate that, freckles."

"And the podcast isn't exclusive to ghosts. It's about anything supernatural, really. And it's just Little Spencer talking."

"He talks to himself?"

Blake grins. "Well, he talks to the audience. But yes. Big Spencer doesn't like how his voice sounds on tape." She picks up her book. "Anyway, I want to keep reading. What are your plans for the rest of the day?"

"Writing. I'm gonna hole up in the sunroom. Probably skip dinner."

She raises a brow at me. "Is it finally coming to you? *The song*?"

"Starting to," I admit. "But don't get your hopes up."

"Nah, I'll get my hopes up for the both of us. Go get that song, Graham."

She flashes me one of those unbridled smiles, and I force myself to look away because I have no willpower when she smiles at me like that.

We go our separate ways for the rest of the afternoon. I grab my guitar and escape to the sunroom at the side of the house. Fueled by a smile, I scribble lyrics and strum the melody I've been hearing in my head since we hiked to the sex tree. It's got so much potential that I do something I rarely do. I pull out my phone and record myself singing it, then send the raw file to Cole for an opinion.

Because holy shit.

This song...might be good.

Later that night, I reward myself for a solid day's work by swiping a bottle of whiskey from the liquor cabinet. It's my mom's favorite and stupidly expensive, but I don't think she'll mind if I indulge.

Balancing a tumbler on my knee, I settle into a chair on the deck and gaze out at the quiet lake. A faint breeze carries the scent of pine and campfire smoke. Someone is having a fire nearby. But all I can smell is the sharp, warm burn of whiskey.

"Can I have some of that?"

Blake curls up in the chair beside me, holding out an empty glass. I eye it for a second before shrugging. Whatever. I can't keep policing her. Besides, from what I've seen so far, she barely drinks, and when she does, she knows her limits. I slosh some amber liquid into her glass, then sip mine.

A comfortable silence settles between us. We drink our whiskey, staring at the water. Our floating swim dock is barely moving, that's how still the lake is tonight.

"What were you thinking about when you were jerking off?"

I almost choke on my drink.

Shit. Here I was, mentally patting her on the back for handling her alcohol so well. Turns out you give Blake Logan one whiskey and she's asking about my jerk-off fantasies.

"Yeah..." I keep my gaze straight ahead. "Not telling you that."

"Come on, tell me. What were you thinking about?"

*You. On your knees. Sucking me dry.*

I take another gulp of whiskey. "Nope," I say firmly.

"Do you remember when you were annoying me in the kitchen?"

"Which time?"

"Any time I'm cooking. But I'm talking about the night you called me bossy."

I don't remember at all, but clearly it was memorable enough for her to bring it up again. When she continues, I realize why it flagged in her memory.

"You said you liked bossy girls as long as it was out of bed." Blake polishes off her drink and reaches for the bottle, but I lean in and grab it before she can.

"No. You're cut off."

"One more," she protests.

"Half a shot."

I pour a scant amount of whiskey into her glass. She glares at me but accepts the compromise. As she sips, I feel her gaze boring into the side of my face.

"So you're the bossy one in bed?" she prompts. "You like taking charge?"

I groan, rubbing a hand over my jaw. "I am not having this conversation with you."

"Why not?"

"Blake..." Her name leaves my mouth, but I don't know if it's a warning or a plea.

"What? It's not like I'm asking for a demonstration. Why can't we talk about this?"

"Because you and I..." I gesture between us. "We're friends. I'm not about to ruin that by telling you things I shouldn't."

"Friends talk about sex. Come on. Bossy how? Bossy like handcuffs and safe words?"

My groin throbs at the images her words just conjured.

*Blake handcuffed to my bed. Begging for my dick.*

I exhale slowly, already regretting what I'm about to say next. "I don't know. Bossy like intense. I'm not laid-back, not when it comes to sex. I like it when the woman I'm with gives me everything."

"What do you mean everything? Like anal?"

I burst out laughing. Jesus Christ.

"No," I say between chuckles. "I mean, sure, if she wants it, I'm happy to accommodate. But I mean everything as in not just physically." My voice becomes gruff as a strange sensation moves through my chest. "I want...trust. Vulnerability. I want her to look me in the eye, to be right there with me. No walls. I want every thought, every look, every breath focused on me and what I'm making her feel."

I notice Blake's hand trembling as she picks up her glass and gulps down some whiskey. "Oh. That does sound intense."

"Yeah." I lick my lips. Her eyes stay on me, pinning me in place. "I don't want half of someone. I want all of them. Mind, body, all of it. That's what gets me hard."

Jesus, I sound like a dick. I've never articulated any of this before, but now that I hear it, it triggers a pang of shame, this notion of asking someone to give me everything and then bailing afterward. I reciprocate in the moment, though. I do. I never ask for anything I'm not willing to give in return.

I just...don't stay.

I notice that Blake's cheeks are flushed, either from the whiskey or my words. Hopefully the former. I don't want to turn her on. Well, I do, but I also don't. God. This girl does my fucking head in.

"That's not bossy," she says, and her voice isn't too steady. "That's just honest."

My fingers tighten around my glass. "Yeah. I guess that's what I want. Honesty. I want someone who will let me see all of them."

"That's...not a bad thing."

I don't miss the way her tits rise as she sucks in a breath. The whiskey has loosened my tongue, and I can't stop the next words from tumbling out.

"You'd hate it," I say roughly. "You'd hate me like that. It's too much."

I can't look away from her, not when she's watching me with those big blue eyes. Even when I know I'm showing more of myself than I want.

"You'd hate how much I'd want from you. How much I'd take."

Her gaze doesn't leave mine. "What makes you think I'd hate that?"

I hear my pulse thundering in my ears. I need to pull out of this tailspin. Now. This is not friendship etiquette.

"It's getting late," I say, scraping back my chair. "I wanted to turn in early tonight, try to get some real sleep. Night, freckles."

You Know

I'm not good enough for you
~~You're too good for me~~
You know that, baby
You know
I drink too ~~much~~ slow
and talk too ~~little~~ fast
I was somebody once,
but I think I forgot

You look at me like maybe
you see something
Maybe you know something
Maybe you need something
And maybe that something is me

# Chapter 16

## WYATT

*Anyone but the muse*

"THIS IS GOOD," COLE SAYS.

"Yeah?" I bite back a smile, forcing myself to temper my excitement. But Cole usually takes a lot longer to get back to me about shit, so the fact that he called in less than twenty-four hours is promising.

"It's really fucking good, bro. Come back to Nashville. We need to get you in the studio."

"No, I'm not ready for that. I don't want to come back with only one track on deck. I want to be able to send Dodson a few song options. I'm working on another one now."

"Fair enough." There's a long pause, and then Cole chuckles. "So who is she?"

I play dumb. "What do you mean?"

"Who's the song about?"

"Nobody."

He laughs even louder now, a deep bellow in my ear. "Bull-fucking-shit, G. That song is about a living, breathing woman. And she, my friend, is your muse."

Shit. That's what I was scared of.

But deep down, I knew it was true. She's under my skin. Burrowed deep. This morning, I lay in bed like a lovesick fool remembering all the sarcastic remarks and dumb jokes she made yesterday. Then I jerked off to the memory of her big eyes watching me in the shower. Yet somehow, the obsessive replaying of every word she says is the more embarrassing act.

"It's the one you're spending the summer with, isn't it?" Cole guesses. "The forbidden fruit."

"Yes," I admit. "And it's bad."

"What are you talking about? It's phenomenal. You found a muse."

I don't *want* Blake to be my muse. That means spending more time with her. Immersing myself in her. What I need to do is see *less* of her.

But she's everywhere. In the house. On the dock. In my fucking dreams. And she's not even doing it on purpose. She just exists, and I'm a goner.

"Dude, it's a problem," I grit out. The confession eats at me. I hate voicing it. "The lyrics come when I'm with her. They just pour out."

"Again, how is this a bad thing?"

"Because I want to fuck her." A groan slips out. "And if my behavior of the last twenty-four hours is any indication, I'm probably gonna do that soon."

"Shit." Cole goes quiet for a moment. "Well. You obviously can't do that."

"I can't? I mean, right, I can't." I hesitate. "Remind me why?"

He snorts. "Because you can't sleep with your muse. Too big of a risk."

I rise from the deck chair and approach the railing, gazing out at the lake. The sun is dropping low in the trees, casting orange streaks across the water.

"It could go either way when you fuck a muse," Cole continues. "Best case—it releases a creative wave that makes you even more productive. Remember my weekend in Munich with Anastasia? Jeezus. I wrote 'Pretty Girl' that weekend. Album went platinum last month, by the way."

"Nice."

"Yeah. But then there's worst case. Remember that December I spent with Tansy? The Vegas blackjack dealer? She inspired the hell outta me for weeks, and then the moment I slept with her, the music died. I couldn't write again for months." His tone becomes stern. "You can't screw the muse, no matter how tempting it is."

"Might be less tempting if I wasn't goddamn celibate," I mutter, unable to keep the accusation from my voice. This is his fault after all. *Just try celibacy, bro. Trust me, it'll help.*

There's another long pause.

"All right," Cole says. "I give you permission."

"For what?"

"To go get laid. Pick anyone but the muse."

"Really," I say dubiously.

"Look, you tried. You gave the whole celibacy thing a shot. But it's obviously not working for you, and if you're in danger of compromising the only source of creative output you've had in a year, then we need to get ahead of this. Find a beautiful woman, get your rocks off, and preserve the muse." He curses suddenly. "Shit, I gotta go, G. Aimee and I are about to lay down the track. Send me the rest of the song when it's ready."

He disconnects, leaving me trapped in my own thoughts.

Maybe he's right. Clearly, the celibacy didn't work. I wrote nothing but shit when my dick was dormant. So maybe it's time to let him loose.

But not with Blake.

And *not* because she might be my muse. Because all the reasons why I shouldn't get involved with her haven't changed. She deserves more than a one-night stand, and our families will literally murder me if I use her for sex and break her heart.

I stare at my phone, my thumb hovering over my chat thread and Mira's last message. The nude might be gone, but the invitation remains.

*Hit me up if you feel like it.*

After several seconds of indecision, I type.

You around tonight? Want to grab a drink?

Then I tap Send before I can overthink it.

"You going out?"

Blake appears on the stairs as I'm rummaging on the hall credenza for the Jeep keys. I was the last one to drive it, and I swear I dropped them in this glass bowl. But all I see are decorative acorns.

I keep my head down. "Yeah."

"Where you off to?" she asks curiously, bounding down the steps.

"Nowhere really."

"Right, because that's not suspicious." Her laughter tickles my back. "Let me guess—you're going to a secret underground poker ring? Moonlighting as a stripper?

I move my key search to the credenza drawer. "Nah, just meeting someone in town."

"Who?"

My fingers collide with the key fob. Thank God.

"Who?" Blake pushes when I don't respond.

"Just a girl," I say vaguely.

Silence.

I don't want to see the look on her face, but I'm a masochist so I turn around. Her expression is too bright, her smile forced.

"Anybody I know?" she chirps.

"Doubt it."

"Is it the girl who sent you the nudes on the boat?"

Her hurt tone triggers a prick of guilt. Which only makes me want to distance from it.

"Yes. Her."

I could've stopped there. Could've walked out without another word. Instead, I force myself to twist the knife.

"She's a fun time," I add. "We hooked up last summer."

I watch it land. The wounded flicker in Blake's eyes. The way her shoulders pull back like she's been slapped but doesn't want to show it.

Good. Let her hate me. It's better than the alternative. If this friendship between us is going to stick, then I need to quash the attraction. On both sides.

"Uh-huh. Cool." Blake pauses. "Your vow of celibacy is null and void then?"

I exhale through my nose but say nothing. I'm a dick.

"If the sex is good, are you going to write a song about it?"

I stifle a sigh. "Blake—"

"Whatever, it's fine. Have fun tonight."

Her cavalier shrug is betrayed by the stiffness in her shoulders. She strides into the kitchen. I don't follow her.

Instead, I slide out the front door to go pick up Mira.

# Chapter 17

## BLAKE

*We've got absinthe*

WYATT'S ON A DATE TONIGHT. That's fun. I hope he has the best time.

Like the best time.

I don't care that he's on a date. Why would I? It's not like I wanted to hang out with him or anything. I'm perfectly content to stay in and work on the puzzle. I love this puzzle. I'm not purposely jamming this piece into a spot I know is wrong, just to feel the resistance and bask in the power trip of doing something I know will make Wyatt angry.

Of course not.

JULIETTE

You should key his car.

I peek at the message that popped up, grinning.

Can't. He took it on his date.

I try to focus on the puzzle, but the ticking clock above the kitchen doorway is too distracting. Has it always been this loud? It's making me hyperfocused on the time. 8:38. He left less than an hour ago, but it feels like it's been two days. And who is this girl he's out with? He said they hooked up last summer, and my nosy brain is now cycling through every female I remember seeing here last year.

Was it that blond from the mini golf place? I think her name was Cassandra?

No. She hooked up with Gray, I recall.

Maybe those two punk-rock chicks from the music festival at Commons Beach?

Wait. That was also Gray. His dad found them on the boathouse roof after the concert, and we all had to listen to Uncle Hunter's lecture the next morning about how threesomes—"however awesome," Uncle Dean had interjected—are not appropriate during our Tahoe family summer.

Wyatt better not be having a threesome tonight.

My phone lights up again. I expect to see Juliette's name, but it's Isaac. It's taken him three days to respond to my last message.

THE CHEATER

Be honest, Blake. Is this even about a toaster? Because I'm starting to think you want me back.

I gape at the screen. Wow.

I don't want you back.

THE CHEATER

It's okay to admit it.

You cheated on me. For a whole year.

THE CHEATER

And I'm willing to work things out if that's where your head is at.

He's willing to work things out? What in the actual fuck. Fuming, I type back one word at a time.

You

Cheated

On

Me

THE CHEATER

I made a mistake.

Really? Was it a one-night stand? Because a repeated mistake is a choice, Isaac.

I don't want you back.

I just want my fucking toaster.

THE CHEATER

Well, you ain't getting him.

I'm debating whether to do the unthinkable—dispatch my father to my old building to beat that toaster out of Isaac Grant—when I'm distracted by an Instagram alert. It's a DM from someone named Landon Kerns. The name sounds familiar, but it isn't until I open the notification that I make the connection. The bartender with the mullet. The one I was chatting with before Wyatt went all caveman on me and made me leave the bar.

LANDON

Hey, girl. I hope you don't mind me sliding into your DMs, but I didn't grab your number before you took off the other night.

He's still typing, so I wait for his next message before responding.

LANDON

It's sort of last minute, but I'm having some people over tonight. Not a huge blowout or anything, just a small gathering at my place. Come by if you feel like it. Would love to see you.

I don't even hesitate, because...gee, what a conundrum! I can stay in and sulk about Wyatt being on a date, or I can go to a party.

Why should Mr. Good-Time Fuckman be the only one who gets to have fun tonight?

Any chance you can pick me up?

Landon shows up twenty minutes later in a shiny black sports car, and we make the twenty-minute drive to the north shore. Despite his expensive car, he lives in a more affordable area on a quiet street lined with older cabins and single-family homes. Since I'm a responsible person, I let Wyatt know I'm meeting up with friends and text him the address, but it's radio silence in response. Guess he's too...occupied to be overprotective about me tonight.

I'm not sure why, but that stings. A lot.

I expect a bigger crowd inside, but I guess Landon wasn't kidding when he said it was a small gathering. On the well-worn leather couch, three guys are playing a racing video game, trash-talking loudly as their little cars hurtle across the screen. A young woman with a dyed-red bob and tattoos on every visible inch of skin is curled up in the armchair, while a pretty blond in gray sweats and a crop top sits near the redhead's feet, scrolling on her phone. There's music playing from a nearby speaker, but the volume is low, and the vibe in the house is chill.

"This is Blake," Landon tells his friends before introducing the guys to me. "Sammy, Zan, Gio." He nods toward the girls. "Kelly and Christina."

"Nice to meet you guys." I awkwardly sit on the other couch, an upholstered love seat, while Landon ducks into the kitchen to get me a drink.

He's gone a while, and I hear the sound of cupboards opening and rattling closed. His friends seem cool, though. Kelly tells me she hosts paint nights in Tahoe City every Thursday and Saturday, which sort of sounds like a blast. Christina works at the boat rental place at the marina in Zephyr Cove. The three boys ignore me completely, too caught up in their game.

"Okay, I have good news and I have bad news," Landon announces, reappearing several minutes later. He's holding something behind his back.

"Bad news first, always," Christina says.

"We're out of beer."

That finally gets the boys' attention. Sammy pauses the game in sheer outrage. "Dude! But we need beer!"

Landon's mouth stretches in a shit-eating grin. "Ask me what the good news is."

"What's the good news?" Zan says suspiciously.

With a grand flourish, Landon whips his hand out to reveal an ominous-looking black bottle.

"We've got absinthe."

# Chapter 18

## WYATT

*Who the fuck is Landon?*

MIRA'S TONGUE IS DOWN MY throat. We're in the front seat of the Jeep, her hair tickling my jaw as she kisses the ever-loving fuck out of me. It's the kind of kiss that would normally get me rock-hard. Passionate. Hungry. But as she devours my mouth and grinds her ass against my fly, I can't convince my dick to cooperate.

"Missed this," she murmurs between kisses.

Her hand is already working its way south. She cups me over my jeans, trying to coax a response I can't seem to give her.

I want this.

I do.

I mean…

I *want* to want this.

"I need your dick so bad." She squeezes, and finally my body starts to react.

I let my head fall back against the seat as she undoes my jeans, sliding her hand inside my boxers. I'm semihard by the time she pulls my cock out.

Kissing me again, she wraps her fingers around me and gives a teasing stroke.

"Yeah, that's it," I mutter. "Jerk me off."

Her hand moves more deliberately now. But I'm not getting any harder.

"Wyatt," she whispers, her lips trailing along the side of my neck. "Relax."

I'm trying.

I close my eyes and try to focus on the sensation of Mira's hand on my dick. Instead, my mind flashes to Blake, and now all I can picture is her sarcastic smirk. Her hair.

"Use your mouth," I grind out.

She kisses her way down and circles my cockhead with her tongue. A jolt of heat travels through me.

My head lolls back.

Okay. We're getting somewhere.

I thread my fingers through her hair. It's too…straight. For some reason I expected it to be thicker, wavier—

Fuck!

I still her with my hand. I've never stopped a woman mid blowjob, but this is wrong. I'm trying to pretend she's Blake, and Mira doesn't deserve that.

"Just relax," she urges again as my phone suddenly buzzes on the dash.

I ignore the incoming text, touching Mira's cheek to lift her off my rapidly deflating cock. Not that it was overly inflated in the first place.

"Mira," I start. "I'm not—"

My phone buzzes again. And then again and again. I realize it's not a text. It's a call.

Annoyance flashes in her eyes as I reach for it. "Seriously? I'm sucking your dick, Wyatt."

"I'm sorry. It might be important." When I check the screen, my stomach drops, and all traces of arousal leave my body. I already wasn't feeling this hookup, but seeing Blake's name on my phone has cemented that.

I answer without delay. "Hey. You okay?"

Her urgent voice fills my ear. "Wyatt. Oh thank God. Can you come get me?"

Is she slurring?

"Get you from where?"

"North shore. Like, a house. I want to leave but there's no drivers and Landon won't drive. I mean, he would if he could, but he can't drive because we're really, really, really drunk."

Who the fuck is Landon?

Mira touches my arm and tries to ask a question, but I shrug her off and silence her with a look.

"Where on the north shore?" I'm already starting the engine. "Where did you go?"

"A party. I texted you the address earlier." Her voice slurs again. "Can't be here anymore. I don't feel good. Dizzy and..." She trails off.

Fear fills my throat. "Are you hurt?"

"No, I'm—" She hiccups. "I'm too drunk. I don't want to be here anymore. Can you come get me? Please? I didn't know who else to call."

"I'm on my way."

I throw the Jeep in reverse and pull out of our parking space behind the bar. Because yes, I was hooking up in a parking lot behind the bar.

After Blake disconnects, I click on our chat thread. I hadn't checked my phone when Mira and I were inside, and now I wish I had, because if I'd seen these messages from Blake? She sure as hell wouldn't have gone to some party at *Landon's* house.

Who the fuck is Landon?

"What's going on? Who was that?" Mira asks suspiciously.

"Blake. Family friend."

"You mean Blake Logan? I didn't realize she was in town too."

"Yeah. She's drunk at some party, and I need to go get her." I turn onto the main road, glancing over. "I'm sorry. I'll drop you off at home first."

"I can go with you," Mira offers.

"It's fine. I can handle it."

That isn't the answer she wants to hear, but I don't care. I ignore her stony expression and drop her off with a muttered "Sorry about tonight," and she gives a dramatic flip of her hair and slams the door with more force than necessary.

I barely notice.

Anxiety twists in my stomach. What the hell is Blake doing at some random party? And how did she get so wasted she can't even find her own way home?

And. Who. The. Fuck. Is. Landon.

The drive is a blur, GPS bringing me to a small cabin near Kings Beach. It's not a bad area by any means, but considering she mentioned a party, I'm expecting thumping music and a lawn overrun with drunk people. But it's eerily quiet, and the only person I see is the slumped-over figure on the front porch.

My heart jumps into my throat when I realize it's Blake.

I throw open the door and race toward her. "Blake!" I shout, fear racing up my spine.

She's half sitting, half lying on her side, her cheek pressed against her bent arm. One strap of her floral sundress hangs off her shoulder, and her feet are bare. Where the hell are her shoes?

"Blake," I say urgently.

She lifts her head, and relief floods my gut to find she isn't passed out. While her blue eyes are hazy, she doesn't look completely out of it. Mascara isn't even smudged.

"Are you okay?" I kneel in front of her and cup her cheeks. "Are you hurt?"

"No. Fine. I'm fine. Just a bit dizzy. Was lying down."

"Why are you lying down on this asshole's porch? Where is he?"

"Oh." She glances around as if realizing she's alone. "He went inside to use the bathroom. Thought he was coming back out..." She blinks a few times. "Guess he forgot to come back..." She trails off.

I am going to strangle this motherfucker's throat until his eyes pop out of the sockets.

"How much did you guys drink?"

"Not how much. What."

"Huh?"

"I only had a few shots. But it was absinthe."

"Goddamn it, Logan."

"It was good." To my utter chagrin, she's grinning. Pleased with herself. "Maybe not the taste. It's like...a bag of black licorice exploding in your throat. But then...it's good!"

I swallow a sigh. "Come on, let's get you up." I help her to her feet, but she's wobbling hard. "Where are your shoes?"

She stares at her feet, but it takes several seconds for it to register there's nothing on them. "Oh. I...don't know."

I nudge her toward the short railing so she's leaning on something. "Don't move a muscle. I'm going in there to find your shoes and have a talk with this asshole."

"Who? Landon?" She gasps. "Oh no, he's great. Don't be mad

at Landon. He's not a car. I mean, he can't drive a car. He's wasted."

My anger doesn't ebb. "He left you out on the porch like a piece of trash, Blake. Wait here."

I reach the front door just as it swings open and I encounter a familiar mullet.

The bartender from town staggers out, looking worse for wear. Mullet sticking out in all directions. Eyes bloodshot. But his expression brightens when he spots me.

"Yeah! We got a driver!" He peers past my shoulder to grin at Blake. "See! Told ya someone would come."

"Someone came!" Blake confirms, and they beam at each other like a pair of drunken idiots.

I'm spitting mad. This jackass is just standing there grinning while Blake was alone on the porch steps for God knows how long, her feet dirty and bare, her dress riding up her thighs for the whole goddamn neighborhood to see.

Clenching my jaw, I advance on the mullet. "What the hell is wrong with you?"

He startles. Blinking rapidly. "Wha..."

"I showed up here to find her half-asleep on the porch. You left her out here? At midnight?"

"I was pissing," he protests. "She was fine."

"Anybody could've walked by and found her like that."

"What are you, her dad—"

I cut him off by grabbing a fistful of his collar and slamming him against the side of the house, hard enough to rattle his teeth.

"She could've been hurt, you piece of shit," I growl. "You left her outside, drunk out of her mind, for who knows how long."

Landon raises his hands in surrender, gulping visibly. "She's fine, man. Jesus."

"She couldn't even sit up because she was dizzy." I push him again. "You think abandoning a woman after pouring absinthe down her throat is something men do? Real men? You fucking loser."

"Wyatt," Blake protests from the bottom of the steps. Her voice sounds weak.

I draw a calming breath. Force myself to release his collar.

"Good," he mutters. "Glad you've come to your senses—"

"Shut the fuck up," I interrupt, pinning him with a deadly look. "Don't ever come near her again, you hear me? Don't text her. Don't call her. Don't even *think* about her. You're done."

I give him a final shove and then twist on my heel.

"Let's go," I tell Blake, but she can barely take two steps before stumbling.

When I try to steady her, she bats my hand away.

"I can walk," she objects.

The last semblance of patience abandons me. "Nope. We're not doing this."

Before she can argue, I scoop her up into my arms.

"Wyatt!"

"Shut up," I grind out. "We're done talking right now."

I stalk forward, and her hands instinctively clamp around my neck, holding on tight. She doesn't fight me, though. She tucks her face against my shoulder and lets me carry her to the Jeep.

# Chapter 19

## BLAKE

*Sunrise*

IT'S NOT EVEN MIDNIGHT WHEN I emerge from the shower after letting the icy-cold spray beat down on my head for more than twenty minutes. I don't know if this is common to all absinthe partakers, but that green shit turned my body into a furnace. I've never gotten so overheated drinking alcohol before. Or that wasted. Even now, hours later, I still feel a lingering buzz in my veins. Still a bit unsteady on my feet as I wrap myself in a short white bathrobe.

I'm startled to find Wyatt in the hall, leaning against his closed bedroom room.

"Have you been waiting out here the whole time?"

"Yeah," he says gruffly. "Wanted to make sure you didn't slip in there and crack your head open."

"That's…very sweet. Thank you."

He gives me a thorough once-over. "You seem more alert. You feeling better?"

"Oh my God, yes. My head is so much clearer. The cold shower helped." Along with the bottle of water he made me chug and the two ibuprofen he made me swallow before we barely even walked through the front door.

"Good." He pushes away from the wall. "I'm going out for a smoke. G'night."

"Night," I murmur to his retreating back.

I go to my room and put on my pj's, but that shower was too successful at waking me up. Rather than climbing into bed, I roll on a pair of warm socks and head outside. It's cooler out than I expect, so I grab the throw blanket off the deck chair and wrap it around myself on my way to the stairs.

When I step onto the dock, Wyatt smiles at the sight of me all bundled up. Then he takes a quick drag of his cigarette before exhaling a puff of smoke into the night.

I wrap the blanket tighter around my shoulders and stretch out on the lounge chair next to his. "How was your date?" I ask reluctantly.

"Short."

I bite my lip. "I'm sorry. I didn't mean to ruin it."

"You didn't." He blows out another smoke cloud. "I mean, okay, yeah, you did. But I was about to cut it short anyway."

I ignore the traitorous flipping of my heart. "How come?"

"Wasn't into it." He glances over at me. "How was your night? Before the absinthe?"

"Shitty. Isaac accused me of wanting to get back together and using Hot Boi as my excuse."

"Any truth to that?"

"Not in the slightest. I have no desire to get back with him. Once a cheater, always a cheater, right?"

Wyatt shrugs. "Life isn't that black and white."

"Cheating is," I say simply. "For me at least. It's not about whether he cheats on me again. Even if he didn't stray again for the rest of our lives, I'd never forget that he cheated before. I'd never trust him."

"Fair enough."

"Also, I sort of had an epiphany earlier at the party," I confess. "An absinthe-induced breakthrough."

"Yeah?"

"Uh-huh."

I go quiet for a moment, and Wyatt patiently waits for me to continue. I appreciate that about him. He never rushes me through my own thoughts.

"I was thinking about Isaac and our relationship and why I was even with him. He came on so strong at first, and..." I sigh. "And yeah, fine, it was love bombing. It was all a big show. I see that now. But I didn't at the time. I thought it not only meant he was madly in love with me but that he had depth. He seemed so in touch with his emotions. A lot of men can't access those intense feelings, you know?"

Wyatt nods.

"I was wrong, though. The thing about Isaac is that he likes everything big and shiny and perfect. He's all about the surface, the aesthetics. His whole identity is wrapped around grand gestures and flashy things. I mistook it for passion maybe. But it was distraction, a way for him to avoid growth. He wants the sparkly, shallow version of life, not the messy parts."

"You could never be shallow, Blake. *You're* depth. And that terrifies people like him."

His conviction leaves me a little breathless. I swallow, letting Wyatt's words sink in.

"It's frustrating," I admit, "because for the first time in my life, I really did want something deeper. I was ready for someone to actually *see* me, when before I used to go out of my way to avoid that."

"Why's that?" Wyatt asks roughly. He reaches toward the table and puts out his cigarette, but his focus remains on me.

"Because..." I exhale, trying to vocalize my thoughts. "You know what it was like to grow up with our dads. You had a famous mom too, so you probably know even better than I do. All the cameras, the attention. Especially in a hockey town like Boston. Everyone recognized my dad everywhere we went."

"Yeah, I get that."

"I hated it. Not because I wanted to be anonymous but because I never got to be *me.*" The confession pours out before I can stop it. "I couldn't be, because if I showed any cracks, it would be photographed, or worse, turned into gossip. I know other celebrity kids—real celebrities—have it so much worse when it comes to living under a spotlight. But I didn't like even a hint of that light on me."

I tighten the blanket when a cool breeze wafts off the water.

Noticing me shivering, Wyatt says, "Come sit with me. You look cold."

I hesitate. His demeanor isn't flirty or sexual, and we're in the middle of a serious conversation, yet it feels too intimate to share a lounger with him.

But then he scoots over to make room for me and extends a hand, and I move toward him as if hypnotized. Awkwardly, I stretch out beside him, still cocooned in my blanket. He wraps one arm around me, the warmth of his body instantly surrounding me.

"I got really used to hiding," I tell him. "Putting on a blank face or making a sarcastic remark. I'm not like Alex, who craves the attention. I *liked* not being seen. But it's not because I didn't want people close. It's because I was afraid of being seen wrong. Until I started college and I started opening up more, and I realized I was craving that closeness."

I feel his chest rise on a slow, pensive inhale. "And the spotlight?"

"God, no. I still want nothing to do with that. I'm okay staying in the background, being the plus-one. But I *was* ready to find that deeper connection with someone." I give a weak laugh. "And then I went and picked the most surface-level guy on the planet. I mean, he's fighting for a toaster with more passion than he ever fought for me or our relationship. That tells me everything I need to know about how deep we got."

Wyatt's grip tightens around me. I lean against his shoulder, breathing in his spicy, smoky scent. God, I'm becoming addicted to it.

"I'm the opposite," he says. "I used to think if the connection was there, that was it. Instant click, soulmates, ride off into the sunset, cue the strings." He chuckles to himself. "But real life's not like that. The instant clicks always burned out just as fast. I got tired of confusing chemistry with something deeper."

We fall silent for a moment.

"Can I tell you something kind of vulnerable and not have you write a song about it?" I ask him.

Wyatt holds up his hand to make a fake signal with his fingers. "Songwriter's honor."

"I'm sort of scared of being known. *Really* known. Every time someone gets close, I feel this urge to run. Like I'd rather be alone than risk disappointing them when I'm not what they thought."

His fingers toy with the edge of my blanket now. "Yeah, I know all about disappointing people. Women especially. I'm probably the worst person to be in a relationship with."

I tilt my head to frown at him. "Why do you think that?"

"Just not built for it. Long-term shit. That's why I never let anyone become too attached. I get so fucking restless. My family calls it wanderlust, because I always need to be in a different place, but it's not about the travel." He inhales again, sharp and ragged. "My mind never stops. There's so much noise inside my head, like this storm that just won't settle."

I stay quiet, because I want him to keep going and I'm afraid if I speak, he'll stop.

"I daydream a lot. I live in my own world, especially when I'm making music. That's the only thing that lets me focus. Everything else feels fuzzy. Like I'm trying to catch smoke with my fingers. I..."

Wyatt pauses, and I can't stop myself from pulling my hand out of my blanket cocoon and slipping it into his. I want him to feel something solid, to know that I'm not smoke. That this conversation isn't smoke, and it's not going to blow away.

He freezes for a second before relaxing, and my pulse speeds up when he links his fingers through mine.

"I think that's why I can't sleep. My brain refuses to shut off, and I lie there in the dark while all these ideas and worries and half-written songs crowd in. Sometimes it gets so loud, fucking deafening, and I don't know how to quiet it. And when it happens..." His voice breaks. "I'm scared, I guess."

"Scared?" My heart is beating even faster. Talk about *depth*. I don't think I've ever gotten this deep with anyone. "Scared of what?"

Wyatt falls silent, but just when I think he won't answer, he speaks again. Voice low, stripped raw.

"That if I show someone all the dark parts, how messy and chaotic and fucked-up I really am, they won't want me."

I can't conceive of a world where someone doesn't want Wyatt Graham. He's everything I've always been drawn to. That rare combination of strength and vulnerability.

"I don't think you have to worry about that," I say softly.

"I'm just saying, I hear you about not wanting to be seen."

I rest my head against his shoulder, a tired smile tugging on my lips. "At least you have something to show people. I've got nothing."

Wyatt stiffens. "What do you mean?"

"I mean I'm not extraordinary." Embarrassment tickles my throat, and I have to choke it down. "I'm not an accomplished attorney like Jamie or drop-dead gorgeous like Alex, being paid millions of dollars to get my picture taken. I'm not a hockey prodigy like Gigi or a talented ballerina like Ivy. I don't have any talent or something amazing about me that makes people look at me in awe."

"You don't actually believe that, do you?" He shifts so that he's peering down at me with those deep green eyes. "That you're not extraordinary?"

"I'm not. At least not compared to everyone else."

"Never compare yourself to anyone," he says. "It's a surefire way to destroy your self-esteem. If I compared myself to other singers, I would've quit music years ago."

He's right. But it's easier said than done.

Another silence descends, accompanied by another cool gust that floats over the dock. I feel bad being so cozy in my blanket burrito, so I quickly unwrap myself and spread the throw across both of us. Wyatt protests at first, then accepts his fate, and I can't help but snuggle closer. I'm worried he'll push me away, but he doesn't.

"This is nice," he finally says, so softly I can barely hear him.

"What is?"

"Talking under the stars."

"Are you going to write a song about it?"

"Maybe." I hear the smile in his voice.

"Will you tell me more about your brain and all the chaos in it?" I'm half joking but also desperate for more.

"Might take all night," he says lightly.

And it does. We stay out on the dock, talking for hours. It doesn't feel like hours, though. It feels like I blink and suddenly the first hint of gray-blue light breaks over the horizon. Cuddled up on the lounge chair, we listen to the lapping water and the early birds singing in the trees, watching the sky slowly blush pink and orange. It's mesmerizing.

"You don't get sunrises like this in the city," I remark.

He turns his head toward me, and the light catches the planes of his face now, brushing gold over the sharp line of his jaw and the scruff that makes him look older and softer at the same time.

"You've always liked the mornings. When we were kids, you'd sneak out here to watch the sun come up."

"You remember that?"

"Yeah." His eyes shift to the sky again. "You'd sit cross-legged on the dock with your knees tucked to your chin like you were trying to hug the whole lake. And then your parents would wake up and find you gone. Your dad would start banging on doors and organizing a search party, and I'd be laughing in my bed because I always knew exactly where they would find you."

Something warm flickers through me. I didn't realize he'd paid that much attention to me, especially when I was seven and he was eleven, and I was sneaking out to watch sunrises.

Finally, the sun breaks through the trees and shimmers across the lake. I shift under the blanket. My arm brushes Wyatt's.

"You should get some sleep," he says.

"Maybe," I answer, still admiring the sunrise. "But this feels better than sleep."

When I turn my head toward him, he's looking back at me, his expression unreadable.

"Don't look at me like that." His voice is quiet, but there's some heat in it. It makes my pulse skip.

"Like what?"

He doesn't respond. His lips curve slightly, and those intense eyes suddenly focus on my mouth.

"What?" I murmur.

His hand comes out, fingers curling over my cheek. His touch unleashes a flurry of shivers. Oh my God. I think he's going to kiss me for real this time. It's the same heavy-lidded look he had in the bedroom when he asked to take my hair down.

He moistens his lips, and now I'm staring at *his* mouth. Begging him silently to press it against mine.

His thumb gently sweeps my bottom lip, but then he sucks in a breath and lets his hand fall from my face. Disappointment slams into me.

"Know what I was doing when you called?" he says without meeting my eyes.

"What?"

"Getting my dick sucked."

A hot pang of jealousy stabs me in the chest. "Oh."

"I stopped it right before you called."

"Why?"

He shrugs. "Wasn't into it."

"You weren't into a blowjob?"

"No."

"Why are you telling me this?"

"I don't know. I shouldn't."

I wait for my jealousy to transform into anger, for a sharp retort to exit my mouth. We just spent the entire night talking, and he decides to punctuate it by revealing he got a blowjob from someone else earlier? I should be livid.

And yet...I'm not.

The last time he brought up his dick and how he puts it to good use, I suspected he was trying to convince me what a big, bad fuckboy he was in order to push me away.

But I don't think that's what's happening.

He's not trying to convince *me*—he's trying to convince *himself*. But I can't for the life of me figure out why.

Wyatt eases the blanket off us, and I try to mask my frustration as he slides off the chair. "I should get some sleep," he says, and then he leaves me on the dock to watch the sunrise alone.

# Chapter 20

## WYATT

*Absolutely no more soul baring*

I'M FUCKED.

Fucked.

And ironically, I didn't even get fucked.

Blake and I stayed up all night talking like a pair of teenagers, watching the stars fade into sunrise. Not a single item of clothing came off.

I stumble into the blue room and face-plant on my bed, burying a silent scream in my pillow.

I knew it was a bad idea sometime around one in the morning, but I ignored the alarm bells in my head. By three a.m., my defenses were starting to slip, because it felt so damn nice, lying there and talking to her. Once four and then five a.m. rolled around, my brain stopped screaming for me to leave and just accepted my fate.

There's something about Blake Logan that I can't escape. Maybe it's the way she looks at me like I'm someone worth knowing. It's an addictive feeling.

But it wasn't just the talking that did me in. It was the way her head felt against my shoulder. The smell of her hair. The sound of her laughter in the dark and the way her hand slipped so easily into mine.

She bared her soul to me last night, and I bared mine right back. I don't do that. I don't just open up with anyone and let them peek inside. My sister is probably the only person who has that power, but she's my twin. It's inevitable.

Yet with Blake, opening up felt as natural as breathing.

And that scares the hell out of me.

I'm not supposed to want her this badly. But God, I do. I wanted to kiss her so badly I could taste her, and it took every ounce of my willpower not to. But it's all I think about when she's near me. Tangling my fingers in her hair and bringing her face to mine. Kissing her. Touching her. Fuck, I want to touch her. I want to slip my hands underneath her shirt and play with her tits. Slide my hand inside her panties and play with her clit, then drop to my knees and suck on it until she's moaning my name.

I roll over, trying to shake off my rising anxiety as my brain cycles through the litany of familiar warnings that crop up whenever the attraction feels too real.

She's younger.

She's the daughter of my father's best friend.

She's close with my sister.

She's my muse.

In other words, she's not someone whose heart I can break and then never see again. But both my brain and body don't seem to care about any of those things. Because she's not *just* those things.

She's so much more.

I groan into the pillow. I need to keep my distance going forward. No more staying up all night on the dock with her.

And absolutely no more soul baring.

Like a coward, I avoid her most of the day. I take the bowrider out alone. I sit with Betty and my notebook and scribble the torrent of thoughts gushing out of me. I can't remember the last time I was so inspired.

Of all the muses the universe could've sent me, why her?

Why torture me like this?

It's late afternoon by the time I'm ready to head back to the house. I'm raising the anchor when my phone rings with a call from Gigi.

"Hey," I answer as I make my way back to the pilot's seat.

"Hey, this a bad time?"

"No, I'm just out on the lake. Heading home, though."

"Where's Blake?"

"Back at the house."

"You're not still being a dick to her, are you?"

"No. Did she say I was?"

"Not at all. But I know you," my twin says. "You can't help yourself."

"I'm not being a dick, Stan. Simply minding my own business and writing music."

*Pulling an all-nighter talking to her...*

*Jerking off in front of her...*

You know, things you do when you're minding your business.

"How's the music going?" Gigi asks.

"Good," I admit. "I've been having bursts of inspiration. Wrote two songs already and working on a third."

"Want to send me something?"

"Nope, not ready. But I might record in the next few weeks."

"Shit. You *are* making progress. Have you shared anything with Mom?"

"No. You know I don't like getting her input until later."

Gigi's sigh echoes in my ear. "I don't know why you fight it so hard. I mean, just imagine a collab between you and Mom! It would be brilliant."

"I don't want to collab with her, Stan."

"Jeez. Fine. Then don't. But at least be nice to her."

A frown mars my lips. "I am nice to her."

"No, you're not," Gigi says flatly. "Any time she tries to help you, you shut her down—"

"Really, because *you* let Dad open hockey doors for you?" I interject. "Remember all the favors he tried to pull with the Olympic committee? You refused to let him help."

"Yeah, but I was nice about it. You hurt her feelings sometimes, Wyatt. She's so proud of you. She just wants to see you succeed, and you're always snapping at her like she's doing something wrong by trying to support you."

I squeeze the phone tighter, trying to ignore the shards of guilt slicing into my gut. "Oh, come on, G. Stop."

"Truth hurts, doesn't it, kiddo?"

I snort. "Don't call me kiddo."

"I'm older than you."

"By less than a minute." Guilt continues to swirl inside me, so I try to change the subject. "When are you and BIL showing up in Tahoe?"

"July, same as everybody else. We can only stay a week, though."

"Fuck that. You need to stay longer. I've barely seen you this year." I know she's busy with her agenting career, but I miss her.

"Ryder has to go back to Dallas for sure, but I'll see if I can swing a second week and work remotely. Don't worry. You'll have Mom and Dad and the Logans all up in your personal space for the full month of August. Which will give you plenty of time to apologize to

Mom," she says sweetly.

"I have nothing to apologize for. Mom knows the rules. She doesn't help unless I ask for help."

"Oh, and you can help Dad when he shows up," Gigi says. "He wants to set up a recording studio for Mom in the basement. He's planning on getting started when he's there."

"Why does she need a Tahoe studio? Do they want to move here full-time?"

"I think they plan to spend the winter. Makes it easier if Mom has a place to record."

I hurry my sister off the phone before she can start lecturing me again, then speed back to the house. When I walk into the great room, I find Blake sprawled on the couch, her laptop on her stomach.

"How's the research going?"

"Slow," she says without looking up. She taps a few keys. "I'm sending another email to the records office. They keep ignoring my information request for Darlie's death certificate. If it even exists."

"What do you want to do for dinner?"

"Nothing. I'm going out with Annaliese."

I can't stop the rush of relief. After staying up all night talking, I think we're in need of some space. So while Blake goes upstairs to get ready, I grill myself a steak and throw a baked potato on the barbecue, then eat dinner alone on the deck.

Blake pops her head out to say she won't be late because Annaliese has to work early, then leaves me to enjoy my solitude. I will say, leaving Nashville was a solid decision. The change of scenery has rejuvenated me.

*The change of scenery or the muse?* taunts the annoying voice in my head.

"Fuck off," I tell the voice. Out loud. Which is never a good sign. Usually once I start talking to myself, it means I'm nearing the delirium point of the insomnia cycle. Might be time to crack open a few beers.

I grab an IPA from the fridge and carry it outside, but the alcohol doesn't stop the thoughts of Blake from surfacing. Why is she so damn easy to talk to? I told her things last night that I've never shared with anyone else. Like how a part of me is envious of the connection my dad and Gigi have. It's a bond I know he and I can never have, and that hurts sometimes.

I love my dad, but his brain is all hockey all the time, whereas my brain, as I told Blake, is chaos. It's music. It's incoherent thoughts and snippets of inspiration. It's melodies, ones that speak through me, and others I can hear so clearly in my head only to never be able to recreate with any instrument. It's so loud inside my head, louder than someone like my dad, who has a one-track mind, can ever understand.

*Hasn't been that loud lately...* that voice points out.

No, I realize, gulping. My head's been quieter these past couple weeks with Blake here. You'd think all our bickering and arguing would create more tension and stress, more noise, but it's had the opposite effect.

Blake isn't even gone two hours, home before ten. I'm lying on the couch when she returns, but rather than go up to bed, she plants herself in the dining room to work on the puzzle. Usually we puzzle together, but I'm trying hard to maintain this space bubble right now, so I stay on the couch, scrolling on my phone. But my gaze keeps unwittingly drifting toward the dining table, where Blake is scrutinizing a puzzle piece like it offers the meaning of life.

"What are you?" she mumbles, because she always talks to herself when she puzzles. "Are you sky? Or are you water? What in tarnation *are* you?"

I choke down a laugh, then get up to grab another beer from the fridge.

"That's your third beer in an hour," she remarks, and I don't miss the disapproval in her eyes.

I suddenly remember what happened the last time I tried to conquer insomnia by getting loaded, and I find myself putting the beer back on the shelf.

"I think I'll turn in," I say without meeting her gaze.

I'm halfway to the stairs when her voice stops me.

"It was just talking."

Her blue eyes meet mine across the room.

"We stayed up all night talking. It's not a big deal, Wyatt."

She says this as if I've never encountered a straight human woman in my life.

*We stayed up all night talking.* Yeah. Exactly. And that *is* a big deal. *I* recognize how big a deal it is, and I'm a man. So I can only imagine the fantasies swirling through her mind right now. She's probably designing the wedding invitations in there.

But sure, if she wants to be dishonest, then so will I.

I shrug. "You're right. It wasn't a big deal."

"Then why were you avoiding me today?"

"I wasn't. Just thought we might need some space to do our own thing today. So neither of us would read too much into what happened."

"You mean me," she says darkly. "*I'm* the one who's going to read too much into it, right? Because I'm some naive idiot who now thinks you're in love with me because we spilled our guts to each other last night." Her lips curl in a frown. "Trust me, I am *well* aware that you don't want me, okay?"

Jesus.

My chest tightens.

*I want you.*

The confession burns my throat, but I refuse to let it escape. If I do, I'll never be able to take it back.

"I know you're not in love with me. And it's hilarious to even think it, right?" Bitterness laces her tone. "So funny, right, Wyatt? Just like when I was sixteen and stupid enough to have a crush on you. You laughed then too."

"Blake—"

"No," she interrupts. "You don't have to explain. I get it. I was a joke then, and I'm a joke now. It's fine."

Misery clamps around my throat. She thinks I see her as a joke?

At the table, Blake throws down her puzzle piece and pushes the box away. "You know what? I think I'll turn in too."

As she tries to bulldoze past me, I reach out and grab her hand, stilling her.

"You're not a joke," I say, my voice low, rougher than I mean for it to be. "You've never been a joke."

She stares at me, eyes hard, then offers a tight shrug and brushes my hand off. "Could have fooled me."

She disappears upstairs, and a moment later, I hear her bedroom door latching shut.

Fuck!

Since I got here, all I've done is piss her off and hurt her feelings. I should just go back to Nashville, let Blake enjoy Tahoe without my broody, complicated ass dragging her down.

We spend the rest of the night in our respective rooms. I shoot off some texts and watch a tutorial about classical guitar, because why not. Around midnight, when I'm about to try to force sleep, I hear stomping in Blake's bedroom, followed by stomping in the hall as she stomps past my door and stomps down the stairs. Someone's trying to annoy me, it appears.

I assume she's getting something from the kitchen, so I tense up when I hear the sharp beep of the alarm disengaging. That sounded like the back door.

Where the hell is she going?

I stay in bed for a moment, telling myself she's probably just going to sit on the dock and look at the stars again. But I hate the idea of her out there alone. Which is stupid, because she's an adult, and it's not like this lake is crawling with psycho killers, other than possibly the Spencers.

Still, I climb out of bed, because I know I'll never be able to sleep now.

I quietly go downstairs. The back doors are closed, but the alarm is off, and the doors are unlocked. I step onto the deck, but I don't see Blake down on the dock. All the loungers are empty. Worry pulls at my stomach, tugging harder when I suddenly catch a flicker of motion against the black sky.

At first, my brain can't register what I'm seeing, but as I near the railing, there's no mistaking her. She stands on the flat roof of the boathouse like a statue, arms at her sides, hair cascading down her back.

With my heart in my throat, I watch as she approaches the edge.

## THE CHEATER

You know what? I'm fucking pissed now. And I'm sick and tired of you constantly calling me a cheater like I'm the worst person on the fucking planet. I'm not going to apologize for this shit anymore, especially when YOU basically pushed me into doing what I did.

You act like you're so above everything, Blake. You're so calm and collected and sarcastic, like nothing ever fucking touches you. I never knew what you were thinking. Ever. Being with you felt like I was constantly trying to impress someone that can never be impressed.

So yeah, I messed up but don't act shocked, because YOU made it easy to look somewhere else. I'm a passionate guy. I just wanted some fucking passion. So I had to go and find that fire somewhere else.

I'm not saying it was all bad. It was really, really good at times. You felt like my safe place, like you were this steady thing in my life and I wanted that.

But I also wanted you to look at me like I was the most exciting guy in the world. I always felt like I was chasing some version of myself you might actually care about, but you never cared about making me feel wanted. You never let me in and you were never really there with me. So maybe think about that before you decide I'm the only one who ruined this.

# Chapter 21

## WYATT

### *Forgettable*

BY THE TIME I REACH the dock, I'm already half running. The boards groan under my weight. I stand at the bottom, staring up at her. The moon carves silver edges into everything. The roof, the lake, the defiant hardness of her features.

"Blake," I snap. "What the hell are you doing?"

"Facing my phobia." Her voice floats toward me from the roof.

My jaw clenches. "You've got to be kidding me. It's almost midnight. Get down. Now."

"Why?"

"Jesus Christ. This isn't a joke. It's late. Get down here."

She seeks out my eyes in the moonlight. "I chickened out that day with Annaliese and her friends. I should've jumped."

"Great. You can jump in the morning."

"What's the big deal? You and the Golden Boys jump off at night all the time."

"Yes, because we're damn idiots. *You* are not. It's pitch-black, and you can't see the bottom. This is reckless. Actually, no, it's irresponsible."

"Fine, then I'm irresponsible. And why do you care anyway? We've already established you're not my dad. You're not even my friend most days. You hover and scowl and act like I'm some dumb teenager."

"I'm just trying to keep you from doing something stupid."

"Maybe I want to do something stupid," she shoots back. "Maybe I'm tired of everyone assuming I won't. That I've got no *passion.*"

"What the hell are you talking about?"

Frustration tightens like a vise at my ribs, but something beneath it burns hotter, more dangerous.

Fear.

And not just the kind that comes with watching someone you care about do something reckless. It's the fear of losing *her*.

And that fear makes me angry, because I hate feeling it.

"What, you're up there because you have something to prove? Why? Because you wanted to kiss me last night and I wouldn't do it?"

She flinches but doesn't back down. "Screw you, Wyatt. You wanted it."

I let out of breath. "Even if I did, we're not going there, okay?"

"Yeah, sure, keep saying that. In the meantime, I'll stay up here, thank you."

My anger boils over. "Is that what it'll take to get you down? You want me to stick my tongue down your throat? You want to ride my dick? Want me to screw you till you can't see straight? Throwing a tantrum isn't going to get you what you want."

She blinks, stunned into silence for half a second. Then her incredulous laughter echoes in the night.

"Wow. You really think you're that important, huh? You're so goddamn full of yourself. I don't need to prove anything to you. If anything, I'm proving something to *him*."

I falter. "Who? Isaac?"

"Yeah." She peers over the edge again at the water, her tone thickening with bitterness. "He blames me for his cheating. He sent me this long-ass message tonight saying I'm to blame for what he did because I wasn't 'passionate' enough. I wasn't exciting. I was the boring, steady presence that he needed, but she was his fire."

"And you're listening to this dickhead? You're up on the roof at midnight to prove something to a guy who doesn't deserve it?"

I'm already climbing the rickety staircase as I talk. Because enough. I'm done arguing with her. I take the steps two at a time, emerging on the roof in seconds.

Blake turns to face me, her expression awash with resentment. "He said I was his safe place but that I never made him feel wanted."

I swallow my irritation, all of it directed at Isaac Grant. "He's an idiot, Blake."

"Maybe, or maybe he's right. Maybe that's who I am. The safe, comfortable one." She gives me a pointed look. "The one men come to for comfort or to talk to when the world is too loud. But then when they crave the heat, when they want to burn, they go somewhere else."

"That's not who you are."

She ignores my gruff statement. I don't even think she notices me anymore.

"But you know what?" she says angrily. "Fuck him and everything *he* wants. What about what I want? You know what *I* want, Wyatt?"

I step closer, careful, as if I'm approaching a wounded animal. "What do you want, Blake?"

"I want someone to *need* me. Not just love me. I want to be wanted so badly it hurts. I want to be someone's obsession. Their *undoing*." Her voice shakes, but she doesn't look away, and I suddenly can't breathe. "I want to be someone's passion. Not their safe place. Not their steady plus-one who makes them look good because I'm John Logan's daughter. I want to be the thing they lose themselves in."

I can't take my eyes off her. The fire burning bright in her eyes. The moon glinting off her skin like frost. She's incredible. But she's also a live wire right now, and I need to temper that fire before it consumes us both.

I inhale, filling my lungs with much-needed oxygen. "I get you're upset about that message. But jumping off the boathouse isn't the solution. It's just you being reckless."

"Maybe I want to be reckless for once. Maybe I'm sick of everyone thinking I'm safe and small and forgettable."

"Jesus, Logan," I say hoarsely. "No one who's ever looked at you could forget you."

"*You* did."

Her hard, emotionless eyes crack something wide open inside me. I move closer, but she shifts her gaze back to the water, banishing me from her gaze.

"I'm so forgettable that you didn't even remember mauling me on Christmas Eve," she mutters. And then she's laughing again, a high, hysterical tinge to it. "We hooked up, Wyatt, and *you didn't fucking remember*. So that's the effect I have on people, apparently. They don't want me, and they forget all about—"

"I remembered."

She spins around, her gaze flying to mine. "What?"

"The next morning. I remembered." Shame constricts my throat, and I have to clear it before continuing. "I remember exactly what happened that night in the kitchen. I just pretended not to."

"Why?" she demands, stunned by the confession.

"Because I'm an asshole, and I knew if I opened that door, we would never be able to close it."

Her breath catches.

"Of course I want you," I say quietly.

"Stop," she says, but her voice trembles. "I don't need your bullshit right now. I told you I had a crush on you, and you laughed at me."

"You told me that when you were sixteen and I was almost twenty. What was I supposed to say, Blake? You were too damn young, and you'd been part of my life since forever. But the moment you said it, it changed everything, and I've been shoving it down ever since. Because we can't go there."

"Why not?"

"Because your dad would kill me for one, and when it ends—"

"When?"

"Yes, when. I told you, I'm not good at relationships. If we hook up, I'm going to hurt you."

She stays quiet, watching me uncertainly.

"I'm a goddamn head case. And I'm selfish. Trust me, you don't want some self-absorbed, struggling musician who can barely quiet his own thoughts." I shake my head in frustration. "All I can give you is a good lay."

Her breath hitches again.

"You deserve more than that."

She still doesn't say a word. And I still can't pull my gaze away from her. From those big eyes and the perfect Cupid's bow in her lips. The freckles, visible even in the shadows.

I've never wanted to kiss anybody more than I want to kiss her right now. And I think she knows it. Her tongue darts out to moisten her lips, and I almost groan. I want to suck on that tongue. I want to suck and lick every part of her. I want to know what she sounds like when she comes.

Instead of moving away, I take a step closer.

One step, then another, until I'm right in front of her.

Now I see her breathing pick up. The sharp rise of her tits beneath her tank top. If I looked closer, I bet I would see the shadowy outlines of her nipples.

Her head tilts up to look at me because she's so much shorter. Our faces are inches apart. Gazes locked. It feels like she's peering into my soul.

When I'm only a foot away, Blake reaches up and touches my face. A hot shiver travels up my spine. Her fingers scrape the stubble along my jaw.

"Stop," I warn.

"You don't really want me to stop."

She's right. I don't.

Time stands still as I lean into her touch. The soft slosh of water against the dock fades. All I can hear is my own pulse pounding in my ears. And all I can feel is my body betraying me, inching toward her, drawn by a pull I've never been able to understand.

"I'm going to ruin you," I say roughly.

"Maybe I'll ruin you too," she whispers back.

She already fucking has.

We need to walk away. Go down those stairs, march inside, and return to our respective beds. I'm about to tell her this when her hands suddenly bunch up the collar of my T-shirt.

She rises onto her toes, her mouth finding mine before I have a chance to object. Not that I would. Common sense abandons me, all my willpower dissipating in the night air the moment she kisses me.

The first press of her lips is soft, tentative, but there's no stopping the rush of urgency that courses through me, years of restraint snapping all at once. In a heartbeat, the kiss is fierce and hungry and unforgiving. God help me, but I can't stop it. Her lips part under mine, and I fucking claim them. I chase her tongue into her mouth, then swallow the tiny moan that she lets out. It's such a sweet sound. She tastes even sweeter. Like mint toothpaste and temptation.

I shiver when her hands slide into my hair, stroking, pulling my head closer. This kiss is goddamn *everything*. It's a drug. Deep and desperate. I'm so hard it hurts, unable to stop myself from cupping her ass and tugging her against me. Letting her feel what she does to me. How bad I want her.

She thinks she's not fire.

Christ.

She's the fucking sun.

Her tongue gains confidence, stroking mine, and I make a low sound in the back of my throat. I lose myself in the wet heat of her mouth, my body reacting to every glide and flick and stolen breath. I've never been this hard from one kiss. My cock strains against my pants, eagerly pressing against her thigh, craving relief.

*Stop this.*

The warning finally penetrates, and it's almost violent how I tear my mouth from hers. Our faces drag apart. Her eyes flicker with surprise. Her lips are still parted, swollen from our kisses, and the sight makes my dick twitch.

"I'm sorry," I mutter. "We can't. This is a mistake."

"Why?"

*Because you mean too much for me to destroy you.*

"Because I've had too much to drink," I lie. "I'm not thinking clearly."

Disbelief fills her eyes. Then she starts to laugh. "Do you ever get tired of it?"

I gulp. "Of what?"

"These stories you tell yourself. That you're too drunk. That you're a fuckboy who's incapable of catching feelings. That your dick is all you can offer a woman. That you can't succeed as a musician unless you do it without a shred of help from anybody."

The accusation throws me off-kilter. I don't even know what to say to it, but she doesn't give me the chance anyway.

"You're like some old dude who's so set in his ways that he can't adapt to new experiences or change with the times. Except in your case, you've committed so fucking hard to this story of who Wyatt Graham is, it's like you can't see all the other paths you can take. And that's what keeps you stuck in your life."

"I'm not stuck," I mutter, discomfort squeezing my chest. "It's just writer's block, for fuck's sake."

"No, it's everything. But fine. Pretend I'm wrong." She brushes past me, jostling my shoulder.

"Blake, stop. Come on."

"What?" she says, keeping her back to me. She sounds cold and unimpressed. "I'm not jumping off the roof anymore, so just relax. I'm going inside, back to my room, where I don't have to listen to your goddamn bullshit anymore." She pauses at the stairs, finally sparing me a look. "Is that all right with you, Daddy?"

I clench my teeth. "Blake—"

"Fuck off."

She gives me the finger, then disappears down the stairs.

## THE CHEATER

You know what? I'm fucking pissed now. And I'm sick and tired of you constantly calling me a cheater like I'm the worst person on the fucking planet. I'm not going to apologize for this shit anymore, especially when YOU basically pushed me into doing what I did.

So I'M to blame for YOU cheating? Go fuck yourself.

You act like you're so above everything, Blake. You're so calm and collected and sarcastic, like nothing ever fucking touches you. I never knew what you were thinking. Ever. Being with you felt like I was constantly trying to impress someone that can never be impressed.

You never knew what I was thinking because you never fucking asked, Isaac. You fawned all over me in public, and then in private you were only sweet when you wanted sex or attention.

I'm not saying it was all bad. It was really, really good at times. You felt like my safe place, like you were this steady thing in my life and I wanted that.

I'm glad I was your safe place. Too bad you were never mine.

But I also wanted you to look at me like I was the most exciting guy in the world. I always felt like I was chasing some version of myself you might actually care about, but you never cared about making me feel wanted. You never let me in and you were never really there with me. So maybe think about that before you decide I'm the only one who ruined this.

You wanted me to look at you like you were the most exciting guy in the world? Well, I wanted you to look at me, period. But I was invisible until you felt like taking me off the shelf to play with me.

Now give me my fucking toaster back.

# Chapter 22

## BLAKE

### *Mind Games*

I NEVER BELIEVED ANY OF those romantic notions about one kiss having the power to knock the earth off its axis. A kiss so world-changing, so soul-fueling, that you feel a cosmic shift right down to the marrow in your bones. When in one heart-stopping moment, you just feel…complete.

If you'd asked me before last night if a kiss like that existed, I would've said, "God no." I would've laughed and told you that sounds like a silly schoolgirl fantasy.

Joke's on me.

That kiss and I are now well acquainted.

In fact, I can never go back to regular kissing now, not after Wyatt Graham shattered my entire kissing worldview.

I feel almost sick. Not emotionally but physically, like I have a fever. My breathing is shallow, and I feel flushed, even hours after the fact. A part of me feels changed, which is so ludicrous because it was *just one kiss.*

Not only that, but it was a "mistake." At least according to Wyatt.

With him, everything is a mistake.

Flirting? Mistake.

Kissing? Mistake.

Staying up all night pouring our hearts out to each other, letting our insecurities spill out? *Big* mistake.

His mixed signals make my head spin like a carousel. They're exhausting.

I sit at the kitchen counter stewing about it, wishing he would make *sense* for once in his stupid musician life. Instead, he spews things like "I'm going to ruin you" and then kisses me like the world is ending and I'm his salvation. He says "We can't go there" and then admits he's been shutting down his feelings for me for years.

He *lied* to me on Christmas morning.

He looked me in the eye, donned a blank expression, and pretended he didn't remember what happened on that counter.

Dick.

I turn toward the doorway when I hear his footsteps. He's fresh out of the shower, dark hair damp and curling behind his ears. He's wearing joggers and a white T-shirt, his feet bare.

"Morning," I say, then lower my gaze to my breakfast. "There're hard-boiled eggs and tomato slices in the fridge if you want."

He nods at that but makes no move toward the fridge. "Can we talk about last night?"

"What's there to talk about? It was a mistake, isn't that what you said?"

Tension lines his shoulders as he prepares himself a cup of coffee. He doesn't join me at the counter, leaning against the sink instead.

"I was drinking." He sounds regretful.

"Yeah. You're always drinking." I pop a tomato slice in my mouth and chew.

"I told you it helps with my insomnia."

"Is that why you get started before noon?" I can't keep the mocking note from my voice. I'm not trying to be an asshole, but I woke up this morning with zero fucks, as evidenced by my no-holds-barred responses to Isaac's bullshit messages. And I'm tired of Wyatt's excuses. "I saw you crack open a beer at eleven yesterday. In fact, since I got here, you've had a beer in one hand and a cigarette in the other."

His expression is one of wry amusement. "So the smoking is a problem for you too now?"

"No. It's your life, Wyatt. But just so you know, chicks don't love it."

"Never had any complaints before."

"Then they're lying to you." I shake my head irritably. "Either way, I don't care. If you want to give yourself lung cancer, go for it. If you want to be the living embodiment of the drunk rock star cliché, knock yourself out."

Sliding off the breakfast stool, I pick up my empty plate and march toward him.

"Move," I snap.

He stiffens for a beat before stepping out of the way to let me use the sink.

"Here's the thing," I tell him as I rinse my plate. "I've officially reached the point of not caring what you do or why you do it. So as of right now, we're going back to the ground rules we established when I first got here. You stay the hell out of my way, and I stay the hell out of yours."

"But it was a good kiss?"

I glare at Annaliese from across the booth. We're at a sports bar in Tahoe City, and I just told her everything that happened last night, including how Wyatt blamed our kiss on being drunk and insisted it was a huge mistake, and all she's taken away from this is that the kiss was good?

"It was a great kiss," I grumble. "A *magnificent* kiss. But apparently it was a mistake."

She brushes that off. "Bullshit. That's just a cope."

"My cope or his cope?"

"His cope. Listen, Logan. A man doesn't passionately kiss you on a roof at midnight because he's had a few beers. He *wanted* to kiss you. The only reason he's backpedaling now is because that's what fuckboys do. They feel something deeper than just their dick twitching, and suddenly the commitment apocalypse is looming over them, and they run."

"And, what, I'm supposed to chase him?"

"Fuck no. We don't chase. We attract." Shrugging, Annaliese grabs the last couple french fries on her plate and pops them into her mouth. "If we want them, we do things to make them chase *us*."

"I don't like playing games."

She grins. "Games are fun."

I sigh and pick up the vodka cranberry I'm still shocked the bartender served me without asking for ID. I have my fake one if needed, but it's rare I don't get carded, especially in a family town like Tahoe.

"No, they're not fun," I finally answer. "I don't want these weird mind games. I don't want to chase or be chased. All I want is someone who makes their intentions clear."

Not someone who kisses me and then cries about it afterward.

And certainly not someone who stays with me for almost *three years* while secretly thinking I'm the most boring, least passionate woman on the planet.

Isaac's words continue to prickle at me. To sting. But deep down, I know there's some truth to them. I loved him, but I didn't *crave* him. And he didn't crave me. Maybe he did at first, with all the love bombing, but once he won me over, his enthusiasm waned. When we were in bed together, Isaac never looked at me like…like he might *die* if he couldn't have me.

"Okay, then let's find that someone," Annaliese declares. She twists in the booth and surveys the bar. "Because I don't know if you've noticed, but… It's like a firefighter porn in here."

I did not notice, but now I do. I realize the counter is littered with young men and several women in navy-blue fire department shirts and sweats. I see a lot of roped forearms and defined biceps, probably honed from long days at the academy, and all the guys are loud and boisterous, shouting and laughing as they loiter at the bar and pool tables.

"Why are they all so young?" I ask Annaliese.

"Oh, it's the recruit class. My brother's there too." She nods toward the end of the bar, where a cute guy with big dimples chats with two other fire cadets.

"Eddie wants to be a firefighter?" I say in surprise.

"Yup, and don't even get me started. This fool was in *college*. Did *two* years and then boom—drops out and enrolls in the fire academy. My parents almost had simultaneous cardiac arrests when he told them." Annaliese waves at the group. "Edward!" she calls. "Come say hi to your sister!"

Breaking away from the group, Eddie strides over to our booth. Last time I saw him, he had a wild head of hair, but it's all been shaved off, giving him a clean-cut, professional air now. He greets us with a broad smile, slinging his arm around his sister in a side hug.

"Do you remember Blake?" Annaliese asks him.

His brown eyes brighten when they meet mine. "Oh, hey. Yes. Beau's cousin."

"Well, not cousin, but we're really close, yeah." I grin at his shirt. "How's the fire academy?"

He grimaces. "Ugh, we had the worst day. They made us run a hose advance, like, a million times."

"What's a hose advance?" I ask curiously.

Eddie groans and rubs the back of his neck. "Okay, so picture dragging an anaconda the size of a tree trunk and it's thrashing around, full of water, while you're crawling on your knees in fifty pounds of gear. Oh, and the anaconda hates you."

Annaliese and I burst out laughing. "That sounds awful," I inform him.

"You have no idea. By the end of the day, my arms were shaking so bad I couldn't even open a water bottle. Had to get Dave to do it for me." He glances across the bar and signals to the friends he abandoned, gesturing for them to join us. "You gotta hear about this prank Mikey pulled on our instructor today. Mikey, get over here!"

Three guys amble up to our booth, one of them instantly catching my attention. He's not super tall, but he's got a great body, a crooked smile, and flirtatious blue eyes. Eddie introduces him as Dave.

As he slides in next to me, he checks me out, but not in a creepy way.

I check him out too, also not in a creepy way.

Annaliese doesn't miss the current of awareness that travels between us. Her lips curve in a smile.

"So," she says brightly. "Shots?"

# Chapter 23

## WYATT

*Are you listening to yourself?*

I CAN'T SLEEP. AND IRONICALLY, it's not because of insomnia. After a shitty day that saw the return of my writer's block and a general sense of discontent, I was genuinely pumped to go to bed tonight.

But then Blake went out with Annaliese. To a bar.

So now I'm lying in my bed counting the minutes until she comes home, because I can't rest until I know she's all right. Don't get me wrong. I trust Blake. Annaliese too. It's everyone else that I don't trust. Especially all the drunk, horny dudes who are probably drooling over her right now.

What if she meets someone else tonight?

I choke down the groan that's lodged in my throat. The idea of her with somebody else rips at my insides. I can still taste her. I can still feel the press of her lips again mine and the heat of her tongue. That kiss wrecked me. And it only whetted my appetite, leaving me craving another taste, wanting so much more. I hate how badly I want to open that door again.

Resting my forearm over my eyes, I release the groan, the frustrated sound echoing in the bedroom. I force myself to sit up. No more wallowing. It's pathetic. Might as well put all these volatile emotions to good use.

I grab my songbook and flip it open to my latest draft of "Stop the World." I'm not sold on the song title, so it's a placeholder for now. I pull up Cole's last message on my phone, the one with his most recent list of suggestions. I wasn't able to write anything new today, but I can at least be productive and work on something I know is good.

My pencil moves quickly over the page as I try to work in Cole's notes. He's right. The second verse is better this way. Shorter, snappier.

You smile at me
and I feel like I could love you forever
just for that.
Just for the way you say
"yeah?"
when you're half listening.

When did you become what I measure time by?
Before you
After you

Yes. I like that.

I sing the lines under my breath. Fits nicely with the melody too.

See? I'm not stuck. Blake has no idea what she's talking about. Those accusations she lobbed my way have been bothering me all day, but she's wrong. Nothing is keeping me stuck in my life, and I'm not avoiding other paths. I keep my relationships casual because it's all I can offer. I'm barely capable of calling my folks once a week. How the fuck am I supposed to devote time to a girlfriend?

I'm putting the notebook away when I hear the front door alarm disengage.

She's back.

Relief washes over me, a weight lifted off my chest at knowing she's home safe. But the tension returns in full force when I hear not one set of footsteps on the stairs but two.

Every muscle in my body coils like a spring. Hushed whispering fills the hallway, the unmistakable murmur of Blake's voice.

"We have to be quiet."

Someone else speaks now. Someone male.

"Mmmm. Can't wait to get you naked."

In the blink of an eye, I go from mild discomfort to capable of committing murder.

There's a thump, as if someone bumped into the wall. Then a thud on the way past my door, followed by a quiet moan.

This asshole's making her moan?

Over my dead body.

I stalk out of my room and burst into the corridor, rage fueling my every step.

"Let's get these off." Blake. Muffled and breathy.

The hall is bathed in shadows, but there's enough light to illuminate her door, which is wide open, providing me with a perfect view of Blake.

On her knees.

She's on her goddamn knees in front of another man.

"You've got the hottest mouth," he mutters as she unzips his pants. He reaches out to nudge the door closed. "Show me how you use it."

A red mist obscures my vision as I charge toward them. I shove the door before the guy can close it, and the resulting crash when it hits the wall has both of them glancing over in surprise.

"Oh my God, Wyatt!" Blake cries in outrage. "Go away."

"Get up," I bark at her.

"Go. Away." She stays on her knees. Her features are tight with anger.

"Get. Up."

The guy's wary gaze flicks toward me. "Who's this?" he asks Blake.

"Nobody. Just a family friend who's also staying here. And now he's leaving." She glares at me. "Good night, Wyatt."

"What are you doing?" I snap at her. "You're bringing home random townie trash now?"

"Hey," the guy objects.

I ignore him. "What the hell are you trying to prove?"

"Get out of my room," Blake orders through gritted teeth. She finally stumbles to her feet, advancing on me. Trying to push me out the door.

I cross my arms and hold my ground. "No fucking way. Your dad asked me to watch out for you this summer."

"Your dad?" the townie echoes in alarm. His head swivels back to her. "I thought you said you were twenty."

"I *am* twenty," she growls. "My dad is just overprotective."

The guy is already zipping up his pants, not even trying to be discreet about it.

"No," she bursts out, looking annoyed. "Dave. Come on. We're not stopping because of this asshole."

"Yes, you *are* stopping because of this asshole," I say coldly. I gesture to his fly. "Come on now. Finish up."

Fury burns in Blake's eyes. "Get the fuck out, Wyatt."

"No. This is not happening. I get that you're drunk—"

"I'm not drunk," she interrupts in disbelief. "One shot." She holds up one finger. "We each had *one* shot."

That doesn't faze me. She can scream at me all night long, but there is no way on God's green earth that this man's pants are coming off tonight. I don't care if it makes me a possessive caveman or a psycho or whatever other accusation she wants to hurl my way.

It. Ain't. Fucking. Happening.

"You know what?" Her date edges away from her. Guy's not dumb, I'll give him that. "I think this might be too messy for me."

"It's not messy," she protests. "Wyatt's just a friend. A controlling asshole friend."

"Yeah, that's messy," Dave says dryly. He steps sideways between me and Blake as we continue to face off. "It was really nice meeting you, Blake. But, uh, yeah, I think I can let myself out."

We hear his footsteps on the stairs and then the main floor before the front door closes louder than necessary. Dude's not happy leaving here with blue balls. Too bad, so sad.

Blake and I barely notice he's gone. Our eyes never leave each other's. Her cheeks are bright red, her hostility thickening the air.

"I cannot *believe* you did that. You had *no* right."

"Trust me, you'll thank me for it in the morning."

"Oh, fuck off, you condescending prick!"

I don't even flinch. "Your parents would kill me if they knew I let that happen while I was down the hall. That I just sat by while you sucked off some stranger you've known for five minutes. Is that what you wanted? To suck his dick? To let him come in your mouth while I'm in the next goddamn room?"

She releases out a harsh laugh. "What does that have to do with my parents? Let me worry about my own parents, how about that? And you can worry about yours."

"I get that Isaac bruised your ego—"

"Oh my God!"

"But this isn't you," I finish. "You don't have random hookups with guys you barely know."

"You don't know me at all," Blake says angrily.

"Yes, I do, and this isn't who you are. It's who *I* am. *I'm* the fuckboy. I'm the one who sleeps with half the lake, remember?"

"First of all," she snaps, "I think we can be done with you telling me you're a fuckboy, considering you haven't had sex *once* since I got here despite numerous opportunities. And you *don't* know me, Wyatt. Clearly you don't. Because I'm not just a good girl with freckles. I am a whole-ass complex woman who might want to hook up with a guy I've only known for two hours. Did you ever think about that? Did you ever think maybe that makes me feel desirable?"

"Your self-worth shouldn't be determined by validation from a man—"

She cuts me off again. "Save the self-help quotes for someone who gives a shit. I have agency. I know what I want, and I know what I wanted *tonight*. I wanted *him*. And you had to storm in like some overgrown guard dog and ruin my night."

"I was doing you a favor."

"You humiliated me! You humiliated Dave. You weren't doing anyone a favor. You just wanted to play alpha male and throw a temper tantrum."

I clench my fists against my sides. "I was trying to look out for you. You would've regretted it."

Her laughter is dripping with incredulity. "You don't get to tell me what I will or won't regret. Are you listening to yourself?"

"You and I kissed last night," I say roughly while my heart beats wildly in my chest. I can't temper my emotions when I'm around this woman. "You expect me to believe that in less than twenty-four hours, you suddenly decided you want someone else?"

Her eyes narrow. "So that's what this is. This isn't about me. It's about *you. You* don't like the idea that I might be attracted to someone who isn't you."

My jaw twitches. "No, that's not what this is."

"Yes, it is. You couldn't stand the thought of me being with someone else tonight. Just admit it. That's why you burst in and broke it up. Because you were jealous. Because that kiss affected you as much as it affected me."

I grind my teeth, determined not to take the bait. That's what she wants. She wants me to give in. To throw her up against the wall and kiss her again.

And to not stop at kissing this time.

"Fine. Whatever." I let out a frustrated breath. "There's obviously nothing left to talk about tonight. And I need a fucking cigarette."

# Chapter 24

## BLAKE

*Wyatt Graham doesn't follow the rules*

IT TAKES NEARLY FIFTEEN MINUTES to calm myself down. I spend that time pacing my bedroom, reminding myself that strangling him to death wouldn't be in my best interests. I wouldn't enjoy prison at all. And although tonight's humiliation still boils in my blood, there's also a surge of satisfaction.

Because I *saw* it.

The crack in his armor.

He was jealous tonight, and men only get jealous when they genuinely feel something for you. I sensed it when he kissed me, but tonight only cemented it. He can make as many excuses as he likes, but it's clear to me now. Wyatt cares about me a lot more than he lets on.

*This isn't who you are. It's who* I *am.*

His words keep buzzing in my head. I don't get it. Why is he so devoted to this man-whore story he's written about himself? What does he think will happen if he admits he might actually care about someone?

As the last of my anger melts away, I pull a sweater over my head and leave the bedroom.

I find him on a lounge chair, fingers gripping a cigarette, eyes on the moon. It's surprisingly quiet outside. Usually, you'd hear the buzz of mosquitoes, but right now everything is still and silent other than the occasional rustling of trees.

"Is it just me, or did all the mosquitoes disappear?" I mutter.

Wyatt exhales a wisp of smoke. "Maybe Darlie sucked them all into the lake with her."

A smile tugs at my lips, which only pisses me off. He's not allowed to make me smile, not after what he pulled up there.

Rather than sit down, I loom over him, arms crossed.

"So," I say.

He takes one last drag, then leans over to extinguish the butt. When he meets my eyes, I expect to see the same anger from before. The same indignation.

But all I see is remorse.

"I fucked up," he says.

I nod tightly. "Correct."

"I turned into a possessive, crazy caveman."

"Also correct."

"I made judgments, and I infantilized you."

"Very good."

Wyatt chokes out a laugh. "Oh, fuck off with that strict schoolmarm tone."

My stern face collapses. I can't keep it up anymore. Sighing, I sit at the edge of his chair. When he moves over to make more room for me, I can't help but remember how we stayed up talking until the sun came up. I wonder if he's thinking about it too.

"We watched the sunrise together, Blake."

Guess he is.

"I know," I say.

"That's not normal."

"I mean, there's nothing more normal than the sun coming up."

He runs a hand through his hair. He's jittery. "I need another cigarette."

Before he can reach for the pack, I capture his hand and hold it in place, and I feel a rush of warmth when he stops fidgeting. He falls silent for several seconds. I see his Adam's apple dip as he swallows.

"I wasn't trying to protect you," he says. "You were right—I *was* jealous. I wanted him to stop touching you."

The warm sensation in my chest expands. "I know."

"I hate that he had his hands on you. I hate that your hands were down his pants."

"It didn't get that far. Someone interrupted," I remind him with a pointed look.

His lips curve slightly. "Yeah, and I don't regret it."

"Wait, so we're *not* apologizing?" I say in amusement.

"We're apologizing for interrupting you, acting like a jackass, and telling you that you don't know what you want." His smile becomes smug. "But we are not apologizing for being happy that his dick never made any contact with you."

A laugh pops out. "Fine. That seems fair."

He focuses on the moon again, and I follow his gaze. It's so clear and bright, you could probably guide a boat across the water without requiring a headlight. Even still, the notion is daunting.

"I'd be too scared to take a boat out right now," I confess.

He blinks at the change of subject. "What do you mean?"

"Darlie. She'd be sneaking out around this time to meet Raymond at the sex tree. But I think I'd be too scared. What if something happened? Like the boat hits a log and I fall overboard? What if I drown without anyone knowing I was ever on the lake?"

"That's grim."

"I know." I pause. "It must have been really good sex."

Wyatt snorts. "I mean, there's literally an iconic landmark in Lake Tahoe to honor their fucking."

That makes me laugh, but the sound dies in my throat when I notice his serious eyes. I suddenly feel self-conscious.

"Your ex is an idiot, Blake. And he's a manipulative bastard."

"What?" I say in surprise.

"He cheated because he wanted to cheat. Because he wanted to get laid. Because he wanted the excitement and the thrill, and now he's twisting it around to make it look like you're the reason he did it. But you're not. It's always been him. You don't need some bar hookup to feel desirable."

"Again, telling me what I need," I murmur.

"I'm not doing it in a judgmental or possessive way. I promise. I'm just saying if Isaac doesn't see it, then he's a moron."

My pulse quickens. "See what?"

"You," Wyatt says simply, and that sends my heartbeat into overdrive.

I know I should still be mad at him for the overbearing way he behaved. But something about the raw note in his voice makes it impossible to stay angry.

His eyes burn with intensity as he fastens them on me. "You want to be seen. That's what you said, isn't it?"

I nod, because I can't make my vocal cords work. There's a lump growing in my throat, pressing against them.

"I see you," he says quietly.

"You do?"

"Yeah." His teeth dig into his lower lip. "This is messy, Blake."

"Yes," I agree.

"I don't want to hurt you."

"You're not going to hurt me."

"I think you might be wrong about that." He lets out a ragged breath. "If we do this..."

That elicits a laugh, even as my pulse speeds up again. "If we do what? What exactly are we negotiating here?"

His lips twitch in a faint smile. "Us kissing again without me running off afterward."

"Bold of you to assume I want to kiss you again."

The humor fades from his eyes. "Shit. No. You're right. I'm a presumptuous prick—"

I press my lips to his before he can finish.

He's startled for a moment, freezing, and I'm worried he'll push me away. But then he makes a strangled sound and pulls me closer, his fingers in my hair, guiding my head for another kiss.

Heat rushes through me as I lose myself in him. He tastes faintly of smoke and mint and something darker, addictive. My heartbeat is out of control, thudding in my throat and pulsing in my fingers as I cup his cheek, stroking it. When his tongue slides against mine, I can't stop a soft whimper from slipping out.

Groaning, Wyatt reaches between us and cups my breast over my skimpy tank top. My bra is paper-thin, and I know he feels it when my nipple hardens and scrapes against his palm, because he makes another husky noise and squeezes harder.

With our lips still fused, I climb onto his lap and straddle him, moaning when I feel him against my ass. Hard and ready for me. One hand still caressing my breasts, he brings the other one to where my filmy skirt has ridden up to reveal my thighs. He strokes bare skin, teasing, his thumb grazing my inner thigh.

I'm breathless by the time he breaks the kiss, and then I see the arousal burning in his eyes and forget how to breathe altogether.

"You got on your knees for him," Wyatt grinds out. He doesn't sound angry, only tormented. "This goddamn asshole should've been on *his* knees worshipping you."

"I didn't want that."

His hand stills on my thigh, inches from my panties. "No?"

"You don't get it. That's not what I wanted tonight. I mean, obviously it's nice to be worshipped. But sometimes a girl doesn't want to just feel good. She wants to be desired. She wants a man to want her so bad that he's begging for her."

He swallows. "You want a man to beg for you, freckles?"

I swallow too. "Yeah."

"You want *me* to beg for you?"

Slowly, I nod.

"Then take off my pants."

I gulp harder, hesitating. Because I know if we do this, there's no going back. And if we take things further than kissing and he pushes me away again after? I don't know if I'd survive it.

But the same way he sees me, I see *him* now. I see how hard he fights himself. How badly he wants to believe this image he's projected onto himself. That he's a nomad musician who uses women for sex and then moves on to the next one. I see a beautiful lost boy who needs to recognize he's got so much more to offer than sex and songs.

And maybe it makes me a foolish, lovestruck idiot, but I think I might be the only one who can help him recognize that.

Despite the pang of fear, I can't stop myself from bringing my hand to his groin and running my palm over his very noticeable hard-on.

He groans in response.

God. Yes. This is what I wanted tonight. For a man to become undone by my touch.

And as I watch Wyatt's expression darken with unadulterated need, I'm glad that man won't be a random firefighter from a bar. I don't think I'd care as much about the noises a stranger makes, not the way I care about Wyatt and how his breath hisses when I drag the heel of my palm along the thick ridge of his arousal.

I lower myself onto my knees in front of him, never breaking eye contact. His chest rises and falls faster. I glimpse the hunger in his gaze as he watches me, waiting. I run my hands up his thighs, feeling the muscles tense under my touch. He's so damn sexy, and I love knowing that I'm the one who gets to do this to him.

"So..." I look up at him through my lashes, my fingers tracing the outline of his penis. "I was told you have a really good dick."

He barks out a laugh. "Oh yeah?"

"Uh-huh. I heard everyone loves it," I say, half teasing, half mocking.

"Don't care about anyone else," he mumbles. "Just you."

"Really. You want me to love it?"

"Yes."

I tug on his waistband and ease his sweatpants down, stifling a moan when his erection springs up. Long and thick, making my mouth water.

Wyatt's lips quirk at whatever he sees in my eyes. He reaches down and wraps his fingers around his shaft. "You want this?" he says hoarsely.

"Yes."

"Then take it, baby."

Nudging his hand away, I gauge his reaction as I stroke him. His head falls back against the back of the lounger, and he hums in approval.

A flicker of uncertainty goes through me. As confident as I was five seconds ago, the truth is… I don't know how to make a man beg.

"I…I need you to tell me how to please you."

"Jesus," he mutters.

"What?"

"You don't get it, do you? You breathe, and it gets me hard. It won't take much to please me."

Pleasure dances through me. Nobody's ever said anything like that to me before. I like it. It empowers me, renewing my confidence.

"At least tell me if I do something you don't like?"

"Sure," he says, and he seems amused, as if that's impossible for me to do.

Anticipation coils inside me as I lean forward. I flick my tongue over his tip, and Wyatt's entire body tenses. Then I draw him into my mouth, my hand gripping the base of his shaft. When I suck gently, his hips jerk up.

"That's it. Just like that." His hand rests on the back of my head, guiding me but not forcing. "Jesus. You look so fucking hot sucking my cock."

I hum around him, loving how he feels in my mouth, filling it completely. His fingers bunch in my hair, and his breathing changes, becoming more ragged, more desperate. Good. I want him desperate. I pull back, smiling at the agony that floods his eyes.

"Keep going," he pleads. "Please."

A thrill shoots through me. Wyatt Graham is begging me to blow him. I never would've dreamed it.

Lowering my head again, I lick a circle around his tip, then tease the underside with my tongue, making his hips jerk. I feel his cock throbbing beneath my tongue.

"*Jesus.*"

He releases a tortured noise when I drag my tongue along the full length of him. And then he's begging again.

"Suck it. Please."

Emboldened by his pleas, I give him what he wants, sucking him as deep as I can.

"Yes," he growls when I tighten the suction. "Keep going. Christ, you have no idea how often I've thought about your mouth."

I release him with a soft pop. "Really?"

"Really." He slides his hand down to my lips, tracing them with his fingertips. He looks at me with something close to reverence. "This perfect mouth. Made to suck my dick."

His dirty words make me even more determined to push him to the edge. I encircle him with my hand and give a long, slow stroke before sucking him down to the base, my tongue dragging along his throbbing shaft.

When my eyelids flutter closed, he grips my hair and tugs on it. "Eyes on me," he says roughly. "I want to see you."

Oh my God. Our gazes meet, and my breath gets trapped in my lungs. It's difficult to function when he's watching me like that. So intense. So locked in on me.

*I want every thought, every look, every breath focused on me.*

My mind flashes back to the husky words he'd uttered the night he told me what he likes in bed. When he said that he doesn't want half of someone but all of them.

*That's what gets me hard.*

He wasn't lying. The eye contact makes him impossibly harder. He's like steel in my hand, precome leaking from his tip as we stare at each other. I lap up those pearly drops with my tongue, then engulf him with my mouth, and he lets out a strangled moan.

As my hand moves faster, working in tandem with my lips and

tongue, his body tenses beneath me.

"Freckles," he rasps. "I'm not gonna last if you keep that up."

I ease my mouth off him, my lips swollen and wet, but I don't stop moving my hand. "That's the point," I say, then take him deep again, determined to finish what I started.

His hips buck up, his grip on my hair almost painful. "You're gonna make me come," he warns.

"Good," I mumble around his cock.

I suck harder and enjoy the way his body shudders.

"*Goddamn*," he grunts. "Coming, baby."

He thrusts deeper into my mouth, and I feel a rush of power, knowing I've completely unraveled him. The salty, heady flavor of him coats my tongue. I swallow it down, moaning around him while he curses and shakes with release.

His body is still twitching when I pull back, wiping my mouth with a wicked grin.

Wyatt opens his eyes, his chest heaving. He gazes down at me, completely wrecked. He's still trying to catch his breath, but his sated, heavy-lidded eyes tell me everything I need to know.

"You were right," I say solemnly. "You have a really good dick."

I wake up the next morning in Wyatt's bed, the little spoon to his big one. It's disorienting but nice. He surprised me last night by not letting me go to my own room when we went up to bed. I changed into pajamas and he stripped to his boxers, and then we brushed our teeth side by side and climbed into his bed. He curled one strong arm around me, pulled me close, and it honestly felt like we'd been sleeping together for years.

I twist my head to check if he's awake. And, God, he's beautiful. His hair is tousled. Lips parted in sleep. I like him like this, with his brow uncreased and his features relaxed and unguarded. Wyatt only shows vulnerability when he's performing, but he looks vulnerable right now. Younger, less intense.

I don't want to wake him, so I turn back, burrowing closer to his warm body, my ass pressed against his groin.

He must be a light sleeper, because my gentle movements summon a sleepy noise from him and he murmurs, "Morning."

"That was cute," I whisper, feeling myself blush.

"What?"

"That noise you just made."

I feel a soft laugh against my hair. Then he holds me tighter and makes that low, satisfied noise again.

"Did you sleep?" I ask him.

"All night." He sounds surprised.

"It's the power of my blowjobs."

That gets me a chuckle. "I don't think we moved from this spot the entire night." He runs a hand along my bare arm up to my shoulder, where he toys with the strap of my tank top. "Usually I'm tossing and turning and getting everything tangled up."

"Yeah, because you don't actually sleep. But I remmed you."

"I'm sorry—did you just say you rammed me?"

"No, I remmed you. Like, I made you feel so good that you fell into a deep REM cycle."

He trembles with laughter. "I got remmed all right. Remmed real hard by that sweet LMD."

Now I'm the one howling. "Oh my God."

"What? You're denying you gave me some Logan Mouth Delight last night?"

"No." I'm laughing so hard, I can't stop hiccupping. "But that's my *dad's* drink. Now I can never have it again without thinking about blowing you." I gulp in a breath, trying to compose myself.

Wyatt tugs me toward him again. When his forearm brushes my breasts, teasing a nipple, a shiver runs through me. Feeling that, he cups my breast, then gives the nipple a light flick, drawing a tiny moan from my lips.

"Do you like that?" he murmurs, and in the blink of an eye, the air in the bedroom goes from light to heated.

"Uh-huh."

It's impossible to form words when he's toying with my nipple like that. He pinches it, and I moan again. He teases my breasts for a bit before lowering his hand to the waistband of my shorts. He curses when he realizes I'm not wearing underwear beneath them.

"No panties?"

"Nope." I gasp when he slides his hand inside my shorts. "What are you doing?"

"Playing. Do you want me to stop?"

"No." My voice sounds breathy to my ears.

His index finger brushes over my clit before he cups my pussy in his palm. Heat jolts through me. I rock my hips slightly, and though I can't see his face, I can practically hear him smiling.

"You're so wet this early in the morning," he muses. "Are you into morning sex?"

"Are you offering?"

"No," he says, even as he slips two fingers through my slit to tease my opening.

"Then what is this?" I challenge.

"Playing," he repeats. "Lift up this leg, freckles."

Disappointment clenches in my stomach when he abruptly moves his hand, but it's only because I'm apparently not lifting my leg fast enough for him. With a deliberate pat, he grips my knee and slides it up, giving him better access to the spot that's aching for him. Then his hand is back, stroking and teasing, dipping into the arousal pooling at my core.

"You're soaked," he mutters.

The pads of his fingers are coated with wetness, and he brings them to my clit, rubbing slow circles over the swollen bud. His touch is precise yet indolent, as if he has all the time in the world. His teeth graze my shoulder, sending pleasure dancing through me. I feel his erection against my ass, but he doesn't release it from his boxers. Doesn't try to kiss me. He just rubs my clit until I'm mindless with need, desperately grinding against his palm.

"I'm going to come if you keep doing that," I whisper.

"And that's a problem because…?" His voice is a husky tease.

I'm practically fucking his hand now. My muscles coil tight. Every inch of skin starts tingling, pleasure building in my core. I try to draw a breath, but it happens to be at the same time as he summons the orgasm from me. I choke in surprise, crying out as waves of bliss spread through my body, from my fingers to my toes and everywhere in between.

"Such a good girl," he says in approval while I gasp for air.

The orgasm short-circuits my brain. I trap his hand between my thighs, my pussy spasming from each delicious, blissful pulse. Finally, I can't take it anymore. I roll onto my back, heaving as I stare up at the ceiling. I feel him watching me, so I turn my face toward his.

"Is this awkward?" I ask him.

"No, but it should be," he says gruffly.

I fully agree. I search his uneasy expression. "So why isn't it?"

"I don't know."

He stretches out beside me, one arm tucked behind his head, the other resting on his abdomen. He's silent for so long, I wonder if he's fallen asleep, but then his chest rises on a long inhale.

"I figured something out a while ago." He exhales in a rush. "You're my muse."

My heart skips a beat. "I am?"

"Yeah. Since you got to Tahoe, I've been writing nonstop. And none of it is trash. I'm writing good shit, freckles."

I smile at that. "So why do you sound so upset?"

"Cole told me I can't bang my muse."

"I mean, technically we didn't bang," I point out.

"True... And I do like a good technicality." He sounds more upbeat now. "Maybe it won't go away then. The inspiration."

"Is this a real thing?" I wrinkle my forehead, a part of me wondering if he's messing with me.

"Sort of. It's an unspoken rule that you don't sleep with your muse."

"Then you're in luck. I have it under good authority that Wyatt Graham doesn't follow the rules."

He laughs, but the humor dissolves fast. "Probably should, though," he says. "About this at least. About us."

I roll onto my side, studying his serious profile. "You want us to come up with rules?"

"Yeah, maybe. If we do this—"

"What do you mean *if*? We've already given each other orgasms."

"I mean if we continue giving each other orgasms. We can't let it get messy." His voice strains. "We can't, Blake."

"Okay. So what rules are you proposing?"

He's quiet, thinking it over. "It ends when the summer ends," he finally says.

I raise an eyebrow at him. "You think it'll even last that long? Because you keep telling me you're only good for a short time, remember? Now you're okay with a monthslong fling?"

He falters for a moment. "As long as we keep it casual, I guess I'm cool with it."

Something about his smooth, careless response has me hiding a smile. He's cool with it, huh? I should be bristling about the way he phrased it like he's doing me a favor, but I'm not. If he needs to tell himself that "casual" is the only way we can move forward, then I won't get in his way.

Besides, this *has* to end when summer's over. How can it last beyond that? I'm going back to college at the end of August. He's going...wherever he's going. Wyatt can barely handle an actual relationship, let alone a long-distance one.

"But we don't drag it out," he says. "Summer's over, and we walk away."

"Okay," I agree.

"And the friendship comes first." He speaks without hesitation now. Brisk and self-assured. A line drawn in the sand. "It comes before everything. If hooking up gets in the way of it, we stop the hookups. Not the friendship."

"Friendship first. Always." I snag my lip between my teeth, a thought occurring to me. "What if one of us wants to stop before the summer ends?"

"Then we stop." He shifts onto his side, meeting my eyes. "No questions asked. No explanations required. You say the word, it's done."

I search his face for a beat, then nod. "Okay. So those are the rules."

Wyatt nods back. "Those are the rules."

**1 NEW EMAIL**

**From**: County Records Department

**Subject**: Re: Records Request

Dear Ms. Logan,

The County Records Department has completed processing your recent request. Please find attached the certified copy of the death certificate for Darlene Beth Gallagher.

As for your request of medical examiner records, please note that no such report exists under this name.

We also conducted a search for death certificates for the additional two individuals you listed; however, no records were located for them in our files. Regarding your inquiry into property records to determine house purchases in Nevada under those names, please note that such records are maintained by a different office.

This link can provide further assistance with regard to property ownership and transfer documentation.

If you have any further questions regarding death records, please feel free to contact our office.

Sincerely,

Fiona Baker

County Records Department

# Chapter 25

## BLAKE

*Be a good girl and watch the fireworks*

"YOU STILL HAVEN'T HAD SEX." Annaliese sounds dubious.

"Nope," I confirm.

"Why are you stalling?"

"Oh, you sweet, naive girl. I'm not the one who's stalling."

Laughing, I reach for my Diet Coke and bat away the persistent wasp that's been buzzing around, determined to land on my straw. We're having lunch at an outdoor patio in town today.

Her jaw drops. "Bullshit. Wyatt Graham, the guy who's fucked half the lake, refuses to have sex with you?"

"Jeez, when you say it like *that*, it's terrible for my ego."

"Oh, shut up. He undresses you with his eyes any time you're within a hundred feet of him. That's why I'm so mystified."

I'm not. I'm starting to understand Wyatt's modus operandi: distance. He always maintains just the right amount of distance to prevent you from getting too close to him.

Unless it's in bed. Then? He's all in.

He lamented about women always falling for him. Claimed his

dick is so good that they inevitably want more. And there's no denying his penis is downright enchanting. It hasn't even been inside me, yet I would already sign a statement declaring it the world's greatest dick.

But his dick isn't the reason women fall. They fall because he makes them believe he loves them. Not with words but with his actions. He's attuned to every breath, every soft noise, while his eyes devour you, burning into your soul. The first time he went down on me, he spent an eternity tracing his lips over every inch of flesh. Listening to every microscopic bodily response, every whimper. Taking the time to learn and memorize what I liked, what made me shiver.

In the moment, Wyatt Graham makes you feel like you're the only woman in the world. Like you're his oxygen. His one true love.

It's no wonder women are left bereft when he moves on. Who wouldn't want that intoxicating feeling back?

"I think he's afraid of breaking my heart," I tell Annaliese, sipping my soda.

"I mean, he has the track record for it. Remember what he did to Rosie Tipper? Girl was so devastated she forced her parents to sell their house."

"I don't actually believe that. Yes, she was upset and showed up at our dock crying and begging, but there's no way that's why they sold their house."

Annaliese is smug. "Logan, my mother is *the* Tahoe Realtor. And that is literally what happened. Mom's the one who sold their house."

Wow. I'm legit shocked that the rumor is true. Enchanting penis indeed.

"Anyway, he thinks he's going to hurt me," I say with a shrug. "He makes comments about it sometimes when we're fooling around. He's probably terrified that full-on sex will make me fall in love with him."

"Well, joke's on him, right? Because you're already in love with him."

I glare at her. "I am not."

She snorts. "You've been in love with him since you were a kid."

"That wasn't real love," I protest. "It was puppy love. It was a *crush*."

"Okay, so what is it now?"

I bite my lip. What is it now? It's...

It's magic.

Ugh. I hate even thinking that, because it only demonstrates I'm probably way more into him than he is into me. But something happens when Wyatt and I are together. Something magical and emotional and infuriating. He stirs all my emotions, not just one or two, and it's terrifying to feel *everything*, all at once.

I'm so tempted to ask him if he feels it too, that magic. I want to ask him what it means that he texts me all the time, even when we're in the same room. It's cute. And sweet. And I want so badly to know if I'm misreading it. Because I behave the same way, and I know what it means when *I* do it. He's always on my mind.

Fuck.

Maybe I *am* falling, just a tiny bit. But I'd never admit it to Annaliese, because she'll tease me mercilessly.

We're interrupted by an incoming message on my phone. I check it and chuckle at the screen.

"Is that him?" Annaliese grins.

"No, it's my ghost-hunting buddies. Little Spencer claims he heard Darlie at the lighthouse yesterday. His hypothesis is that she takes a break from lake haunting sometimes to indulge in some lighthouse haunting as revenge for her sister meeting Raymond there."

"Girl, you need to stop associating with crazies."

"The Spencers aren't crazy. They're hilarious."

"Crazy people can be funny. There's no rule that says they can't be."

"Nah, I like them. And I'm enjoying the research. Oh! And guess what!" I brighten at the reminder. "The county sent me Darlie's death certificate. We've got official confirmation that she's dead."

"Oh, thank God," she mocks. "*We* needed that confirmation so badly. I was suffering sleepless nights because of it."

"We both know you're invested now. Stop pretending you aren't."

"Didn't you say you were going to be looking at possible jobs this summer? What happened to that?"

"Ugh, yeah," I say with a sigh. "I'm doing that research too, but this is way more fun. Oooh, and now that I know she's actually dead, I can hit up all the local cemeteries and look for her tombstone."

"Wow." Annaliese stares at me for a moment. "Maybe that can be what you do after graduation. Cemetery stalker."

I flip up my middle finger, then reach for the bill that our waiter just dropped off. "On me," I say. "Since you drove."

"Are you still coming to the fireworks show tonight?" she asks as we leave the restaurant.

"Me, yes. Not sure about Wyatt yet. If he comes, we can meet you at Commons. Otherwise, pick me up?"

"You got it."

After she drives me home, I head to the dock in search of Wyatt. His guitar and notebook are on a lounger, but he's not with them. He's lying down on the swim platform fifty feet out. Sunglasses on, black swim trunks hugging his muscular thighs. A golden feast on display for my hungry eyes.

"Hey, Graham!" I shout toward the water.

He rises on one elbow and props a hand on his forehead to shield his eyes, peering in my direction. Then he gets up and dives off the platform, barely leaving a splash in the water. I admire his long, graceful strokes as he swims back to the dock.

A moment later, he climbs the ladder, his muscular torso glistening and water dripping from his wet hair.

A devilish smile forms at the sight of me. "Hey, freckles."

Forget the sun beating down on my head. His words are what make me melt. I'm a fucking goner every time he smiles at me like that. Every time he drawls that endearment. For the first time in my life, the word *freckles* doesn't feel like a slur.

He strides toward his lounger and grabs a towel, drying himself off. Then he flops down and stretches his legs out. "When'd you get back?"

I wander toward him. "Just now. I came down to see if you want to go to the fireworks tonight with me and Annaliese and her brother."

I don't think Wyatt is listening. He's too busy staring at me. Or, as Annaliese would call it, undressing me with his eyes. That hot gaze starts its journey at my feet in my red flip-flops, traveling up my bare legs, resting on the hem of my short, flouncy skirt. He focuses only briefly on my thin tank top before those hungry green eyes lower again.

"Lift up the skirt," he says.

I gulp. "Why?"

"Because I want to see your pussy."

My breath stutters in my chest. I'm standing in the middle of a dock, not exactly a discreet spot, yet a thrill shoots through me at the prospect of giving him what he wants.

Biting my lip, I gather the white fabric between my fingers and ease my skirt up, flashing him just a hint of my striped panties.

He curses softly. "Move the panties aside. Let me see."

Oh my God.

I nudge the narrow scrap of fabric aside, baring myself to him.

His eyes blaze as they settle between my legs. He swipes his tongue over his bottom lip.

"Goddamn. I want to go down on you right here."

*Do it*, I almost beg, but the bold request dies on my tongue when I hear loud laughter behind me. A boat speeds by, and I instantly shove my skirt down, heat scorching my cheeks.

"Aw, look at that. My good girl is blushing," he says, which only makes me blush harder.

"Stop calling me that in public," I chide.

"We're not in public. We're alone on our dock, and you almost let me eat you out."

"Nope," I insist. "I was just playing around. I never would've let you."

"Liar. You were seconds away from riding my tongue."

"Fireworks," I say, jabbing a finger in the air. "Yay or nay?"

He shrugs. "What the hell. Yay."

Commons Beach hosts a fireworks show every Fourth of July, but although we've been coming to Tahoe my whole life, this is only my third time attending. My family doesn't usually show up till August, so we're always a month too late. Wyatt and I meet Annaliese and the others an hour before the show so we can procure a good spot on the grassy area directly facing the lake, where the fireworks will be launched from a barge on the water.

We haul our gear to our chosen spot, laying out blankets and setting down a cooler. Annaliese's brother brought two lawn chairs that he calls dibs on for him and his girlfriend, Shaye. Annaliese brought a date too, though I use that term loosely. She met the guy on a hookup app only a couple hours ago. They literally met for the first time just now on the grass.

Since alcohol is strictly prohibited on all the county beaches, we're drinking sodas and nonalcoholic wine coolers. "Also known as fizzy juice," Eddie scornfully says, then reveals he snuck in some vodka disguised as mineral water. To be honest, I'm not even angry about it. There's a chill in the air tonight, so I'm grateful as Eddie passes the bottle around and we all take secretive sips to warm up.

Wyatt and I brought an extra blanket, and I nestle beside him as he spreads the thick fleece over our laps. He tucks it at my side, his expression earnest as he murmurs, "You warm enough?"

I don't miss Annaliese's very obvious smirk, but damned if his fussing doesn't make my heart swell. God. Never in my life would I have thought I'd be snuggled under a blanket watching fireworks with Wyatt Graham.

Does he see this as a date? We have our rules, but none of them addressed whether the things we do together out of bed are considered dates. He'd probably insist they're not. That tonight's outing isn't a romantic one. Just two lifelong friends watching the dazzling display lighting up the world. Nope, not romantic at all.

The first rocket streaks into the night sky, vanishing for a heartbeat before bursting into a canopy of color that shimmers across the lake.

"Oh my God," Annaliese breathes.

It's stunning. Red, green, and gold sparks rain down in majestic arcs, while their reflections on the water's surface create a mesmerizing mirror effect. Two explosions of color happening at the same time, sky and water. The other groups scattered around us are all our age or older, yet everyone oohs and aahs and gasps and screams like a bunch of excited kids. Each boom and crack of fireworks echoes off the surrounding mountains, and the entire sky feels alive with layers of glittery bursts and crackling light trails.

"Come closer," Wyatt says. "You're too far away."

I'm really not. Our shoulders are plastered together. But I love that he can't seem to get close enough whenever we're together. And he always needs to be touching me. I smile when he tugs my body and positions me in front of him so that my back is resting on his chest. Strong arms encircle me, his face nuzzling my neck.

"Freckles," he whispers.

I tilt my head to meet his eyes, then sort of regret it because all I find is pure lust reflected back at me.

He brings his lips back to my ear. "I'm horny."

I tamp down a laugh. "Do you want to leave?" I whisper back.

Wyatt shakes his head, a filthy gleam sparkling in his eyes. The next thing I know, his hand is traveling beneath the blanket.

My breath hitches when I feel his fingertips teasing my waistband. The skirt is light and filmy, the elastic stretching easily to allow him to slip his hand inside my underwear. The moment he makes contact with bare skin, a rush of moisture pools between my legs.

I glance around to check if anybody notices what he's doing, but I'm fairly confident it just looks like we're bundled up under a blanket with his arms around me. A few feet away, Annaliese and her date are paying us no attention, their eyes focused on the sky.

When he massages my clit with the pad of one finger, a shiver skitters through my body.

His lips tickle my ear again. "You're shaking. Does that feel good?"

"Mm-hmm." I force myself to stare straight ahead. To pretend that the ministrations of his fingers aren't turning me into a puddle of aroused mush.

He starts toying with me in earnest, his finger moving up and down, dipping inside my slit. He makes a low noise when he discovers how wet I am.

"You like this..." His soft voice is barely audible over the booming explosions of light. "Having me play with you with everyone around us."

I'm desperate to rock my hips, craving deeper contact, but he denies me. He keeps his touch light, his fingertips dancing over my clit.

A mocking whisper ghosts over my earlobe. "You're such a good girl, Blake. Sitting there so nicely, not making a sound."

I gasp when his free arm suddenly pulls me closer to his body so I can feel the erection pressing against my ass.

"You feel that? Rock-hard, baby, just from feeling that wet pussy under my hand."

A moan slips out, and I cover it with a cough. Annaliese turns to give me a funny look, and Wyatt's hand freezes.

I hastily pick up my water bottle. "Sorry," I tell her. "My throat is so dry."

"Gotta keep that shit lubricated," she says, and Wyatt chuckles against my hair.

I force down a sip of water while Annaliese refocuses on the fireworks and Wyatt continues to torture me with his fingers.

"When we get back to the house," he mutters in my ear, "I'm gonna need you to take care of my dick. Can you do that for me?"

In response, I grind my ass on him, and his fingers tighten over my thigh in warning. Oh, so I'm allowed to be tortured in front of hundreds of strangers, but he isn't?

I peek up with an innocent smile. "What's wrong?"

"Behave," he cautions, "or I'll stop."

Calling his bluff, I move my butt again, rubbing it over his prominent erection.

The decision backfires horribly on me as Wyatt proves he doesn't make idle threats. I almost weep when his hand abruptly disappears from my underwear.

"Noooo!" The wailing complaint flies out before I can stop it, this time drawing not only Annaliese's attention but everyone's.

Eddie leans over on his lawn chair and grins at me. "You okay there, Logan?"

I'm so mortified, my cheeks nearly burst into flames. "Um, no, I'm not. I'm just *so* disappointed by this fireworks display."

Every single person in our vicinity gapes at me like I'm a crazy person.

"The fuck you talking about?" Eddie says. "It's magnificent."

Meanwhile, Wyatt sits there all smug and obnoxious, both his hands on top of the blanket when at least one of them should be making me see stars instead of fireworks.

Gritting my teeth, I twist my head to glare at him.

He merely shrugs. "I warned you what would happen if you didn't behave."

"I'll be good," I blurt out, wincing at the pleading note in my voice.

That gets me an arrogant smile. "No. You had your chance. Now be a good girl and watch the fireworks."

# Chapter 26

## WYATT

### *The cure for insomnia*

IT'S RAINING TODAY, SO BLAKE and I spend a lazy afternoon in the great room. My fingers wander over the piano keys, laying out the chords. Nothing fancy. C major to E minor, a quick pivot to G major, dancing down to D. It's a soft, sweet love song from Blake's dock playlist. She put it on yesterday, and it's been stuck in my head ever since, so last night I carried Mom's electric piano upstairs from the basement and set it up by the windows, because I enjoy looking at the lake while I play, and the acoustics in this room are surprisingly decent.

The chords spill into each other like watercolor on canvas. I like this song. And it isn't Mollie May, thankfully. It's Crystal Soto, a young singer who sort of came out of nowhere last year and skyrocketed to fame.

On the couch, Blake is slouched on her back, reading on her phone. She's got one knee up and her other leg crossed over it, drawing my gaze between her legs like a magnet. I glimpse the shadow of her pink panties beneath her thin white shorts, and my mouth waters, distracting me from the song.

After nearly two weeks of fooling around, my desire for her hasn't dimmed one iota. I keep waiting for it to fade. Because it *always* fades. But I want her all the damn time. Can't even be in a room with her for more than five seconds without needing to kiss her. And once her lips are on mine, I can't stop myself from touching her. From sliding my hands all over her body and exploring every perfect inch of her.

I should just fuck her. She'd be into it. I'm the one resisting, though. I've been telling her it's because you can't sleep with your muse, but at this point we both know I'm feeding her a load of bull. My inspiration hasn't waned in the slightest, and we make each other come on a daily basis.

But while I'm confident that sex won't silence the music, it *will* complicate things. I know the moment I bury myself inside her, I'll want to stay there forever. I'll never want to stop, because she's quickly becoming an addiction.

I tear my gaze off her and continue playing, trying to figure out how Crystal Soto transitions into the bridge. I think I'm missing a chord maybe. It takes a few attempts to get it right, and then I start the song from the top, because I'm the kind of perfectionist who needs to play something right the entire way through.

I'm at the first chorus when I realize Blake is singing along. It's barely audible, but the sound of her soft, pure soprano is so unexpected that I stop mid-chord.

Her gaze flicks toward me. "Why'd you stop?"

"You can sing." I stare at her in shock.

She quickly shakes her head, cheeks reddening. "No, I can't. That wasn't even singing."

"That was totally singing." Excitement tickles my chest. "Do it again. Sing with me."

"Oh my God. We are not singing a *duet*."

"Oh yes, we are. Come on." I crack my knuckles, and she laughs at my antics. "I'll sing the first verse, you come in for the chorus, and then you take over verse two."

"Wyatt—" she protests, but I'm already playing the intro again.

My voice is a bit raspy as I sing the verse. I don't know why this thrills me so much. Lots of people can sing. It's just... Blake isn't an attention seeker. She isn't the first to sign up for karaoke like Alex Tucker or belt out show tunes like Stella Davenport after you get a few beers in her. The fact that Blake even feels comfortable singing around me does something fierce to my heart.

When I hit the G major of the chorus, her voice slips in, reluctant at first, but it's so sweet, bringing a smile to my lips. I join her, letting the high notes ring so her voice has somewhere to land. And it does. She's perfectly in tune, carrying the melody like she's the one who wrote it, and I tap into the harmony on instinct, our voices twinning.

Fucking magic. There's no harmony in the original, but here, with nothing but us and the piano, it's perfection. Her light, airy voice balances my deeper tone, and the song suddenly isn't a cover anymore. It's ours.

As the final chord fades to silence, our eyes lock, and I shake my head at her.

"What?" she says, sounding insecure. She pulls her knees up to her chest, hugging them.

"That was amazing."

"It was fun." She smiles at me over her knees, that gorgeous smile that utterly devastates me, and for a second, I have to look away.

Everything about her gets to me. Her smile. Her voice. Her energy. I want more of it. More of *her*. I want her to show me every part of herself, shed every last layer and let me look inside. And the fact that

I'm thinking any of this while we're fully clothed scares the shit out of me. Feelings like that aren't casual. They're dangerous, because if she lets me in the way I'm craving to be let in, I'll have to do the same.

I've never been in this position before—I'm *never* the one who wants more—and I don't like it one damn bit. Yet that doesn't stop me from sliding off the piano bench and climbing onto the couch with her. She giggles when I lie directly on top of her, propped up on my elbows so I can peer down and kiss her. She kisses me back, but I nip at her lip when she tries to slip me some tongue.

"Don't start something we can't finish right now."

"Why can't we finish?" she asks mischievously.

I give her another soft peck before sliding lower so my head is resting on her chest. "Because I'm taking a nap. You kept me up all night."

"You wouldn't have been sleeping anyway."

That's where she's wrong. About a week ago, something miraculous happened. I discovered the cure for insomnia.

It's called Blake Logan.

If she's in my bed, I sleep. At first, I thought it was a fluke. That her blowjobs are just so goddamn good that they short out my brain and send me into a post-BJ coma.

But then one night last week, my dick didn't enter the equation. I was too tired after frying my brain writing all day, so the only action in my bed was me eating Blake out for forty-five minutes. She came all over my face and curled up in my arms, and then we fell asleep.

*Both* of us.

Telling a girl "You put me to sleep" isn't exactly a flex, though. I'm worried she won't take it as the compliment it is, so I've been pretending I'm still not sleeping great. But this streak has held up every night. Even daytime naps don't affect it.

"Are you really napping right now?" she teases.

"Mm-hmm."

I press my cheek against her breast, sighing happily when she starts playing with my hair, and it isn't long before I feel my breathing slowing, steadying, as her fingers softly stroke and lull me into slumber.

We're fixing dinner later when my phone lights up, an unfamiliar New York number flashing on the screen. Normally I don't answer calls from numbers I don't recognize, but this past month, I've been lunging for the phone no matter what. It's been weeks since my mom told me Tobey Dodson was going to call me. To be honest, I'd given up hope, and considering it's nearly ten p.m. on the East Coast right now, I'm expecting a telemarketer or attempted scam recording when I swipe to answer.

"Hey," a baritone voice rumbles in my ear. "Is this Wyatt?"

My heart stutters. "Yes. Who's this?"

"Wyatt, my man, it's Tobey. Dodson. Got your number from Hannah. I hope you don't mind that I'm calling?"

"No, not at all." Now my pulse is racing. Blake glances over curiously, brow raised, but I step away from the pot of boiling spaghetti and duck out of the kitchen. "It's nice to meet you. I mean, over the phone. It's nice to phone meet you." *Jesus, shut the hell up.*

"Pleasure's all mine," he replies, his tone sincere. "I've been meaning to call you for a while, but I got called away on business in Tokyo. I work with this *sick* K-pop girl group over there, and we had to re-record a few tracks for their new album. Anyway, I'm stateside now, so I wanted to touch base with you. See what's what."

"Yeah, sure," I say awkwardly. "So...um...what's what?"

There's a deep chuckle in my ear. "You tell me, my man. Hannah says you're working on some new material?"

"Uh. Yeah. I am."

"Love to hear it, if that's something you're interested in. I was telling your mom, I'm obsessed with this track of yours—'Silver'? It's the exact vibe I've been craving lately, you know? There's so much pop and bubblegum right now, market's oversaturated with it. Don't get me wrong, I love my pop divas. Been doing some great collabs. But I need to sink my teeth into something different, you feel me?"

"I think so, yeah."

"Figured we'd open up a dialogue, see if the chemistry is there. But I'm heading back to Tokyo this week until the end of the summer, so if your new material speaks to me, we realistically wouldn't be able to get into the studio till September. That work for you or no?"

"It totally works," I blurt out, then cringe at how overeager I sounded.

"Brilliant. In the meantime, send me the new shit. You good with critical feedback, or am I dealing with a diva over here?"

I laugh. "Nah, criticize away. Only makes me better, right?"

"That's what I like to hear." Dodson sounds enthusiastic as he says, "I'll have my assistant send you all my deets. Email, phone numbers, whatever. And we'll touch base soon, my man."

He disconnects without a goodbye, leaving me a little dazed.

Did that really just happen?

I stumble back into the kitchen and collapse onto a breakfast stool. Blake is draining the pasta at the sink, but she sets the strainer down at my dramatic entrance.

"Everything okay?" she says.

With my head still spinning, I recap the conversation, and her eyes light up when I finish. She comes to the counter and flings her arms around me.

"Holy shit. Wyatt! This is incredible."

I grip her arm, not quite hugging her back. I'm still too stunned. Noticing my frozen state, Blake pulls back and searches my face.

"What's wrong? Why aren't you happy about this?"

"I am. But..." I clear my throat because it's coated with apprehension. "What if he hates my new material and decides he doesn't want to move forward?"

"He won't."

"He might."

"He *won't.* You are beyond talented, which apparently everyone sees but you. But listen up, Graham—you are way too hot to be insecure."

I can't help but laugh. "I'm not insecure. I just..."

"Don't think you're good enough," she finishes.

Yeah. I suppose so. Sort of. I *know* I'm good. I just always fear I can't be *great.* And that's a hard pill to swallow when everyone around me is. My mother. My father. My sister. All great.

"It's the curse of coming from a family of overachievers, I guess," I say wryly. A lump fills my throat. "It's like... What if I can never measure up?"

"I feel that way too," Blake reminds me. She pulls out the stool next to mine and sits, reaching for my hand. "Everyone else is destined for greatness, and I'm destined for a boring office job I hate and my dumb hobbies."

"I mean, most people work jobs they don't love. That's just life." I squeeze her hand. "But your hobbies aren't dumb."

"I research things for *fun,*" she grumbles.

"Yeah, and you enjoy it. Isn't that all that matters? Who cares what everyone else is doing?"

"See, you keep saying that," she teases, "and you tell me to never compare myself to anyone else unless I want to destroy my self-esteem. Yet you're sitting here comparing yourself to your family."

"Haven't you learned by now that people are shit at following their own advice?"

Blake laughs. "We should make a pact. Promise to keep reminding each other not to fall victim to the trap of comparison."

A warm sensation washes over me. "I like that."

This time, when she loops her arms around my neck, I don't resist. I just hold her tighter.

# Chapter 27

## WYATT

### *The lighthouse*

THE NEXT DAY, THE RAIN has let up and the sun peeks through the clouds. Blake and I make omelets for breakfast and eat them on the deck while she types one-handed on her phone. Then she sets it down and takes another bite, only for the phone to buzz again. Her braid falls over her shoulder as she peers at the screen.

"So chatty," I say dryly.

"It's impossible to send the Spencers one text and not have it turn into a whole conversation."

"What are our paranormal podcasters up to now?"

"They visited the lighthouse on the island a couple days ago, and Little Spencer insists he felt a presence."

"We both know that didn't happen."

She laughs. "Probably not. But either way, I want to go out there. Wanna come?"

I pop the last bite of omelet into my mouth. "Sure. When?"

"Let's go today. Make up for being trapped indoors all day yesterday."

"Hey, I enjoyed our indoor time yesterday." I wink at her. After we woke up from our nap, I rolled onto my back and made her ride my face. She didn't seem to be complaining at the time.

She blushes, which only makes me grin harder. "It was very nice," she says primly. "But now I'm stir-crazy. Let's go to the lighthouse."

"Is this where Raymond supposedly met up with Darlie's sister?"

"Yep. And it's also not far from the cinnamon ghost house, so who knows?" Blake waggles her eyebrows. "We might encounter *two* spirits today."

"Yes. That is for sure gonna happen." I push my chair back and reach for our plates. It's my turn to do the dishes.

"So we're going?" she prompts.

Truth is even if I didn't want to go, I still would. It's impossible for me to say no to her. One smile from this girl, and I'll give her the parka off my back in the middle of the tundra.

So I shrug and say, "Of course."

"How much farther?" Blake asks a couple hours later, huffing with exertion.

I check my phone, shocked to find I'm still getting enough service to load a map. I dropped to one bar almost the second we stepped foot on the island.

"Maybe ten, fifteen more minutes."

She sighs. I don't blame her. The climb was steeper than I expected, and my legs are burning from the effort. I heard the view is worth it, though. Yes, *I'm* here for the view and not the ghost, because I don't believe in ghosts, and there is absolutely nothing otherworldly about a lighthouse on an island in Lake Tahoe. Come on now.

We power forward on the trail. I took my shirt off about half a mile ago, and it's tucked through one of the straps of my pack. Blake keeps checking out my chest, and I keep smirking each time she does it, but she's unrepentant. That's fine. I like having her eyes on me.

Tall pine trees line either side of the narrow trail, their needles slick with moisture. It must've rained up here this morning. I suspect it will again, judging by the cooling, damp-smelling air.

"Why isn't it busier up here?" she wonders. "Big Spencer said this spot is popular on the weekends."

"Maybe we got lucky?"

As if to voice its disagreement, the universe unleashes a low rumble that rolls across the sky.

We exchange a wary look.

"Did you check the weather before deciding we were going to scale a cliff?" I ask her.

"Nope," she says cheerfully. "Did you?"

"Sure didn't."

The wind shifts suddenly, and the branches all around us begin to move, pine needles floating down to the ground. I lift my gaze to the dark clouds gathering above the lake.

"Shit," I say just as the sky rumbles again. It sounds closer now.

Seconds later, the raindrops begin to fall, hitting my chest and sliding over my pecs. The trees sway harder.

Blake purses her lips. "We're closer to the lighthouse than the boat, right?"

I calculate the distance on my phone. "Yes."

"Then let's keep going."

We can't run because the trail is too steep, and now it's wet too. The rain soaks us within minutes. It turns the dirt beneath our feet to mud, making it harder to navigate, and when the lightning cracks, I feel the first flicker of concern that we're going to get fried to a crisp. Fortunately, it isn't long before I see the silhouette of the lighthouse in the flashes of light. By the time we reach the base of the old structure, the wind is howling, and the rain is deafening.

I shove the heavy wooden door with my shoulder. It stays stubbornly closed, creaking from my effort, before finally pushing open. Inside, the air is musty, but the small space is blessedly dry, which is more than I can say for us. We stumble inside, dripping and breathless.

"Holy shit, that was intense." Blake shakes water from her sleeves and turns in a slow circle, taking in the spiral staircase and iron railing, her features softened by the dim light filtering through the broken shutters. Then she sits on an overturned crate and starts wringing her hair out.

I pull off my backpack and fish through it. All it contains is two granola bars, one bottle of water, and the hoodie I thought I might need.

"Do you have reception?" I ask, and we both consult our phones.

"No bars," she says. "Useless."

"Same."

"We might as well wait it out here, right?"

"I think so."

As the rain beats against the dirty windows, we make ourselves comfortable and spend the next several minutes listening to the storm and feeling the wind shake the old bones of the lighthouse. I sit on the dusty floor and stretch my legs in front of me, propping my hands behind my head while Blake wanders toward a window to watch the storm roll across the lake.

I sweep my gaze over her wet hair, her cheeks pink from the wind. She's gorgeous. Windswept and wild. I tuck the line away, wishing I'd brought my songbook with me.

The wind hissing in the cracks of the wooden facade sounds almost human, a ghostly wail. "Uh-oh," I joke. "Do you think Darlie's here?"

"Maybe." Blake turns to face me. "You know what? What if we're wrong? Maybe what *actually* happened is Darlie killed her sister."

I lift a brow. "Ooh. Go on."

"She found out that Raymond was meeting Dolly at the lighthouse and followed them here one night. Then she killed them both and drowned herself in the lake."

"You still haven't found any records showing whether Raymond and Dolly are dead or alive?"

"Ugh, no. I finally confirmed that Darlie is dead, but not the other two. These information requests take forever. Honestly, if I had one wish in life, it would be to cut through all the red tape of the bureaucracy."

"Really, *one* wish, and that's what you would do? We don't want world peace? Not interested in curing hunger?"

"Oh, shoot, yeah, those are probably better options," she says, and I snort out a laugh.

She sits down again and kicks off her wet sneakers and socks, leaving her feet bare. The rain settles into a steady rhythm. It's not as violent as before but still persistent.

"This is kind of romantic," she remarks. "Trapped in a lighthouse during a storm, dramatic lightning strikes, near-death hike. It's very..." She mulls it over. "Jane Austen meets *National Geographic.*"

I snicker. "What a combo."

"Hey, don't laugh. I bet you're already writing a love song about this."

She's not off base. Lyrics are dancing through my mind like

dust motes.

"Maybe," I say vaguely.

"No maybe about it, songboy. I can practically see you composing."

"Hey, you said so yourself. It's romantic. The song practically writes itself." I begin strumming invisible chords on my thigh. "*The ocean's wild, but her eyes are calm. Guiding me home like a beacon in the storm. Falling...we're falling...into the crash of the tide, our hearts open wide...*" I trail off, smiling sheepishly.

Her jaw drops. "Did you seriously just make that up on the spot?"

"Yeah."

"Wow. It was kind of perfect." She gasps. "Wait, you said *falling*. Is that your way of saying you're falling in love with me?"

Mischief twinkles in her expression, indicating she's just teasing, but the question, joking or not, throws me off-kilter.

"No," I say quickly. "Of course not."

"Uh-huh." She looks back to the window, but not before I glimpse a hint of a smile.

Thankfully, she doesn't push it. Doesn't force me to defend the denial. If I opened my mouth again, I'm not sure what would come out. Because I see how easily it could happen. Falling for her. When I let myself go there, it happens fast and fierce.

But it also doesn't last. Love is too messy, and I'm bad at it. I get bored and move on. I leave broken hearts in my wake. And I refuse to break Blake.

Yet I also can't stop myself from getting deeper and deeper with her. It's like a hand reaching out from the water, pulling me under. But not in a horror movie kind of way. I *want* to go deeper. I want that warm water to engulf me whole.

I don't understand it. All I know is that when we're together, I crack open my soul to her, and I think she does the same with me.

Our eyes lock across the room. There's something between us, something that I fight so damn hard, but here in this old lighthouse, with the thunder cracking in the sky and the streaks of lightning from the thin gaps in the slats, it's impossible to deny.

Her throat dips as she swallows. "Can I ask you something?"

"Of course," I say gruffly.

"Why won't you have sex with me?"

I blink. I wasn't expecting that.

"Because I don't think it's about me being your muse," she continues. "So...why?"

"I just think..." I hesitate. "If we do that, there's no turning back."

"Turning back from what?"

"I don't know."

"Yes, you do."

I don't answer.

"This is ending when the summer is over," she says softly. "I haven't forgotten that rule."

I want to believe her, but I've had women say that to me before, insisting they were okay with their temporary status. I always make it clear they're on borrowed time with me, which makes me sound like a total fuckboy prick, but at least I'm honest. I'm not built for long-term entanglements. Eventually, I'll be drawn elsewhere. To another place, another woman, another song.

Blake fixes those blue eyes on me with an intensity that makes it hard to breathe. But she doesn't speak.

"What are you thinking about?" I ask.

"You don't want to know."

"No, tell me."

"I was just thinking it would be a real shame if I never got to feel you inside me."

Jesus Christ.

I choke back a groan. But looking at her right now, I share that sentiment entirely. She's a sight to behold. Her hair in that messy braid, dark strands falling onto her face. Perky breasts hugged by that tight tank top. Long legs emerging from those indecent denim shorts. She's so beautiful it almost hurts to look at her.

"Yes," I say, my voice hoarse. "It would be."

Our eyes meet again.

"Take your pants off," she says.

This time, the groan slips out. I'm always the one bossing her around, and my dick twitches at her commanding tone. He likes it.

"If I do that, there's no going back," I warn.

"I don't want to go back. Back is boring. I want the here and now."

I'm usually a lot smoother than this, but my fingers are shaking as I undo the button of my pants.

"Zipper," she prompts.

I drag the zipper down.

"Take it out."

Jesus, someone with this many freckles shouldn't be saying those words. I'm already stiffer than a post as I take my dick out, wrapping my fingers around it.

Blake licks her lips, and damned if that doesn't get me even harder.

She reaches for her backpack and pulls it toward her by the strap while I sit there with my dick in hand, watching her remove a small blue pouch and unzip it. When she stands, she's holding a condom.

I raise a brow. "Were you planning to seduce me on our hike?"

She smiles. "No, it's my emergency pouch. It has everything in it. I brought it for the lip balm, but we might as well take advantage of the condom."

"Might as well," I agree, even as I worry this is a bad idea. Which is ridiculous, really. We've been fooling around every day. Sex shouldn't make a difference. But it does.

She tosses me the plastic packet. I catch it but don't rip it open yet. I'm too distracted by her undressing. She peels off her top, revealing the skimpy triangle bra underneath. Then she takes that off too, baring her breasts at the exact moment that lightning strikes again, brightening the shadowy space we're occupying to offer a perfect view of her perfect nipples.

My mouth runs dry. I can't tear my eyes off her. She undoes her shorts, wiggles out of them. Panties disappear next. She's fully naked when she climbs into my lap, and I'm shaking again.

Resting her hands on my shoulders, she presses her lips to mine in a slow, teasing kiss. A hint of tongue and a lot of temptation. I could probably stop this now before we let it get too far, but I don't want to. Instead, I thread my fingers through her hair, tighten it in my fist, and bring her face even closer, deepening the kiss.

I swallow her quiet whimper. I'm obsessed with every sound that escapes her lips. I want to kiss every inch of her body, but there isn't much of an opportunity for foreplay here. Not on this dirt-covered floor. It's also uncomfortable as hell, but it's difficult to dwell on that when her hands are roaming my bare chest. Then I blink and she's pushing me down onto my back.

I shove my backpack under my head as she eases my pants and boxer briefs off my hips. I run my fingers over her skin. It's impossibly soft, like silk beneath my fingertips, which are calloused and rough from years of playing guitar. It feels criminal to be scraping them over her perfect flesh.

I kick off my pants, and something sharp digs into my bare ass.

Maybe a pebble, hopefully not a rusty nail. I don't care, because I'm rock-hard and Blake is putting a condom on me. She rolls it down my shaft and squeezes, igniting a burst of pleasure.

When I reach between her legs to test her readiness, I discover that she's soaked. Jesus. She's never been this wet before. She lowers herself onto me, letting my cock slip in one inch at a time until I'm so deep inside her, I feel like she's a part of my body. It feels as incredible as I knew it would. A feeling of complete...fucking...belonging.

For the first time in my life, I don't want to be anywhere else. Just here. Inside this girl.

Her pussy grips me like a hot glove, squeezing my shaft and rippling around me each time she rises and then sinks down again.

"Feels so good," she whispers. Her hair falls like a curtain over us as she bends down to brush her lips over mine.

"Yeah?" I whisper back. "You like that dick?"

She moans, and I swallow the sound with another tongue-tangling kiss. Then I break away and watch her as she starts to move. She rides my dick slowly, drawing out every tight glide, every rotation of her hips each time she's seated fully. Her pussy is so tight and warm, and I suddenly curse the condom, because I can't feel her wetness, but I *see* it clinging to the latex every time she lifts up. I want to feel her soaking my dick, damn it.

When her eyes close, I keep one hand on her hip but slide the other up to her face, cupping her cheek. "Keep your eyes open."

Her eyelids flutter open.

"I want you to look at me as you fuck me, okay?"

She nods wordlessly, and I stroke her hip in encouragement, groaning my approval when she rides me a little faster. I need her to come. I've seen what she looks like when I send her over the edge with my tongue, my hand, my fingers. Now I need to know what it's like with my cock lodged inside her.

My breathing goes shallow as her hips undulate in a slow, dirty rhythm. That pebble digs into my ass cheek again, bringing a sharp sting that matches the sting of pain in my chest when Blake's nails scrape my pecs a bit too hard. Her face is flushed. Hips moving faster.

"That's it," I urge. "I don't come until you do."

The noises she's making are a goddamn symphony. I want to record them, listen to them when I'm alone, inject her melody into my blood.

I don't know how I'm managing to stave off my release. My balls are aching, so tight they've damn near disappeared. Every drop of blood in my body is concentrated in my dick. Her pussy feels so good surrounding me, it brings black dots to my vision. I resist the urge to thrust upward and fuck her senseless. This is her show, her pace, and I'm just lucky enough to be here.

But then she lets out an anguished moan and bends over me again, her lips finding mine in a desperate kiss before she says, "Stop holding back." She buries her face in my neck. "Fuck me back, damn it."

The plea breaks the dam inside me. I lift my hips and drill into her hard, drawing a choked groan from her lips. Meeting her thrust for thrust, all I can hear is the sound of the rain on the walls and roof and Blake's sweet moans and hushed gasps. And then finally, her hoarse cry of release as she comes all over my dick.

It's the permission I need to let go. My fingers dig into her waist as the orgasm shudders through me and spills into the condom.

As my heartbeat regulates, I realize the storm has calmed as well, the thunder trailing off into distant grumbles. Rain still taps the windows, but it's quiet, lazy almost. Even the darkness has lifted, the afternoon sun peeking back out and spilling shafts of gold light through the cracks of the lighthouse.

The storm is over, but Blake doesn't seem to notice. She's lying on top of me, nestled close.

I was wrong. There is something otherworldly about this lighthouse.

Her.

Lightkeeper

The ocean's wild, but your eyes are calm
Calling ~~Guiding~~ me home, a beacon in the storm.
Falling...we're falling...
into the crash of the tide,
~~our hearts open wide.~~

Windowpanes streaked with rain
~~Rain on the windows~~
and the waves ~~sea~~ swelling close
like ~~it knows~~ they know
what we've done.
You light the lantern anyway,
AND You say, "let the ships see,
let them stay."

And the storm keeps raging
but this is where we ~~rest~~ stay
In the lightkeeper's room,
where the sky kisses the ~~sea~~ waves
and you reach for me
And you smile
The kind of smile
That makes the ~~whole~~ ocean hold its breath.

I'll remember every kiss
every touch
every whisper
I'll remember this
~~until the light fades.~~
I'll remember that you're the lighthouse
And I'm the storm
And you'll always, baby, you'll always
guide me home.

And we'll leave the lamp burning
long after the storm strays.
Just in case.
Just in case
someone else needs to find the way.

cut this? might be overkill

# Chapter 28

## BLAKE

*Take it from me*

WYATT SAID SEX WOULD CHANGE everything. He was right. It has.

Because now it's all we do.

Two, three, sometimes four times a day. It's an obsession, a drug I can't get out of my system, and I know he feels the same intoxicating pull. We spend most of the time in his bed or mine. Or on the dock. The boathouse. The boat. The kitchen counter. Pretty much anywhere the security cameras don't cover. Which means all doors, entrances, and property boundaries are off-limits, but that's fine. We don't need to fuck on the front porch or against the back doors. Plenty of other surfaces to go around.

It's been a full week since we rode out the storm in the lighthouse, and these days, it would take extraordinary measures to lure me out of bed. I don't even think you could pay me. We've barely left the house since except for a couple of trips to the library and one lunch with the Spencers.

When they found out Wyatt and I have been hooking up,

Little Spencer shrieked so loudly, everyone on the patio thought he was getting attacked. Of course, the Spencers insist that this "love connection" was Darlie's doing.

"We told you," Big Spencer said smugly. "Darlie loves love. She wants everyone to have the happy ending she was deprived of."

"Well, there's lots of happy endings happening over at our place. Two this morning alone," Wyatt replied with a cheeky wink, at which point I punched him in the arm while the Spencers howled.

Tonight, we're in Wyatt's bed. I'm naked and sprawled on my stomach near the foot of the bed, because that's where he was bending me over when he made me come so hard, I almost blacked out. He's got his boxers on as he sits at the headboard, leaning against a mountain of pillows and strumming his guitar.

My eyes flutter closed as he sings, his husky voice echoing through the bedroom. This song… Wow. The lyrics are hauntingly beautiful.

It takes a second for me to register what the song is about, and when it hits me, my eyelids pop open. "You're singing about the lighthouse."

He nods, looking uncharacteristically bashful. It's adorable. "Is that all right?"

A smile tugs on my lips. "Of course it's all right. Nobody's ever written a song about me."

"Who says it's about you?" he taunts good-naturedly. "Could be about the other ten girls I've fucked in lighthouses."

"Oh really?"

I lazily shift onto my side, and those green eyes home in on the breast that's now exposed. My nipple tightens under his thorough appraisal.

"No," he finally says, his eyes softening. "You're my only lighthouse girl."

A ribbon of warmth unfurls inside my chest. When he looks at me like that...when his voice gets rough and smoky like that...I can almost convince myself that he's falling in love with me.

But I know that's just a foolish dream. Wyatt doesn't do love, at least not the kind of love that I want. He craves the love he can sing about, the love that comes with pain and angst and heartache. I'd never say this to him, because I worry he'll take offense, but part of me believes that's the real source of his commitment issues. Why he can be so present during sex, so emotionally connected, only to run away afterward. Because I suspect he's not running from something—he's running *to* it. He *wants* to feel the tragic, soul-crushing emotions that come from a love denied.

I want the love that I can feel safe in. I might've joked about me being the one to break his heart, but we both know that isn't true. If anyone's heart is getting shattered, it's going to be mine when he leaves me. When he finds a new muse. A new girl to sing about. A new girl to gaze at with those hooded eyes when he's moving inside her.

My chest clenches painfully. I don't want him to leave me. I want to stay with him in this room forever.

"Keep going," I urge when I realize he's no longer singing.

"Those are all the lyrics I've got right now," he says absently. "The rest will come."

"Do you think this lighthouse song is the one? *The song*?"

"I don't know." He's pensive. "It might be." He's still watching me. "Get on your back."

I do what he asks, because, well, because I want to. Not just to please him—I know anything we do in here will make me feel good.

His eyes trail over my naked body, eliciting pinpricks of heat.

"Squeeze your tits," he says softly.

Swallowing, I cup my breasts, giving one nipple a light pinch that sends a jolt of pleasure through me. Wyatt continues to play a slow melody on the guitar, but his intense gaze never leaves me.

"Move your hand between your legs. Play with yourself."

I lower my hand to the juncture of my thighs and strum my clit while he strums his guitar. Pleasure skates through me as I tease myself, touching myself for him.

A lock of hair falls onto his forehead, but he doesn't push it away. He keeps playing. Keeps watching me. My hips rock faster, chest rising and falling as my breathing quickens. He knows I'm getting close, because his eyes smolder.

"Give it to me," he says.

My fingers swipe over my clit, stroking, pressing harder, but it's not enough. Because we just had sex, and my body knows it can feel *so much better* if he's involved. As good as this feels, it's like eating one small dish when there's a whole buffet in front of you.

"Give it to me," he repeats.

"Take it from me," I say, and his eyes flare with desire.

He pushes the guitar aside and then he's crawling toward me, his bare chest and strong shoulders hovering over me. Two long fingers slip inside my pussy. He pushes them in deep while I rub my clit, and a moment later, I come with a sharp cry, my inner muscles contracting around his fingers.

"There you go, freckles. You're squeezing my finger so tight. You want my cock again?"

"Please," I beg, and then he goes to get a condom and we're off to the races again.

Afterward, we find ourselves in yet another position on his bed. Now I'm the one reclined against the stack of pillows, Wyatt's head in my lap. His eyes are closed, breathing steady as I gently stroke his hair. I watch him in slumber, my throat tight with emotion. I let him sleep, because it's such a rare occurrence for him.

I lie there and think about how much I don't want this to end, even though I know it's inevitable. We agreed it would be.

But he's here now, and as long as he is, I want nothing more than to keep feeling this pure, unfettered contentment as Wyatt Graham sleeps in my arms.

# Chapter 29

## BLAKE

*Is this growth?*

I COME DOWNSTAIRS THE NEXT morning to find breakfast on the eat-in counter. And not just any breakfast. A stack of golden, steaming pancakes ringed by fresh berries and a drizzle of syrup. Beside the plate is a mug of coffee, a tall cup of OJ, and a candle.

"What is this?" I exclaim.

Wyatt looks up from the stove, spatula in hand.

"Happy birthday," he says gruffly.

Joy explodes in my chest. This is… I can't even… Embarrassment floods my cheeks when my eyes well up. Oh my God. I *cannot* cry. That'll only give the impression that I'm starting to see this thing between us as something more.

And I'm not.

Not really.

No matter how much Annaliese teases me, I am *not* in love with him. The only reason I've got tears in my eyes right now is because I'm touched. This is a sweet, thoughtful gesture, and I'm *touched.* That's it.

Despite my vehement internal monologue, my heart flutters treacherously, and I'm blinking a bit too fast as I approach the counter.

"You didn't have to do this," I tell him.

"Of course I did. It's your twenty-first birthday. Now sit down and eat."

I plop down on a stool and reach for the fork, but before I can cut into the pancakes, I notice they're dotted with tiny dark-brown spots.

A frown furrows my brow. "What are these dots?"

Wyatt gets a sheepish look. "Um. Freckles. Chocolate-sauce freckles."

It takes every ounce of emotional restraint not to blubber like a baby and soak my breakfast with tears. But this might be the sweetest thing anyone has ever done for me.

Noticing my expression, Wyatt grumbles under his breath. "Don't make a thing of it, Logan. It's just a birthday breakfast."

I can only nod, because my throat is too tight to release any words.

His gesture stays with me all morning, circling my heart in a warm, gooey aura of pure joy. And my spirits only soar higher when I'm upstairs changing into my bathing suit and a much-awaited email arrives.

**1 NEW EMAIL**

Dear Ms. Logan,

Attached are the documents you requested. You can also access them via this link. Please consider this ticket resolved.

For future, please deal directly with me regarding these types of requests.

Cordially,

Mary Holmes

"Holy shit," I exclaim, racing outside.

I run to the railing and peer over it. Wyatt is on his usual lounge chair but without the usual cigarette dangling from his mouth. We haven't been to town in a few days, and I think his pack ran out and he's too lazy to replenish.

"Guess what!" I bound down the steps to the dock. "The records office *finally* sent me the documents I've been harassing them about."

"Is this the office that burned down and all the records were lost?"

I grin. Half the time, I wonder if he's actually listening to me or just making up more song-worthy situations in his own head. "It didn't burn down. The catalog was digitized, but there was a data breach, and everything got erased."

"Oh, right. That was it. My reason was better."

"Your reason was fiction! Anyway, they luckily didn't destroy any of the originals, but it's taking them forever to redigitize, and the woman who runs the department was refusing to dig through the boxes for me, remember?"

"Right. So she finally caved?"

"Oh. No," I say dismissively. "I convinced one of her staff to do it, and now she's pissed. Her email was passive-aggressive to the max. She signed it *cordially*. But she still sent the documents. On my birthday too! It's, like, the best present ever!"

His lips twitch. "I mean, I thought my freckle pancakes were pretty good."

"They were also the best. But listen to this..." I pause for dramatic effect, which summons that smile he was fighting. "Raymond Loughlin did hook up with Darlie's sister, Dolly. In fact," I say triumphantly, "he married her!"

"No shit."

"Yes. Their marriage certificate was filed in a county on the

California side of Tahoe. They were married six months after the date on Darlie's death certificate. Which is close enough to when Raymond was with Darlie that it stands to reason he and Dolly really were having an affair." I'm brimming with excitement as I pace the dock. "And I also have a purchase agreement for a house in Reno, but then they sold that and listed their forwarding address as a place in Albany. Do you know what *that* means?"

"Do I *want* to know?"

"The game's afoot!" I declare. "And it's going to New York. Digitally anyway. I'm moving my search efforts to New York."

"Gonna flood all those unsuspecting counties with your information requests?"

"Oh, fuck yes. I need to grab my laptop—"

I stop when I notice a familiar boat approaching. Perfect. It's the Spencers. At least *they'll* appreciate these new developments.

"Guys," I holler. "I might've tracked down Dolly!"

"How the hell did you do that?" Big Spencer asks after they cut the engine ten feet from our dock, their boat bobbing in the water. "Mary at the records office refused to budge no matter how much we flirted."

"Because you are *terrible* at flirting," Little Spencer informs his partner. "Like, god-awfully bad."

"Oh, and it worked when you tried with her? Do we have those records, Spencer?" Big Spencer lifts a hand to his forehead and mimes searching for something. "I don't see those records anywhere."

Little Spencer has the decency to look abashed. "Fine. We were both abysmal at wooing Mary."

"Nobody can woo Mary," I assure them. "I recruited her underling Kyle."

Big Spencer heaves a sigh. "Of course it's a Kyle. Kyles are so dumb. They'll do anything for pussy."

His partner snorts. "Says the gay man who has no idea what straight men will do for pussy."

"I'd dig through a few dusty boxes for pussy," Wyatt offers, and I turn to glare at him. "I mean, not *any* pussy," he amends. "Yours, obviously."

The Spencers howl with laughter.

I spend the next few minutes filling them in on everything I managed to uncover this week while Little Spencer gasps and *oohs* at the appropriate moments and Big Spencer nods along and not ironically.

As Little Spencer and I dissect the Raymond and Dolly marriage bomb, I notice Wyatt smirking at us, but there's also an odd gleam in his eyes.

"What?" I grumble at him.

He pushes his sunglasses onto his nose. "Nothing. I just find you guys entertaining. I feel like I'm watching a talk show with two overly enthusiastic morning hosts, only they're not annoying."

Little Spencer gasps again. "That's the nicest thing anyone's ever said to me."

"Ever?" his partner says dryly.

"Well, today." He spins back to me. "You should come on the podcast!" Another gasp flies out. "You should be my cohost!"

"Uh-huh, okay."

"I mean it," he insists.

"I don't think I'm interesting enough to be on a podcast."

"You wouldn't be talking about your own life," Wyatt points out, and I can't believe he's entertaining the idea. Any venture with the Spencers feels like it would be exhausting. "You'd be discussing actual topics. You know, like hauntings and vampires or whatever the hell your thing is about." He directs the last part at the Spencers.

"I don't know," I say, shrugging.

"At least agree to a guest appearance," begs Little Spencer. "We can record an episode for the Darlie mystery. And if we have crazy chemistry, then maybe we'll do more."

"Sure, I'd do that," I say, because why not. I wouldn't mind chatting about Darlie.

But I have no intention of making it a regular occurrence, especially since the podcast has a video component. Next to Spencer's larger-than-life personality, I'll probably come off as the most boring, unimpressive person on the planet. Plus, the idea of being on camera and uploading it to the internet for all to see makes me break out in hives. I feel more comfortable in the background. The support staff, if you will. Not everybody needs to be the CEO.

Little Spencer breaks out in a broad smile. "Excellent! What are you two up to tonight?"

"Oh, I can't tonight. I'm going out to get drunk."

"No, she's not," Wyatt says immediately.

I ignore him. "Today's my birthday," I tell the Spencers. "Guess who's twenty-one, gentlemen?"

Their faces light up.

"It's your birthday?" Little Spencer's outraged gaze shifts to Wyatt. "And you're not letting her celebrate?"

"She can celebrate here," he says firmly. "At the house. I already told her she's more than welcome to invite whomever she wants and drink whatever she wants. In the house. Where I can keep an eye on her."

"First of all—Daddy," Big Spencer says in a sultry voice.

Wyatt rolls his eyes.

"Second of all," I interrupt, "I don't need you to keep an eye on me. But if you insist on it, you can keep an eye on me in a bar," I finish sweetly.

"Yeah, but then that means *I* can't drink. I'll need to stay sharp to make sure you're okay and that nobody's taking advantage."

"Got it. So I can't go to a bar because *you* want to drink on *my* birthday."

"Exactly," Wyatt says. Then he sighs. "Okay, I just heard it out loud. Let's go to the bar."

And that's how we end up at a karaoke joint in town later, watching Big Spencer and Little Spencer perform a duet of Mollie May and Stylo Lewis's latest collaboration—with both of them singing Mollie May's part.

"How is this song so good?" I shout over the music. The melody is so catchy that I can't stop dancing along. I have both arms thrust in the air, one hand gripping my third fruity cocktail of the night. I'm more than a little tipsy. Veering into very drunk territory, in fact.

"My mom wrote it." Wyatt leans in so I can hear him better. I think he's on his way to drunk too, because his green eyes have taken on a hazy glow.

"Seriously?" I exclaim.

Then I wonder why I'm surprised. It's Hannah frickin' Graham. The woman is downright remarkable. She can sing circles around most people—her performance at Gigi's wedding didn't leave a dry eye in the house—yet she chooses to remain behind the scenes and just write banger after banger for other people. Hannah claims she doesn't like the stress of performing, but I can only imagine the level of stardom she would've reached if she'd chosen to write *and* perform her own music.

"Your mom is incredible," I tell Wyatt.

"I know." He takes a quick sip of his beer, his features straining.

"Goddamn it."

"What?"

"Just realized my sister was right. I need to be nicer to Mom. I'm such a prick when it comes to this music thing. She doesn't deserve me snapping every time she tries to help me."

I mock gasp. "Oh my God! Wyatt! Is this growth?"

He sighs. "I think it's growth."

The song ends, and the Spencers amble off the stage and rejoin us. We do shots because Big Spencer orders a round for the birthday girl, and then we do more shots because Little Spencer orders a round for the birthday girl, and then more shots because Annaliese arrives and buys another round. And then Eddie decides, yes, he too must be part of the shot buying.

By the time Wyatt and I pile into an Uber and head back to the lake house, we're both annihilated. So plastered that neither of us can see straight, speak without laughing, or sit in the back seat for more than three seconds without sucking each other's faces off.

I feel bad for the driver, or at least I would if I was capable of feeling anything other than horny, because anytime Wyatt is kissing me, I can't concentrate on anything but the ache between my thighs.

It takes us three tries to punch in the gate code. We stagger out of the Uber a few minutes later, and then it takes us four tries to get the alarm code right. Finally, the front door swings open and we stumble inside, laughing our asses off. Which lasts about two seconds because suddenly we're kissing again. Wyatt pushes me up against the wall, his greedy mouth latching on to my neck. My head spins as he kisses and explores my heated flesh, dragging his tongue up the side of my throat.

When he reaches my ear, he growls, "Need to fuck you."

Somehow, we make it up to his room, which smells like fresh

citrus and pine cleaner. "The house mouse was here," I mumble between kisses. "I mean mouse. No, I mean *man*. The houseman was here."

"Harry," he mumbles back. "I mean Herny. Horny?"

Laughing hysterically, we fall onto the bed in an alcohol-induced sex fog, and then he's peeling off my tube top, my shorts, my underwear, his pants. It all comes off and he's kissing his way down my body until his mouth finds me. Devouring. Licking and sucking and moaning against my clit.

"I could eat this pussy for the rest of my life," he mutters as I rock my hips against his eager mouth.

It takes me a record-breaking two and a half minutes to come, the unexpected orgasm blowing through me in a gust of ecstasy that makes me tremble. With one last lick and eyes burning with satisfaction, he climbs up my body and pushes his cock inside me.

When he fills me to the hilt, his groan is one of relief and utter appreciation. "So tight, baby. So perfect. Want to be in here forever."

God, I want him here forever too. I wrap my legs around him, my heels digging into his ass.

"Faster," I beg.

He quickens the pace, plunging into me, over and over and over again, while I rake my fingernails down his back and sink my teeth into his shoulder. I don't know what's happening, but I'm like a feral animal. I think I drew blood with my nails.

Wyatt grunts in pain, and then he's grinning down at me, grabbing both my hands with one of his. He locks my wrists together and thrusts them over my head.

"Enough of that," he chides.

"Can't handle a little pain?" I taunt.

"I can handle pain. Just rather make you scream."

He withdraws until only his tip remains at my opening while my pussy tries to cling tight and not let him escape. Then, without warning, he slams back in and fucks me hard enough to make me see stars. The bed is shaking, headboard banging against the wall. It's raw, unfiltered, pure animal heat.

"Why does this feel so good?" he moans in dismay.

"I don't know," I answer helplessly, and then I squeeze my eyes shut and come.

Wyatt curses as I spasm around him. "Oh Jesus. That's gonna make me come too."

He drives into me one last time, pressed deep inside as he finds his release. Groaning, he collapses on top of me, and I wrap my arms around him, and we both start laughing, because holy shit, that was intense.

I glance over at the clock, only to find there's no clock. I blink, disoriented all of a sudden. Then I say, "This...isn't the blue room. I think we're in the mountain room," and Wyatt laughs even harder.

# Chapter 30

## WYATT

*Look at us, being so adult*

I WAKE UP IN AN unfamiliar room on an unfamiliar bed to a familiar voice speaking in the doorway.

"We might have a problem."

I look at Blake and squint in agony against the morning light. Christ. It feels like knives stabbing me in the eyeballs. I dig the heels of my palms into my eye sockets and groan.

"Yeah, a very big problem," I mumble. "I don't think I've ever been this hungover. How are you standing in the sunlight and not dying a slow death?"

"Oh, I'm dying. There is literally a hamster running around in my brain and smashing against my skull."

"Literally a hamster?"

"Yes, literally. But we have a bigger problem than that."

"All right, hold on. Let me open my eyes really slowly."

I try it, a fraction of an inch at a time, until finally I manage to crack open my eyelids and not collapse in excruciating pain.

"So I thought maybe I peed my pants," she starts.

"Okay, not where I thought this conversation was going."

"Because I woke up in, like, a puddle—"

"If you're trying to turn me on, this is not the right strategy."

"I'm trying to say we didn't use a condom last night, and all your...um...offerings were everywhere."

I freeze. "Everywhere, like I came on your stomach?"

She shoots down the hope. "Nope."

"Shit."

"I know."

"And you're not on the pill." It's not a question. That's the first thing she told me when we started hooking up. She went off the pill two years ago because it gave her migraines, so we've been using condoms. Diligently. Until last night, it appears.

"Nope, not on the pill," she confirms before offering a sliver of hope. "But I did check my app, and I'm ninety-five percent certain we're out of the danger zone."

Relief trickles through me. "Really?"

"I mean, it can't give us the *exact* moment of ovulation, but I think that window has passed and we should be okay."

"You sure the egg isn't just hanging around in there for funsies?"

She snickers. "It does for a day or two, I think. And even though I'm pretty sure we're safe, I'd probably feel more comfortable if we drove into town and got, like, Plan B or something. Can we do that?"

I'm already sliding out of bed. "I'll grab a shower and meet you downstairs in ten."

Thirty minutes later, we're on the road, and I'm feeling a little more human after two cups of coffee. Sunglasses protect my eyes from the knives in the sky AKA the sun, and Blake protects us both by not putting on any music.

"Look at us, being so adult," she says from the passenger seat.

I chuckle. "Well, I believe I probably speak for both of us when I say we don't want a little Graham baby running around."

"Logan baby," Blake corrects.

"Sorry to inform you, but you'll have to fight my dad for the title."

"You'll have to fight mine."

"We can let them fight each other."

"Deal."

When I stop at a red light, I reach across the console and cover her hand with mine. "I'm really sorry," I say softly. "I fucked up."

Blake shakes her head. "No, we both did."

"We had sex without a condom. That's on me."

"It's on both of us," she says firmly. "I'm responsible for my own birth control."

"Yes, but there're other things that can happen when you don't use protection. And I just want you to know, I don't have any of those things, and I'm happy to go to a clinic with you to prove it."

She smiles. "I appreciate that, but I wasn't worried."

The light turns green, and I drive through the intersection. The pharmacy is at the end of the block, but it doesn't have a parking lot, and the street is packed with cars. I find an empty spot two blocks past the CVS, and Blake and I hop out of the Jeep and start walking.

I reach for her hand again, and she notes our intertwined fingers with a wry smile.

"Everyone's showing up tomorrow," she says glumly.

"I know."

We've sort of been avoiding this subject. The reality that all the families will be here tomorrow and we won't be able to keep doing what we're doing. No more daily sex marathons. No more cuddling on the couch. My chest clenches. The idea of not touching her for a whole month is worse than this hangover.

"We're going to have to find ways to sneak around while they're here," I tell her.

"Ooh, scandalous. I thought you said we should cool it when the families come."

I stroke her knuckles with my thumb. "Changed my mind. Unless you don't want to?"

"Oh, I want to."

"Good."

"Honestly, I doubt most of them will even notice if we sneak off here and there. The dads are clueless, and the Golden Boys are too obsessed with themselves." Blake purses her lips. "What we'll need to watch out for is the women. My mom. Gigi."

"Alex," I supply, because Alexandra Tucker can detect a romance like a bomb-sniffing dog.

"Jamie will figure it out instantly," Blake says. "But she'll keep her mouth shut."

I agree. Tucker's eldest daughter knows how to mind her own business. She also happens to be one of my favorite people. Jamie can cut a man down with one word, just like her mother.

"Have you and Alex ever hooked up?"

Blake's question comes out of left field. "What?"

"You're badminton partners," she points out. "And you visit her in New York all the time."

I could lie, but we don't do that with each other. So I shrug and say, "We've made out."

"That's it?" She sounds surprised.

"That's it. And it's always so goddamn awkward. Zero sparks."

"Wait, you've hooked up more than once?" Blake starts laughing. "Even though you're not into each other?"

"Yeah," I admit sheepishly.

"How many times?"

"Maybe, like, three?" I say, thinking about it. "Alcohol has a way of making you doubt yourself. Like, we'd get drunk and look at each other and say, we're both so hot, maybe we *are* attracted to each other. But nope. Always ends the same way. With laughter and regret."

"Laughter and regret? Jeez. You're lucky Alex is drowning in self-esteem."

"That and she's hung up on this hockey player guy."

Curiosity fills Blake's eyes. "Ooh, *who*?"

"Luke's brother. I mean, Ryder," I correct. I always forget my brother-in-law doesn't like anyone calling him Luke. He only lets Gigi and my mother get away with it.

"Are you talking about Owen McKay? Alex told me it was a one-time thing."

"Nah, definitely more than once. Last time I went out drinking with her, she bitched about him the entire time. I think he spurned her. But she might've spurned him first? I'm not sure. I don't get involved. Anyway, Alex is the one we'll have to watch out for."

"And Stella," Blake reminds me. "Maybe Ivy."

"Stella is a menace, so yes. But Ivy is too sweet to pry into other people's sex lives."

We arrive at the pharmacy where I open the door for her, earning me a big smile from Blake. She's always so overjoyed when I do basic things like opening her door or pulling out her chair, which makes me wonder what kind of heathen Isaac Grant was. Jackass definitely didn't deserve her.

We make a beeline for the family planning aisle, only to find the shelf that normally contains the emergency contraceptives is empty.

"Maybe they keep it behind the counter?" Blake says.

"Let's go ask."

To my dismay, when we go to the pharmacist's counter, the white-coated man shakes his head and says, "Sorry. We ran out of stock."

"Can you call the other pharmacies in the area and check if they have any?" Blake asks with a worried frown.

"They're all having the same issue, I'm afraid. There was a shortage due to a supply chain problem, so supplies were already low, and then that jackass running for office decided to make the ban of emergency contraception one of the issues he's running on, and it created a panic in the community. Customers started stockpiling, and now here we are."

Fuck.

Sympathy fills his eyes when he notes our disappointed faces. "We have an order coming in on Monday," he says.

"But today is Saturday," Blake frets. "Will it still be effective on Monday?"

The pharmacist nods. "It's effective up to seventy-two hours. When did the intercourse take place?"

I choke down a nervous laugh. I'm twenty-four years old, yet the word *intercourse* still makes me uncomfortable. "About eight hours ago?"

"You're still within that window then. I'm in on Monday morning. If you'd like to leave your number with me, I can set a box aside when the shipment arrives, and you can come pick it up."

"Thank you," Blake says gratefully while the pharmacist slides a pen and paper across the counter.

We leave the pharmacy empty-handed, Blake's teeth worrying her bottom lip the entire walk back to the Jeep.

"Hey, it's going to be fine," I assure her. "That is just the backup anyway. We're not in the ovulation window, remember?"

She nods slowly. "Right."

"It'll be fine, freckles." I take her hand and lace our fingers together. "Come on. Let's go home and clean up for the circus."

**BADMINTON BLOOD MATCH**

TOURNAMENT BRACKET

ROUND 1

| | | |
|---|---|---|
| ALLIE + LOGAN | VS | DEAN + GRACE |
| GARRETT + HANNAH | VS | GRAY + STELLA |
| AJ + JAMIE | VS | ALEX + WYATT |
| BLAKE + BEAU | VS | GIGI + RYDER |
| TARA + KATE | VS | TUCKER + SABRINA |

# Chapter 31

## BLAKE

*It's going to be a long month*

FIRST RULE OF TAHOE FAMILY Summer: Come and go as you please.

Second rule of Tahoe Family Summer: Stay as long as you like.

Third rule? Embrace the chaos.

Because that's what it is. Every summer, like clockwork, pure chaos descends on the lake house. It's bound to happen when there are so many people and so many of us in our late teens and early twenties. Which means there will be partying. There will be drinking. There will be trash-talking. And there will be—apparently this year—a fuck ton of badminton.

The brackets are locked in, but my partner isn't getting in until this evening. He's been texting all morning saying we need to find a quiet place to discuss strategy *the nanosecond* he arrives. And yes, he said nanosecond.

The Tuckers arrive first, Alex strutting inside like the supermodel she is. Dark glossy hair, big brown eyes, and the kind of body most women would kill for. Huge boobs, tiny waist, perky ass, long legs. And it's all natural, every inch of her from top to bottom. She's the spitting image of her mother, Sabrina, while her older sister, Jamie, inherited their father's auburn hair and is equally stunning.

They greet us with hugs and birthday wishes for me, Alex pulling me aside to say, "Come up when I'm unpacking. I brought you something from Milan."

"And I brought you something from Paris," I reply with a grin. "Because I missed *your* birthday." Hers was in the spring.

"How's your summer been?" Sabrina asks, looking from me to Wyatt. "You two been getting along?"

"Splendidly," he says lightly, and Sabrina narrows her eyes.

Shit. Can she sense it somehow? Does she know we've been having sex?

Luckily, Tucker calls his wife over, and her attention shifts to him. Then the four of them climb upstairs to get settled in their rooms.

My parents arrive a couple hours later with Wyatt's parents in tow. They all took the same flight from Boston.

"Happy birthday!" Mom says, throwing her arms around me in a tight embrace. When she pulls back, she searches my face and then smiles. "You look good. Tanned and rested."

My dad hugs me next before giving me the same once-over. "Are we over the potato yet?"

I roll my eyes. "We were over the potato the day his potato sex tape leaked."

Dad snorts. "That's my girl." He glances at my mom when she reaches for her suitcase. "I've got it, gorgeous. Go hang out with our girl."

Dad and Garrett lug their bags up to their respective suites. Most of the parents have a suite, while the Connellys and Davenports always share the apartment above the boathouse. Only the Davenports are coming this year, with AJ representing the Connellys solo. His parents, Brenna and Jake, are spending the summer in Boston to help out Brenna's dad who just had knee surgery.

AJ and the others aren't arriving until tomorrow, though. Today we're waiting only for the Di Laurentises, who show up after dinnertime looking like their perfect blond selves, each one more exquisite than the last.

I greet Beau with a big hug. I haven't seen him since the semester ended at Briar, and I missed those sparkling green eyes and dazzling smile. He releases me to exchange a quick side hug with Wyatt.

"Hey, dude," Beau says. "Where's Gigi?"

"She and BIL are flying in from Dallas tomorrow morning."

Everybody congregates on the main floor. Except for Tucker, who always unpacks every single item in his and Sabrina's suitcases because "we can't stay for a month somewhere, darlin', and live out of a suitcase," he tells Alex, who laughs and says, "My whole life is out of a suitcase, Daddy."

"Doesn't make it right," he chirps.

The rest of the men stomp down to the dock and crack open their beers, their boisterous laughter echoing in the warm evening air and wafting up to the deck. Wyatt is with them, and I keep stealing glances at him from the upper deck, where Jamie is telling me about her recent case. A defense attorney, she practices criminal law. So does her mother, except Sabrina doesn't represent criminals but tries to get the wrongfully accused out of prison. Her innocence organization has had some high-profile convictions overturned, making her one of the most sought-after attorneys in the country.

In a nearby chair, Beau's sister Ivy is on her phone, texting with Stella Davenport. They'll both be freshmen at Briar this fall, and I wonder if their friendship will survive this new life stage. The two of them are inseparable, but they couldn't be more different. Ivy is pure as the driven snow, while Stella is a born hell-raiser. College has a way of making you gravitate toward like-minded people.

"I'm so bummed Hudson isn't here this summer," Ivy tells her mom after she puts away her phone. She's referring to Hudson Fitzgerald, whose family isn't joining us this year either.

Even though all the families are close enough that the hockey kids could probably call themselves cousins, Ivy and the Fitzgeralds actually *are* cousins. Her aunt Summer is Dean's sister. Summer is a fashion designer and has a new line out, so she and her husband are dragging their five kids all over Europe this summer to attend her international shows. Which, honestly, doesn't sound like a chore.

I'm in the middle of complaining to Jamie and Alex about my toaster battle with Isaac, who still refuses to surrender Hot Boi, when my phone vibrates with a message from Wyatt. I wait until the girls are distracted before taking a peek.

SONGBOY

I'm gonna bend you over that railing after everyone is asleep and drill you from behind.

I almost choke on my tongue, a cough flying out. On the dock, his head tips up toward me, and I swear I see him wink. Gulping, I type back a warning.

Stop.

SONGBOY

Stop what? Thinking about your pussy?

Impossible.

Oh boy.

It's going to be a long month.

# Chapter 32

## BLAKE

*Pics or it didn't happen*

THE BADMINTON TOURNAMENT IS AS intense as I expected it to be. If it were any other family, this might be a pleasant day of some sports, some beer, and some laughter. But this is *my* family, and every single one of them is competitive to the extreme. Aggressively so.

My dad and Allie win their heat against my mom and Dean, which only intensifies the hostilities because Dean is the king of tantrums, and when Garrett and Hannah come from behind to knock out Gray and Stella in an upset for the ages, the entire playing field goes wild.

The day devolves into a barbecue and drinking session that ends at the firepit with all the younger people gathered on chairs and blankets, getting wasted and skewering marshmallows over the flames. I sit with Alex, Gigi, and Stella, drinking my third glass of white wine and catching up with the girls, while several feet away, Wyatt chats with Gigi's husband and sneaks looks at me.

By the fire, Gray and AJ laugh their asses off about something. Beau sits on an Adirondack chair nearby, talking to AJ's girlfriend, Tara, a petite girl with shiny blond hair and a Disney-princess face.

AJ, Tara, and the Davenports arrived yesterday morning, courtesy of Wyatt, who grabbed them all from the airport, mostly because we needed an excuse for him to stop at the CVS first and pick up our Plan B.

Tara is currently perched on the edge of Beau's chair, leaning in close every time she says something. She touches his arm too, more than once, which raises my hackles.

"Are you seeing this?" Alex murmurs as we watch AJ's girlfriend flirt with Beau.

Beau, of course, doesn't seem to notice how obvious Tara is being, because men are clueless. He's just being his usual lovable self.

"Oh yeah. This girl is shameless," Stella says, rolling her eyes.

I glance over. "Is she?"

I don't know Tara well at all. She and AJ started dating freshman year at Briar, but this is her first time coming to Tahoe with him. He clearly adores her, though. He's been doing things for her all day. Refilling her drinks, bringing her snacks, always asking if she needs anything.

"Shameless," Stella confirms. "And AJ is *such* a simp for her, which she takes full advantage of. Ivy and I were talking about it the other day. Like, after two years, he still can't figure out she's using him."

"Using him for what?"

Stella shrugs. "Clout, probably. His dad's won two Stanley Cups."

"Your dad won a cup too," I point out. "She could've gone for Gray."

"Nah, Tara isn't stupid. Gray is a forever fuckboy," Stella says of her brother. "Everyone knows that."

I glance toward the fire at the dark-haired guy. With his bronzed skin, piercing eyes, and killer smile, Gray could get any girl he wants.

And he does. Often. Stella's right. Of the three Golden Boys, Gray's the one I can never see settling down.

"If she's angling for a ring on her finger and to marry into hockey royalty, she knows her best bet is AJ," Stella says, cynic that she is. "Poor dumb Connelly. She'll cheat on him first chance she gets."

"I mean, she already has," Ivy chimes in from the other end of our blanket. Beau's sister is so sweet and unassuming, I sometimes forget she's there. "Remember Christmas in Miami?"

"What happened in Miami?" Alex asks curiously.

"Oh shit, we never told you about that?" Stella grins. "So Ivy and her brother and AJ and Tara come to Miami with us over the holidays to spend a few days at my grandparents' place. Tara says she has some sorority sisters down there and disappears for the entire day, supposedly to hang out with them."

"But," Ivy pipes up, "we already knew from stalking her IG page when she first got together with AJ that she has an ex who lives in Miami. We saw all their pictures before she deleted them."

"So we're all supposed to go out to dinner, but this bitch just disappears and then strolls into the restaurant forty-five minutes late—"

"After AJ's been trying to text her for hours," Ivy says.

"Smelling like cologne that definitely wasn't AJ's," Stella finishes, "and thinking no one notices. Please." She mimics a high voice. "*Oh my God, you guys, traffic was crazy.*"

Ivy giggles. "And Stella goes, *traffic doesn't leave bite marks, sweetie.*"

Alex and I snicker. "You are such a bitch," Alex informs Stella.

"Oh, I'm more than a bitch. I'm a total cunt," Stella drawls, and we all howl with laughter. "Anyway, so she tells this *insane* story about her sorority's sister's dog getting too excited when it was greeting her, and that's why she had a bite mark on her neck."

"And AJ's just sitting there, nodding along," Ivy says, sighing.

"This dumbass believed every word." Stella again. "She's babbling, making up shit about exuberant dogs, and AJ's like, oh man, some dogs really need obedience training, huh?"

I sigh too. Why are men so blind when it comes to toxic women?

"Best Christmas I've had in years," Stella says, grinning wickedly.

Our attention is diverted when we hear AJ calling out to his girlfriend. "Hey, babe, get over here!"

Everyone but him notices how reluctant she seems to slide off the arm of Beau's chair. When she joins AJ, he wraps both arms around her from behind and kisses her neck, and to Tara's credit, she does tip her head back to meet his lips for a kiss. Then again, she just spent the last hour flirting with his best friend, so...her pity kisses mean nothing in my eyes.

I get up and brush a twig off my shorts, then make my way to the now-solo Beau. When I reach him, he tugs me into his lap and slings an arm over my shoulder. There's nothing romantic about it, but considering I was having sex with Wyatt only a few nights ago, it sort of feels like I'm doing something wrong.

Beau flashes that beautiful smile of his, the one that never fails to make you take a second look. He truly is one of the best-looking people I've ever seen in my life, though I suppose it's in the genes. His father is basically a male model. His mom is a gorgeous actress. His aunt could stop traffic. Both his sisters are stunning—Ivy is the ethereal fairy-princess ballerina who belongs in live-action Disney movies, and Kate, who's only fifteen and should be going through her gangly teenage phase, could already sign an exclusive modeling contract.

"You've barely spoken to me all day," Beau complains. "Should

I be insulted?"

"I mean, it's hard to speak when our parents are vowing to murder each other over badminton."

"Yeah, that was intense."

I feel my skin prickling as if someone is watching me, and sure enough, I find Wyatt's gaze on me when I turn my head. He's still talking to Ryder, but he's got his phone in hand now, typing something.

Seconds later, mine buzzes in my back pocket.

Beau grins when he feels my butt vibrating. "Not gonna check that?"

"Nah. Probably my mom saying they're going to bed."

I swipe Beau's plastic cup from his hand and take a gulp, trying to cool myself. Wyatt's heated gaze is making me feel flushed. But the beer has been warmed by the fire and only spikes my body temperature.

"So listen," I tell Beau. "The girls and I had front-row seats to the show, and...you might not want to be so friendly to Tara."

His forehead wrinkles. "Why? We were just talking."

"*You* were just talking. *She* was having sex with you in her head."

Beau snorts. "Come on."

"Trust me. We all see it."

"She's with AJ."

I tip my head in challenge. "According to Stella, it wouldn't be the first time Tara strayed."

"If you're talking about the Miami thing, they worked that out."

"By worked out, do you mean she made up a bullshit story and he bought it?"

"Pretty much."

"Either way, she strayed."

"Okay, well, if she's trying to stray with me, that isn't gonna happen." He flashes that boyish, all-American smile again. "I'm a classy boy."

"Just saying, don't encourage her. We were all getting bad vibes."

"Or maybe you're jealous," he counters, winking at me. "Want me all to yourself, huh?"

"Yes. That's exactly it."

His hand brushes mine when I pass his drink back, and I notice his eyes are starting to look out of focus. We sit and chat for a bit until Stella raises the volume of the music playing on the outdoor speakers. The sultry beat snakes into everyone's blood, and soon we're all dancing. Stella and Alex challenge each other to a dance battle while Ivy watches and giggles. In the shadows, Gigi and Ryder sway as if in a world of their own, his intense eyes locked on his wife's face. Lord, that man adores her.

AJ and Tara are wrapped all over each other as they move to the beat, and it isn't long before Beau pulls me off his lap and convinces me to dance with him.

Gray joins us, and I take turns dancing with both Golden Boys, all the while feeling Wyatt's green eyes tracking my every move. Maybe it's all the wine I consumed, but I'm feeling more relaxed than usual, allowing myself to get lost in the music. I never dance when I'm sober because I feel too self-conscious, but once I'm loosened up, I love it.

Gray wanders off to get another drink, and Beau closes in again, pulling me tight to his body. I'm startled by how much bulkier he feels. Going into his junior year, I know he's angling for the hockey captain position, and I realize he must be spending a lot of time in the gym and on the ice lately. He's broader now.

I throw my arms up, and he moves in behind me, sliding his hands up and down my hips. It's fun and boozy and we're both breathless, faces flushed. I laugh when he spins me and then tugs me close. In the flashes of firelight, I catch Wyatt's eye, but I can't make out his expression.

I spin around again before tossing my hair over my shoulder. The move inadvertently gives Beau access to my neck, and I falter when he nuzzles it, his mouth ghosting over my skin. Then he thrusts a thigh between my legs, and that's when I realize he's hard.

Beau's lips find my ear. "B... I wanna fuck you."

Shit.

Resting my hands on his shoulders, I try to make a joke of it. "I think someone's had too much to drink."

He counters with, "I think someone is the hottest girl I've ever known in my life." He bites his lip, desire straining his chiseled features. "Let's go somewhere. Boathouse? Sauna? Please."

"Not a good idea," I murmur back, and then I'm saved by Alex, who waves me over to dance with the girls.

I leave a frustrated Beau behind me, feeling pretty frustrated myself. I know he's drunk, but...*fuck*. Why did he have to go there? We've been doing the platonic thing for years now. I assumed the attraction was long gone on his end, same way it is on mine.

Sensing Wyatt's gaze on me again, I edge away from the girls and check the message on my phone.

SONGBOY

Meet me behind the boathouse. I want to make you come.

My pussy clenches. I glance toward the fire, where Wyatt stands in the light of the flames, eyes fixed on me. Fingers trembling, I finally respond.

Ten minutes.

With as much nonchalance as I can muster, I rejoin the girls and dance with them for precisely one and a half minutes before blurting out, "I'm going to pee."

They give me strange looks. "Okay," Stella says.

I casually leave the firepit and make my way to the path. Luckily, the boathouse is on the other side of our sprawling compound. I pick up my pace, passing the lower deck and the dock, and hurry toward the boathouse. The security cameras only cover the doors, so I creep along the side of the dark structure, past the outdoor shower where I caught Wyatt jerking off that day.

The second I round the corner, he steps out of the shadows and wraps his arms around me.

I squeak in surprise, but he muffles the sound with a kiss.

"These fucking shorts," he mutters against my lips. He's already undoing the button and pulling on my tiny zipper. They're so small they barely require one.

"Why are you so angry at my shorts?"

"Because they're keeping me from your pussy," he says, "but also taunting me with it at the same time. I can see your ass cheeks coming out of them."

He wiggles the shorts down my thighs, along with my skimpy panties.

"Not even gonna say hello?" I tease.

He cuts me off with a kiss, his hand already slipping between my legs. Pleasure skates through me as he cups my pussy and massages my clit with his fingertips.

"Lift this leg up," he groans against my mouth.

He smacks my ass cheek, and I obey, lifting my leg and propping it on his hip. It opens me up to him completely, and he pushes two fingers inside me. He curls them slightly, hitting a spot that makes me gasp, and a shock wave ripples through my body.

"I want to fuck you so bad, baby. But we don't have enough time right now, so I want you to pretend my fingers are my cock, okay? Pretend it's me inside you, fucking you so good and deep." He withdraws his fingers, then thrusts them back in. "You feel that?"

I feel *everything*. My hips buck against his talented fingers, my breath caught in my lungs. Normally I would require stimulation to my clit, but this spot he's hitting is so exquisite that I feel the telltale tingles of orgasm fluttering in my core.

"Jesus, you're soaking my hand," he mutters.

He keeps finding that spot with his fingers, and my whole body starts to shake.

"You're gonna make me come," I gasp.

He gives me a low, filthy laugh. "That's my girl."

Then he curls his fingers again and I cry out with release. He cuts off the sound by covering my mouth with his palm while his other hand continues to finger me until I finally go limp and he has to steady me before I topple over.

Wyatt looks mighty pleased with himself as he slips his fingers out, and I moan when he slides them into his mouth and sucks my orgasm off.

"Fucking delicious," he hums.

Catching my breath, I attempt to fix my hair so it doesn't resemble a bird's nest.

"Go," Wyatt tells me. "Before anyone notices we're missing."

My gaze lowers to the very visible bulge at his crotch. "I feel like I shouldn't be leaving you in this condition."

"I'll take care of it later."

I fight a moan. "Pics or it didn't happen."

"If you're good, I'll send a video," he drawls, and then he smacks my ass before I disappear into the shadows.

## MAN CHAT: STEALTH MODE

GRAY DAVENPORT:

Yo wtf is this? You created a new group chat without AJ??

DEAN DI LAURENTIS

His dad's not in it either. This is a Connelly-free zone.

JOHN LOGAN

Good riddance.

JOHN TUCKER

Your jealousy is getting sad, man.

JOHN LOGAN

Don't care. He doesn't respect the best friend hierarchy.

BEAU DI LAURENTIS

Guys I can't be in a new man chat. I can barely keep up with the OG man chat.

DEAN DI LAURENTIS

Don't worry, it's just temporary. We're opening a forum to discuss the girl.

GRAY DAVENPORT

What girl?

GARRETT GRAHAM

Wait, that's what this chat is for? I thought it was to plan a surprise party for Jake's birthday.

JOHN LOGAN

Wow. You would plan a party for him? Why don't you suck his dick too?

GARRETT GRAHAM

I should. He'd probably be grateful and say thank you after, unlike my other best friend who would probably act all petty and insecure.

JOHN TUCKER

I don't like this analogy.

DEAN DI LAURENTIS

Focus. Should someone tell AJ his girlfriend sucks?

GRAY DAVENPORT

Hahahahahaha

BEAU DI LAURENTIS

Yeah, we're not doing that.

GARRETT GRAHAM

It's his business.

DEAN DI LAURENTIS

She hit on Hunter last night.

JOHN LOGAN

Really???

HUNTER DAVENPORT

Why are you dragging me into this, Dean. I told you not to say anything.

GRAY DAVENPORT

Wait, she hit on *my dad* and not me? Wtf

Not that I want her to hit on me.

But still.

GARRETT GRAHAM

Define "hit on."

HUNTER DAVENPORT

I woke up around 2am to grab a glass of water and Tara came into the kitchen in a skimpy outfit and started flirting.

JOHN LOGAN

Flirting how?

HUNTER DAVENPORT

She called me Daddy and said she's always wanted to be a sugar baby.

JOHN TUCKER

Yikes.

HUNTER DAVENPORT

She was drunk. I didn't take it seriously.

DEAN DI LAURENTIS

So which one of the Golden Boys has the honor of telling AJ?

*BEAU DI LAURENTIS HAS LEFT THE GROUP CHAT MAN CHAT: STEALTH MODE*
*GRAY DAVENPORT HAS LEFT THE GROUP CHAT MAN CHAT: STEALTH MODE*

DEAN DI LAURENTIS

Cowards.

# Chapter 33

## BLAKE

*God forbid I might want to hydrate*

WE ARE FLIRTING WITH DANGER, Wyatt and I.

Over the next four days, we manage to hook up without getting caught, though that isn't to say we don't come close. Somehow, we successfully explain our way out of ridiculous situations, and somehow, not a single person, in a group comprising some of the smartest people I've ever met, catches on.

After a particularly risky boathouse blowjob in the middle of the day, Demi Davenport catches me scurrying away, and I pretend I was chasing a bird because, you know, I'd gotten into bird-watching. Which then forces me to look up bird facts later so I can tell everyone about the mountain chickadee at dinner while Wyatt barely contains his laughter.

The next day, we're bolder. With everyone tanning or dozing on the beach and dock, I start jerking him off in the lake. To anyone watching, it looks like we're just chilling, resting our elbows on the floating swim platform, but beneath the water? Hand job galore. I don't let him come, though, and it's ten long minutes before he can safely get out of the water. I *think* I see Stella giving us a funny look that day, but you never know with Stella because of her resting bitch face.

The biggest risk came last night, when Wyatt texted around midnight.

SONGBOY

I haven't slept since the circus arrived, freckles. Come sleep with me.

Way too dangerous. You know we'll do more than sleep.

SONGBOY

Just sleep. I promise.

Please, baby.

I can't deny Wyatt a thing when he calls me baby. Or when he begs. So I snuck out of my room and into his, he held up the blanket to let me crawl underneath, and then he slept in my arms for hours. I crept into the hall at dawn, terrified someone would catch me, but the coast was clear, thank God.

Still, I refuse to take the chance again when he tries to lure me into his room the following night. No way am I pushing our luck.

Beau and I have moved on to the next round in the badminton tournament, and he insists on practicing every morning for at least thirty minutes. You'd think it would be awkward considering he tried to fuck me the night of the bonfire, but things seem normal with us. He apologized the next day, said he was wasted, and went right back to platonic.

When I told Wyatt about it, he raised a brow and told me there's no way it's platonic on Beau's end. "A man doesn't want to fuck you one day and go back to viewing you as a friend the next one," Wyatt warned, but I'm choosing to believe that Beau will let any lingering attraction he feels for me fade. At least I hope he does.

Today I'm spending the afternoon with Mom on the beach. We've claimed two chairs on our little stretch of sand, and I'm filling her in on all the research I've done this summer.

"So these Spencers," she says, "are we sure they're not serial killers?"

"Pretty sure, but you never know."

"And what's this podcast you're doing with them?"

"Oh, I'm not officially doing it. Little Spencer won't stop badgering me to be his cohost, but I only agreed to record a guest episode about Darlie." I glance over with a broad smile. "I'm having *so* much fun with this mystery, Mom. Every time I send an email request for information and they send back a report, it's, like, the most exciting present ever."

I can tell she's trying not to laugh at me. "Your nerdiness knows no bounds, sweetie."

"I know." I shrug ruefully. "Poor Dad. I'm sure he wishes I was cooler. Or into sports."

"Of course not. Your father doesn't care what you do as long as you're happy." She smiles at me. "And clearly the summer of Blake is a success."

I furrow my brow. "I mean, not really. I still have no idea what I want to do after college."

"I don't know... It sort of seems like you do."

The groove in my forehead deepens. "What, like researching stuff? I'm pretty sure 'research assistant' isn't exactly a lucrative career."

"Hey, you never know. This podcast sounds promising too, and that's certainly something that could eventually make you money.

What if it blows up?"

I shift awkwardly. "I don't want that kind of attention."

She flicks up a brow. "Hmm, really. So you don't want the world to know how smart and insightful and captivating you are?"

"Mom, chill. I've spent the summer researching a ghost story. You hyping that up is the equivalent of someone hanging their toddler's artwork on the fridge."

She laughs. "You really need to give yourself more credit."

I shrug in response.

After a beat, Mom's tone turns cautious. "Is there any update on Isaac?"

I sip my water. "Nope. Other than our continued custody battle over Hot Boi."

"You know, we could just buy you another toaster," Mom sighs.

"That's not the point. It's the principle of it. I bought that one, therefore it's *mine*. And he didn't even want that brand," I fume. "He's fighting for Hot Boi, while if it'd been up to him, we would've gotten the dumb toaster with only two slots. *Two*."

"Are you sure you're not hung up on this boy? Because… That was a lot of passion."

"Trust me, it is not passion for Isaac. I don't have feelings for him anymore. I haven't thought about him romantically in months."

We head back to the house for lunch, which is a chaotic affair since we've still got a full house, every bedroom occupied and the boathouse jammed to the gills. There are so many people that we need both the dining room table and the one on the deck to accommodate everyone.

I'm at the outside table next to Beau's sister Kate, polishing off my burger, when I get a text from Little Spencer.

I glance at Wyatt, who's sitting a few chairs down from me.

"Little Spencer says hi."

"Did they go back to New York?" he asks as he reaches for his water glass. "We haven't seen 'em in a while."

"No. End of August, I think. They've just been busy. I'm going over there next week to record the Darlie episode with them."

"These Spencers," my dad says to Wyatt. "They're really not creeps?"

"No, they're just fucking weird," Wyatt answers, and the Golden Boys break out laughing.

Tara, of course, is draped over AJ's lap, but that doesn't stop her from checking out Wyatt every chance she gets, which annoys me. Yes, he looks delicious today—eating lunch shirtless will do that—but this girl can keep her eyes to herself, thank you very much. She's got her own gorgeous boyfriend to ogle. And I mean *gorgeous*. Any son of people as beautiful as Jake and Brenna Connelly is destined to be stunning, but AJ surpasses expectations with his bottomless brown eyes, chiseled features, and dark hair that always falls so artfully on his forehead.

"I love this podcast idea," Gigi pipes up, joining the conversation. "You should do more than a guest episode, Blakey. Do you realize how much money people are making with podcasts these days?"

"Bullshit," AJ says dubiously.

"It's true," she argues. "You can make a killing, especially if you offer a video version. My friend Diana started a cheerleading channel—her videos are like a day in the life of a cheer coach kind of thing, and she also does a weekly podcast for it. She has over two million subscribers and earns four or five figures per video."

My dad whistles. "Jeez." He glances at me. "What are you waiting for, sweet pea? We're a podcasting dynasty now."

I roll my eyes. "Let's see how this guest episode goes first."

"Fine," he grumbles, then scrapes back his chair.

"Where are you going?" I ask.

"Inside to make after-lunch cocktails. Who wants some LMD?" Dad asks the group, and Wyatt chokes mid-sip, spewing water all over his chin.

I diligently avoid his gaze because I know I'll bust out in laughter if I do.

"You okay there?" Gigi asks her twin.

"Fine." He coughs and wipes his face.

"You sure?" Beau says, leaning around AJ so he can grin at Wyatt. "Because from where I'm sitting, you're drinking water. You realize there's beer here, right?"

"God forbid I might want to hydrate," Wyatt says.

"No, Beau's right," Gray chimes in, frowning. "You haven't gotten wasted once since we got here."

"What, we're not cool enough for you anymore?" AJ cracks.

"You were never cool enough for me," Wyatt answers frankly.

"You're hardly smoking too," Gigi suddenly says, eyeing him curiously.

"Trying to quit," he says with a shrug.

Gray snorts. "Since when?"

Another shrug. "Since I heard chicks don't love it."

I clamp my teeth over my lip to keep the big, dumb smile off my face. God. He means me. I thought he wasn't smoking because he was too lazy to drive to town to buy cigarettes. The realization that he stopped for *me* has my heart soaring like a helium balloon.

I help clean up the mess left over from lunch, then pop upstairs to pee and change into a swimsuit. The girls and I wanted to sunbathe for a while, but that plan changes when a message from Wyatt pops up.

SONGBOY

Come take a nap with me.

I abandon the bikini on the bed and slip out the door, my bare feet scampering in the direction of the blue room.

Like I said, I can't deny this man a thing.

# Chapter 34

## WYATT

*Everything you do turns me on*

I OPEN MY EYES TO find the muted wash of afternoon light coming in through the window. Blake is curled up against me, her ass nestled against my groin, her arms trapping my hand against her chest.

Fuck, sleep feels nice.

I never slept properly before this summer in Tahoe, and it's like someone who's been deprived of a vital sense suddenly getting it. Before Blake, my mind kept racing and racing, especially at night, stretching those quiet hours into forever. Now, it feels like someone turned down the volume in my head. The noise is still there if I really listen to it. But I'd rather listen to Blake's steady breathing and the barely audible noises she makes in her sleep.

And it scares the hell out of me, because I can't lie to myself anymore. I can't pretend anymore.

I don't just want her.

I *need* her.

Not only to sleep. But…for everything. The thought of lying in a bed alone again makes my skin itch. The thought of walking into a room and not seeing her engrossed in some nerdy webpage or book evokes a sincere sense of loss. She's an addiction I'm not sure I can break.

Or want to break.

Blake stirs, letting out a tiny sigh. "That was such a good nap."

She rolls over and tilts her face toward mine. Her cheeks are flushed from sleep, brown hair a mess, and my heart squeezes so tight it hurts. She's so pure and unguarded like this. It's beautiful.

She reaches up to stroke my chin, scraping the stubble over it. Her touch sends a shiver through me, and for some reason, my body reacts to that innocent caress.

I bite back a groan. She notices, of course.

"Did that turn you on?" she teases. "Me touching your jaw?"

"Yeah," I admit hoarsely.

"Why?"

"Because everything you do turns me on."

I brush a strand of hair off her cheek, and she smiles. "Your fingers are always so rough."

"I know. I'm sorry. Guitar callouses."

"I like it. I like how it feels on my skin."

She presses her cheek against my hand, rubbing herself on it like a cat. But that just brings her body closer to mine, and I know she can feel how hard I am.

She parts her lips slightly, and I take that as an invitation. I kiss her. Slow at first, teasing, but then her hand slides between us to cup me over my sweatpants, and my control snaps. I deepen the kiss, my tongue plunging, stealing a gasp from her throat.

"Quiet," I murmur.

When she reaches into my pants and pulls my dick out, I still her hand.

"This bed is too squeaky," I remind her. "We can't fuck."

"Who said anything about fucking?" Smirking, she lifts my shirt up and kisses my stomach before moving lower.

She reaches my dick and plants a soft kiss on the tip, followed by a bratty little lick. My hand moves to the back of her head, fingers tangling in her hair.

"We don't have time for teasing," I warn.

"Mmm, really?" She peers up at me, and there's no sexier sight than Blake on her knees with her mouth hovering over my cock. "You're saying you want it fast and hard?"

"I want that hungry mouth sucking me dry."

Smiling, she bends her head, and a low groan slips out when her hot, wet mouth engulfs me, right down to the base. She hums around my shaft, and I feel the vibration in my entire body. Jesus. My hips jerk up involuntarily. She grips my thigh, fingernails digging into my flesh as she moans happily around me.

I smirk down at her. "You like this, don't you? My cock in your mouth?"

She moans again and curls her hand around my base, squeezing hard enough to make me curse. I thrust my hips again, my cockhead touching the back of her throat, and when I feel her swallow around it, I damn near pass out.

"Yeah, just like that." My voice is rough and desperate. "Take it all."

She strokes me as her mouth almost entirely withdraws, then sucks me in again. Deeper. Faster. My jaw clenches as I watch her blow me. As I feel my control slipping.

"You're so good at this, freckles. So goddamn perfect with those lips around me." My grip in her hair tightens. "You want me to come for you?"

"Mmm," she mumbles around my dick.

"You gonna swallow every drop?"

"Mmm."

"That's my good girl." My hips start moving, pleasure building in my balls, skittering up my spine.

Blake's tongue scrapes the sensitive spot under my cockhead on each upstroke. She picks up the pace, determined to get me there, and my head falls back against the pillow, body tensing.

"Jesus, I'm close. Don't stop, baby, don't fucking stop."

She moans again, and so do I. My voice comes out in broken gasps as I hurtle toward release. My body jerks as I spill into her mouth, and she does exactly what I told her. Takes it all, every last drop, her throat working as she sucks me dry. Her lips are swollen and wet by the time she finally lifts her head and looks up at me with a satisfied grin.

My chest is heaving. "Goddamn. You really are a dirty little thing—"

"Wyatt?"

A knock sounds on the door, accompanied by my dad's brusque voice.

We freeze.

"Champ, you in there?"

Blake's eyes widen in panic. She scrambles up so fast that she thumps the night table. Dad and his superhuman hearing don't miss that, of course.

"Oh good, you are. Can I come in?" he asks.

"Shit," I hiss, bolting upright.

I shove my sweatpants over my dick, but I'm still hard, and it's a struggle to get the material over my raging erection.

Blake dives off the bed as the doorknob starts turning.

"Your mom and I were just talking about..."

He enters like a brazen asshole, seconds before Blake hurls herself into the bathroom. She doesn't even manage to close the door, just flings herself behind it, while it stays ajar.

"Oh." Dad stops talking when he notices me on the bed. "You're busy."

His gaze dips to the erection I'm trying to conceal with my hand. I stifle a groan as he quickly backs away.

"Dude," he sighs. "You should really lock your door when you're doing that."

Yeah. I should.

**DI FAMILIA**

DEAN

Children, we do not support your mother's final game. I will be hosting my own event at the same time.

I'm sure it goes without saying, but you will be attending my event.

IVY

Mom, please tell us what to do.

KATE

I don't like the new group chat name. It's dumb.

BEAU

What's the event?

# Chapter 35

## BLAKE

*I'm ready now*

THE FINAL DAY OF TAHOE Games comes and goes. Beau and I do not manage to beat Allie and my dad in the semifinals, which means they move on to the finals, where they utterly destroy Alex and Wyatt. And because they're both sore winners, they proceed to gloat for the rest of the day and then go into town to buy a thousand dollars' worth of steaks. Everyone grumbles when they announce they're hosting a barbecue to celebrate themselves, but the steaks smell so good on the grill that nobody can stay away.

Over the next week, the lake house gets progressively quieter. The Tucker women leave; Jamie and her mom have court cases to get back to, and Alex is jetting off to Saint-Tropez. Tucker remains, as does Dean, but the other adults all head out, leaving the kids behind, and Ryder has to return to Dallas to prepare for hockey training camp.

I hang out with Gigi, Stella, and Ivy, enjoying Stella's wisecracks, most of which are directed at the Golden Boys. She refers to Beau as Mr. Perfect, which annoys the shit out of him, but she's not wrong. He *is* infuriatingly perfect.

Later that night, we congregate on the boathouse roof, the boys passing around a joint while Stella tosses out mocking remarks—some at Tara, which sail right over the blond's head, and others at her brother, who fires them right back at her. She and Gray have a good-naturedly contentious sibling relationship, constantly riding each other. As an only child, I find it entertaining.

Wyatt is hanging out with his dad tonight. They're playing cards inside, and I hope Garrett isn't ragging him too hard about walking in on Wyatt "jerking off" the other afternoon. That was a close call. Close enough that I refuse to take a chance like that again.

I shake my head when AJ offers me the joint. The secondhand smoke is clouding my brain, in fact, so I get up and wander toward the edge of the roof, just close enough to be able to see the water. Not that I have a phobia or anything.

Ugh, fine. I do. Heights terrify me. I can't believe I stood up here last month, prepared to jump off the roof in the dark because Isaac sent me a text that triggered my insecurities.

When my phone vibrates, I pull it out to find a message from Little Spencer, who prefers to text with an unhealthy number of exclamation marks and all caps.

LITTLE SPENCER

Editing the episode now and it is SO FUCKING GOOD!!! Spence thinks it's one of the best episodes we've ever done!!

I quickly type a response.

I can't wait to see/hear it! Send it to me the moment you're done editing?

LITTLE SPENCER

THE EXACT MOMENT!!

I tuck my phone away when Beau joins me, hands burrowed in the pockets of his gray Briar U hoodie. He doesn't speak, quietly staring out at the lake, but I sense the tension radiating from him. I turn to study his profile at the same time as he turns toward me. His light-green eyes convey frustration.

"What's wrong?" I ask him.

"I really want to kiss you right now."

Goddamn it.

I shift in discomfort. "Beau..." I trail off, not sure what else to say.

"Fuck. Sorry." He moves his gaze back to the lake.

I scramble for a way to make this less awkward. "We can't go there" is what I come up with.

Beau cocks his head. "Remind me again why not? Because as I recall, we've already gone there before."

"Almost four years ago," I point out. I can't stop a laugh now. "You waited four years to ask for a repeat?"

"I mean, I thought I made it pretty obvious I would've been down for a repeat any time," he says wryly.

I swallow a rush of unhappiness. I did get that feeling sometimes, but I always ignored it, hoping it would go away. Not because I couldn't see myself going there with Beau—we might've been good together, actually. But that's the problem. I think deep down I knew that choosing Beau would mean he'd try to get deep with me, and I wasn't ready to be seen back then.

I'm ready now.

But maybe the only reason I am is because of *who* is seeing me.

"You're thinking too hard," Beau accuses, sighing.

"I know."

"Why can't we go there, B?" he pushes.

I gnaw on the inside of my cheek, ignoring the sting of pain. "I'm sort of seeing someone."

"Who?" he says in surprise.

"Not someone I'm ready to introduce to the family yet," I lie. "It's still early." I hesitate, because I don't want this hanging over us, unresolved, if I'm single in the future. "But even if he wasn't in the picture, this still wouldn't be a good idea. You and I."

Hurt shadows his eyes. "Why not? Because you're a year older than me?"

"No, I don't care about that. I care about our friendship. You're one of my best friends. I would never want to lose that."

"Hooking up doesn't mean we'd lose it."

"Hooking up always means you lose it."

My own words suddenly echo in my head, evoking a pang of concern. Because if that sentiment is true, what if getting involved with Wyatt just cursed us to a lifetime of awkwardness? Our families will always be friends. That means he'll always be in my life, for better or worse.

Which is an even better reason not to add Beau into the mix.

# Chapter 36

## WYATT

*I never know what I'm doing*

MY DAD IS ONE OF the best people I know. I think that's why the idea of disappointing him has always filled me with crippling anxiety. My whole life, I tried so hard to love hockey the way *he* loves hockey, but it's just not it for me. Never has been. And that has created a disconnect between us.

The worst part? I'm *good* at hockey. Naturally athletic. If I sucked, at least Dad would've been relieved I wasn't out there embarrassing myself on the ice. Unfortunately, I'm talented enough that if I'd put in the work, I probably could've gone pro. I played in high school mostly just to make him happy.

But music is what called to me. By the end of tenth grade, I finally told him I was quitting the team. And because he's a good dad, he didn't freak out. Didn't try to talk me out of it. He simply said I needed to follow my own path. I should've taken that as proof he supported me, but there was always—and still is—that niggling doubt. That fear I've let him down. It's in the back of my mind nearly every time we're together.

This morning, we're working out in the basement gym, Dad spotting me as I lie on the weight bench, lifting heavier than I usually do.

"Damn," he says with a whistle. "Didn't realize you were going so hard this summer."

"I mean, there's not much else to do."

My summer routine has been pretty consistent. Write music, swim, nap, work out, fuck Blake. Repeat.

"Thanks for watching out for Blake while you've been here," he says as he sets the bar back on the rack.

I sit up and roll out my shoulders. "Wasn't much of a chore. She's great."

"When are you heading back to Nashville? Still aiming for the end of the summer.?"

"I think so. But maybe not Nashville. That producer, Tobey Dodson, works out of a New York studio, and he's back in town in September."

"How are you for money?"

I rise from the bench and walk over to the shelf of towels that Houseman Henry comes every few days to launder and replenish. I swipe one and mop up the sweat on my neck.

"I still have a lot left in the trust," I assure him. "Plus the money I make gigging and the cash I've saved from all those construction jobs. To be honest, I've barely touched my trust."

"That's good. Getting paid for gigs means you're a real musician." Dad winks at me, but I don't miss the spark of pride in his gray eyes.

"Yeah. And I make a decent amount on streams and the videos I upload using my ad account."

"Well, if you need any help from me and your mom, just let us know."

I nod, but I don't plan on asking for help any time soon. I'm turning twenty-five in two months. I shouldn't be accepting handouts from my parents anymore. But I appreciate the offer. Not everybody has a safety net like I do, and I would never take that for granted.

We're done in the gym, but before I can go to the stairs, Dad says, "Hold up. I want to show you something."

We bypass the screening room and game area toward what used to be a huge storage room. Now it's a gaping space, all the contents moved out.

"This is where I want to set up your mom's studio. I was hoping you could help me out with it. Pick out equipment and whatever else she needs." He looks sheepish. "I could build you a hockey arena with my eyes closed and fill the locker room with everything you'll ever need, but this isn't my forte."

What I love about my dad is that he's not some blustering macho man who pretends he can do everything. He's able to be humble. Probably because he grew up with a parent who didn't know the meaning of the word. I never liked my grandfather. The rare times we saw him, he came off as phony. Manipulative. I'm reminded of what Blake said about Isaac being shiny. That was Phil Graham too. Shiny on the surface, and then you look closer to find he's all scratched up.

"Sure, I can help." I wrinkle my forehead. "But wouldn't it make more sense to just ask Mom what she wants?"

"I would if it wasn't a birthday surprise," he says with a grin. "She has no clue what I'm up to. I recruited Houseman Henry to empty out this space. He's been moving boxes all summer into the boathouse storage room, a bit at a time."

"*All summer*? How have we not seen him even once?"

"He's like the wind," Dad says solemnly.

"For real."

We spend the next ten minutes walking through the room, going over the logistics of installing a music studio. Later, Dad goes off to drink beers with his friends, and I wander into the kitchen, where I find my mom at the stove.

"I'm making grilled cheese," she says when she spots me. "You want one, honey?"

"Yes, please." I plop down at the counter, smiling as I watch her flip the sandwich in the pan.

It reminds me of when Gigi and I were little. Whenever Mom was cooking, Gigi would always hurry off to watch hockey with Dad in the den while I'd sit in the kitchen chatting with Mom. Sometimes, she sang when she cooked, and I'd sing along with her, practicing harmonies. Those are some of my best memories.

"I'm sorry I haven't been nice to you," I blurt out as a rush of guilt seizes control of my vocal cords.

Mom turns from the stove, eyes wide. "What are you talking about?"

"I know you're only trying to help when it comes to my music. And I'm always biting your head off about it." I gulp down the lump obstructing my throat. "I feel bad. And I'm sorry."

She gives me a gentle smile. "It's all right. I get it."

"Do you really?"

Mom slides the spatula under the grilled cheese and flips it again, browning the other side. "Of course. It feels like a hit to your pride. Reminds me of your father. He's way too proud sometimes. But even your dad knows when to accept help."

"It's not that I don't want your help—"

"I promise you, I get it. And I appreciate the apology. But for what it's worth, the reason I try to offer my assistance—within the parameters of the rule book, of course," she adds with a grin, "isn't because you're my kid. I do it because you're so talented, Wyatt."

I bite my lip.

"I love you and your sister equally, and the two of you are my world. But you...you're also my soul. You feel music the same way that I do. I've been writing songs my entire life, just like you have." She pauses, her voice softening. "I've never told you this before, but I went through a difficult time when I was a teenager. A pretty bad trauma."

Concern tickles my stomach. I want to ask her what happened, but a part of me isn't sure I want to know the answer.

"It took years of therapy and being kind and gentle with myself to work through it. And whenever I felt like I couldn't bear it, I'd distract myself with music. Lose myself in songs." She laughs. "Sometimes I hear music in my head when I'm trying to sleep."

"I know the feeling."

"Of course you do. Because you got it from me. And I want you to know that if I ever push you, it's only because I want other people to experience your gift."

"So you're saying if I couldn't carry a tune, you wouldn't be pushing me like some nepo baby onto all these industry folks?"

Mom snorts. "God, no. I would've found a nice way to encourage you to seek a different career path."

I believe that. Mom might be teeming with compassion, but she doesn't allow for delusions. She's grounded in reality.

She slides the plate across the table, and I take a bite of grilled cheese, even knowing it's fresh off the pan. As I try to blow on the food while it's in my mouth, she laughs and gets me a glass of water. I gulp it down, and then, because I'm a masochist, take another bite right away.

"Just wait for it to cool," Mom chides, sputtering with laughter

"No. It's too good. Tastes best when the cheese is still sizzling."

I chew slowly. "Hey, so... I have a few tracks I'd love to get your opinion on. I want to send them to Tobey this week."

Her eyes light up. "Oh, I would love that. I'm dying to hear what you've been working on this summer."

"I think it's some of my best work," I confess.

"Wow. You never compliment your own music."

"I know, but...yeah," I say gruffly. "This is good material. Found my inspiration, I guess."

*Her name is Blake.*

I keep that part to myself, though.

All the parents go into town that night, leaving the boathouse empty for the Golden Boys to party in. My social battery is in desperate need of recharging, so I beg off and stay in the main house. My sister decides to stay in too, which puts a damper on my plans to lure Blake upstairs and screw her until she can't see straight.

Instead, the three of us end up puzzling together in the dining room.

"Whoa, you guys got so much done just the two of you," Gigi remarks. She admires the puzzle, which is about three-quarters filled in. "How much time did you spend on this?"

"We did a little bit every night," Blake says. "I did most of the sky because this asshole is apparently black-blind."

Gigi grins. "What the hell is black-blind?"

"When you can't tell the difference between shades of black."

"Because there's only one shade of black!" I say in protest. "It's called black." I snatch two pieces out of the box. "See this? This is black. And see this one? It's also black."

"That second one is clearly five shades lighter," a haughty Blake replies. "It's closer to charcoal. Dumbass."

My jaw drops. "You know, I didn't try to shame *you* when you couldn't tell the difference between the center of the moon and the swan neck."

"Because those are *actually* the same shade of white." She jams her finger on the swan, then the moon. "White and white."

"Yeah. White with feathers. White with moon dust."

"What the hell is moon dust? You know what? I don't care. Fuck you."

"Fuck *you.*"

"I said it first."

"I said it second."

"Ahem." Gigi clears her throat.

We both glance toward her.

And my stomach drops. Because this is my twin sister, which means I'm familiar with every single facial expression she possesses, every glint in her eye, and right now...

"You're hooking up," she accuses.

Silence crashes over the dining room. Blake gets the panicky look of a deer that ran in the middle of the road and is seconds from smashing through a windshield.

Then, in the worst impression of a truth teller, she says, "No, we're not."

"Holy shit." Gigi heaves a long, arduous sigh. "Oh man, you two are screwed. How long has this been going on? The whole summer? Or did it start recently?"

"Neither, because nothing is going on," Blake says stubbornly. When I remain silent, she implores me with her eyes. "Tell her it's not happening."

Gigi's lips twitch. "Yes, *twin*, tell me it's not happening."

I grit my teeth. "Are you gonna keep this to yourself, Stan?"

"Wyatt!" Blake says, looking betrayed. "Tell her it's not true."

I sigh. "Don't worry, freckles. It's between me and the twin."

My sister takes an alarming amount of time to consider my question. But then she grins, and I realize she's messing with me. "Relax. I won't say a word to anyone but my husband."

Blake's eyes fill with panic again.

"Relax," Gigi assures her. "Ryder doesn't speak to anybody. Literally."

I snort, because she's right. My brother-in-law is not Mr. Chatty.

Accepting her fate, Blake searches Gigi's face. "And you're...cool with this?"

"I mean, depends on what *this* is. Summer fling, I can get behind." My sister gives me a warning look. "Unless it's more?"

"It's a summer fling," Blake answers immediately, and although that's the rule we laid out, the conviction in her voice bothers me for some reason.

Still, I nod in agreement. "We're just having fun till the end of the summer." When Gigi's skeptical gaze shifts between us, I roll my eyes at her. "Don't make more of it than it is."

When I scrape back my chair, Gigi frowns. "Where are you going?"

"Need a smoke."

"Thought you quit," she says in disapproval.

I ignore that and say, "Be right back."

With casual strides, I head outside, but when my sister finds me on the dock ten minutes later, I'm already on my third cigarette.

Gigi marches toward me, her dark ponytail swinging. "Look, I didn't want to say this in front of Blake, but..." She shakes her head in disbelief. "What the hell are you thinking?"

Yeah, I knew this was coming.

"It's not a big deal," I say, even as I suck nearly half my cigarette in a nervous drag.

It was easy to pretend I wasn't doing anything wrong when it was our little secret, but now that someone else knows, all the reasons that caused me to deny my attraction to her come rushing back.

"She's practically our sister," Gigi scolds.

"Trust me, I've never thought of her as my sister."

"God. Men will justify anything in their minds for sex."

"Hey, don't make this a gender thing."

"If you hurt her, she's not going away. You get that, right?" Gigi's features are hard, but her voice is soft. "And you have a bad track record with flings. They always fall for you. Without fucking fail. If you break her heart, it won't be like one of the girls you leave in the rearview mirror and never have to see again. You can't just fuck off to Boston for a few months until they forget you. You're *going* to see her, probably for the rest of your life, unless for some completely implausible reason, Dad stops talking to Logan."

Which we both know will never happen. They're brothers for life.

"When this ends, you're going to see her next summer in Tahoe," my sister continues. "You'll see her for Christmas, on birthdays. Are you sure you know what you're doing?"

I chew on my cheek, feeling uneasy. "I never know what I'm doing, Stan."

Gigi shakes her head at me. "Yeah, well, maybe you should start figuring it out."

My sister's warning stays with me, yet it's not strong enough to stop me from sneaking into Blake's room every night for the rest of the week. I know it's risky as hell with every room occupied, and when I sneak back into my own bed at dawn every morning, I try not to question why I'm taking such a huge risk for this girl.

All I know is that everything is quieter when she's around. In a good way. She eases the chaos in my head, sometimes even silences it completely. When I'm curled up beside her, I don't stay up all night, staring at the ceiling. I haven't slept this well in years, not since I was a child.

But Gigi's right. I need to figure out what we're doing. Whether Blake is truly on board with saying goodbye in a few weeks.

*Blake?* mocks the voice in my head.

Okay. *Me.* I need to figure out why the idea of going our separate ways fills *me* with so much fucking anxiety.

But what's the alternative? Blake is returning to Briar for her senior year. I've got an album to record. Are we going to have a long-distance relationship? A relationship, period? I don't fare well when it comes to relationships. I always screw them up.

My mind is a jumbled mess as I make my way down to the dock. It's a gorgeous, sunny morning, so everyone is either in the water or lounging on the beach. The Golden Boys are executing backflips off the swim platform. All I catch is flashes of tanned skin and wet hair as a bunch of rowdy hockey players hurl themselves into the lake. Nearby, Blake and Kate float on their backs, long hair stretching out behind them like strands of seaweed.

I find Tucker napping on a lounge chair, a red baseball cap brandishing the logo of one of the gyms he owns covering his face. I don't want to disturb him, so I settle on the chair farthest from him and scribble in my songbook for a while.

Around noon, my mother shouts down from the railing saying lunch is ready if anyone's interested. I hear a happy shriek as AJ grabs his girlfriend's hand and they both jump off the platform to swim back to shore. Gray and Stella follow suit, diving cleanly into the water, but Blake goes to the ladder rather than jump, gripping the rungs as she climbs down.

I can't tear my gaze off her. Her skin is golden brown from being out in the sun all summer, and her teeny white bikini only emphasizes that tan. I watch as the bottoms ride up on her ass, baring one perky cheek. My dick stirs in my trunks. I want to smack the hell out of that ass.

There's a blur of motion as Beau dives off the platform without noticing Blake descending the ladder. His left foot clips her temple, and my heart slams into my ribs when I see Blake's head jerk back a second before she goes under.

And doesn't come back up.

I don't think. I don't hesitate. Instinct takes over. I'm off the lounger and diving off the dock before I even realize what I'm doing. I swim toward her at a breakneck speed, arms cutting hard through the water.

"Blake," I shout and inhale a mouthful of water.

For one terrifying second, I see nothing but bubbles and ripples near the ladder, but then she surfaces with a cough, flinging out her arm to clutch the side of the platform.

My dramatic dock dive and shout caught everyone's attention, because I suddenly hear concerned voices from the sand. I ignore them and close the distance between us, pulling her against my wet body as we tread water and hold on to the wooden edge.

"Are you okay?"

She blinks water from her lashes, rubbing the side of her head. "Yeah."

"Can you swim?"

When she nods, we push off from the platform and swim toward shore. We stumble onto the sand, where I cup her face with both hands, gently rubbing her temple. My body is still experiencing phantom fear, pulse racing, skin ice-cold in response to that moment she went underwater and how it felt like my entire world had stopped.

"Fuck, baby. When I saw you go under..." I take a breath.

"I'm fine," she says, shoving wet hair out of her eyes. "I just got stunned for a second and then disoriented. I wasn't sure where I was."

"That scared the shit out of me." The relief coursing through my veins has me leaning down to give her a quick kiss, just to make sure she's really there.

She makes a strangled noise when our lips touch. At first, I mistake her reaction for anger.

But then I realize it's panic.

And that's when I remember we're not alone.

I called her "baby."

I kissed her.

And *we're not alone.*

Someone clears their throat, and I turn my head to see every single person we know on this earth staring back at us.

## DAD CHAT

DEAN DI LAURENTIS

So. That happened.

JOHN TUCKER

*JOHN LOGAN REMOVED GARRETT GRAHAM FROM DAD CHAT.*

DEAN DI LAURENTIS

Real mature.

JOHN LOGAN

Fuck off, Dean.

COLIN FITZGERALD

DEAN DI LAURENTIS

*JAKE CONNELLY ADDED GARRETT GRAHAM TO DAD CHAT.*
*GARRETT GRAHAM REMOVED JOHN LOGAN FROM DAD CHAT.*

JOHN TUCKER

Add him back, G. The father of the penis needs to grovel to the father of the vagina.

DEAN DI LAURENTIS

Agreed.

COLIN FITZGERALRD

I dunno...

DEAN DI LAURENTIS

I see you, Fitz. You're only saying that because you have 4 penis sons.

GARRETT GRAHAM

That's bs. I'm not the one who has to grovel.

JOHN TUCKER

I'm putting up a poll.

All right, submit your votes.

**WHICH FATHER SHOULD GROVEL?**

**PENIS DAD** 7 VOTES

**VAGINA DAD** 2 VOTES

DEAN DI LAURENTIS

And that's a victory for the vagina.

GARRETT GRAHAM

Goddamn it.

***GARRETT GRAHAM ADDED JOHN LOGAN TO DAD CHAT.***

GARRETT GRAHAM

Stop being a whiny baby, dude. He didn't do it on purpose.

JOHN LOGAN

Oh, so he accidentally had sex with my daughter?

***JOHN LOGAN REMOVED GARRETT GRAHAM FROM DAD CHAT.***
***JOHN TUCKER ADDED GARRETT GRAHAM TO DAD CHAT.***

GARRETT GRAHAM

DO THAT ONE MORE TIME ASSHOLE. I FUCKING DARE YOU

# Chapter 37

## BLAKE

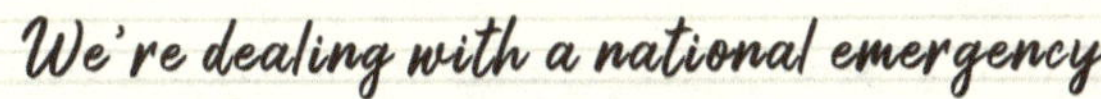


"HOW LONG HAS THIS BEEN going on?"

"Who initiated it? It was him, wasn't it?"

"Oh, fuck off. That's so sexist of you."

"How is that sexist?"

"What, you think just because he's a man, that means he made the first move? This is the modern world, John. Women initiate all the time."

"Don't fucking call me John, Garrett."

Oh no, they're full naming each other.

This is dire.

From my spot on the sectional, I send Gigi a silent plea. *Help us. Please.* She's the only "nonparty" (as my father phrased it) who was allowed entry to the great room, because apparently this is a Graham/Logan interrogation only. Everyone else has been banished outside to the deck, which I'm grateful for. I didn't miss the hurt on Beau's face when he realized Wyatt and I have been hooking up. I'm not ready to have to explain myself to anyone.

"It doesn't matter who initiated," Gigi puts in. "So they've been hanging out. Big deal."

"What is 'hanging out'?" Garrett demands at the same time as my father growls, "Define hanging out."

Hannah exchanges a look with my mom. "Okay," she interjects. "Let's all take a breath and calm down."

"Yes, let's calm down," a voice pipes up.

"There's no reason to freak out," another voice chimes in. "We always knew this was gonna happen someday. I just assumed it would be a Golden Boy."

We all turn to see Tucker lurking at the kitchen counter. Then Dean pops up too like a whack-a-mole. They must've snuck back inside through the front door and crept up without anyone noticing.

"Go away," my dad snaps at them. "We're dealing with a national emergency."

"Fine, we'll go, but we need an update in the group chat later," Dean begs.

"Obviously," Dad huffs.

Their footsteps thud in the hallway, and we hear them laughing as they exit the house.

On her end of the couch, Mom loosely clasps her hands in her lap and glances at me. "Look, obviously you don't owe us any explanations—"

"Like hell they don't," Dad and Garrett say in unison.

"Oh my God," I mutter, my cheeks hot with embarrassment. "We're just spending time together. It really isn't a thing."

"So it's a rebound?" Dad grumbles. "Rebounds are always a bad idea, sweet pea."

"No, they're not. Sometimes they're a nice palate cleanser." From the corner of my eye, I see Wyatt's lips twitch, as if he's amused by the notion that he's a palate cleanser. "Would you rather I was still with Isaac?" I direct the challenge at my father.

His jaw drops. "Don't put me in this impossible situation. The potato versus the fuckboy?"

"Hey," Hannah cuts in, jabbing a finger at my father. "I get this is your only daughter and you're—how do I say this nicely?—*psychotically* overprotective—"

My mom snorts softly.

"But you've known Wyatt his whole life," Hannah finishes. "He's got a good head on his shoulders."

"Thanks, Mom," Wyatt murmurs.

It's the first word he's spoken since the interrogation began. But he doesn't seem uncomfortable in the slightest. He just sits there looking like the easygoing, unbothered bad boy he is, looking at his sneakers and twisting his rings around on his fingers. I'm not the only one who notices, as my dad suddenly narrows his eyes on Wyatt.

"Stop acting all cool," my dad says to him. When I laugh, it earns me another glare. "Don't laugh at him being cool."

"I'm not laughing at him. I'm laughing at *you*." I heave an exhausted sigh. "Guys. You seriously need to chill. We've just been hanging out this summer. Enjoying each other's company."

"Have you had intercourse?" Dad demands.

"I am *not* answering that."

"Yeah, I don't think you want the answer to that," Wyatt concurs, while his twin laughs into her arm.

Dad promptly goes back to glaring daggers at Wyatt's father. "Are you hearing your son, Garrett? What if he gets her pregnant?"

"Oh, because he's knocked up so many other girls? I don't see a bunch of grandbabies running around, *John*."

"You wouldn't, because babies can't run," Dad says smugly.

"Let me introduce you to something called a figure of speech, jackass."

And on and on it goes. They talk in circles. They scowl. They demand details.

Until finally, I do a very un-Blake-like thing. I hold up my hand and snap, "Would you both shut the fuck up?"

"Language," my dad chides.

"I'll mind my language when you mind yours." Tamping down my frustration, I focus on my mom and Hannah, because they're clearly the most reasonable people in this room. "Wyatt and I formed a connection while we've been here. We like spending time together. But I'm going back to college in the fall, and he's going back to Nashville to record his album." Now I turn toward the dads. "Nobody is pregnant. Nobody is dropping out of school. Nobody is breaking anyone's heart. And even if any of that happened, we are adults and perfectly capable of handling it on our own. With that said, we love you all very much—"

"Well, not right now," Wyatt drawls, then grins when I flash him a dirty look.

"And our families are going to be just fine," I finish.

"I'm not fine at all," Dad gripes. He shakes his head at Garrett. "I don't like this."

"Oh, because I'm jumping for joy?"

"I hate it more."

"Would you prefer it was a Di Laurentis?" Garrett counters, at which point my father rises to his feet and stomps out of the room.

I spend the rest of the day in my room faking a headache. Which isn't a total lie. My head is throbbing from all the nonsense it had to endure today.

After the fallout from the hookup bomb, it was decided that everyone was going to "digest" things. As if it's anyone's business but mine and Wyatt's. But I should've anticipated this.

Fortunately, the girls know to back off when I tell them I don't feel like talking about anything tonight. And the Golden Boys have disappeared for the night, thank God. I think they went drinking in town.

Deciding to go to bed early, I shower and change into my pajamas, returning to my room to find Mom sitting on the bed waiting for me.

"Got a minute for me?" she asks. "Or are we still hiding out?"

"We're still hiding, but never from you."

I close the door and get comfy on the bed. Mom comes up and lies beside me, both of us curled on our sides. Growing up, this was one of my favorite things to do with my mom. We used to cuddle in bed and talk for hours. I would ramble on about school and friends and whatever other random topic I had on the brain. Mom would tell me stories about her college days, meeting my dad, her time at the news network where she worked as a producer for almost twenty years.

"So. I don't need details. In fact, please don't give me details," she begs, and I snort. "All I want to know is are you being safe, and are you happy?"

My heart expands from a rush of emotion. I love my mom so much. "Yes, we're being safe, and yes, I am happy."

She hesitates for a beat.

"Say it," I urge.

"Look, you know I love Wyatt. Your father is just being dramatic right now, because that's who he is. But I'm not worried about Wyatt's intentions. I don't think he'd ever set out to hurt anyone..." Mom pauses again.

"But you think he'll hurt me," I finish.

Her tone is careful now. "I think...he'll leave."

Pain shoots through me. "He'll leave me, you mean?"

"No, he'll just leave. That's what Wyatt does. He left Nashville and took off for Tahoe without telling his own family. He doesn't like to be rooted to one place. He never has."

*Because he's trying to outrun the chaos.*

*Because he's lost.*

I don't express any of those thoughts; I don't feel right revealing the vulnerabilities Wyatt has shown me. I know that's why he fled to Tahoe, though. Because his head gets too loud, and he's desperate to quiet it, but more than that, because he's stuck in this narrative he's created for himself, like a car spinning its wheels in the mud.

I don't know if he'll ever break free of this rigid perception he has of himself, but I've definitely noticed a change in him. He's not the same man he was when I arrived here at the end of May. He doesn't chain-smoke on the dock anymore. Doesn't pour alcohol down his throat to help him sleep. Doesn't snap at me in frustration or insist I'm not worth his time.

These days, he sneaks into my room at night and stays sound asleep until morning. He spends hours writing music instead of fighting it. He asks for his mom's input about his songs when before, he would've rather swallowed broken glass than ask for her help. He's starting to find peace within himself, and maybe that's all he needs to...not leave.

To stay.

After Mom says good night, I reach for my phone to text Wyatt. Even though we've kept our distance, we've still been texting all day.

I'm going to bed soon. Today was intense.

SONGBOY

Baby, I believe you've perfected the art of the understatement.

"The art of the understatement" would be a good name for a song.

SONGBOY

Nah too wordy.

Are you sleeping here tonight?

SONGBOY

I probably shouldn't.

Disappointment lodges in my chest, but I understand his reluctance.

SONGBOY

It's too risky. Your dad's probably patrolling the hallway.

I don't think you need the word probably in that sentence.

SONGBOY

Let's give it a couple days? Let them get used to the idea.

Okay. Good night, songboy.

SONGBOY

Good night, freckles.

I'm about to burrow under my blanket when a knock sounds on the door. For a moment, I wonder if Wyatt changed his mind, but when the door cracks open at my hurried "Come in," it's Beau who appears.

He doesn't come all the way inside, just lingers in the doorway. He's wearing sweats, his blond hair damp from a shower. When our eyes meet, I don't miss the glint of disapproval in his.

"Just say it," I sigh.

"Wyatt? *That's* the guy you're seeing? You could've told me that the other night."

"We were keeping it on the down-low."

"Well, you did a shit job, because now it's on the fucking"—he pauses—"*up*-low."

"Wouldn't it be up-high?"

He ignores that. "You don't even understand the shitstorm you've unleashed. The dads are all holding a meeting about it right now."

"Let them meet," I say irritably. "This has nothing to do with them."

Beau shakes his head. "You're smarter than this, B. I love the guy to death, but we both know his track record. He's going to break your heart."

"Maybe. Or maybe not." I huff out a breath, annoyed that everyone is sticking their nose where it doesn't belong. "Either way, it's nobody's business but mine."

# Chapter 38

## WYATT

*Ooh, we're taking risks again?*

THE DADS ARE FEUDING. WHICH would be funny if I weren't part of the feud. Like, if this was AJ hooking up with Ivy? Or Beau hooking up with Alex? Hilarious.

Unfortunately, it's me hooking up with Blake, and that means we're the ones caught in the middle of this storm and the ones everyone glares at when the feud gets particularly annoying. For example, during tonight's dinner.

"Can someone please tell Mr. Logan to pass the mashed potatoes?"

"Can someone please tell Mr. Graham that he needs to lay off all the butter because he's starting to look flabby?"

"Can someone please tell Mr. Logan to piss off and that if he's so inclined, I will challenge him to a push-up contest on the dock?"

"Can someone please tell—"

"No!" my mother bursts out. "No! We're done here!"

Grace nods firmly. "Get your plates, everyone. We're eating outside. *They're* staying in here."

"Oh, no, thank you," Dean says, and Tucker nods in agreement.

"We'll stay and watch if you don't mind."

"Suit yourselves," Grace says.

Everyone else scrapes back their chairs and marches toward the french doors. AJ snickers under his breath, glancing over at me.

"Damn, Wyatt, you broke their brains."

Logan overhears that and growls at AJ. "Shut it, Connelly. You're already on thin ice because your father tried to steal my best friend and—you know what? Jake can have him." He flashes a big, fake smile at my father.

It's been three days of this.

It's also been three days of insomnia, because apparently, if Blake isn't wrapped around me, I can't sleep.

And it's been three days of blue balls, because I can't fuck her.

Which means three days of jerking off, an activity that isn't that much fun when I know my girl's tight pussy is two doors down.

But I'd never risk it in the house now, not with her father scowling at me any time I enter a room. It sort of makes me want to head back to Nashville early, but the idea of saying goodbye to her…

Agony.

Fuck. I need to get ahold of myself. This isn't who I am. I don't panic at the thought of moving on. Blake and I will still be friends once the sex runs its course. We'll always be friends.

*You don't want to be her fucking friend,* an incredulous voice says, but I silence it before the accusation can take root in my mind.

After dinner, the Golden Boys and I drive into town to shoot pool. Tara tags along, but she passes the time sitting at a high-top table on her phone, legs crossed and miniskirt riding up her tanned thighs. We team up—Beau and me versus AJ and Gray. But it's sort of hard to enjoy the game when my partner keeps giving me surly looks.

I tried to warn her. I told her that Beau has a thing for her, but

Blake just shrugged it off. Women don't want to see the things that make them uncomfortable.

Despite the rising tension between us, Beau and I win the first game. While Gray racks the balls for round two, AJ goes to get another pitcher of beer. The Golden Boys are twenty, so they all use fake IDs. I find that hilarious, as I'm sure most of the bartenders in Tahoe know who their fathers are and could easily google their ages and find out they're minors. But AJ strolls back with a second pitcher, no problem.

Pouring myself a pint, I notice AJ and Gray smirking at me.

"What?" I say, rolling my eyes.

"Are we seriously not gonna address this Blake thing?" AJ demands.

"Seriously," Gray agrees. "We've been so patient."

"Giving you space," adds AJ.

"Trying to be cool about it," continues Gray. "But…dude. It's been three days."

"I know you like to live on the edge," AJ says in amusement, "but pissing off Logan by banging his baby girl? You've got balls of steel, bro."

I notice Beau draining more than half of his pint glass—which he filled literally five seconds ago.

"Slow down," I murmur.

That gets me a derisive snort. "Why? I'm on fucking vacation." Then, as if to spite me, he chugs the rest of the glass and pours himself another.

Okay then. If he wants to get loaded, go nuts, buddy.

I end up drinking more than usual myself, at least compared to this past month. I started the summer pounding beers like mints, sometimes before noon, but I've cut back significantly since getting a handle on the insomnia. However, after three days of nonstop tension and feeling like I'm under a microscope, I've earned the right to let loose.

I'm unsteady on my feet by the time we leave the bar. AJ's girlfriend is our designated driver and surprisingly patient as she helps her boyfriend into the passenger's seat. Tara's been nothing but bitchy and entitled since they got here, so it's nice to see she actually cares about the guy.

AJ is even drunker than I am. He collapses in his seat and cranks open the window, then passes out with his arm hanging out of the car. I sit in the back with Gray and Beau, texting Blake because I'm drunk and horny and I miss her.

Be home in 15. Meet me behind the boathouse.

FRECKLES

Ooh, we're taking risks again?

Yes.

FRECKLES

Thank God.

It's pitch-black later when I stumble through the shadows behind the boathouse. I find her leaning against the wall, wearing a loose T-shirt that hangs over her shoulder, no bra strap. That's my girl. And she's in a skirt. Definitely my girl.

"Hi—" she starts, but my hands slide under the hem of her shirt, and her hello dissolves into a quiet sigh.

She smells so good. Like summer and sex and lavender. My lips skim her neck, and I drag my tongue along her soft skin, tasting her. Meanwhile, I'm already pushing my hips against her body, trying to get closer.

When she reaches down and squeezes my ass, I groan. Loudly.

"Someone's going to catch us if you do that again," she whispers, even as she's wrapping her arms around my neck and pulling me even closer.

As much as I want to take my time with her, sink down on my knees, bring her pussy to my face, and fuck her with my tongue, we're on borrowed time, and every second we drag out this encounter, we're in danger of someone catching us.

"Freckles, you know I could spend the rest of my life on my knees making you come..." My hands slide under her skirt, and I stroke her thighs before gripping her ass cheeks. No panties. God, she's perfect.

"But?" she prompts.

I lick my lips, trying to remember what I was saying before her ass distracted me. "But tonight I need to be selfish and use this tight body before I fucking explode. Are you gonna let me do that?"

With a tiny smile, Blake rises on her tiptoes and leans in until her mouth is a scant inch from mine. "Wyatt?"

"Hmm?" I'm still squeezing her ass.

"Give me your dick."

And then my good, obedient girl turns around and lifts up her skirt.

Goddamn perfect.

I undo my pants and slip my fingers in the crease of her ass, dragging them lower until I find her pussy. She's wet and ready for me, and while I'd love nothing more than to slide my bare dick in there and feel her soaking me, we've already been there, done that, gotten the Plan B T-shirt. I'm not taking that risk again.

I fish out the condom I stashed in my back pocket and roll it on, then follow through on my seductive threat—I bend her over and thrust deep inside her. When she moans, I curl my arm around her body and bring my hand to her mouth to cover it. She bites my palm, and I have to choke down my own moan.

"Be quiet," I say. "Just let me use you."

Rather than take offense, she bucks against me, her inner muscles clamping tight.

I smile. "Oh, you like that, don't you?"

The back of her head moves as she nods.

"Can I take my hand off your mouth?"

She nods again.

I move my hand and slide it through her hair, wrapping a hunk of it in my fist. And that's how I fuck her—fast, deep strokes, one hand pulling her hair, the other hand squeezing her tits. I drive my cock into her until we're both breathless. I come without telling her, jerking with pleasure, my teeth digging into her shoulder to stifle a groan. I don't know if she has an orgasm, but she looks sated when she twists around to kiss me.

I pull out and wrap the condom in a tissue I also brought for this exact purpose, then shove it in my pocket.

"That was fun," Blake murmurs, and I grin.

"You head back first. I'll wait a few minutes."

Before she can go, something thuds inside the boathouse. We both freeze. That sounded like footsteps.

Her hand closes around mine. "Did you hear that?"

I nod warily. "Raccoon maybe?"

"Raccoons don't sound like human footsteps." Blake creeps along the wall. "I think someone's in there."

It's one in the morning. There's no reason for anyone to be inside the boathouse. On the roof, maybe, if you're smoking a late-night joint. In the apartment, sure, if you need somewhere to crash. But among the boat slips? No.

I move ahead of her and quietly round the side of the boathouse. I wince when the wooden planks creak under my shoes.

"Stay behind me," I murmur. "Could be someone breaking in."

I reach the door, my hand hovering over the handle. Before I can ease it open, there's another muffled sound. A giggle.

I turn to Blake, whose lips have twisted into a frown. "There's a girl in there," she whispers.

She comes up beside me as I open the door just a tiny crack for us to peer inside.

At first, all I see are shadows. The cruiser is tied off on the pier, but the bowrider and motorboat bob gently in their wells, and I don't see anybody on them. My gaze travels across the huge space toward the old workbench against the back wall. I glimpse another shadow. No, two shadows. The bench jostles and a coil of rope falls to the ground, the soft thud reverberating through the boathouse.

As my eyes adjust to the darkness, the two shadows become two figures. A woman falling back on her elbows while pulling up her shirt. Platinum-blond hair catches in the moonlight slicing in from the small window.

"For God's sake, get inside me already." A female voice, soft and breathless.

There's another flash of blond hair. Beau is undoing his pants. He shoves the zipper down and reaches inside. I close the door before I see the rest.

Blake and I back up, eyeing each other in shock.

"That was Tara," she hisses.

I nod grimly. Yes. Yes, it was.

From inside the boathouse, we hear a low moan, followed by a higher-pitched one and then the unmistakable sound of the workbench rattling as Beau pounds into his best friend's girlfriend.

# Chapter 39

## BLAKE

### Brilliant drunk logic

BREAKFAST IS TENSE.

For me anyway.

Everyone else is living their lives in blissful oblivion while I steal glances at Beau, wishing I could see his expression behind those dark glasses. What the hell was he *thinking* last night? AJ is his *best friend.*

This is bad. Very, very, very bad.

The parents attribute his sunglasses and surly demeanor to his hangover, which I'm sure is also bad—he looked beyond wasted last night—but I don't think that's the only reason he's shielding his eyes from the table.

Dean is clearly trying not to laugh as he glances at his son. "Doing okay there, kid?"

Beau grunts. He shoves some bacon into his mouth and chews fast. He once told me his go-to cure for hangovers is piles and piles of bacon, and he's already eaten an entire tray to himself this morning.

Tara and AJ are both conspicuously absent. They haven't missed a single breakfast since they got here, so this doesn't bode well.

I feel like that psychic in the thriller I read this summer. The heroine could see all these horrific accidents coming and couldn't do a damn thing to stop them. Yet the one thing she couldn't see was her husband's affair with her mother. The irony.

It doesn't take long for my premonition to come to fruition. Less than ten minutes later, the french doors fly open. One of them hits the frame with a crash, startling everyone.

"Hey," Allie chides. "Go easy on the door, AJ."

He doesn't pay her any attention. He stomps toward the table.

"*You fucking asshole.*"

As everyone watches, stunned, AJ hauls Beau out of his chair, gripping him by the collar.

"AJ," Garrett warns, while Dean's shoulders square up at seeing his son manhandled.

"You want to tell them?" AJ's voice thickens with rage. "Or should I?"

Beau doesn't answer. He just stands there, shame carved into every line of his face. Even hungover, with his eyes bloodshot and features gaunt with pain, he's still one of the most attractive people at this table.

"Oh, for God's sake," my dad mutters. "What's going on now?"

AJ's lips curl into a sneer. "He fucked my girlfriend last night. In the goddamn boathouse while I was asleep upstairs. He *fucked* my *girlfriend.*" AJ spits out the words like they're burning his tongue.

"Ah, hell," I hear Dean murmur.

Beau finally speaks. "AJ—"

AJ's fist connects with Beau's jaw, the resulting crack echoing like a gunshot on the deck. Beau's head rears back, but he doesn't defend himself. He staggers backward, grunting. He doesn't try to block the second punch or the third. He locks his stance and takes it, flinching with every hit but making no move to fight back.

"Garrett," Hannah orders. "Stop this."

But none of the men at the table move to stop this.

"Let them work it out," Dean murmurs.

"Fight me, you goddamn prick," AJ roars, lunging at Beau again.

He slams his fist into Beau's stomach, and I wince at the solid *thud* it makes. Then he does it again, sending Beau staggering back against the railing.

Gray rises to his feet as his two best friends go at it, but he doesn't interfere either. He simply watches with a stoic expression.

"I'm sorry," Beau says quietly. "I was drunk."

That gets him another uppercut to the face. Only when blood pours out of his nostrils do the parents get involved.

"All right, enough," Garrett commands. "You got it out of your system."

My dad pries AJ off Beau while Allie hurries over to her son with a napkin. She tries to press his nose, but he shrugs her hand off.

"Mom, stop," he mutters. Blood trickles from his nose and lip, leaving red streaks all over his jaw. "I deserve it."

Near the railing, AJ is fighting my dad's hold. His breathing is ragged, dark eyes wild. He's shaking with rage.

"Calm down, son," Dad urges.

Finally, AJ pushes out of the hold. "I'm done here." His hard eyes settle on Beau, his jaw grinding. "We're fucking done here. Don't talk to me ever again."

It's then that I notice Tara in the doorway, frozen, her eyes red and wet with tears. AJ notices her too and scoffs at her.

"You can find your own way to the airport," he spits out.

When she reaches for him, he shoves her hand off him and stalks past her without a backward look.

I find Beau on the beach a while later, sitting with his hands on his knees, staring at the lake. At the sound of my footsteps, he glances up, and I almost gasp. He looks wrecked. Lip swollen. Blood caked at his nostrils.

"What the hell were you thinking?" I sigh, sinking down beside him on the sand.

He curls his hands tighter over his knees, his broad shoulders hunched over as if he's trying to disappear into the sand. "Don't start, B. Not now."

"He's your best friend. Since you were in diapers. You threw a twenty-year friendship away for a girl? What was going through your head?"

Beau barks out a bitter laugh. "Nothing. My head was a blank space because I was drunk off my ass. It was a mistake."

"A mistake. That's what you call screwing your best friend's girlfriend."

"I was completely hammered. I don't even remember half of it."

"That makes it better? You fucked her in the boathouse while he was sleeping upstairs, totally oblivious. You think that's just a little mistake? That's goddamn nuclear, Beau."

He visibly swallows. "I'm not proud of what happened, okay? I feel like shit. Is that what you want to hear?"

I shake my head in disapproval. "Is this about me?" I have to ask.

"Oh, fuck off, Blake. Don't flatter yourself. I was wasted and stupid and horny, and she came on to me, and I was too drunk to say no. That's it."

"Really. It had *nothing* to do with me turning you down the other night and you finding out about me and Wyatt."

"It had nothing to do with you," he replies through clenched teeth. "It was just me being a dumb, drunk asshole who didn't think beyond the next five seconds."

"So your brilliant drunk logic was to blow up AJ's relationship and your lifelong friendship? Because that's what you've done."

He tries to shift his gaze back to the water, but I grab his sleeve and force eye contact. The shame lining his features softens some of my anger.

"You need to fix this," I say firmly.

"I know." His voice cracks with guilt. "Stop looking at me like that. I hate what I did, okay?" Bleakly, he staggers to his feet.

"B—"

"Just leave me alone. I can't do this right now. I already feel like shit, and I don't need you making me feel worse."

"Maybe you should feel worse," I call after him. "Maybe you deserve to."

He stops for half a second, shoulders tensing. But he doesn't turn around. A moment later, he marches off, leaving me alone on the beach.

## DAD CHAT

DEAN DI LAURENTIS

All right. Let's have it. Go ahead, Connelly. Remove me from the chat.

JAKE CONNELLY

For what?

DEAN DI LAURENTIS

My kid stole your kid's girl.

JAKE CONNELLY

Bro, he deserves a medal. Brenna and I have been praying for the downfall of Tara for two years. Can't stand her.

DEAN DI LAURENTIS

Wait, so you're not pissed?

JAKE CONNELLY

Nah. Tell Beau thanks.

DEAN DI LAURENTIS

See? This is how adults handle conflicts between their children.

# Chapter 40

## WYATT

### *Just three*

I ASSUMED THAT THE DRAMATIC end of a Golden Boy friendship—something I never dreamed possible—would also mean the end of the dramatics for the day. But I was wrong.

I'm in bed later that night, once again fighting insomnia because I can't sleep without Blake, when there's a soft knock on my door. Seconds later, my dad pokes his head in.

"Get dressed and meet me on the pier."

Huh?

Confused, I pull on a pair of sweatpants and an old band hoodie and shove my feet into my slides. The house is dark and quiet as I head downstairs, the kitchen illuminated only by the strip of lighting underneath the cabinets. I exit through the back, letting the moonlight guide me to our pier.

I spot the bowrider bobbing in the dark water with two shadowy figures on board. That should've been my first sign to turn away. But I'm too curious, and then it's too late because they've spotted me. My dad and Logan. Like me, they're in hoodies, only they're also in all black and wearing baseball caps.

"What is this?" I say warily.

"Get in the boat," Logan orders.

I look at my dad. "This feels like a trap."

He sighs. "Just get in the boat."

I don't want to, but I do. Soon, the engine purrs softly as we glide across the water. I sit in the back, only about eighty percent certain I'm not about to get murdered. My dad would never kill me, but there's a twenty percent chance he won't be able to stop Logan in time.

"Hey," I realize. "So you guys are talking again?"

"Shut up," Logan says without turning around from the pilot seat.

Okay then.

I shift my gaze to the lake. It's glossy and black tonight, reflecting the stars above as little pinpricks of silver across the water.

When the silence drags on, I clear my throat. "You guys aren't gonna kill me, right? Because I've seen this movie, and it never ends well for the guy in the back of the boat."

Dad chuckles. "Your mother would kill me if I killed you. Don't worry."

That does provide some solace. My dad hates angering my mom.

When we're about a hundred yards from the house, Logan cuts the engine and lets the boat drift. Finally, he turns to face me, his expression deadly.

"What are your intentions with my daughter?"

I swallow a sigh. "We already had this talk. Blake and I are just—"

"Hanging out," he finishes coldly. "Well, guess what? *My* daughter? She deserves a helluva lot better than *hanging out*."

"No, I know that. It's not..." Discomfort rises inside me. "Look, I'm aware of my track record with women, but Blake isn't someone I'm just going to mess around with and discard. She means a lot to me."

"Told you," Dad says smugly, glancing at Logan.

Logan crosses his arms. "Your father's trying to convince me that you're not just using her for"—he grimaces—"sex, and that is the *last* time I'm ever gonna say the word *sex* in connection with my daughter."

"I'm not using her."

Heat creeps up my neck. I hate being forced into a position where I need to articulate my feelings to other people when I haven't even figured them out myself.

"All right," Blake's dad says. "You want to prove you're not playing with her? Tell me three things you like about her."

"Just three?" I say dryly, and I see my dad trying not to smile.

"Told you," Dad gloats.

I glare at him. "What exactly have you been telling him?"

"I mean it," Logan says firmly. "Name three things you like about her. Go."

I groan. "Can we please not have this conversation on a boat where I can't escape?"

"Nope. We're not leaving here until you convince me that she's not just a toy for you."

"Of course she's not a toy." Aggravation spirals through me. "Fine, you want three things? She's smart. And not in the obvious book-smart way. She's sharp and analytical and notices things that other people don't notice. And she's got a stupid amount of discipline. She spends hours researching the most random bullshit, except it's not bullshit to her. She's genuinely fascinated with learning new things. She's always solving these puzzles that the rest of us don't even know exist. And it's really fucking amazing."

Logan blinks in surprise.

"She argues with me about *everything*, but it never annoys me. It makes me feel like I'm...awake. Like I'm not just going through the motions."

Now they're both staring at me, but I can't fucking stop. The words are pouring out.

"She has the most calming energy of anyone I've ever known, and I feel at peace just being around her. And yes, she's gorgeous, obviously, and..."

I trail off, my cheeks burning. Fuck. I wish I'd kept my mouth shut.

"Oh shit," Logan says, looking at my father. "You might be right."

"No, he's not right," I grumble. "Whatever he told you, he's not right."

"So you're not in love with my daughter?"

I falter. "No."

"You just recited a dozen reasons why you think she's incredible," Dad tells me, grinning like the asshole he is.

"I'm saying I like her," I mutter. "And that I'm not using her. That this isn't some joke to me, and she's not a toy." I shove my hands through my hair. I don't get embarrassed often, but I'm glad it's pitch-black out, because I'm pretty sure I'm blushing.

Logan studies me before letting out a long, slightly overdramatic sigh. "Look. I've known you your whole life. I know you're not a bad guy, even if your dick *has* done some questionable things in the past. But... If my daughter's going to fall for anyone, I guess I'm okay if it's you."

"She hasn't fallen for me," I protest. "No one's falling for anyone."

"But," he continues, ignoring me, "if you hurt one hair on her head, we will take another midnight boat ride, and I will fucking drown you."

"I'll probably stop him," Dad says to neutralize the threat.

My gaze slides between the two of them. "So you're friends again?"

Dad looks confused. "We were always friends."

"You kept calling each other Mr. Logan and Mr. Graham at dinner."

"Yeah. In a friendly way."

Logan's tone takes on a note of regret. "I'm sorry I called your son a whore, G."

I scowl. "When did you call me a whore?"

He waves a hand. "Oh, you weren't there for it."

Dad shrugs from his perch at the copilot's seat. "It's all good," he tells Logan. "He sort of earned that rep."

"Blake will straighten him out," Logan assures him.

"Obviously. She's a great girl. He's lucky to have her."

I rumble in frustration. "Seriously? Now you're both happy about this?"

"Of course," Dad says. "We've been dreaming about this since we were boys."

"You met in college!"

"College boys," he shrugs.

I sigh. I will never understand this friendship. Ever.

But it's not as confusing as all the emotions currently racing through me. As we start to head back to shore, I slump against the side of the boat, feeling like I'd just been ambushed and exposed at the same time.

# Chapter 41

## BLAKE

*They can't relate to big thinkers like us*

THE LAKE HOUSE HAS CLEARED out of everyone but me, Wyatt, and our parents. In other words, the most uncomfortable configuration of people you can ask for. I'd kill for an AJ and Beau fistfight right about now. But the Golden Boys are gone, Gigi's not here to back me up, and Wyatt's been acting weird the past couple days, leaving me on my own to field constant questions from the dads about our relationship.

Making my mood worse, I feel myself coming down with a cold, so I've been trying to take it easy today. I work on the puzzle with Wyatt, then go for a walk with my mom.

At dinner, we talk about our fall plans and lament about how there are only a few weeks left to summer. My parents are going to Paris in September to visit my grandma, Josie. I'm envious because I'd way rather go back to Paris than to Briar for my senior year. I still can't muster any enthusiasm for this broadcasting major of mine. Or school in general. And my goal of figuring out what the hell I'm going to do after graduation remains unmet. At this point, I think I'm destined for mediocrity, and I should just accept that.

Beside me, Wyatt pushes his chair back to get seconds, glancing at me as he rises. "You need anything from the kitchen while I'm up, freckles?"

"More water would be great, if you don't mind."

"Of course."

When he returns, he sets a full glass next to my plate while planting a sweet kiss on the top of my head. I think it's a reflexive action, because he then abruptly straightens as if remembering he's supposed to be the cool and collected Wyatt Graham. Mr. Bad Boy with his messy hair and chunky rings.

As he retakes his seat, I notice our two fathers beaming.

"This is amazing," Garrett declares.

"Everything I've always dreamed of," Dad says happily.

"Oh really," I challenge. "Suddenly you're A-OK with this? You didn't speak for *three* days."

"We were always speaking in our hearts," Dad says. "I don't understand why they don't get it, G."

"They're small thinkers," Garrett agrees. "They can't relate to big thinkers like us."

I stifle a sigh while our moms laugh.

"What's everyone up to tonight?" Mom asks the table. "Should we play a game? Monopoly?"

"Oh, we're going to see the Spencers," I tell her. "They're heading back to New York tomorrow, so we're hanging out with them on their last night."

"Are you sure you want to take the boat out?" Mom frets, studying me. "You're looking pale. Still trying to beat that bug?"

"It's fine. We won't be long." I glance at Wyatt. "Just a couple hours, right?"

He nods. "Yeah. But you know what, let's take the car. The drive's longer, but you do look a bit pale. Don't want you getting seasick."

While the parents hang out on the deck, Wyatt and I clear the table and clean up, then make the drive to the Spencers. We're not even halfway there when he suddenly pulls off onto the shoulder.

I look over with a frown. "What are you doing?"

He has already flicked the hazards on and is climbing into the back seat. "Quick. Hop on."

Despite the laughter that sputters out, I waste no time wiggling out of my denim shorts. We haven't had sex since the night we caught Beau and Tara, and I am going through major withdrawal.

When I join him in the back, naked from the bottom down, I notice he's already got a condom on. "Were you wearing that the whole time?" I demand.

"No, I put it on while you were taking off your shorts," he says with a snort. "I'm not *that* much of a sex maniac." He pauses. "With that said, sit on my dick, baby."

Laughing, I straddle his lap, and he's instantly all over me, gripping my waist, caressing my sides, my breasts. His breath is hot against my neck as he kisses me there.

"I've been thinking about your body all day. Thinking about how good it feels under my hands." His voice is low, rough, sending chills down my spine. "Your body was fucking made for me, Blake."

My heart races. His words ignite something deep inside me, that wild side he coaxes out of me so easily. I sigh as his lips trail down to my collarbone, and I can feel the heat between us rising fast.

There's no foreplay save for his tongue on my nipples and his hand cupping my pussy to test my readiness. He finds me wet and aching for him, and we both moan eagerly when I sink down on his dick. Pleasure rockets through me, seizing control of my hips because

I need to *move*. I ride him fast and hard, racing toward the orgasm I've been craving for days. My favorite kind of orgasm—the one when his cock is so deep inside me it feels like he's part of me and his fingers are in the place where we're joined, stimulating my clit.

He rubs that throbbing spot and whispers filthy words in my ear, and it isn't long before the knot of pleasure detonates and sends a rush of bliss coursing through my veins. I keep riding him until he's shuddering, squeezing my waist as he thrusts upward and finds his release.

I would've preferred a lot more than a quickie, but it's difficult to be alone (or quiet) in the house, and we can't constantly be banging behind the boathouse like animals. Sometimes a girl needs a bed.

Wyatt pushes his hair out of his eyes, breathing hard. "I needed that."

"Me too." I lean in to kiss him, but all that bouncing made me a bit nauseous, so I reluctantly ease my mouth away and fumble for my shorts.

The first thing Little Spencer says when he lets us in ten minutes later is, "You have sex hair, sweetie."

Grinning, I check my hair in the hall mirror. He's right. It's a disaster. I finger comb the messy strands and tuck them behind my ears while Wyatt drifts into the kitchen to say hi to Big Spencer. They set out a cheese and fruit plate on the cedar counter, but I don't partake. I lean against the stove while the Spencers chat with Wyatt for a few minutes before Little Spencer suddenly clears his throat.

"So," he starts, his sheepish eyes seeking out mine. "One of the reasons we invited you over tonight wasn't just to say goodbye. We... um...sort of did something."

My suspicious gaze travels from one Spencer to the other. "Oh God. What have you guys done?"

"Okay. Well. Hmm. So."

"Stop speaking in monosyllabic riddles," I order.

Big Spencer takes over for his stammering partner. "I know you wanted to listen to the guest episode and watch the video before we finalized it, but we uploaded it already."

"And you can't be mad at us because the video has more than a million views," Little Spencer blurts out.

Shock slams into me. "What? What do you mean over a million?"

"We mean over a million," Big Spencer says, chuckling. "And the podcast has about a hundred thousand downloads. It's free to subscribe, so we don't earn much through downloads, but—"

"You put it online without asking me?"

Anxiety ripples through me as I try to remember everything we talked about. Damn it! They were supposed to let me approve the final edited cut. And they uploaded the *video* too? Oh God. I don't even remember what I was wearing that day.

"What was I wearing?" I demand.

They blink at me. Even Wyatt gives me a strange look.

"What? You can't just put a girl on the internet like that," I moan. "I didn't even wear makeup that day. This is so embarrassing."

"Focus," Little Spencer says, snapping his fingers in front of me as if I'm a parakeet whose attention he's coveting. "One *million* views, Blake. And it's through our ad account, so do you realize how much money we made? Ten thousand dollars! Half of which is yours, obviously."

My jaw drops. "Seriously?"

"It's the most we've ever made on one of our videos. And the comments are all positive. *All* of them! That's unheard of. Usually there are at least a dozen saying how annoying I am."

"A million people listened to us talk about Darlie and Lake Tahoe?"

"Yes," Big Spencer confirms.

I feel dazed. It's unfathomable to me that so many people watched—and *enjoyed*—me and Little Spencer chatting about our silly ghost story.

"If you really want, we'll take it down," Little Spencer promises. "We did a shitty thing putting it up without your permission."

"We're really sorry," Big Spencer says with genuine remorse.

"Say the word and it'll be taken down. Or..." Little Spencer tips his wineglass, taking a dainty sip before setting it down. "We can make it official."

"Make what official?"

"The podcast. There are *so* many comments asking when episode two is coming. Like, this can be a real thing." Little Spencer is practically bouncing with excitement. "We even have a name for it!"

His partner nods and says, "Fringe Benefits."

"We thought we could structure it in seasons. You know, like every season we discuss one topic. Season one: ghosts. Season two: aliens. There's so much cool shit we can do with this, Blake." Little Spencer implores me with his eyes. "Please say yes."

"I have to go back to school," I remind him.

"We can do it while you're in school. New York isn't far from Boston. You can take the train, stay for a weekend. We'll knock out a bunch of episodes, stockpile them, and stagger the releases. Or we'll do a video call setup. We've got options."

"We can make a lot of money," Big Spencer says, which is definitely a selling point.

"And you'll have fun," Wyatt says quietly, finally joining the conversation.

He's right. I will have fun. Because all the research I've done about this one measly mystery? I've had more fun this summer than in my three years of college combined. The only time I enjoyed doing schoolwork at Briar was when researching and writing papers about topics I was able to choose myself. The rest of the time, it's been a boring chore.

"Okay," I say slowly.

Little Spencer's eyes light up. "Okay as in *yes*?" He gasps. "Are you accepting my podcast proposal?"

A smile springs free. "I think I am."

"Oh my God!" He claps his hands together. "This definitely calls for a champagne toast!"

Although I'm not feeling a hundred percent, I can't resist accepting the wineglass he hands me. This does feel toast-worthy. Our Darlie episode earned us *ten thousand dollars*. Even if we never get a fraction of those views again, that is still pretty fucking cool.

"To our new venture," Big Spencer toasts.

"Oh, you've gotta dream bigger, honey," Little Spencer chides. "To our new podcasting empire!"

The four of us clink our glasses. But the moment the champagne slides down my throat, my insides rebel. Oh no. My stomach starts to gurgle, and I gag when I feel the bile burning a path up my throat.

"Oh shit," I blurt out. "I'm gonna be sick."

Gagging, I shove my wineglass at Wyatt and sprint to the hall bathroom. I shut the door and proceed to empty the contents of my stomach.

And as I curl over on my knees, retching and hugging the toilet of Spencer and Spencer Hanz, paranormal podcasters, it occurs to me that my period is two weeks late.

# Chapter 42

## BLAKE

*We'll figure it out*

THE TILES ON THE FLOOR feel like ice beneath my bare feet. I'm sitting on the edge of the tub, staring at the plastic stick in my hands.

Two pink lines.

Not one, two.

I repeat: two.

I blink. Then blink again. And again. Waiting for the image to blur or fade or do something that will prove I'm hallucinating this.

But the lines remain, taunting me.

*Two* of them. Did I mention that?

I honestly didn't think it would be positive. I felt silly when I asked my mom to take me to the pharmacy this morning. I was embarrassed to tell her I was late, but part of me was convinced there was another reason for it. Otherwise, I might not have even recruited Mom for the errand. I might have kept it to myself. I don't regret telling her, because right now, I don't think I can process this alone. My entire body has gone numb.

I barely register the knock on the door. "Honey, it's Mom." She sounds calm, but I can hear the twinge of worry. "Are you okay in there?"

Okay? I almost laugh. No, I'm not okay. My life has just turned upside down. I can't make my vocal cords work. So, knees wobbling, I stand up, open the door, and hand her the test without a word.

She looks at it, closes her eyes briefly. Then she sighs and pulls me to her arms for a tight hug. "Oh, my girl," she murmurs, running her hand over my hair like I'm a kid again.

Tears spill over before I can stop them. "You can't tell Dad," I blurt out. "Please. Promise me you won't tell him."

"Blake—"

"No, not yet." My voice breaks. "*Please.*"

After a beat, she nods. "I won't tell him."

"You promise?" I know they don't keep secrets from each other. But her face is the picture of reassurance.

"I promise, not until you're ready. This is your choice. No one else's."

"Oh my God." My breathing becomes shallow. "What... I can't... I'm not..."

I can't even finish a sentence. All I know is that I'm not ready for this. It's too big. And saying it out loud would make this real in a way that I can't take back.

She brushes my tears away with her thumbs. "You don't have to decide anything today. You can take your time, and whatever you decide, I'll support you."

"What about Dad?"

"He'll support you too, or I'll divorce him."

I laugh weakly. To be fair, I'm not sure she's even joking.

A question tickles my throat, bringing a queasy sensation to my stomach. "Do you think I should get rid of it?"

There's a long pause.

"I think that might be easier," she finally says. "But easier isn't always right. Only you can know what's right."

"But I *don't* know."

"You don't have to know right this second. We'll figure it out."

"What about Wyatt? I have to tell him."

"Yes, you do. But again, it doesn't have to be right now, okay?"

"He's not going to want a baby," I mumble, and my body starts shaking again. "You know him. He can't be tied down. He can't even stay in one place for too long. He'll hate me if I keep it."

"Aw, honey, you don't know that."

"Yes, I do." I let out another laugh. There's nothing funny about this, yet it's all I seem capable of doing. Laughing at the absurdity of it. "He'll feel like I trapped him, and then he'll run, or even worse, he'll try to do the right thing when he really doesn't want to." The tears start falling again. "I wouldn't be able to stand that."

"Blake," she says firmly. "You're spiraling. Take a breath. Take a step back. You don't need to tell him until you're ready." She cups my face, forcing me to look at her. "You don't need all the answers. You're scared, and that's okay. But you are *not* alone in this. Whatever you decide—to keep it, not to keep it, talk to Wyatt, don't talk to Wyatt—I will stand with you always."

I bury my face against her shoulder and let myself cry harder than I have in years. Or maybe ever. This isn't only about a pregnancy. It's about Wyatt and me and everything I feel for him. Everything I fear for us.

What if I tell him and he looks at me like I ruined his life?

What if I want to keep it and he doesn't?

What if he wants to keep it and *I* don't? That one's unlikely, but it could happen. Anything could happen.

The fear gnaws at my insides like a scavenger until my stomach feels like it's torn to shreds. Mom holds me and lets me cry, stroking my hair in a slow, soothing gesture.

"We'll figure it out," she says as I sob in her arms. "I promise."

# Chapter 43

## WYATT

### *Forever, maybe*

BLAKE IS ACTING WEIRD. SHE'S barely argued with me about anything these past couple days, which is unsettling on its own, but she's also not initiating sex, naps, jokes. She claims she's not feeling well, and Grace did make her soup for dinner last night, but I can't shake the feeling like there's something else going on, a piece of the puzzle that I'm missing.

She seems lost in thought, and I wonder if it has to do with school. Maybe agreeing to do the podcast with the Spencers has made her rethink going back to college altogether. But she only has one more year. She might as well power through it and earn her degree. You never know when one of those could come in handy. Not that I know. I skipped college. Wasn't for me.

Tonight, I'm in the studio Dad's been toiling over since he got here. His labor of love. I can't even make fun of him for it, because I get it now. I spend an unhealthy amount of time thinking about ways to make Blake happy.

As the speakers play the last notes of the melody before fading out, I shift nervously in my chair. Although the studio is still missing some equipment and furniture, it's mostly done, and Dad wasted no time taking my mother downstairs, blindfolded, to reveal her surprise. She cried when she saw it. Mom rarely cries, so I know how much this must've meant to her.

"So?" I ask, holding my breath.

From her perch near the mixer, Mom simply says, "It's beautiful."

I feel a burst of joy. "Really?"

"I think it might be the best thing you've ever written."

I search her face, but I don't see even a hint of dishonesty or bullshitting. I think she means it.

"Is it ready for Tobey Dodson?"

"Absolutely." She smiles at me. "Do I even need to ask who it's about?"

I played "Lightkeeper" for her, which is, of course, about Blake. But so is "Stop the World." So is "You Know." So is every other line and verse I wrote this summer.

Before I can answer, my phone lights up with a text from Blake. Her ears must be burning. I lean over to check the message, then frown.

FRECKLES

We need to talk. Meet me on the dock.

*We need to talk*. Shit. Those words are never good.

But this is also what I've been desperate for. She's been shutting me out for two days, and that worries me. I *want* to talk.

"Can we finish this in a bit?" I ask, sliding off my chair.

"Of course. Whenever you want," Mom says.

I waste no time slipping my feet into a pair of slides and striding outside. A minute later, the dock is creaking beneath my shoes as I make my way toward Blake. She sits cross-legged with her phone beside her. She doesn't even look over when I join her. That's concerning.

"Hey," I say. "What's going on?"

She doesn't answer. Just sits there quietly, twisting her fingers together in her lap. The lake is still tonight, the moonlight dancing across its dark surface.

"Blake," I urge. "Talk to me."

"I'm pregnant."

The world stops.

It just…stops. My lungs seize. My heart freezes. The crickets go silent. The buzz of mosquitoes ceases.

For a second, I wonder if I misheard her.

"You're w-what?" I stammer.

"Pregnant."

"As in?"

"Pregnant." She finally glances at me. Her eyes are tired and sad but also a bit amused. "You put a baby in there, Graham."

"How?"

"With your sperm."

I choke out a laugh. "No, I mean, I know that. But we took the Plan B."

"Must've missed the window," she says dully. "I found out two days ago. I'm sorry I didn't say anything sooner, but I've been trying to figure out how to tell you."

"Do your parents know?"

"Only my mom. I wanted to tell you before we destroyed our dads' friendship again."

I have no clue how she's managing to make me laugh when she just changed the entire trajectory of my life with two words. *I'm pregnant.*

Jesus. Her father is going to take me out on the boat again, and this time, he'll drown me.

"I got a blood test done yesterday at the clinic in town, and I spoke to my doctor today. We had a video consult. She thinks I'm about five weeks. She's bringing me in for a seven-week scan, and we'll be able to see if everything is going smoothly or normal or whatever..." Blake gulps. "So we have two weeks to sit with this before we even know what's happening."

My mind is still spinning, free-falling. Pregnant. Baby.

"I know you'll want me to take care of it, but I haven't decided."

I frown at her. "Why is that what you think I want?"

"Because..." Her voice starts shaking. "You're not the kind of guy who wants a baby this young, Wyatt. You don't want to be tied down or trapped."

"Who's trapping me? Because the last time I checked, it takes two people to make a baby, and I'm equally responsible for this."

"And you should have a say in what we do." Her bottom lip trembles. "It's okay to admit you don't want it."

"Hey." I reach for her hand.

She flinches, just slightly, and it kills me.

"Blake, look at me."

Her eyes meet mine. They're full of fear and...guilt. And that kills me too. She has nothing to feel guilty about.

"We did everything properly," I remind her. "We fucked up, and we tried to fix it with Plan B, and it didn't work. But we did this *together*."

"I don't know what I want to do," she tells me. "So I'm not saying I'm keeping it. I just want to wait to decide until after the scan. Maybe there isn't even a decision to make."

I go quiet for a moment, absorbing that. "Okay. Then we'll wait."

She gawks at me like I've grown horns. "You're calm," she accuses. "Why are you so calm? Why aren't you freaking out?"

"I am. I'm terrified. My stomach's doing backflips. But..." I hesitate, searching for the words. "I'm not as terrified as I thought I'd be. Not with you. Not when it's us."

"What does that even mean, us? This isn't... I don't know what this is." Frustrated, she pulls her hand back and hugs her knees. "You can't say it's fine, because it's *not* fine."

"I'm not saying it's fine. I'm saying I'm not going to run. If you decide to keep it, I'll be here. I'm here now."

Tears well up in her eyes, clinging to her thick lashes. "You're not the settling-down type. You've made that clear. This isn't you."

"Maybe it is," I say softly. "Maybe I just didn't realize it until now."

She focuses on me, uncertain. "Are you only saying that because I'm pregnant? You're trying to be some hero now because you feel responsible?"

"No, I'm saying it because I care about you. Because I..." I stop, exhaling slowly. "Because I love you."

I've said those three words to a girl before. Many times, in fact. Back when I mistook sexual chemistry for true love, before I realized what I was feeling wasn't real. Didn't last.

It's been years since those words left my mouth, but the second they do, I know without a doubt this isn't about chemistry or sex or some idealistic version of love I write about in songs.

This is the most real thing I've ever felt in my life.

Blake Logan owns me. Heart, body, and soul.

"You love me." She bites her lip. "Since when?"

"I don't know. Forever maybe. I've just been too scared to say it."

She stares at me like she's trying to read every thought in my mind. “You’re not just saying that?”

“No.” I reach for her hand again, and this time, she lets me hold it. “I’m saying it because it’s true. I’m in love with you.”

Her face crumples, as if she doesn’t know whether to cry or laugh. She doesn’t say it back. That should bother me, but it doesn’t. She’s going through a lot right now. I don’t want her to feel forced to say things or pressured to feel something that she doesn’t.

For a moment, we sit there. Fingers laced together, staring at each other like the rest of the world doesn’t exist.

Then she says, “What if I’m not ready? If I can’t do this? I’m not someone’s mom.”

I tighten my grip on her hand. “We’ll figure it out. Whatever you want, whatever you need, I’m in this.”

She sniffles, peering at the water. “It scares me that you don’t sound scared.”

Chuckling, I press her hand to my chest, where my heart is pounding harder than it ever has before.

“Feel how fast that’s beating? I’m fucking terrified. But…two weeks,” I remind her. “We sit in this together for two weeks. No rushing, no pushing. Just us.”

“Us,” she repeats slowly, as if testing the word out for size.

I gently stroke her knuckles. “Can you do that for me, baby?”

“Yeah.” Blake leans toward me and rests her head against my shoulder. “I can do that.”

# Chapter 44

## BLAKE

*If*

DESPITE OUR AGREEMENT TO KEEP it between us, we decide to do the unthinkable and tell the dads. Not because we're desperate for transparency but because morning sickness has descended on me like a swarm of locusts. It hits out of nowhere the day after Wyatt and I have our conversation on the dock, turning my life into a state of pure misery.

Mom told me that when she was pregnant with me, she only felt nauseous at night. *My* nausea begins in the morning, and then (fun times) continues well into the afternoon, and then (lucky me) stretches out long past evening.

Pregnancy sucks.

Day one, we were able to convince my father that I had a twenty-four-hour stomach bug.

Day two of me marrying the toilet was harder, because he got worried and suggested we go to the emergency room. Mom convinced him it was probably a *forty-eight*-hour bug, then secretly drove to town and picked me up some pregnancy-safe stomach remedies. They didn't help.

On day three, when Dad was ready to drive me to the ER himself, Wyatt and I finally called a family meeting.

Sixty seconds ago, we told my father and Wyatt's parents about the pregnancy. Now we're sitting on our respective deck chairs, awaiting the explosion.

It doesn't come.

Dad and Garrett look at each other for a moment. Then they nod and turn back to us.

"Okay," Dad says.

"All right," Garrett says.

I wrinkle my forehead. "What's happening right now?"

"You're pregnant," Dad tells me.

"Yes, I know that! I'm asking what's happening *here*." I wave my hand between them. "You two are cool with this?"

They shrug, which heightens my suspicion. Wyatt told me about that midnight boat ride my father forced him on. What if they take him out on the boat again?

"Please don't drown him," I blurt out.

Everyone startles.

"Honey," Mom starts.

"No," I cut in. "That's totally what's happening right now. Why they're so calm about it." I plead my case to Wyatt's parents. "You can't let him kill your son."

"I'm not killing anybody!" Dad protests, doubling over with laughter.

"No, she's right," Wyatt says uneasily. "You guys are too calm. I don't trust this."

Wyatt's mom eyes him curiously. "You're pretty calm yourself."

"Yeah, because like we just told you, we're waiting until the scan before we make any decisions."

Hannah nods. "And we'll support whatever you two decide."

Relief flickers through me. I wasn't worried about Hannah, though. She's levelheaded like my mom. Our dads are the crazy ones. And yet neither of the crazies looks bothered.

"Dad," I say, "you can't possibly be happy about this."

"Happy?" He mulls it over. "Well. I can't say that my twenty-one-year-old daughter having a baby was in my five-year plan for you. But..." He shrugs. "Things happen."

"Things happen?" I echo. "What's going on here?"

A gasp sounds from the phone in the center of the deck table. It's Gigi. She's back in Dallas, but Wyatt didn't feel right telling their parents and not including his twin. I don't blame him. If I had a sibling, I'd include them too.

"Oh my God," Gigi says. "I know what's happening. They *want* this."

My gaze swings back to our dads.

"You *are* happy," Gigi accuses. "Admit it."

"Again, I don't know if *happy* is the word I'd use," Garrett says carefully. "But we sort of came to terms with it already."

"What the hell does that mean?" Wyatt demands.

"It means once we accepted the relationship was happening whether we like it or not, we obviously talked through all the steps that might follow. Marriage, for one," his dad says.

"We're splitting the cost of the wedding," mine pipes up. "That way, we have equal say."

"You have *no* say," Mom says in exasperation. "It's their wedding."

"There's no wedding!" I interject, starting to get frustrated.

"Anyway, after the wedding, what naturally comes next is

babies." Dad gives me a reassuring look, which doesn't reassure me in the slightest. "Don't worry, sweet pea. We've already negotiated everything."

Oh my God. I rub my forehead.

"Graham will come first in the hyphenated name. Graham-Logan. Because Grahams are always in first place," Garrett explains.

"But Logans always come in clutch to get the job done," Dad says smugly.

"If it's a boy, Grahams have middle name rights."

"If it's a girl, Logans obviously."

"And then the grandfather babysitting schedule will be—"

"Okay, we've heard enough," Hannah interrupts while Gigi's uncontrollable laughter floats out of the phone speaker.

"All right, guys," chirps Wyatt's twin. "I gotta get on a work call. But...maybe congratulations? Either way, Luke and I will keep this to ourselves. I promise."

"Thanks, but I wasn't worried about you or BIL blabbing," Wyatt says before she disconnects. He turns to glare at his father. "*You're* the one I'm worried about."

"Yeah," I chime in. "I know we have this whole incestuous family dynamic where everyone is up in everyone's business, but I don't want anyone to know. If we keep it, the pregnancy stays a secret until the first trimester's over."

Dad is stricken. "We can't even tell Dean and Tuck?"

"*Especially* not Dean," Wyatt grumbles.

Meanwhile, I'm tripping over the last thing I said. And the word *if*.

*If* we keep it.

We only told our families because I needed to explain why I'm throwing up every other minute, but now that we've brought them in on this fucked-up journey, it's feeling a lot more real. Like maybe this isn't an "if we keep it" situation anymore.

Maybe it's *when* we keep it.

# Chapter 45

## WYATT

*All paths lead to you*

MY FATHER JOINS ME ON the dock later that night, where I'm sneaking a cigarette. I cut back almost entirely this summer, but the past few days have been...overwhelming, to say the least.

"You okay?" He comes up beside me at the edge.

I exhale a cloud of smoke and let the night breeze carry it away. "Well, my girlfriend's pregnant so..."

Dad chuckles. "Is it too late to give you the condom talk?"

I groan. "Don't even start. It was one drunken night. And we were so responsible."

"Clearly not."

"Seriously, we even drove to the pharmacy the next day for Plan B. We had to chase some down, and we thought we took it in time, but..."

"But fate had other ideas."

"Fate? You think I was fated for this?"

"Nah. Not really." He shrugs. "I believe in making your own fate."

I go to rake my hand through my hair, but I forget I'm holding a cigarette and almost burn the ends of my hair off. I take a deep drag instead and blow out another puff of smoke, watching it float over the water.

"You seem to be handling it okay," Dad remarks.

I bark out a laugh. "I started smoking again, so obviously not. I'm trying to, though. I have to figure out how to be someone who can handle this."

"Of course you can." His tone goes gruff. "But I will say..."

"What?"

"Being a father isn't something you can half-ass. You can't get lost in music for days."

"I know. If she keeps the baby, I'll do whatever I need to do." A lump fills my throat. "I love her."

His expression softens.

"I'm not gonna let her go through this alone." I take another drag. "It's weird, but when she told me, we were sitting right there," I say, nodding to the end of the dock. "Time just stopped for a moment. But then...it kept going."

He chuckles. "Well, yes, that's usually how time moves. Forward."

"No, I mean... I wasn't panicked. I was calm. I thought, okay, I guess maybe we're doing this, or maybe not. Blake even commented that I wasn't as scared as she thought I would be." I exhale another cloud. "Were you scared when Mom told you she was pregnant with us?"

"Beyond scared," he admits. "I reacted poorly."

I frown at him. "Poorly how?"

"We got into a big fight because she kept it from me for weeks. I only found out because she started bleeding and had to go to the hospital."

"That doesn't sound like Mom. Why didn't she tell you?"

"Because she was scared of how I would react, and rightly so. I didn't want kids that young. I was still in the NHL. But not only that—I didn't know how to be a father. Because mine was a piece of shit who only spoke to me if it was about hockey or when he was beating the shit out of me and my mom."

I nod, because I've heard this before. And while I feel sick about the childhood he had, I'm proud of who he's become. He's a good man in spite of his father. He could've taken a whole different path, perpetuated the cycle of abuse, but he broke free of it.

"I lashed out," he continues, and I hear the grief in his voice. "I said shit that I regret. The thing about your mom is she always sees through my bluster and cocky remarks. She knew it was coming from a place of fear and was able to forgive me. We made up, and then we had you guys, and it's the best thing that's ever happened to me."

He reaches over and slings one arm around me, squeezing my shoulder before releasing me.

"You're already ahead of the game, Wyatt. You're standing here saying you'll do whatever it takes. And that's something I had to learn the hard way. I had to learn to be your dad."

"Well, I had—have," I correct, "a great father. I know I can do this if she wants me to. Maybe not perfectly. I'll probably screw it up half the time, but I think I can do it."

I can't believe the words that are exiting my mouth. Who the fuck is this guy? My entire life, my head has been pure chaos, pushing me in a thousand different directions. One summer with Blake has tethered me. Not in the way she fears, though.

Not a trap but an anchor.

When I check on her a short while later, she's curled up on her bed, her cheek pressed against the pillow. The ashen shade of her face tells me she just threw up.

"You okay?" I ask quietly. "Need me to bring you some crackers? Water?"

"No, thank you. I'm just gonna lie here until my stomach settles."

I stretch out next to her, and she rolls toward me and rests her cheek on my chest. I run my fingers through her hair.

"You were right," I find myself saying.

"About what?"

"When you said I've been stuck in my own life by telling myself stories about who I am, who I'm supposed to be. I've been so fucking stubborn about everything. Refusing to even consider playing pop music, refusing to let people help me. Convincing myself I can't ever have a relationship because I'm self-centered and music comes first and I'm destined to be alone on the road." There's a strange ache in my chest. "Fuck. All I ever did was hold myself back."

"And you're not holding back anymore?" she murmurs.

"I don't think so. It's...sort of fucked up, but the moment you told me you were pregnant, it's like I could suddenly see all these new paths available to me." I swallow. "Not necessarily ones that lead to fatherhood. I'm not saying we should keep it. But all those paths have one thing in common."

"What?"

"You. All paths lead to you."

She tilts her head up at me, and her bottom lip starts trembling. I don't miss the flood of emotion in her eyes, so I pull her close again, gently stroking her hair. After several beats of silence, her whisper tickles my neck.

"You don't have to stay here if you want to go write."

"No." I kiss the top of her head. "I'm not going anywhere."

## THE DEAN MACHINE

DEAN

They're acting weird, right?

ALLIE

Who?

DEAN

G and Logan and their respective clans. Something's up. They've barely texted me this week.

ALLIE

Just because they're not texting *you* doesn't mean something's up. Contrary to popular Dean belief, the world doesn't revolve around you, sweetie.

DEAN

Beau—back me up. Blake and the twins have been quiet, right?

BEAU

I don't know. I haven't noticed.

IVY

Leave him alone, Daddy. He's sad.

ALLIE

Aw honey. AJ's still not talking to you?

KATE

LMAO AJ's never talking to him again. Not after what he did.

ALLIE

Maybe don't laugh at your brother's misery, Katherine?

KATE

Maybe don't bang your best friend's girlfriend?

DEAN

You're fifteen. Don't use the word bang. Ivy—weigh in?

IVY

Not until you change the name of this group chat.

*DEAN DI LAURENTIS CHANGED THE NAME OF THE GROUP CHAT TO THE BEST-LOOKING FAMILY EVER.*

IVY

Better.

# Chapter 46

## BLAKE

*Don't look so proud of yourself for snitching*

IN TEN DAYS, I HAVE to go back to school.

In eight days, I have my seven-week scan.

Coincidence? I think not.

The universe is forcing me to choose. I see you, universe. Transparent bitch.

The idea of not finishing my senior year feels like a waste. I mean, it *is* a waste. It's a waste of my parents' money, because they paid for my tuition. Which means I *have* to finish college.

While possibly pregnant.

Ugh. And, what, have a baby in the middle of my graduation ceremony?

I mean, Sabrina Tucker did it. She got pregnant with Jamie right before she started law school. That woman is a rock star, though. Her work ethic isn't sustainable for us mere mortals. I don't know if I have that kind of discipline.

Wyatt and I are taking the boat out for a few hours, so I put on a pair of shorts over my bathing suit and look for my tote bag. We're eager to escape the grandfathers, who've been very politely asked not to discuss anything baby-related until a decision has been made, yet they're constantly sneaking off, and we can hear them giggling together. I fear they'll be devastated if we choose not to continue with the pregnancy.

An *if* that continues to haunt me.

The kitchen smells like pancakes. Usually, it's an aroma I'd welcome, but it triggers a twinge of nausea. Stupid morning sickness. There's also a dull ache low in my stomach today. It's been there since I woke up, this knot of discomfort. But Mom says some cramping is normal.

I hold my breath as I pass the stove and go to the fridge to grab some water.

"You want pancakes?" Dad offers.

"No. It'll make me throw up."

"At least try one."

"Dad, seriously, the smell is so awful."

"Aw, and I thought these were my best batch."

"No, it smells fantastic, but it still makes me want to vomit." I shut the refrigerator door. "Anyway, we're going out on the boat now."

"Without eating anything?" He folds his arms. "You're eating for two now, sweet pea."

"I'm also puking for two," I reply, and he chuckles before his expression snaps back to serious.

"Also, are you sure you should be going out on the boat? It's too dangerous."

"Dangerous how? It's not like we're going cliff diving."

"I know, but you still need to be careful. What if the boat capsizes?"

I glance at him over my shoulder. "You and Wyatt need to get together and discuss your irrational fear of boats capsizing in Tahoe."

Mom wanders in from the deck, carrying two empty plates. She and Hannah were eating their breakfast outside. "Leave her alone, John," she chides.

I set down the water bottle when I feel another cramp. Sharper than before. Taking a breath, I press my hand against my lower abdomen.

Mom notices instantly. "Are you okay?"

"I think so. It's just, I don't know, it's this weird feeling. Like a stretching sensation. But I read that's normal." I'm kind of embarrassed to admit I've been reading up on early pregnancy, but they know me. I'm not going into any situation without a healthy amount of research.

Mom relaxes, but a flicker of concern remains. "Cramping is normal, yes. Do you have any spotting?"

I shake my head.

"You're a touch pale," she says, scrutinizing me. "Are you sure you're not overdoing it?"

"See!" Dad says triumphantly. He glances at Mom. "And she's going on a *boat ride*."

I glare at him. "Don't look so proud of yourself for snitching. Also, there's nothing to snitch. Yes, we're going out on the boat for a while. It'll be fine."

Mom shrugs. "All right, have fun. Just try to take it easy. Don't swim if you have cramps."

"I won't."

The ache doesn't subside during our lazy cruise of the lake. By afternoon, it's deepened, radiating to my back and down my thigh. Deciding maybe I do need to take it easier, I lie on the couch after lunch, scrolling on my phone while Dad watches a movie and Mom and Hannah clean up in the kitchen.

Wyatt is fishing with his dad, which I was quick to encourage. They've been hanging out a lot this week, and I can see how happy it makes Wyatt to connect with Garrett over something that isn't hockey. I wonder if he'll ever tell his father about all the times he hit up the rink this summer.

My phone buzzes with another message. I'm texting with Little Spencer, who's back in New York and just sent a picture of his home podcasting studio.

LITTLE SPENCER

See, I can totally get a second chair in here!! And we'll design a professional backdrop behind the table so it looks like a real studio. OMG I can't wait for you to move to the city!!!

For the last time, I'm not moving to NYC.

LITTLE SPENCER

Fine, we'll stick to our weekend plan. FOR NOW!

I grin at my screen, but all of a sudden, the words blur as a wave of nausea hits, forcing me to sit up abruptly.

"You okay?" Dad glances over.

"I'm fine. Just feeling queasy again."

"Grace, get the bucket," he calls.

"I don't need a bucket. There's a bathroom, like, fifteen feet away."

I get up, and the room tilts when that sharp pain radiates through me again. My skin feels clammy, and my heartbeat is now pounding in my ears, making me lightheaded.

"What's going on, kiddo?" Alarm laces his tone.

I hold on to the back of the couch, my vision blurring again. As my knees buckle, I try to steady myself. "Something's wrong," I say.

Dad stands so fast that the remote clatters onto the floor. "Talk to me. Where does it hurt?"

I gulp through the nausea, and the pain stabs me deep in the side. White hot and relentless.

A wave of dizziness overtakes me. And then everything goes black.

# Chapter 47

## BLAKE

*You don't have to pretend*

WHEN I OPEN MY EYES, the world feels slow and heavy, like I'm surfacing from the bottom of a deep, dark lake. All I feel is confusion. A bright light stings my eyes. A monitor beeps softly nearby. There's the sterile smell of antiseptic in my nose and a dull throb in my abdomen.

The last thing I remember, I was feeling sick. I was dizzy. Stumbling. I remember my dad's worried eyes on me, his arms reaching for me before I fainted. Oh my God. He brought me to the hospital because I *fainted*? He's so melodramatic.

I swallow through my arid throat and try to speak. I only manage a rusty squawking noise at first before finally getting out a croaky, "Dad?"

There's a flurry of motion around me. The next thing I know, I see my mother's face, pale and lined with concern. Then Dad is on the other side of the bed, his expression grim.

"Hey, sweet pea, how are you feeling?"

"Sore," I say. "My stomach hurts."

Neither of them answers.

I lick my dry lips. "Why am I in the hospital? Did you overreact and bring me here?"

When I attempt to sit up, Mom firmly touches my arm to keep me down. "Nope, don't move yet, honey. You just got out of surgery."

"Surgery? For fainting?" I say in confusion.

My gaze darts around the room, then focuses on my own body. I realize I have one of those heart monitor things on my finger.

"I don't understand," I finally say.

"You had an ectopic pregnancy," she says gently. "It ruptured, and there was some internal bleeding."

"Scared the hell out of us," Dad says.

"We're so lucky we got you here when we did." Her voice shakes, and I realize how scared they both look.

I try to move again, but Dad stops me. "You need to stay still. I'll get the doctor so she can check you out, okay?"

As he hurries out the door, Mom squeezes my hand. "We were so worried about you. So was Wyatt. The Grahams are in the waiting room. He wanted to be in here with you, but I thought you might want me and Dad to be the first people you saw while you process."

"Process," I echo weakly. "I don't understand. So I'm not pregnant anymore?"

I'm usually not this stupid, and I can sense that the question is dumb, but my brain is fuzzy, and I still can't comprehend what's happening.

"Ectopic pregnancy… That means… The embryo implanted outside the uterus?"

She nods. "In your left fallopian tube."

"It was just cramps…" I trail off when footsteps approach the door.

A doctor in pink scrubs enters, tailed by my dad. She approaches the bed in brisk strides. "My name is Dr. Lechie. How are you feeling, Blake?"

"Confused," I admit. "A bit woozy."

"Yes, that's the anesthesia wearing off." She examines my pupils, making me follow the penlight she pulls out of her pocket. "I'm sure your parents told you, but you experienced an ectopic pregnancy. We had to perform a salpingostomy, which means we repaired your tube rather than removing it. You were lucky. The rupture wasn't severe, and while there was internal bleeding, it wasn't heavy."

She keeps talking, explaining she made an incision in my fallopian tube in order to "remove the pregnancy," and her tone is so clinical and matter-of-fact that it makes me want to cry. Then she assures me they were able to preserve the tube, and as long as the scarring isn't extensive, natural conception shouldn't be an issue in the future since both tubes are intact.

"You'll be discharged tomorrow," she finishes with a smile.

As if that's the takeaway from all this. Good news! No baby! Now go home.

When she notices my expression, her tone softens. "I know this is a lot to process."

"I...don't get it. Was there something I could've done or... Did I overdo it?" My pulse is racing now.

"You didn't do anything wrong," Dr. Lechie says firmly. "Unfortunately, this is just something that happens sometimes. It occurs in about one in fifty pregnancies, and ninety percent of the time, it's a tubal ectopic. You usually can't even detect it until your first scan. If you'd found out next week at your ultrasound, we could've given you medication to clear the pregnancy, but the rupture gave us no choice but to remove it surgically."

She talks me through the post-op, telling me to expect some

soreness from the small incision in my abdomen but that any pain should improve within a week. I'm allowed to return to light activities in a week, heavier activities in about a month. It's all very technical, and my head is starting to hurt. As she drones on, tears prick my eyes, and my hands begin shaking.

I don't want this. I don't want to be here. I want to go back to this morning. Before that dull ache and before the fear, when I still had a future to picture.

Instead, I'm listening to this doctor and to the stupid beeping of this monitor. It's supposed to remind me that I'm alive, but all it's doing is reminding me that my baby is not.

The thought unleashes the tears. Mom instantly clutches my hand and strokes my hair while Dr. Lechie gently touches my arm before leaving to continue her rounds. I barely notice she's gone. Or that she was there in the first place.

"I want to see Wyatt," I choke out.

"Are you sure?" Mom asks.

"Please, can someone go get him?"

Dad nods and disappears from the room. He's only gone for five minutes, but it feels like an eternity before Wyatt appears in the doorway. Relief catches in my throat at the sight of him. He looks beautiful, even in the harsh glare of hospital lighting. And his hair is beyond messy, which tells me he's been dragging his hand through it in that waiting room.

"Freckles," he says, his eyes full of concern.

My parents give us privacy as he approaches the bed. He cups my cheeks and urgently searches my face.

"Are you okay?"

"No," I whisper. "The baby's gone." My throat closes up. "Well, technically, the baby was never even there. It had zero chance of survival."

"I know. The doctor explained it to us." He strokes my cheek, his thumb brushing over my cheekbone, and a few tears spill out. "Hey, it's okay. You're gonna be okay."

Now I'm crying in earnest. Dr. Lechie had said something about hormones and that I still have high levels of HCG in my system. Apparently they'll need to monitor my levels until they return to zero to make sure no "tissue" remains. And I'm going to be a hormonal basket case for at least a few weeks, if not longer. Awesome.

"Oh, baby, please don't cry."

Wyatt sits on the bed, infinitely gentle as he pulls me into his arms. I feel a twinge of pain in my side, but I don't care. I bury my face against Wyatt's chest, breathing in his familiar spicy scent, filling my lungs with it so I don't have to smell that horrible antiseptic anymore.

"I'm so sorry this happened," he murmurs in my hair. "And I know you're upset. But you're young, and you're healthy, and the doctor said you still have both tubes—"

"I wanted it."

He stiffens in surprise.

I lift my head, wiping my tears. "I didn't even realize how much I wanted it until right now, and now it's just gone."

"I think...maybe I wanted it too," Wyatt says, and for some reason, that triggers a jolt of anger.

"Stop lying."

He's taken aback. "I'm not lying."

I turn my head, suddenly unable to look at him. Every breath feels like I'm dragging broken glass through my lungs. The anger has come out of nowhere, making me feel small and embarrassed but at the same time helpless to stop it.

"Please look at me," he says softly.

But I can't. I don't know why. All I know is there's this cynical voice in my head telling me that the grief I see in his eyes isn't real. It's fake. That what he's really feeling is relief.

"It's fine, Wyatt," I mumble. "You don't have to pretend."

His hand finds my chin, gently forcing my head toward him. The shock and hurt on his face evoke a rush of guilt, but the fear has already taken hold, coiling inside my chest like a boa constrictor.

"You didn't want this," I say. "Not really. It's okay to admit that."

"That's not true. Neither of us even knew what we wanted. We agreed to decide after the scan."

I wrap my arms around myself and dig my nails into my skin, trying to steady myself. "It's fine," I repeat. "You pretended to be cool with it for me, and I appreciate that, but—"

"Stop saying that," he interrupts, and his voice breaks. "I wasn't pretending."

He's *lying*. He has to be. He *has* to be breathing easier without the weight of a baby crushing down on him. I'm not a fool. Any man would be relieved, and *especially* a man who's had commitment issues his entire life.

"I was at peace with either option," Wyatt says softly. "I promise you that."

My throat closes around a sob. "You're saying that because it's what I need to hear right now."

His eyes search mine. I sense his frustration, his panic. He pries my hand out of my death grip on myself and squeezes it tight.

"I know what you're doing, and I understand why, but please don't shut me out. I'm here with you. Right here with you. Always."

I shrug my hand away. "Can you go get my mom?"

Wyatt flinches as if I struck him. "I'm not leaving you."

"Please." I twist my face away from him, the tears soaking the pillow. "I just want my mom."

# Chapter 48

## WYATT

### The right thing

BLAKE IS DISCHARGED FROM THE hospital less than twenty-four hours after being admitted. It seems too soon for me, but apparently this is a common surgery, so minimally invasive she'll barely have a scar. Nonetheless, I don't like the idea of sending her home when she's still so fragile. Everything makes her cry, even leaving the hospital. She has to be in a wheelchair because it's policy, and when a mother and her young son can't fit onto the elevator and say, "We'll take the next one," Blake bursts into tears because there was no room.

My mom tells me it's completely normal. Blake's hormone levels are dropping, and it can take weeks for what I'm told is the "pregnancy hormone" to leave her system. But it's hard to watch. No, it's excruciating, especially when she barely looks at me. Barely talks to me. We haven't even been alone since she accused me of pretending to be cool with the pregnancy and then chose to seek comfort from her mom rather than me.

I'm trying not to take it personally. Blake is close with her mom, and I know Grace is her support system—it's only natural she's leaning on her.

But I wish she would lean on me, even just a little.

The day after she's discharged, I decide to fix her some lunch and see if she'll eat it outside with me on the deck like we used to do. She hasn't left her room since she got back from the hospital.

Mom finds me in the kitchen, smiling at the sight. "He's cooking."

"He's cooking," I confirm. "Well, sort of. It's just grilled cheese."

I lift the sandwich out of the pan with a spatula and set it down on the plate. As I grab a knife and prepare to cut the grilled cheese in half, a memory surfaces, making me glance over at my mom.

"Hey, remember that time I asked you and Dad why you cut diagonally and not directly in half, and you said it's because diagonally means you love the person?" I snort. "And then Dad made us grilled cheese that one time and purposely served everyone but me a diagonal cut?"

Mom huffs out a laugh. "And you ran upstairs crying. God, your dad is such an asshole."

"Nah, you have to admit, it was a pretty funny prank."

"Well, obviously. But still an asshole. You bringing that up to Blake?"

"I'm gonna see if she'll come down. Guard the sandwiches, will you? Don't let the dads get them."

"With my life," she promises. Before I can walk away, Mom touches my arm. "She'll be okay, honey. She's just gone through a trauma, but she's strong."

I nod. "I know."

"And those hormones can be a real bitch. Try not to take anything she says to heart. She'll probably feel bad about it later."

"You've heard her snapping at me then," I say wryly.

"Yes, but she's been snapping at everyone, if that makes you feel better."

"Actually, it does."

Upstairs, I find the door to the yellow room closed. I really did disrupt the entire ecosystem of rooms by taking the blue room without thinking. With Blake in the yellow room, Gigi and Ryder had to sleep in the mountain room, which means I got to hear my sister complain endlessly about how she much hates the mountain room because there are too many mosquitoes on that side of the house. Who doesn't like a majestic mountain view? My twin is such a diva.

I knock on the door and am rewarded with a soft, "Come in."

That's promising.

The first thing I see when I step inside is the suitcase on the bed.

I take it back. Not promising at all.

"Why are you packing?" I ask with a frown.

Blake glances up from the stack of T-shirts she's folding. She's wearing blue sweatpants and a white T-shirt, her hair arranged in a loose braid. Clothing-wise, she looks like her usual self. But I've never seen that vacant expression in her eyes before.

"I'm going back to Boston," she answers. "Well, Hastings."

"You're not supposed to be leaving until Sunday."

"I decided to go early." She folds another shirt and adds it to the pile. "I want to get settled at Grandpa's place."

I nod. After she and Isaac broke up, she was living with her parents in Boston, but there's really no reason for her to have to make the commute when Grace's dad lives in an old century home in Hastings, which is only ten minutes from campus. Blake will be living there for her senior year.

"So you're going back to school?"

"Yes."

I press my lips together to stop the flood of words trying to escape.

All the questions. So many fucking questions.

*Are you angry with me?*

*What does this mean for us?*

*Why won't you look at me?*

Instead, I wander over and sit at the bay window, hands on my knees, watching her. She moves methodically, folding each item neatly. It's completely opposite from how I leave a place. Everything's going to have to get taken out anyway, so I just throw it all in a jumble and deal with it when I get home.

"I think I'm going back to Boston too," I tell her.

She doesn't even blink. "Cool."

Cool? That's it?

"I'll be at home for a few weeks working in my mom's studio with her. She's helping me polish some tracks before I send them to Dodson."

Still nothing.

"Yeah, I know, I know. Growth, right?"

No response. Blake pulls several sundresses off the hangers in the closet. Those cute little floral dresses she wore all summer that made my heart pound and got my dick hard.

Finally, I can't take it anymore.

"Freckles."

She doesn't answer.

I get up and stride toward her, capturing her hands as she's rolling up the dresses. Of course she's a rolling packer. She's the kind of person who wouldn't want wrinkles. I disentangle her hands from the fabric.

"Please look at me."

Her blue eyes shift toward me. Behind the blank mask, I glimpse sorrow.

"Do you want to talk about it?" I say quietly. "The baby?"

Her voice is flat and emotionless. "There was never a baby."

Agony slices into my chest. "There was. Just because it implanted in the wrong place doesn't mean there wasn't a baby. You can talk to me about it."

Those eyes suddenly pin me in place. "What are you doing?"

I falter. "I'm trying to comfort my girlfriend."

She sputters out a laugh, which, I'm not going to lie, stings. A lot. I try not to show that it affects me, pasting on an understanding smile because that's what I need to be right now. Understanding. I need to let the hormone-induced jabs bounce off me because it's not who Blake is. I know that deep down, she's kind. She doesn't laugh when someone is offering comfort.

"I'm not your girlfriend, Wyatt."

I slowly inhale. Just the hormones.

"Stop trying to act like you're my boyfriend, okay? We just fucked for the summer."

Now I can't help myself. "It was more than sex and you know it."

"Okay, fine, it was more than sex," she concedes. "It was a fling, a summer romance, whatever you want to call it. But I'm not your girlfriend, and the only reason you're calling me that is because we happened to get pregnant."

"That's not true," I object.

"Yes, it is. Before that positive pregnancy test, we both agreed it was going to end when the summer ended. That was the number one rule, remember?"

"We created those rules at the very start. A lot has changed since then."

"Yeah, I got pregnant."

"No, it changed before that. I fell in love with you before there was ever a baby."

She just stares at me. It's like a knife to the heart.

"And I know you love me too."

She says nothing, and the knife twists in deeper.

"I want us to keep seeing each other," I say. "The pregnancy, yes, would've guaranteed that, but I don't need it as an excuse. I want to be with you."

"You only said you loved me after I told you I was pregnant."

Frustration clogs my throat. What the fuck am I doing wrong here? I *love* her. What more am I supposed to do to convince her?

My hands clench, and I have to slowly loosen my fingers before I break them. "I already told you I was planning on telling you before that."

"Yeah, well, you didn't."

"So you think I..." My voice shakes. "You think I'm fucking lying to you? Saying I love you when I don't mean it?"

"I think you feel bad that I lost the baby. I think you were trying to do the right thing when you said it."

I'm incredulous. "Really. I told you I loved you because it was the *right thing*."

"I don't know, Wyatt." Her eyes get shiny, and when she blinks, a few tears spill out.

My eyes are stinging pretty badly themselves, and I don't have hormones to blame for it. Only the panic of seeing her slipping away from me. And the disbelief and...yes, maybe some anger over the accusation that my "I love you" was nothing but lip service.

For the first time in my life, I fully opened my heart to someone, and she thinks it was fake.

"I think we need to stick to our rules," she says dully. "If one of us wants to stop, we stop. Isn't that what you said? No questions asked, no explanations required, remember?"

"Screw the rules," I burst out, the panic rising again. "You can't walk away from this. You love me. I know you do. I fucking feel it."

She scrubs her hands over her tear-streaked cheeks. "I don't know where my head is right now. I burst into tears every five seconds. My emotions are all over the place. I just need to go back to Briar and focus on graduating and figuring out what to do with my life."

"I can help you figure it out."

"I don't want your help. I don't want..."

"Me," I finish, my tone flat. "You don't want me."

"This is for the best, Wyatt. It was always going to end. Fucking always. It wasn't going to work long-distance."

"You don't know that."

"Just stop. Please." She's crying again, wearing that same helpless look she gave me in the hospital. As if she can't make sense of her own world. "I'm not pregnant anymore. You're off the hook."

"It wasn't a hook," I say hoarsely.

"You don't understand."

"Then help me understand." I run both hands through my hair. Now we're both agitated. "Please don't do this. Don't leave."

A knock sounds on the half-open door as Grace peers inside. "Everything all right in here?" I don't miss the compassion in her eyes when she sees my face.

Blake turns her back to both the door and me, going to the closet to get more dresses.

"I'm almost done packing," she tells her mother, even as the tears continue to stream down her cheeks. "And Wyatt was just leaving."

Pain rips into me. She doesn't want me here. She doesn't want me anywhere.

As I walk to the door, my whole body feels weak. Like I've just been beaten within an inch of my life. Everything aches, and I can barely see through the sheen of emotion obscuring my vision.

Before we even kissed, I told her I was going to break her heart.

Joke's on me.

She broke mine.

**1 NEW EMAIL**

**From:** Mercer County Records Office

**Subject**: Purchase Agreement, 1229 Sycamore Lane

**Dear Ms. Logan,**

Please find attached the requested deed and purchase agreement for the following property:

1229 Sycamore Lane

Trenton, Mercer County, New Jersey 08610

**Lot & Block Reference:** Lot 42, Block 19

**Purchasers:** *Raymond C. Loughlin/Dolly Gallagher Loughlin*

**Seller:** *Evergreen Properties LLC*

Don't hesitate to reach out if you require more assistance. Happy to help!

Best,

Devin Gorchuk

Mercer County Records Office

# Chapter 49

## BLAKE

*Proof of life*

**SEPTEMBER**

LIFE GOES BACK TO NORMAL when I return to Hastings.

If by normal, you mean sudden bouts of paralyzing sadness and random angry outbursts interspersed with feelings of sheer and utter numbness.

After two weeks of this, I'm used to it, and to be fair, it *is* getting better. I had a blood test last week, and my hormones are leveling out. In another couple weeks, I'll know if the reason I want to crawl in a hole and die is because of a hormonal roller coaster or because I broke up with the man I love.

It needed to be done, though. I had to enforce our rule, and not just because a part of me can't shake the fear that he only stayed because I was pregnant. I'll never know if that's true now, if he would've stuck around without a baby in the equation, even though he insists he would have. When I told Mom, she said I should take Wyatt at face value, believe his words.

But the doubt still lingers. It's been there all summer, the knowledge that I'm not enough to keep him. He was always going to Nashville, always going to record his album. One day, he'll be a star. And I'll still be me. Aimless and ordinary. Not a supermodel like Alex or an athlete like Gigi. I don't even know what he sees in me.

*Stop wallowing.*

It's the rational voice, the one that sometimes manages to pierce through my natural inclination toward depression and self-loathing. Sometimes, I'm able to listen to it. Other times, such as now, the insecurities drown it out. *It was never going to work*, those insecurities snap at the voice.

Grandpa Tim has been letting me use his car to go to campus, except on Fridays when he has curling practice. I went with him last week, and it was actually pretty fun. Yes, these days I spend my time *curling* with seniors. A drastic change from a month ago, when I was secretly getting fucked behind the boathouse.

I shove the memory aside. The summer is over. Wyatt and I are not together. He's off in Boston or maybe New York now. I've been forcing myself not to keep tabs on him, but he's posted a few stories on Instagram, and I couldn't resist clicking on them. A story of him at the piano with his mom. Another one showing a blank page of sheet music. Part of me wonders if it's for my benefit, but that's arrogant of me to assume. He's probably not thinking about me at all since I ended it.

My classes this semester are as boring as they were every other semester. Even my politics course, in which I get to do oodles of research on communism, isn't lighting a fire inside me. Nothing is, really.

For the last few weeks, Little Spencer has been blowing up my phone, begging me to record another episode of the podcast, but my heart's not in that either. Hell, I don't even care about the documents that were emailed the other day.

Before I discovered I was pregnant, I was able to learn that Raymond Loughlin and Dolly Gallagher sold the property at the Albany address and purchased another one in Trenton, New Jersey, but no amount of searching has led me to a phone number or even an email. If I want to verify whether Raymond and Dolly still reside at that address, I'll have to go in person. Which, normally? Sounds like an awesome adventure. The Spencers even offered to come along and make a road trip out of it, yet I can't muster up any enthusiasm, not even to possibly solve this mystery.

On Thursday afternoon, I'm leaving my politics class when I get a text from Beau asking if I want to meet at the Coffee Hut. I'm about to decline—I've been avoiding pretty much everyone I know since I returned to Briar—when a follow-up appears.

BEAU

Don't say no. At this point I need proof of life, B. Please. I miss you.

I haven't told anyone about my pregnancy or the surgery. Wyatt and I swore our families to secrecy, because it's our business, and the last thing I needed was dozens of family friends asking if I'm all right or texting their condolences.

It wasn't even a baby, damn it. I don't care what anybody says. *Zero chance of survival* equals *never a person.* It wasn't *real.* Which means I'm not allowed to grieve it.

Except I am. My heart clenches whenever I think about it. And each time I run my fingers over my tiny salpingostomy scar, it reminds me I had to have surgery to remove...an alternate future, I suppose. The path that shall never be walked.

But I know if I keep shutting out everybody in my life, they'll eventually suspect something is wrong. Something heavier than Wyatt and I simply "parting ways," as I told everyone. So I force myself to accept Beau's invite.

I'm on campus now. I can be there in five.

BEAU

See you soon.

I meet him at the campus coffee shop. He's in a white T-shirt and track pants with a backpack slung over his broad shoulder, his blond hair swept away from his forehead, emphasizing his gorgeous features. He's as handsome as ever, commanding attention from every person in our vicinity, male and female.

"Hey." Beau greets me with a hug, frowning when he releases me. "Why do you look so thin?"

I shrug. "I'm on a diet." Truth is I've barely had an appetite. First with all the morning sickness and then the depression.

"You don't need to be on a diet." His frown deepens as we approach the order counter. "You don't look good."

"Thanks," I say dryly.

"No, I mean… Have you been sick?"

Realizing he's not going to drop it, I lie and say I had the flu at the end of the summer and I'm only bouncing back from it now. Beau blessedly accepts the explanation, and we grab our coffees and find a table in the back of the crowded room.

Beau kicks out a chair and sits, thrusting his long legs out in front of him. He's still watching me, his wry smile telling me he *didn't* buy the flu story.

"It's okay to admit it's a broken heart diet."

I've been so numb lately that I've mastered the art of showing no reaction. I don't even blink at the teasing accusation. "What do you mean?" I play dumb.

He shrugs. "You and Wyatt ended it. You're allowed to be upset about that. You doing okay?"

I shrug back. "I'm fine. I knew it was going to happen."

"That he would break your heart?"

"He didn't break my heart," I reply. *I broke his.* "Wyatt and I both agreed that when the summer ended, so would our fling. And that's what happened." I casually sip my coffee. "How's the semester going so far?"

"All good. Classes are fine."

"And AJ?" I prompt.

Beau's expression dampens. "Not good."

Last I heard from our girls' chat, AJ still refuses to accept Beau's apology. They haven't spoken since July, and we're nearing the end of September.

"Why haven't you fixed this?" I ask.

"He doesn't want to fix it. He's done."

"He's not done. You guys have been friends since you were in the womb."

"He's done, B." Beau takes a quick sip. "We went out for beers the other night—"

I perk up. "See, that doesn't feel done."

"—and he told me to stop contacting him," Beau finishes.

"Oh."

"Said he'll never forgive me and that a real friend wouldn't do what I did. Called me a piece of shit and said that no years of friendship could make him look at me like I *wasn't* a piece of shit."

"Oh. Wow. I'm sorry."

"Yeah, me too."

I can't imagine the Golden Boys not being the Golden Boys.

Especially considering they're teammates. "What about hockey? How's that going to work?"

"No fucking clue. We started practice this week. We're not on the same line, so that's good at least, but it's rough. He just treats me like any other teammate. And if it's not about hockey, he looks right through me. We'll see how it goes." Beau lets out a sigh. "Coach Jensen has picked up on the tension, but he doesn't get involved unless it affects gameplay. So far, it hasn't. But yeah, to answer your question, I can't fix it because it's unfixable."

I get that.

That's how I feel right now.

Unfixable.

# Chapter 50

## WYATT

*Who the fuck are you, and why are you this good?*

AT THE END OF SEPTEMBER, I tag along to Manhattan with my mother. She's working at the studio for a few days, and I'm meeting with Tobey, who'd been delayed these past few weeks. He loved the songs I sent him, though, so it's official: I'm cutting an album with Tobey fuckin' Dodson. Our meeting to talk logistics isn't for another two days, so I hang around the studio while my mom dons her producer hat.

She's working with a kid named Frankie Stephens, a baby-faced soul singer from Philly whose label asked my mom to write and produce a track for him.

The control booth is dim save for the glow of the LED meters. Mom leans forward in her chair, one hand on the mixing console, the other cupping a pair of headphones.

"All right, let's roll it back five seconds." When her sound guy twists a dial, she says, "No, right before he hits that note."

I love seeing her in work mode. It's so cool.

Beyond the glass, Frankie waits patiently, looking happy just to be there. And of course he is. He's on the brink of his big break. His whole musical life ahead of him. I feel like I'm on that same precipice.

Mom shakes her head. "Shit." She plays the track back, letting it run for a few seconds. "Yeah. I think we picked up some room slap from the monitor bleed. We'll need to run it again, clean."

Wilmer, the sound guy, nods. "You got it, Hannah."

She taps a button to speak to her singer. "Frankie, we need to do a retake. Same energy, right from the top. We'll fix the rest in the mix, but I need this one clean."

"Yes, ma'am," Frankie says over the talkback mic.

Mom glances at me. "You must be getting sick of listening to the same four lines over and over again. There's an empty room next door with a piano if you want to get some work done."

"Yeah, I might do that. I'm gonna grab some coffee first. Do you want anything? Wilmer?"

"I would love a latte," Mom says, and Wilmer requests a coffee, black.

There's a coffee stand out front that everyone at the studio declares is a million times better than Starbucks, so I go outside and make a beeline for it. While I'm waiting for my order, Cole calls, so I step away from the crowded line to answer.

"You still tagging along to my mom's house before my New York show in November?" he asks. "'Cause she's asking what you'd like for dinner."

Cole's tour launches in six weeks at Madison Square Garden, which means I'll be in the front row cheering my buddy on. He's visiting his mother the night before the show, and apparently, he talks about me so much to her that she's requested my presence too.

I grin. "I need to place my dinner order more than a month in advance?"

“That’s how Ma rolls. I’ll just tell her you’re good with any red meat, yeah?”

“Perfect.” I glance at the coffee stand, but my order’s still not ready. “You nervous at all for this tour?”

“Nah. More like excited. I’m about to have all flavor of female throwing herself at me. American girls. European girls. Australian girls. Those Aussies are hardcore, G. They surf and wrestle crocodiles.”

“I’m pretty sure most of them don’t, but cool. When is the Australian stop?”

“Not till winter. Their summer, I guess. I’ve got six weeks here in the States before I’m scampering across the pond,” he says in a bad British accent. “London first. Ireland. Then Europe and then Australia. That leg’s brutal.”

“You ready?”

Cole chuckles. “Always. You know me. If I stop moving, I lose my mind.”

I nod. I get that. Movement keeps the ghosts at bay.

The barista calls out my order, so I say a quick goodbye and go grab it. I’m shoving the cups into a cardboard tray when a commotion breaks out at the curb. A cluster of people gather around, and I realize they’re paparazzi, all eagerly focused on the road. A black town car with completely tinted windows pulls up, followed by a second one, and then a third.

Two burly men emerge from each vehicle. The way they carry themselves screams bodyguard. Mom didn’t mention anyone famous showing up today, but there’s no way this isn’t a celebrity arrival. It’s presidential-level treatment.

I hang back, watching as one of the big men opens the back door of the second town car. I catch a glimpse of a hooded figure. Gray hoodie with long, chestnut-brown curls spilling out of it. Big hoop earrings that look familiar for some reason.

Although it's not raining, the bodyguard opens an umbrella, and the figure ducks underneath it before scurrying toward the front entrance of the building, flanked by two other guards. The paparazzi start screaming.

"Mollie May!"

"Mollie May!"

"Over here!"

Holy shit, that was Mollie May?

I know she recorded here for the duet Mom wrote, but I heard she usually works out of her private studio in LA. I wonder why she's here today.

I go inside, enduring another security check, then deliver Mom's and Wilmer's coffees before taking her up on that empty piano room offer.

You never put a drink on a musical instrument, so I set my coffee on the ledge behind me and position my fingers over the keys. I play the song that Tobey Dodson went feral over—which, ironically, is not "Lightkeeper." His favorite track is "Stop the World," but he's recommending we strip it bare. Piano only, maybe some strings. I like the idea of going simple so it doesn't feel so produced, but sometimes I worry my voice isn't strong enough to carry a track without a band behind me.

I run through the song, fingers dancing over the piano keys, voice reverberating clearly in the room's perfect acoustics. I'm just reaching the bridge when I catch a flicker of movement up in the control room. Through the glass, I see her.

A moment later, a throaty voice sounds over the speaker.

"Who the fuck are you, and why are you this good?"

I grin despite myself. And though I'm not even a fan, I find myself a little starstruck as I slide off the piano bench. My legs are actually wobbly.

The pop princess opens the door of the control booth and saunters into the room, strutting toward me while her bangle bracelets clank around her wrists. Nobody can deny that this woman is a stunner, with her brown curls and big liquid-brown eyes, the sexy mole over her top lip. A pocket rocket, AJ once called her, because Mollie May is tiny. Can't be taller than five feet, but her presence is larger-than-life.

She's wearing a short skirt and a crop top that shows off both her impressive rack and impressive abs. I glance at the outfit and ask, "What happened to the hoodie and umbrella?"

"Huh?"

"I saw you come into the building," I explain. "Drowning in a gray hoodie."

"Oh, that wasn't me." Mollie May waves a hand, laughing. "It's my decoy. Antonio and I came in through the back, like, thirty minutes before that. Tony is my bodyguard." She nods toward the booth, where an enormous hawk-eyed man stands guard.

I lift a brow. "He's not worried I'll try anything with us alone in here?"

"Nah, anyone who sings that pretty isn't gonna hurt me." Her magnetic eyes sweep over me. Up and down. "Why don't I know you? I should know you."

"I mean… I'm nobody." I shrug.

"Highly doubt that." Despite the flirtatious note in her voice, her gaze is shrewd, gleaming with intelligence.

I'm caught off guard by her entire demeanor. Onstage, at her sold-out stadium shows, she comes off as, well, flighty. Dumb even. Might be a shitty judgment to make, but that's the vibe I got. And she's always hyper to the max, with the fringe and the bright eyeshadow, the high-heeled boots and wild dance moves.

But right now, her energy is mellow. Low-key.

"I'm Wyatt," I say. "Wyatt Graham."

She brightens. "Graham? Related to Hannah?"

"She's my mom."

"Holy shit. You realize your mom is iconic, right?"

Coming from another icon, that makes me smile. "Yeah, she's pretty great."

"She wrote a duet for me and Stylo. One of my favorite tracks to sing live. When he comes in, the crowd goes nuts." Mollie May gestures toward the piano. "Did she write that? The song you were just playing?"

"Nope. That was a Wyatt Graham original."

She looks impressed. "Do you write all your own shit?"

"Yeah. I'm not a great collaborator." I sigh ruefully. "But I'm trying to be."

That makes her grin. "I used to be the same way. Insisted on writing everything on my own. My first album was all me. Every track. And then the second one, I literally cried because I had to give a credit to this producer who made a change to *one* line, and apparently that earns them credit. Third album, I gave credit to fuckin' everyone—because you know what I realized?"

"What?" I'm genuinely fascinated by this conversation.

"That it's arrogant to think other people don't have anything to offer me."

"I'm sort of reaching that conclusion myself," I confess. "I just spent a month in Boston letting my mother point out all the things that were wrong with my song."

"But it made it better, though, didn't it?" She tilts her head knowingly.

"Yes," I grumble. "But don't tell her I said that."

That gets me another delighted laugh. "So. Who is she?"

"Who's who?"

"The girl whose smile stops the world. Who's the song about?"

Pain clenches around my heart. "Oh, just someone I…"

I can't finish. I don't know how to.

Someone I used to love? Well, no, because I still love her with every fiber of my being.

Someone who used to love me?

Someone I created a life with?

Someone who doesn't see a future with me?

"Someone I used to know," I finally say.

"Past tense. I like the past tense." She leans forward and touches my arm. Her nails are painted a glossy black. "How long are you in town for?"

"A few days. I'm meeting with my new producer."

"Who?" she demands.

I shrug sheepishly. "Tobey Dodson."

"Well, fuck me. Tobey took you on? You cutting an album?" When I nod, intrigue dances in her eyes. "When's it going to be ready?"

"I don't know."

"How many tracks?"

"I don't know."

She grins again, then startles me by saying, "Let's grab dinner while I'm in town." She nods decisively, as if it's a done deal.

"Oh." I blink. "Okay. Sure."

"My agent will get your number."

"Mollie May," someone interrupts. Her bodyguard is at the talkback mic. "We gotta go, girl. Sanchez is ready for you."

"No, *I'm* ready for Sanchez," she calls toward the booth. She turns to wink at me. "Don't ever let people think they control your time. They're always waiting for *you*."

"Noted."

As she flounces toward the control room door, I check out her ass in that tiny denim skirt. Damn, she's cute. And not at all what I expected.

After Mollie May and her bodyguard disappear, I suddenly notice my mother is up there too. I walk into the booth, wondering how much of that she heard.

"You realize the biggest pop star in the world asked you to dinner?" Mom says.

Guess she heard everything.

I shrug. "I think she just wants to talk about my album."

"Oh, honey, she doesn't want to talk about the album. That was flirting."

I give another shrug.

Mom searches my expression. "Have you spoken to Blake?"

"You don't need to ask me that every day. The answer never changes. It's a no. She's not speaking to me."

Her gaze softens. "She's just going through something."

"She thinks I never loved her."

"Give her time," Mom advises. "She needs to work through it, come to terms with what happened. She lost a baby."

"I lost one too," I say stiffly. "But everyone keeps forgetting that part, now don't they?"

She looks startled. "Wyatt—"

"Forget it. It's fine." I stalk back into the studio and return to the piano, ignoring my mother's concerned eyes through the glass.

# Chapter 51

## WYATT

*It made me feel things*

**OCTOBER**

I DON'T END UP SEEING Mollie May during my New York trip. She never calls, and it's not like I'm about to contact a global superstar and say, "Hey…about that dinner?"

I meet with Tobey, who's eager to get into the studio with me. So eager, in fact, that I'm coming back next week to start recording with him. Rather than fly down to Nashville, I return to Boston to hang out with my parents until I'm due back in New York. I spend time with our dogs, Dumpy and Bergeron, though it makes me sad to see Bergeron, our energetic husky, slowing down. He's getting old, and the idea of him not being around anymore and following me all over the house with his intense, watchful gaze… It breaks my heart.

Nothing lasts forever, though, does it?

Everything ends, and everyone fucking leaves.

I step onto our sprawling stone patio out back, feeling more melancholy than usual. For the first time in weeks, I'm having a beer and a cigarette, and it reminds me of the beginning of the summer when I was a total mess. Chugging beers in the morning, chain-smoking, brooding and snapping like an asshole.

Is it possible for someone to change in such a short amount of time? To evolve? Because I feel different. I truly do.

She changed me. And for the better, I think. I wish I could tell her, but my last several texts have gone unanswered. I'm worried she's punishing me for not texting her for nearly three weeks after we left Tahoe, but I did that for *her*. I was trying to give her time to grieve and heal, even though it fucking killed me to keep my distance.

The last time Gigi checked in with her, Blake told her she was focusing on school. Against my wishes, Gigi mentioned my unanswered texts, to which Blake responded she thinks we need space from each other. Which, of course, wrecked me to hear.

Gigi told me she sounded better at least. Less depressed. I hope that's true. I can't stand the thought that she's sad and I'm not there to make it better for her.

"Hey." Dad walks out, holding a beer of his own. He's wearing a Bruins hoodie, his hair damp from the shower.

"Hey," I say.

He sits at the patio table, resting the bottle on his knee. For a moment, he's quiet, just staring out at the dark yard. Then he sighs.

"Your mom said something the other day."

I glance over. "What?"

"She told me you made a comment about how nobody cares about your loss."

Fucking hell.

"No, don't look like that. She's not trying to pry in your business or force you to talk about it."

"Then she *didn't* send you out here?"

"Nope." He chuckles. "If anything, she told me not to say anything. But I had to, because it needs to be said."

"What does?"

He lets out another breath, looking a bit troubled. "I just want you to understand something. About being a man."

I sink into the chair across from his, a deep wrinkle in my brow. "What do you mean?"

"There's a lot of pressure on us. We're supposed to be the strong ones, the providers. And even now, with women being breadwinners and men staying home, that expectation is still there. People don't really want to see men break down. No man shows his emotions without paying for it somehow." He pauses as if choosing his words carefully. "But you suffered a loss too. Maybe your body didn't go through it, you weren't the one in the hospital, but you still lost something. And it's okay to be sad about it."

My throat constricts painfully. "I feel like I'm not supposed to be. And I feel like I didn't even have time to process it, you know? Barely even got my head around the idea of being a dad before the option was taken away from me."

"Yeah, I get it."

"At the hospital, Blake said losing the baby made her realize she was leaning toward keeping it. Honestly, I think I would've been cool with that. And that whole fucking situation just makes it sadder, because we never even got to make that decision. It was stolen from us."

"It wasn't stolen from you. It just wasn't given to you. Things happen when they're meant to happen," Dad says quietly. "The people you meet, the situations you face, the traumas you suffer… It's all going to unfold the way it's supposed to."

"Fate again?" I say wryly.

"Not fate. Just life."

A long, pained silence falls over the patio. My heart is on its last legs; it's been aching for so many weeks now, I don't know how it's still beating.

"She doesn't want to talk to me."

He knows exactly who I mean. "Have you tried calling her?"

"Yeah. A couple times. Texted her a bunch too. But she told Gigi she wants space."

Dad waves that off. "Try again."

"But she doesn't want—"

"Wyatt, I appreciate that you want to listen to women here, but I can tell you this from experience: Sometimes they say they want space, but what they really want is for you to hold their hand. To be there."

"She ended it. I'm not going to force her to love me." Jesus. Sounds so pathetic saying that out loud.

"But you love her."

"So fucking much. But I also can't force her to believe me."

Another silence settles between us, this one shorter, because my next words spill out before I can contain them.

"I played hockey this summer."

His head swivels toward me. "Where?"

"The new community center by the library. They have a good rink."

"Great rink," he agrees. "The air is so crisp in there."

"You mean cold, Dad. The air is fucking cold in there."

He grins. "I love it."

"I know you do." My voice turns gruff. "I'm sorry it's not what I want to do."

"What?"

"Hockey. I know how badly you wanted me to follow in your footsteps." Shit, how is one beer loosening my tongue? "I've spent a long time feeling like I'm not good enough."

Dad looks shocked. "What are you talking about, not good enough? Wyatt—"

"No, let me finish. I've always felt like I let you down. Disappointed you because I chose to quit the team in high school, even though I probably could've been good enough."

"Not probably, definitely," he corrects. "But here's the thing about hockey, champ. You can be technically perfect, have all the skills required of a great player. But if you don't have heart, what's the point?" He takes a quick sip of beer. "I listened to your song."

"Which one?"

"'Lightkeeper.'" He cocks his head at me. "It made me feel things."

I can't help but chuckle. My dad might not be the most articulate when it comes to explaining why he likes the music he likes, but I know what he means.

"You're talented," he continues. "And *your* heart is music. Not hockey."

"You really don't care that I didn't want to play pro?"

"Look, when your mom and I talked about raising kids, we agreed that we wanted to show our kids the things we love. Hockey. Music. And if our kids loved those things too, that would be a bonus." He offers a shrug. "I got my hockey player. Hell, your sister is better than I ever was."

"Says the multiple Stanley Cup winner."

"Stan's more disciplined." He smiles. "And you, well, you ended up loving your mom's passion. But see, here's the thing—even if you'd decided that you loved, I don't know, engineering or origami, we would've been rooting for you. I don't care what you do as long as you love it. I'm proud of you, always. No matter what."

"Thanks, Dad." My eyes feel hot, so I chase away the tears with a huge slurp of beer.

"As for Blake, if you love her, then you shouldn't give up on her. Go see her before you leave for New York," he suggests. "Bring her flowers, write a letter, anything to show her that you meant every word."

He's right. I should see her at least one more time before I leave town for who knows how long. I'm not sure about flowers, but...

I do know *one* thing guaranteed to get my foot in the door.

I don't drive directly to Hastings. First, I make a stop in the city, double-parking on the street and praying I won't be here long enough to get towed. In the lobby, I give the desk clerk my name. He picks up the phone, makes a quick call, and I'm surprised when he's given permission to let me up.

I ride the elevator to the twenty-third floor and march with purpose to Apartment 2301. I give the door two sharp knocks. I don't have to wait long.

The door swings open to reveal a smug wide receiver in a sleeveless hoodie.

Christ. This guy is the fucking worst. Who wears a sleeveless hoodie?

Isaac rolls his eyes at the sight of me. "What are you doing here, Graham?"

He remembers me at least. We've only met once, when Blake brought him to Tahoe the first year they started dating. I didn't like him then, and I don't like him now.

"She send you here to beg me to take her back?" he taunts.

I clench my jaw. Along with my fists. But I force myself to keep them pressed to my sides. "I'm here for Hot Boi," I tell him.

His jaw drops. "You serious?"

"Deadly."

Isaac stares me down. I don't even blink. I come from a hockey family. I can handle a guy whose only job is running in straight lines and not getting grass stains on his tight pants.

"Bro," he says. "It's a *toaster.*"

I bare my teeth in not quite a smile. "And yet... Here we are."

# Chapter 52

## BLAKE

*Just you and me*

THE KNOCK ON THE DOOR startles me. My grandfather is still at his curling game, so I hop off the couch and go to answer the door. I'm frowning as I open it, already expecting to be annoyed with whoever decided to show up announced after eight, so I freeze when I find Wyatt standing on the porch.

Holding Hot Boi.

My mouth falls open in shock. I look from the toaster to his bruised knuckles, then lift my gaze to his. "What did you do?"

Wyatt shrugs. "He made it harder than it needed to be."

Despite myself, laughter sputters out. "Oh my God. Come in."

He enters the house but doesn't move farther than the front entrance. He holds out Hot Boi, and I accept the toaster gratefully while sweeping my gaze over Wyatt. He looks good. So good. God, I missed every inch of that gorgeous face.

I'm relieved to see he's free of bruises. As far as I can tell, all the damage is confined to his knuckles, which bodes well. I hope he punched Isaac in his stupid, toaster-stealing face.

"I can't believe you fought him over a toaster."

Wyatt's mouth twitches in a ghost of a smile. "I mean, you've been fighting him all summer. My beef only lasted, like, four minutes."

I feel like I should scold him, but I can't muster up a rebuke. I'm too touched that he did this. And too distracted by how beautiful he looks.

"Anyway. That's all I came for. Just wanted to drop it off." He turns toward the door.

"Wait."

The word flies out before I can stop it.

Wyatt's gaze shifts back to me.

"Do you want to stay for a drink or something? I mean, it's the least I can do after you fought my ex in my honor."

He hesitates. Then his gaze softens, and he nods.

We walk to the kitchen, where I realize I have nothing to offer but red wine. Grandpa Tim doesn't really drink, but he keeps a few bottles of merlot handy for guests.

"We've only got red," I say.

"I'll take a glass."

I pour for both of us and pass him a wineglass. We stand on opposite ends of the counter. My gaze drops to his right hand again, his torn knuckles.

"You probably shouldn't have done that," I say ruefully. "Isaac holds a grudge."

"I'd do it again."

My hand trembles as I lift it to my lips. The heady flavor coats my tongue and slides down my throat, but it does nothing to relax me. The silence that falls over the kitchen is too tense and oppressive. It's too thick with everything that happened the last time we saw each other. Heavy with everything we lost and crackling with everything

I'm still aching for.

I missed him so much. My chest physically hurts from how much.

"How's school going?" he finally asks.

I swallow. I guess we're making small talk then.

"Terrible," I confess. "I'm bored and frustrated. I have a meeting with my advisor this week to discuss my options."

Wyatt's brow furrows. "What options?"

"Graduating early. I might have the credits because of those two summer classes I took sophomore year. And if not, maybe I can finish out the year online instead of attending classes. I'm just so tired of being on campus."

"What about your sorority?"

"I've basically checked out. I tried to officially resign, but Shaye—she's our new president—refused to let me." I roll my eyes. "She said it's a bad look for Delta Pi. So I'm still a member and have to pay dues for the year, but they're not making me participate in any sorority events."

"That's good, I guess."

"Yeah." I watch him over my glass. "How's the album going?"

"We start recording next week. I'm nervous," he admits.

"You'll be great."

Silence settles over the kitchen again. We drink to the sound of the refrigerator humming, and it drags on so long I have to avert my gaze.

He breaks first, his low, husky voice cutting through the tension.

"Nothing's changed, freckles."

I set down my glass because my hand is too unsteady. "What do you mean?"

"Nothing's changed on my end. I still love you. I still want to be with you. I'm just waiting for you to say you want it too."

My throat closes, so tight it ripples with pain. "It's not that simple."

"Yes, it is." Frustration laces his words. "I loved you in Tahoe. And I love you now, here. All you have to do is…believe me."

"I don't know what I believe. I'm still such a fucking mess. My head is always spinning. My hormones are out of whack. I cry all the time. I can't even tell if what *I* feel is real."

Hurt fills his eyes. "You're saying you don't know if you love me?"

A helpless feeling twists my stomach. I lay both hands flat on the counter, needing to ground myself. "I'm saying I'm on an emotional roller coaster, and until I feel like myself again, I can't be sure of what I want. And I can't give you any answers."

His features go taut for a moment, but then he swallows, relaxing his jaw. Slowly, he bridges the distance between us.

I suck in a shaky breath, torn between the longing in my chest and the crushing weight of doubt. He never told me he loved me before I got pregnant. He claims he *felt* it, but my brain keeps insisting that isn't true, and the darkness inside me wants to push him away for it.

But when he slowly approaches and I whisper, "Wyatt," I'm not sure if I'm asking him to come closer or to stop.

He brushes a strand of hair from my face, and his touch is so gentle, so careful, that I almost burst into tears.

"Tell me to leave," he says roughly.

I don't.

I can't.

Instead, I reach up and run my fingers over his jaw, feeling the tension there. "I don't want you to go."

That's all it takes. I blink and his mouth is on mine. He tastes like wine and faintly of smoke, and I wonder if he's picked up the habit again. If so, I hope it's not because of me.

His lips brush over mine, and I'm confused by his kiss. How slow it is, how cautious. It's a restraint I've never felt from Wyatt. He's holding back.

"Kiss me for real," I whisper. "The way you used to. Please."

The request seems to undo him. With a strangled noise, he kisses me again, deeper this time, and my body lights up under his touch. I part my lips for him, and his tongue slides through them. When it touches mine, an electric shock surges through me.

When he pulls back, my breath gets trapped in my lungs. God, that look in his eyes. Like I'm the only thing that matters to him in this entire world. Or maybe I'm just projecting what I *want* to see, but I don't care.

"Let's go to my room," I say.

"Are you sure?"

Am I sure? No.

Is this a bad idea? Probably.

Am I going to stop him? Not a chance.

Rather than answer, I take his hand and pull him toward the stairs. We don't say a word as we go up to my bedroom. I close and lock the door, and we stand in the dim light of the bedside lamp that I forgot to turn off earlier, eyeing each other.

*I miss you.* The words burn my tongue. But I don't think I can say them out loud without unleashing a wave of emotion.

He steps toward me, framing my face with both hands. Then his mouth is on me again. He trails it along my jaw, down my neck, each kiss making my breath hitch. But his control is slipping. I can feel it in the way he thrusts his fingers in my hair and pulls on it to guide my mouth closer to his. I can hear it in the groan that rumbles in his chest when my tongue fills his mouth.

"I missed you," he whispers between kisses. His breathing is labored. "Missed you so fucking much."

I don't say it back. I just kiss him again, and he plasters his body against mine as if there isn't enough space in the world for the two of us to exist apart. When I feel his erection against my stomach, I let out a helpless, needy moan.

"Let me take care of you tonight," he says. "I want you to just... let go. Nothing else matters right now. Just you and me, okay?"

A rush of heat ripples through me. "Okay," I whisper.

I lie back on the bed, and he hovers above me, undressing me slowly, pulling off my sweatpants, my panties, my sweater. Each inch of skin he exposes makes his breathing grow heavier.

"You're beautiful," he says simply.

His clothes come off next, and then his warm, naked body covers mine, calloused hands sliding over my bare skin in slow, teasing caresses. His lips find my neck, teeth grazing the sensitive spot beneath my ear.

I close my eyes and lose myself in sensation. In the feel of his mouth on my breasts, his tongue flicking my nipple. He isn't rushing at all, but urgency simmers behind every kiss, every touch, as if he's forcing himself to slow down.

"Tell me what you want," he murmurs.

"I want *this*." I swallow. "Do you?"

His eyes are swimming with emotion as he rises on his elbow to look at me.

"I've wanted you for so long I can't even remember what it feels like to want anything else."

His words make me dizzy, but he doesn't give me time to fully absorb them. He's kissing his way down my body, his palms stroking my inner thighs before he gently parts my legs. He lowers his head and plants a kiss on my pussy, soft and sweet. Then he licks a gentle circle around my clit, and I gasp.

He looks up with that dark, intense gaze. "Feel good?"

"Yes." I'm almost embarrassed by how fast the word escapes my mouth.

A smile curves his lips before he dips his head again and resumes his slow and dedicated mission to wreck me. And he does. He licks me until I'm mindless, long strokes interspersed with teasing flicks, his lips wrapping around my clit and sucking it, teasing it, making me whimper with pleasure.

By the time he puts on a condom and slides inside me, I'm a live wire waiting for a spark. And the spark comes in the form of his cock filling me to the hilt. I climax from that first, deep stroke, unraveling beneath him. My orgasm only spurs him to move faster, thrusting his hips into me, his eyes open and fixed on my face.

*You'd hate how much I'd want from you. How much I'd take.*

His confession from early in the summer burns through my mind.

He's wrong. I don't hate it.

But it terrifies me.

My gaze stays locked with his as he comes, pleasure darkening his eyes and drawing a low, husky noise from his throat. Afterward, he collapses on me, and I wrap my arms around him. I lie beneath him, breathless not just from his weight on me but from the storm of emotion that swept through the bedroom.

When I feel the moisture on my shoulder, I realize I'm not the only one affected.

"Hey," I say, running my fingers through his hair. "You okay?"

His broad body trembles, and my throat clamps shut when he lifts his head and I see his tears, his red-rimmed eyes.

"We lost our baby, Blake." His voice cracks, and so does my heart. Right in two. Because it's the last thing I need to hear right now. Or ever again.

As agony rips into me, I disentangle from his embrace, easing out from under him. He rolls onto his back, forearm covering his eyes, his breathing shallow.

I don't know what's wrong with me. Why I can't comfort him. The reasonable part of my brain knows that he suffered a loss too. This isn't just about me. It was *our* loss. Not mine.

But I don't have it in me to do this. To carry this for both of us. I suddenly can't breathe. The tears pour out, soaking my cheeks and the pillow as I press my face against it.

Realizing I'm sobbing, Wyatt slides in behind me and wraps his arm around my trembling body.

"I'm sorry," he says against my hair. "I shouldn't have said that. Please don't cry."

I can't stop, though. I cry even harder, because tonight it's not just sorrow fueling the tears but also guilt. Because I'm not strong enough to take on Wyatt's grief. I can barely handle my own.

"You should go," I manage to choke out.

He only holds me tighter. "No. I'm not leaving you like this."

Somehow, I find the strength to pull myself out of his arms. I fumble for my clothes, shoving my pants on. "You need to go. We can't help each other right now."

"Yes, we can."

"No, Wyatt." The guilt is burning my throat. "This isn't fair to you. You're so focused on taking care of me that you haven't even been able to process this loss and deal with your own grief. And I'm barely managing to keep it together for myself, let alone both of us."

On the bed, Wyatt sits up. He looks tired. Numb.

I slip my sweater over my head, seconds from collapsing on the floor and sobbing again.

"My grandpa will be home soon," I finally say.

After a beat, Wyatt reaches for his boxers. "I'll get out of your way then."

Even though my heart is screaming in agony, I let him go.

Because if I beg him to stay, it wouldn't be fair to either one of us.

# Chapter 53

## WYATT

*I hate being wrong*

**NOVEMBER**

I'm doing a small charity set in Nashville tomorrow night and a little birdie told me you're in town. I'll send a car for you. -MM

SHE SIGNS IT MM.

I raise a brow. *I'll send a car for you.* Presumptuous of her to think I'm interested in attending or even free to do so.

Of course, the answer to both those questions is yes.

And fate must want me to, because I just happen to be back in Nashville this weekend to pack up my apartment. The first cut of my album is done, and I'm going to rent a place in New York while Tobey and I polish it up. I'm thrilled with how it's shaping up.

I set down my roll of packing tape and type a quick reply to Mollie May, saying I'm in.

My opinion of the pop princess, with her massive online following and platinum records, hasn't changed per se. I still don't love her shiny, overproduced hits, but there was something about her that I really liked when we met. Her intelligence, her humor. She seemed cool. Plus, the fact that my mom likes her and even wrote a track for her counts for a lot with me. Mollie May's music might not be my jam, but I trust Mom's opinion about people's character.

As promised, a car collects me the following evening at my apartment. The venue is tucked inside an old hotel downtown, the event taking place in a large ballroom featuring tables with ornate centerpieces in gold accents and a stage lit by hundreds of candles.

Security is intense, which I'm starting to realize is par for the course for someone like Mollie May. I read that she had to testify last year at the trial for one of her alleged stalkers. *One* of. I can't imagine living my life being stalked or worried that some unhinged fan is gonna murder me and wear me as a skin suit.

I slip inside the ballroom after security pats me down at the door. I'm wearing a suit, and I actually styled my hair into some semblance of not-messy. I scan the room, not sure where to stand or who to talk to. I expected a lot of industry people, but it seems to be mostly civilians. Older civilian women. *A lot* of women. The sign on the posterboard in the lobby said the charity is called the Later Years Foundation.

I spot her by the stage, laughing with a pair of older women. Her dark hair is piled in an artful mess, and she's wearing a silky gold-yellow gown that looks incredible against her bronze skin. It hugs every curve of her body, and the asymmetrical hem allows her to flash a lot of thigh.

Mollie May waves me over like we're old friends. "Wyatt!"

She separates herself from the group and saunters over. Her heels are black and strappy and wrap around her ankles.

"Look at you," she draws. "You clean up nice. I'm loving the all-black. Very Johnny Cash of you."

I tug at the collar of my dress shirt. "I have a complicated relationship with color," I answer, and she laughs.

A waiter approaches, his tray laden not with champagne flutes but small glasses of something amber.

"Bourbon theme," Mollie supplies, grinning.

"What is this charity?" I ask her, accepting the glass.

"They raise money for senior care, with a focus on women. I helped them out last year too. Had lunch with the chairwoman, and she was telling me how most nursing homes have more women than men. Since men, on average, die earlier. A lot of these women, the married ones especially, suddenly end up alone in these places, suffering from dementia or Alzheimer's or whatever other illnesses."

"That's really sad."

"I know. My abuela is in a similar situation," Mollie May tells me. "So it's sort of a personal cause for me."

We chat about the charity for a bit longer, but soon my mind drifts, because I'm still not sure why she asked me to come tonight.

"You seem bored."

I glance at her amused face. "Sorry. I was just...wondering why I'm here," I admit.

"Got it. You're a right-to-business kind of guy." She sips her bourbon, drawing my gaze to her red lips. "I bribed Tobey to send me some tracks from your album."

I narrow my eyes. "Did he?"

"Oh yeah, that man will do anything for me." She winks. "Most men do. But I've been listening to them nonstop and—"

"Mollie May," someone interrupts. "I need to steal you away for a moment. Veronica is dying to meet you!"

I swallow my frustration as she dashes off. I'm forced to spend the next fifteen minutes waiting for her to return. I'm almost done my bourbon when she gets back.

"Why doesn't anyone ever call you just Mollie?" I ask curiously.

"Because my name is Mollie May. Technically, it's one word. My birth certificate has a hyphen. Mollie-May Rivera." She grins. "Courtesy of an Irish mother and Puerto Rican dad. If anyone calls me by a nickname, it's usually Mol. Anyway, back to business. I wanted to—"

But then we hear, "Mollie May, you're on."

She stops again. "Shit. Hold that thought *again*. Time to shine."

My head is spinning as I watch her saunter toward the stage. I chat with an assistant to one of the record label execs as we wait for her set to start. He whispers that it's ten thousand dollars a head to get into this event. Jesus Christ.

A hush goes through the ballroom. The ambiance is intimate and seductive with the candlelit tables and velvet ropes. There's no band onstage, only a piano, a guitarist on a stool, a cellist, and a lot of candles. That startles me. Mollie's shows are usually such productions that it feels wrong to watch her grace such a simple stage with just her sleek yellow gown. No Auto-Tune, no backup dancers, no pyro. Just her and the mic.

And holy fuck, she's good. She covers a Patsy Cline song, soulful and sultry, then launches into one of her own tracks, only it's been stripped down to acoustic guitar.

For a moment, I have to grit my teeth, because I hate being wrong. Plus, I feel like an asshole. This woman is talented. I've spent years judging her as bubble gum, and it turns out she might have more talent than I can ever dream of having.

When her set ends, she glides off the stage and spends the next thirty minutes chatting with attendees, accepting their heaps of praise, and flitting from group to group like a pro. I can see why they paid her the big bucks to attend. She's probably raking in the cash for this charity.

Finally, she sidles up to me near the silent auction table. "Well?" she says, tipping her head.

I tip my head back. "Well, what?"

"Did you like my set?"

"It was incredible."

She nods, then casually says, "You want to open for me on tour?"

"I'm sorry, *what*?"

"That's what I was trying to tell you before. My opening act got a DUI last week."

"Stylo Lewis?" I say in surprise.

"Yep. Not a good look. So we're hunting down a replacement." She shrugs. "I'm thinking you."

"Are you serious?"

"As a heart attack. You in?"

I'm still battling shock. Never in my wildest dreams did I expect Mollie May, the biggest pop star in the world, to invite me on tour with her.

"But..." My head spins. "Our styles are..."

"Day and night?" she fills in.

"I mean, yeah."

"That's why I want you." She winks and I get the feeling it means *in more ways than one*. "I always go with singer-songwriter openers. It helps ease the audience in before I drop them into chaos."

I have to grin, because I've seen clips of her tours. Fire, pyro, backup dancers in latex.

"I loved what Tobey sent me. Those tracks. Especially 'Lightkeeper.'" She shivers. "Slow in the right places, moody where it needs to be, and then you belt out that last chorus and holy Jesus.

That balance is hard to pull off, but you do it so well. And it doesn't hurt that you have that"—she waves vaguely at me—"face."

"My face?" I echo with a grin.

"You're hot," she says frankly. "And we need to make these straight girlies and gay boys happy. Give them some eye candy."

"You're really selling me on this tour."

She laughs. "I don't need to sell it. You're already saying yes."

I smirk. "Am I?"

"Well, you'd be a fool to say no."

She's called away again then, leaving me reeling from the invitation.

Mollie May wants me to open for her. Am I fucking dreaming? And am I really going to say yes? I've spent years mocking her songs like a pretentious jackass, insisting it's not real music. I'd look like a goddamn hypocrite if I joined her on tour.

But I also just watched her perform without any effects, flash, or gimmicks, and I'm big enough to admit I'm wrong. She *is* a musician.

And like she said...

I'd be a fool to say no.

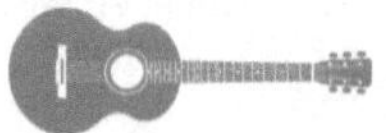

Three hours later, the ballroom has mostly emptied out. I expect Mollie May to be whisked off by her bodyguards at any second. I'm already edging toward the door, wondering if the car that deposited me here is also going to deposit me home.

Mollie May notices me trying to leave and shakes her head no. Then she waves her handlers over and says something to them. Within minutes, the staff and hangers-on are ushered out, doors closing behind them.

"Wow," I tell her when she joins me. "You know how to clear a room."

"Practice." She tugs on my hand, pulling me toward the grand piano on the stage. "Come on. Music's calling," she teases. I watch as she sinks onto the bench, the silk of her gown pooling around her knees and ankles. "Let's play something."

Shrugging, I join her, and we spend the next several minutes messing around with melodies and harmonizing until we find a groove. We sing the duet that my mom wrote for Mollie May and Stylo Lewis, and I'm a bit floored, because we sound like a real duo. Our voices go well together, hers rich with surprising tenderness. Once again, I feel like a piece of shit for thinking she lacked talent.

The last strains of the song echo in the ballroom. Mollie May turns to me, her brown eyes soft.

Then she kisses me.

It's bold and unexpected. Her mouth moves against mine like she knows exactly what she wants, and I hesitate only for a moment before kissing her back, giving in to the teasing strokes of her tongue.

"Fuck, you're a good kisser," she mumbles.

I deepen the kiss and try to drag her closer, but she laughs and then hops up. The ivory keys clang under her thighs as she climbs onto the piano's glossy black top. She pulls me to my feet and yanks my body toward hers. Her dress rides up as she wraps her legs around me.

"You sure about this?" I murmur against her jaw.

"Wouldn't have cleared the room if I wasn't."

Our mouths collide again, rougher this time. I skim my hands along the curve of her spine, stroking the bare flesh that's exposed by her backless gown. She responds eagerly, tugging my shirt out of my waistband. But when she reaches between us, she finds me completely soft.

She eases back, panting slightly. Her lipstick is smudged. Pupils blown. "What's wrong?"

I swallow hard, still gripping her hips. "Fuck. I'm sorry."

Now she frowns.

"I want to want this," I say with a heavy breath.

"But?"

"But I don't. Not really." My hands drop to my sides. "I'm in love with someone else."

I step away from the piano and scrub my fingers through my hair. What the hell is wrong with me? Blake and I are done, and there's a beautiful woman sprawled on top of a fucking piano wanting to have sex with me.

But I can't make my body or my heart cooperate. They're not even at odds with each other—they're in perfect harmony that I don't want to do this. Kissing her felt nice for all of ten seconds before it turned hollow, empty, like trying to light a fire with wet matches.

There's a long beat before Mollie May lets out a little laugh and wipes the corner of her mouth. "Jesus, you musicians. Always bleeding from somewhere."

"Sorry," I say roughly.

"Don't be." She slides off the piano, smoothing her dress as if what just happened between us was no big deal. "Honestly, I was mostly curious if the mouth matched the voice."

My answering laughter is equal parts guilt and relief. "Guess I'm off the tour?" I quip.

"Not a chance." She flashes an impish smile. "That kind of sexual tension makes for great shows. I'm already envisioning at least one duet. Besides, I'm sleeping with one of the guys in the band, and *he's* not in love with someone else." She steps toward me and fixes the lapel of my shirt. "You're allowed to bring someone, by the way."

I blink. "What?"

"My drummer always brings his girlfriend along. It's not a big deal if you want to invite this girl you're in love with. As long as they don't mind living out of a suitcase for six months and don't get in the way, significant others are welcome."

"I haven't agreed to anything yet."

"Yes, you have." She pats my arm. "Tour starts before Thanksgiving. Boston's up first. See you there."

## BREAKING NEWS

### New couple alert?? Mollie May spotted with MYSTERY MAN at charity event!

Looks like the annual Later Years Foundation gala in Nashville last night was a lot more exciting than expected... Cameras caught pop princess Mollie May getting cozy with a mystery man, sources revealing that the pair were inseparable all night.

But who is our mystery man? As of yet, nobody knows, but these photos have sent the internet into a tailspin and the internet *sleuths* on a hunt for answers.

Our exclusive sources reveal not only was the couple whispering to each other during the gala, but Mollie May's staff cleared the entire ballroom after the event so the two could enjoy a little...privacy.

Mollie May is notoriously private about her romantic life, so last night's PDA is raising eyebrows and creating much speculation. Is this a PR stunt, or has Mollie May finally found a **[read more]**

# Chapter 54

## BLAKE

*You could try*

THE BRIAR MEN'S HOCKEY TEAM wins their next game, putting them on an eight-game winning streak. Which is sort of a miracle considering AJ would rather skate over Beau's throat than pass him the puck. Yet that's exactly what happens to secure the win: a quick pass from AJ leading to a one-timer from Beau. The home crowd screams as helmets fly off in celebration, and I watch in dismay as AJ skates away from his cheering teammates and disappears into the tunnel alone.

I'm starting to fear their friendship will never recover.

The last thing I wanted to do was go out tonight, not after the flurry of activity on my phone all day. Literally every woman in my life, including my own mother, texted me a link to the tabloid piece about Mollie May and her mysterious new man.

AKA the gorgeous, dark-haired, green-eyed sex god that the tabloids and gossip sites still haven't figured out is Wyatt.

Eventually, someone will. The internet is rife with photos and videos of him performing in Nashville. *Someone* is going to recognize him and post it online. Until then, only I get to experience the joy of knowing Wyatt has moved on with a fucking pop star. And one he's trashed repeatedly to boot.

Juliette, who I've barely seen since I left Delta Pi, convinced me that the only way to not give that article power over me is to ignore it. Don't sit at home stewing. Don't lie in bed obsessing over it.

Besides, if Wyatt really has moved on, I'm in no position to be mad about it. The last time we saw each other, I asked him to leave. I told him I couldn't be there for him. I have no right to stop him from being with somebody else.

I attend the game with Juliette and Stella but surprisingly not Ivy, who I've barely seen since she and Stella started at Briar. Stella claims she's in the dance studio from morning till night, which I believe because Ivy has dedicated her whole life to ballet. But I do find it odd that I have no idea what she's been up to for nearly two months, and that she wouldn't show up to support her older brother during his first season as team captain.

After the game, everyone heads to Malone's, the sports bar in Hastings, where the Briar players are treated like heroes as they strut inside to cheers and backslaps. A brigade of starry-eyed puck bunnies instantly swarms to stake their claims.

I pile into a booth with the girls, along with Beau, Gray, and a few of their teammates. Not AJ, but he did come to the bar at least, even if he's taking up residence in another booth.

"You guys, Wyatt is everywhere," Gray says, shaking his head in amazement. "I heard his song at the Coffee Hut today."

"Dude's blowing up," Stella agrees.

Juliette squeezes my leg under the table in a comforting gesture. I pick up my Diet Coke and gulp some down. I didn't feel like drinking tonight, but hearing Wyatt's name, I sort of regret that decision.

They're not wrong, though. Wyatt *has* been everywhere lately. He hasn't released his album yet, but according to Gigi, it's all done, and his manager and new PR team have a whole plan for how to roll it out. So far, they've only released one single. "Lightkeeper."

The song he wrote about me.

About *us*, and the first time we slept together.

It shreds my heart to pieces every time I listen to it. And I listen often. Too often. It's basically playing on repeat most of the day.

"Do you think he's hooking up with her? Mollie May, I mean," Gray says, and Beau is quick to elbow him in the ribs. Remembering I'm in the booth, Gray gives a sheepish look. "Aw shit. Sorry, B."

I shrug, smiling like I'm fine. "Don't worry. We're not together. I don't care what he does."

Now I feel Stella's hand on my other thigh, as the normally raging bitch softens her expression.

"I'm fine," I insist. "Jeez, you guys. I'm happy for him. He's living his dream."

Across the booth, Beau's gaze flicks toward me. He doesn't say anything. I don't think he believes me. I don't think any of them do.

Hell, I don't believe myself.

Needing a breather from the pity I feel thickening the air, I slide out of the booth. "I need to use the ladies' room."

The line is long, though, and it's nearly fifteen minutes before I return to the booths, only to find my seat has been stolen by one of the d-men. I'm walking toward the booth, prepared to fight for my spot, when someone in the other booth sticks out their arm and grabs my hand.

I glance down and find AJ's brown eyes twinkling devilishly. He must be drunk, because this is the first time in ages that I've seen his killer grin. I honestly sort of missed it.

I grin back at him. "Well, hi there."

"Hey." He tugs me toward him. "Come sit with me."

I slide in next to AJ, because my other seat has been hijacked and AJ is alone. On the other side of the booth, one of his teammates is making out with a redhead, who's a little too into it considering we're in public. I'm pretty sure her hand is down his pants.

Since I haven't gotten AJ alone since his falling-out with Beau, I decide to take this opportunity to see if I can finally talk some sense into him.

He drapes his arm along the back of the seat, angling his body toward mine. The music is so loud, he has to bring his head close to mine so we can talk.

"That was a hell of a game," I tell him, keeping it light. "Great assist."

He shrugs off the compliment. His hand trails toward my shoulder, then lower, his fingers tweaking the end of my braid. "You look good tonight, B. Well, actually, you always look good, but you already know that."

"Thanks."

He winks. "Not gonna return the compliment?"

"Nope. Your ego's big enough."

"You know what we should do?" he drawls.

"What?" It's becoming obvious he's drunker than I thought.

"Go back to my place."

"You mean the studio apartment you're renting 'cause you're too stubborn to make up with Beau?" I say sweetly. After the Tahoe fight, AJ moved out of the house he shared with the other two Golden Boys. Which is a boneheaded move, because it's a great house.

"I'm not stubborn. I just have no interest in talking to that asshole."

"That asshole is your best friend."

AJ rolls his eyes. "He was balls deep in my girlfriend. There's no coming back from that, Blake."

I sigh. "You could try."

"Or I could move on." He smirks, his thumb brushing my bare shoulder. I shrugged out of my hoodie the moment we got here because the bar is way too hot, but it left me in a very skimpy camisole, which AJ's hungry gaze is currently raking over. "Want to help me move on?"

"You've had too much to drink."

"Nah, I've had just enough." His voice drops, growing husky. "Enough to tell you I can have you bent over this table if you just say the word."

"Jesus, AJ."

"What?" He blinks innocently.

Irritation flickers through me. "This isn't you."

"You're wrong." He leans back, spreading his arms and grinning like he owns the whole damn bar. "This is exactly me. And I forgot how much fun it was to be me."

"What's fun? Banging your way through life the way you did in high school?"

"Yes."

I study him, searching for bravado in his smile or maybe a hollow shadow behind his eyes, but I don't see it. He seems genuinely smug. Pleased with the fact that he's reverting to fuckboy status.

His hand brushes my thigh under the table, and I smack it away.

"I'm not going home with you, Adam," I say, full naming him so he knows I mean it.

"Too bad. Would've been hot."

Shrugging, he takes a long swig of beer, then grabs his phone and proceeds to pull up a hookup app while I'm sitting right the fuck there beside him.

# Chapter 55

## BLAKE

*Life is short*

THE TRAIN FROM BOSTON TO Trenton takes nearly five hours. A flight would've been way quicker, but I wanted to use the time to work on my midterm papers without distractions. The one I'm currently writing explores the invention and history of radio and its impact on modern media, which reminds me I need to text the Spencers to finalize my New York visit next month.

I finally feel back to normal. Hormones settled, depression gone. Sure, the aching pit in my stomach refuses to go away, but at least I'm not bursting into tears every five seconds anymore. If this Trenton trip goes well, maybe Little Spencer and I can record a follow-up episode to the Darlie one. Who knows. Maybe I'm two hours and thirty-eight minutes away from solving the mystery.

And yes, I recognize that I might've just thrown ten hours of my life out the window. I'm riding a train all the way to New Jersey, and all I have is an address. Still no phone number. Still no email or any other way to contact the homeowners. I even called Mercer County this week and begged the lady on the phone to pass along a message to the residents of 1229 Sycamore Lane. "Just tell them to call me," I begged, to which she said, "Uh, yeah, we don't do that."

That left me with two options: mail a letter, which could lead to days of waiting or no response at all. Or hop a train, knock on the door, and see what happens.

Worst case, I get my schoolwork done on the train.

Best case, Dolly and Raymond actually live in that house, and I get some answers.

As we pull into the station, I tuck my laptop back in its case and slide it into my bag. Outside at the taxi stand, I slide into the back seat of a cab and then watch the exciting city of Trenton flash past the window. 1229 Sycamore Lane is located in Trenton's Hillside neighborhood, which my research says is quite affluent. That bodes well, since Raymond Loughlin comes from money.

The taxi stops in front of a large Tudor-style house with a spacious front lawn and three-car garage. I'm happy to see a car in the driveway. I hope that means somebody's home; otherwise, I'm about to make camp on the porch like a stalker.

This was…a really bad idea, I realize.

I've done some ridiculous things for the sake of research, like flirt with a Kyle to convince him to dig through old, dusty boxes. But a day trip to a different state to visit a house whose residents might not even be connected to the story?

That's extreme, even for me.

And yet the lengths I've gone to, as extreme as they may be, remind me of Wyatt saying how much he loves my nerdy pursuits. How my hobby isn't dumb but passionate.

Still, I do feel sort of dumb as I stand awkwardly on the porch and ring the doorbell. My pulse speeds up when I hear footsteps beyond the door. Then it swings open, and a woman answers. An *elderly* woman. I'm not great with guessing ages, but she looks like she could be in her late sixties. Also bodes well. Darlie died fifty years ago, and her sister was nineteen at the time, so that would make Dolly sixty-nine now.

"Can I help you?" she asks with a polite smile.

"Um…maybe? Are you by any chance Dolly Gallagher? Loughlin, I mean. Dolly Gallagher Loughlin."

Her smile falters, joined by a quick flicker of suspicion. But she doesn't slam the door. If anything, she sounds curious as she says, "I am indeed. And you are?"

"Blake." I offer an embarrassed smile. "Blake Logan. I'm a student at Briar University in Massachusetts. I was hoping I could ask you a few questions. About your sister," I clarify.

Now her eyes narrow.

God, this is so awkward. "You know what? I'm so sorry," I tell her, my cheeks hotter than Hades. "I just realized how crazy this is and how incredibly intrusive. I shouldn't have shown up at your door like this, but I couldn't find a phone number or email. This would have been so much better over email."

I guess my nervous babbling eases her concerns that I might be here to kill her, because she laughs softly and opens the door wider. "Why don't you come in, sweetheart? Do you want a glass of water?"

"Yes, please." I glance toward the curb and give the taxi driver a thumbs-up. He's been waiting for my signal to head off.

Inside, I remove my shoes at her request and follow her down a wide corridor toward a large kitchen with sky-blue cabinets and a cedar table by a window that overlooks a beautifully manicured backyard. This house isn't as fancy as the Loughlins' cliffside Tahoe property, but it's still pretty damn nice.

"That's a gorgeous yard," I tell her.

"Thank you! Ray and I do all the landscaping ourselves."

"Ray? You mean Raymond? So he's still alive?"

"Alive and kicking," Dolly confirms. She walks to the kettle on the stove. "I was just fixing myself a cup of tea when you rang. Would you like one or do you prefer water?"

"Tea is great, thanks."

She returns to the table with two steaming mugs. "It's peppermint. I hope that's all right."

"Perfect," I say, gratefully reaching for the tea. "I really am sorry for just showing up here. Sometimes I find a topic I'm interested in, and before I know it, I'm obsessed. My family owns a house in Lake Tahoe, right across the lake from the Loughlin property."

"Lord, I haven't been back there in decades," she muses. "Though I hear my sister is still creating quite the stir."

I'm startled by the humor gleaming in her brown eyes. "So you know about the Darlie legend?"

"You mean that my sister tragically drowned herself because of her broken heart? And that rather than turn evil, she now strives to mend people's hearts and shower them with love? Or whatever it is benevolent ghosts do." Dolly releases a peal of laughter.

"You're saying none of that is true?"

"Honey. I assure you that most ghost stories aren't true."

I feel a pang of disappointment, but at the same time, my curiosity hasn't abated in the slightest. There's clearly a story here.

"All right, what's the real story then?" I ask the smiling woman. "I found your sister's death certificate, which means she did die around the time this legend began."

Dolly's expression goes serious. "Yes. My sister passed on. And it was a difficult time for all of us, especially Ray. But it certainly wasn't as dramatic as suicide by drowning. She died of a brain tumor."

I gasp. "Wow. Really?"

"It came on so suddenly. Heck, we didn't even have a history of brain cancer in our family. Darlie went in for a checkup for migraines and left with a diagnosis of three weeks to live. The tumor was so advanced, the doctors said even the most aggressive treatment wouldn't help." Her breath catches. "She was engaged. She was happy. She had her whole life ahead of her. Lord, we never even saw it coming."

"Why wasn't there a medical report?"

She wrinkles her forehead. "Well, I'm sure there was. Hospital records for her scans, certainly."

I nod. After I found Darlie's death certificate, the first thing I did was call all the hospitals in the area, but it turns out they don't release private medical records to random college girls.

"Her cancer was no secret," Dolly says. "And she died at our house, looking out at the lake, surrounded by her family and Raymond."

Sorrow tugs at my heart. "They were still engaged before she died?"

"Of course. They loved each other very much."

*How did you end up with him*? I almost blurt out, but I resist the urge.

She must read my thoughts, because she laughs again. "If you're wondering about me and Ray, I'm afraid it's not very scandalous what happened after. We grieved together. Darlie's death brought us closer together, and eventually the grief faded and turned into love. But it was too painful to stay in the place my sister loved so deeply, so we moved to the East Coast after we got married."

"Why isn't there a grave for her in Tahoe?" I ask curiously. That was another strikeout for me, trying to locate a headstone for Darlie in all the local cemeteries.

"She wanted to be cremated. We spread her ashes over the lake." Dolly giggles. "Which probably contributes to the ghost story."

I marvel at her. "It doesn't bother you that everyone believes your sister is a ghost who was betrayed by her sister and fiancé? That people think you and Darlie were both sleeping with Raymond all over Tahoe? Meeting up in lighthouses? Secret tree trysts?"

"Oh, the tree was real." Dolly's eyes twinkle. "I used to cover for her when she snuck out to meet Ray. I'd stuff pillows under her blanket so it looked like she was asleep in bed. She and Raymond were quite the wild ones. He still has some of that wild streak, even now. I never did, but I believe that might be a good thing. Every relationship needs that balance."

"One person is the storm, and the other is the lighthouse," I murmur, and my heart clenches as Wyatt's lyrics echo in the kitchen.

She smiles. "Yes. I like that. And no, it doesn't bother me. My sister died at the lake surrounded by her family. Her fiancé found a second chance at love. And this legend... Well, it keeps her memory alive. To be honest, Darlie would love this."

"She would?"

"Oh yes. She was fun-loving, mischievous, always causing trouble. The fact that everybody is still talking about her fifty years later? Spreading the story that she's a ghost who loves love? All that attention? It would delight her."

I sip my tea, letting everything sink in.

No ghost.

No plot twist that makes you gasp.

Just a boring, run-of-the-mill ending. Someone died, two people got married, and now they garden together in New Jersey.

And yet I'm not disappointed. Although it would've been cool if it turned out there really was a ghost—it would make the Spencers happy anyway—I realize I care more about the journey it took to reach the end of this story rather than the ending itself. I don't need to solve crimes and take down killers. I don't need shocking plot twists. I loved the research. I loved the digging. And yes, I loved sending emails to county records offices.

Not to mention the episode I recorded with Little Spencer is at almost two million views now. Two million people enjoyed it, and that is incredibly validating. So maybe my hobby is dorky and dumb, but Wyatt's right. I shouldn't be embarrassed of it. I might not possess a flashy talent or supermodel looks, but I have something I'm good at, something I enjoy. And that's not nothing.

I stay a while longer, chatting with Dolly. We drink a second cup of tea. She tells me about her and Raymond, how they never wanted children, how they've enjoyed every second of their life together. I tell her about school and how much I dislike it. How I feel destined for a boring job and that maybe I shouldn't even bother doing the podcast.

At that, she shakes her head in rebuke. "Do it. It's not as if you can't still work your tedious nine-to-five while you do the podcast. If you want this old lady's advice, Ms. Blake Logan, here it is: Life is short. If I'd done what was expected of me, I wouldn't have married Raymond. My parents weren't thrilled with the idea—they worried he was trying to replace one Gallagher fiancée with another. But I knew he loved me for *me*, and I know I made the right decision. But there are also some things I didn't do, and once you reach my age, you tend to look back and think, well, shit, *that* was a missed opportunity."

I bite my lip, more affected than I thought I'd be by her words.

"You're twenty-one. Your life is swimming with opportunities. Don't squander them."

I gulp down the lump in my throat. "I'll try not to. And I appreciate you inviting me in and talking to me. You have no idea how much it means to me. With that said, I won't take up any more of your time."

If I leave now, I can make it back to the station in time to catch the five o'clock train. I could be in Hastings by midnight. This was a quick trip, but I don't regret it. I got everything I was hoping for.

"Come back and visit anytime," Dolly says, and we exchange phone numbers, because she *does* have a phone, and email addresses, because she has one of those too.

As she walks me to the door, I promise to send her a link to our podcast on Darlie.

"Are you going to record a follow-up now that you know what happened?" she asks curiously.

I shake my head, which surprises her.

"But you solved your mystery."

"Yeah, I did." I shrug. "But I don't think Darlie would want me to ruin the legend."

"No," her sister agrees. "She would not."

"Which is why I'm going to keep this visit to myself. I don't even plan on telling my podcasting partner. So...no. No follow-up. Let Darlie keep haunting Tahoe to her heart's content."

We say goodbye at the door, and I'm already pulling up a ride app as I descend the porch steps. I'm so focused on ordering the car and locking in the pickup spot that I don't even notice him approaching.

Then I hear a mystified, "Blake?"

And I turn to find Wyatt standing there.

# Chapter 56

## BLAKE

*There's no such thing as coincidences*

WE STARE AT EACH OTHER, each of us shocked to see the other standing on this sidewalk. Wyatt is the last person I'd expect to find on a random residential street in Trenton, New Jersey, and it suddenly occurs to me that the only way he can be here is if he followed me.

I narrow my eyes at him. "How did you get this address?"

He looks confused, shaking his head. I notice he's dressed nicer than usual, wearing a pair of dark pants and a hunter-green sweater that complements his eyes. And his hair is longer than the last time I saw him. The night he cried in my arms about our baby and—

I shove the thought aside, because *nope*. I can't go there right now.

"How did *you* get this address?" he counters.

"From the Mercer County records office."

"What the fuck? They just gave you Lorraine's address? That seems unethical."

"What?" I rub my temples. "Who's Lorraine?"

"Lorraine Tanner. Cole's mom?" Wyatt nods toward a house two doors down from Dolly and Raymond's.

"I'm sorry—Cole Tanner's mother lives here?"

"Yes. Isn't that why you're here? You tracked me down?"

I gape at him. Then I point to the house behind me. "*That* is Dolly and Raymond's house."

Wyatt's jaw falls open. "Are you kidding me?"

"No. I tracked them from Tahoe to Albany to this house."

"Jesus fucking Christ."

I'm feeling rather amazed myself, because this is the mother of all coincidences. "So your friend, Cole Tanner, the country star—that's his mom's house over there?"

"Yeah. He bought it for her about a year ago after his album went platinum. Lorraine wanted to leave the south to live near her sister."

"And why are *you* here?"

"Cole's kicking off his tour tomorrow at Madison Square Garden. His mom wanted to meet me. We just finished dinner, and we're about to head back to our hotel." Wyatt stares at me for a moment, as if trying to convince himself I'm actually here. "I can't fucking believe this."

Then he moans. A low, miserable sound.

A groove digs into my forehead. "Why do you look so upset?"

"Because I don't want to give them the satisfaction," he grinds out.

"Who?" I ask blankly.

"The Spencers."

"What do they have to do with this?" My head is spinning.

"No. You're right." Wyatt nods decisively, only confusing me further. "This doesn't have to be a ghost. It could just be fate."

It clicks in my mind. "Wait. You think this is about Darlie?"

"Remember how much they gloated in Tahoe after they learned we were together? They said Darlie played matchmaker. You and I haven't spoken in a *month*, and now you're standing here, visiting Darlie's sister—" He jabs a finger toward Dolly's house. "And I'm two doors down, visiting my best friend's mom—" He jabs his finger at Lorraine's house. "That isn't a coincidence, freckles."

I want to argue, but part of me thinks he's right.

"We might need to apologize to the Spencers," I say solemnly, and for a moment, it's like old times and we're back in Tahoe. For one beautiful moment, he's flashing that lazy smile and I'm smiling back, and my heart feels lighter than air.

Until I remember we're not in Tahoe, and we're not together anymore.

"Hey, so listen..." He bites the side of his lip, shifting awkwardly on his feet.

My good mood plummets.

Oh God. No. I know where this is going. Damage control. He must know I saw the pictures of him and Mollie May, and now he's trying to get ahead of that.

"I have some news."

Now I feel queasy. *News*? What the hell is this? Is he going to tell me he's *dating* her? Is it an official thing?

"Mollie May asked me to come on tour with her. As her opening act."

I blink in surprise. "Seriously?"

"Yeah, the original opener was Stylo Lewis, but he just got charged with that DUI, and her team thinks it's bad PR if he stays on the tour. So..." Wyatt laughs nervously. "She asked me."

"Wow, that's huge."

"I know." He looks amazed. "Honestly can't believe it."

"Have you given her an answer yet?"

"I did, yeah." His eyes meet mine. "I said yes."

My stomach clenches. "Oh, well, great. Congratulations."

"Thanks."

A short silence falls.

Despite myself, I suddenly flash back to those photos. They weren't racy. No one "canoodling" in a corner, thank God. But there *was* one of him standing close to her, and she had her hand on his arm, her touch very deliberate. And another one where he was gazing down at her, smiling at something she said.

Although I hate myself for doing it, I can't help bringing up the article. "I saw the pictures of you at that event in Nashville. She's gorgeous," I say tightly.

"Yeah, she is," he agrees. Then he pauses. "Nothing happened."

A laugh slips out before I can stop it. "Really?"

"Well, no, something did happen," he amends, and it's like a knife to the heart. "She kissed me."

The blade twists harder.

"I kissed her back."

My heart is gaping open now, gushing blood.

"But I didn't let it go any further."

"Why not?"

"Because I didn't want to. I told her I was in love with somebody else." His voice is gruff. "I don't want to be with anyone but you."

My head is still stuck on the fact that he kissed somebody else. Yes, I pretended I was cool with him being with other people, and yes, I really don't have any claim on him, but God, did he have to tell me?

"Nothing's changed," he says, just like he's said every time we've spoken since I woke up in that hospital.

"Wyatt..."

"No, I'm going to say this every fucking time till you believe me, Blake. I love you. I—"

"Yo, G, what are you doing?" interrupts a male voice. "Picking up my neighbors?"

We both spin toward the man sauntering toward us. For a second, I'm starstruck, because Cole Tanner is all over my social media, all the time. I'm constantly bombarded with clips of his music videos, gorgeous shirtless pictures, interviews where he's flashing those endearing dimples. He's even better looking in person.

He reaches us, glancing at me with a faint smile. "And who might you be?"

"Blake, Cole," Wyatt says in way of introduction.

"Blake?" Cole's eyes widen. "Wait, this is the muse?" His head swivels back to Wyatt. "You two made up?"

I don't know how much he's told Cole about our relationship, so now I shift in discomfort. "Actually," I answer for Wyatt, keeping my tone light, "we just bumped into each other. Weird coincidence, huh?"

Cole responds with a knowing chuckle. "Oh, muse, there's no such thing as coincidences." He raises a brow at me. "You should come back to the hotel with us. My manager set us up at a real swanky place. Swanky for Trenton anyway. We're gonna have some drinks—"

"I can't," I interject. "I need to catch the train home."

From the corner of my eye, I see a car turning onto the street, and relief trickles through me. It's my ride. Perfect timing.

"That's me," I tell the guys, taking a step toward the curb.

Wyatt blocks my path. "No, wait."

"I'll give you a second," Cole says, then strides toward his mother's driveway. Two sharp beeps slice the air as he unlocks a silver Mercedes.

Once he's gone, Wyatt clears his throat. "I was told that significant others are allowed on the tour."

I blink, not expecting that. "What do you mean?"

"I mean..." He hesitates for a beat. "Come with me."

My heartbeat kicks up. "On tour?"

"Yeah. It kicks off next week and lasts six months. First show is in Boston."

"You're asking me to come on tour with you." I feel a bit dazed.

"Yes."

"Even if I wanted to, I have school..." I trail off.

"You said you might be finished this semester," he reminds me. "You had that meeting with your advisor. And if you can't swing it, you don't even like school. You could just take the semester off and finish in the summer if you really want to."

"My parents would kill me," I say, as if that's the one impediment to me embarking on a world tour with Wyatt and the pop star he kissed.

"Your parents will understand. They love you. They'll support anything you do as long as they know you're choosing something that makes you happy."

"You say that like you know what makes me happy."

"I think I do," he says softly. "I think a lot of things, actually."

I swallow the lump in my throat. "Like what?"

"I think you miss me. I think you went through something. *We* went through something. I think it scared you. I think it hurt you a lot. But I don't think anything has changed. I love you, and I think you love me."

Tears sting my eyes. I don't answer for a moment. My mind unwittingly flashes back to those pictures of him and Mollie May laughing. Her hand curled possessively over his bicep. And all my insecurities rush in. I feel the same way I did when I went to Fashion

Week with Alex. Everyone fawning all over the supermodel. Me sitting there with my freckles, utterly invisible. I can't even imagine how insecure I'd feel going on tour with Mollie May. Meeting the stunning woman, shaking her hand, watching her command a stage in a sold-out arena.

I believe that Wyatt isn't interested in her—he wouldn't lie to me about that—but part of me still can't fathom why he would want *me* over her.

"Maybe you should be with someone like her," I find myself saying, the words burning my throat.

"Someone like Mollie May?"

"Yes."

"It's not who I want, Blake."

"Why not? She's beautiful and successful, and the two of you could share the spotlight. You'd be a power couple."

With an aggravated curse, Wyatt drags a hand through his hair. "Stop it."

"What?"

"You accused me of believing shit about myself that wasn't true. Keeping myself stuck." He shakes his head at me. "Don't you see that you're doing the same damn thing? You tell yourself this story that you're ordinary, that you belong in the background. Someone's plus-one, that's what you called it, right? Well, you're nobody's plus-one, freckles. You belong in the spotlight too. You *are* the fucking spotlight."

I press my lips together to stop them from quivering. He's wrong. How could I ever compare to someone like Mollie May? Someone who is all confidence and sequins and unrivaled success. Meanwhile, I'm floundering through a degree I don't want, too stubborn to quit school and too scared to open my heart up to him again.

I force myself to speak. "Cole's waiting for you. You should go. Go and live your dream, Wyatt. I know the tour is going to be amazing."

"I want you there." I can hear his frustration.

We both jerk at the sound of a car honking. I glance toward my waiting driver and gesture that I'm coming.

"I have to go," I say.

Wyatt nods. "So do I. But just know that the offer to come on the tour is still there. We're leaving in a week. Say the word, and I'll make the arrangements."

When I give a noncommittal shrug, I don't miss the flash of hurt in his eyes. I slip into the back of the car, and as we pull away from the curb, I force myself not to look back to check if Wyatt's still standing on the sidewalk.

I don't call him the next day. Or the day after. Or the day after that. Wyatt doesn't call either. The ball is in my court. We both know that. He'd never pressure me to talk to him, let alone go on tour with him.

On the weekend, my parents drive down to Hastings to have dinner with me and Grandpa Tim. Afterward, while Mom and Grandpa chat in the kitchen, I join my father in the family room and plop beside him on the couch.

"You were quiet at dinner," he remarks.

I reach for a throw pillow and pick at the frayed threads. I don't answer right away, because I don't typically confide in Dad. Mom is my go-to for that. Yet for some reason, the confession slips out.

"Wyatt asked me to go on tour with him."

Dad's eyebrows shoot up. "Like, actually go with him? On a tour bus? Like a band girlfriend?"

I giggle at his asinine description. "Not a band girlfriend. *His* girlfriend." I bite my lip, feeling anxious now. "He wants to get back together."

"Won't he be gone for six months?"

"Yeah."

"Well, you can't go then. You're in school."

"I don't have to be."

His eyebrows crash together. "What does that mean?"

"I spoke to my advisor a couple weeks ago," I admit. "And he said I could graduate early if I wanted to. It would just require I take one online course in the winter semester. But yeah, I don't have to be on campus if I don't want to."

"Why wouldn't you want to?"

"Because I don't care about it, Dad. I care about learning but not necessarily about school, if that makes sense."

He nods. "Yeah, I get that."

"Really?"

"What, you think *I* was obsessed with homework and couldn't wait to attend all my lectures? Fuck no. I loved Briar because of hockey, because of my friends, and because of your mom. But the school part?" He shrugs. "I could take it or leave it."

A smile breaks free. "I'm sort of the same way. And I learned a lot about myself this summer. For so long, I was feeling like such a loser, like I'm not talented or extraordinary—"

"Are you kidding me?" Dad's mouth is agape. "You're the most extraordinary, brilliant, accomplished kid on the planet."

"Says my dad," I answer dryly.

"It's the truth," he insists.

"I love you for believing that, but the *actual* truth is I don't possess some incredible skill or talent that's going to take the world by storm, like you with hockey or Alex and Gigi and Wyatt. And it was really bringing me down," I confess. "I was supposed to spend the summer figuring out what I want to do after college, but I ended up burying myself under a mountain of random research." A laugh pops out. "And not only did I love it, but it opened the door to this podcast, which might actually earn me some money. Who knows? Maybe I'll even be able to make a living from it one day."

"Podcasting empire," Dad agrees with a nod.

"Anyway, I realized this summer that I don't need some big, flashy career. I just need to be doing something I enjoy. But I will graduate, one way or another. I promise."

"Eh. If you didn't, that's also okay," Dad says.

"Seriously?" I say in surprise.

He scoots closer and slings his arm around me. "Kiddo, I don't care what you do as long as you're happy," he says, echoing what Wyatt said when he asked me to go with him. "I think your mom would probably prefer if you graduated, though."

"I will."

"And this tour... You want to go?"

"I don't know. Part of me does, but another part of me is scared."

"Scared of what?"

My teeth dig into my bottom lip again. "That he doesn't actually love me and that maybe someone like Mollie May makes more sense for him."

Dad chuckles. "Sweet pea, life isn't about what makes sense on paper. It's about who makes you feel like breathing's easier when they're around."

Tears sting my eyes. "I pushed him away after the hospital. Like, I've been so horrible to him, Dad. Partially because of hormones—I mean, I was a dick to everyone."

He snickers. "Yeah, the hormone monster wasn't fun. But we understood. And so does Wyatt."

"But I kept pushing him away after the hormones settled," I moan. "I was insecure, and I ruined everything."

"So fix it."

"Uh-huh. Because it's that simple?"

"Of course it is. You want him back, you feel bad about how you treated him, then grovel."

"Grovel," I echo dubiously.

"Yes. Beg. Apologize. Tell him you messed up. Tell him you love him, because we both know you do. And then prove it to him."

I let out a choked laugh. "Since when are you a romantic?"

"Since always. Ask your mom about the poem I wrote her once."

"Bullshit."

"Nope, I think she still has it in a scrapbook somewhere. It was beautiful."

I narrow my eyes. "I believe you wrote the poem, but I do *not* believe it was beautiful. Also, *why*?"

He grins at me. "Because I messed up and had to humble myself to get her back. The reality is if you let a good thing walk away because you're too proud to beg, you're always going to regret it."

"So…grovel," I say slowly, testing out the word.

"Yes, sweet pea. Because you're a Logan, and Logans grovel."

Anxiety skitters through me. "You don't think it's too late?"

He shrugs. "Only one way to find out."

# Chapter 57

## WYATT

*Go get her already*

I ADJUST MY HEADPHONES, TRYING to act like I'm not sweating under these lights. Or maybe it's the pressure that's making my collar damp. The radio studio is smaller than I expected. Dimly lit and soundproof, with a glowing, red ON AIR sign flashing over the booth window. I don't know how I let my manager convince me to do a live interview instead of a prerecorded podcast or something that could be edited in case I make a fool out of myself.

But no. *Live* radio. Fucking hell. Kill me.

*You're about to perform live for thousands of people for the next six months*, a voice in my head points out.

*True*, I relent. Maybe this interview is a good way to dip my toe in. Prepare for the never-ending spotlight I'm about to be under.

The tour starts in four days, kicking off in Boston because it's the hometown of Mollie May's Irish mother, who'll be backstage for the show. While I'm excited to meet her, I wish the person backstage was *Blake*, but I haven't heard from her since fate brought us together on a street in Trenton.

I'm calling it fate, because I refuse to accept that Spencer and Spencer Hanz were right about a ghost spreading her love magic around.

"And that was Wyatt Graham's 'Lightkeeper,'" Ashley, the host, chirps into her mic.

Her cohost is a big, bald quipster named Hughie, and the three of us are squished into this hot studio like buns in an oven. They're cool, if you ignore Hughie's obnoxious habit of overemphasizing every other word.

"And you guys are in *luck*," Hughie tells the listeners, "because we have *the* Wyatt Graham sitting here in studio with us."

"Looking real fine, if I might add," Ashley chimes in, winking at me.

"That *song*," Hughie says to me. "Streaming numbers are *through* the roof, and it just got a review in *Rolling Stone*. Critics are calling it *raw* and *reckless* and *sad as hell*. So I guess what I want to know is—who *hurt* you?"

I can't help but chuckle. "Sad, huh? I thought it was more romantic than sad."

"Very romantic," Ashley agrees, nodding. "Big song. Big feelings. Is that what we can expect from the rest of the album?"

"I think so. I worked with Tobey Dodson, who's so great at pulling out the emotion and getting the best out of you with every track."

"And how many songs can we expect?"

"Ten, plus a bonus track," I say, because the publicist that the label connected me with said I need to tease the bonus track. Apparently, people love 'em. "I'm excited for everyone to hear them."

Grinning, Hughie wags his finger at me. "Now, now, don't think I didn't notice you dodging my question. So. 'Lightkeeper.' Is it about a *real* girl?"

I scratch the stubble on my jaw. I forgot to shave this morning because I was too busy preparing for this radio spot. My sister was firing questions at me on the phone all day. She tried to catch me off guard with a few, and this was one of them. I'm supposed to say my music is about no one in particular, but as I'm about to deliver the rehearsed line, I suddenly can't do it. Because this whole fucking album is about someone in particular, and it feels wrong to dismiss that.

"It's about a real girl," I say gruffly, and both hosts grin at me now.

"Ooh, *okay*, we've got a muse," Hughie says.

"Yes."

"And you and this muse," teases Ashley. "Are you together?"

"Not at the moment," I admit, then want to smack myself.

The first thing the publicist told me was *don't discuss your personal life*, and here I am, talking about Blake.

I quickly try to redirect the conversation. "Not all the tracks on the album are about love, though. There's one that explores the idea of family," I start, but that only opens the door for them to ask about my mother, which leads to two minutes of gushing about how incredible she is. And yes, Mom *is* incredible, but I was supposed to stay on point and plug my own work, not hers.

We're in the middle of discussing how prolific my mother is because of all the genres she's written in when I notice the producer in the booth pressing a hand to his earpiece. Then Ashley does the same in her plush seat, and the next thing I know, she lets out an elated laugh and cuts Hughie off midsentence.

"Guys, sorry to interrupt, but plot twist. We've got someone on the line claiming to be the muse."

My shoulders tense. "What?"

Behind the glass, the producer is mouthing the words *line three.*

"We're patching her through right now," Ashley announces. She presses a button, which I deduce is muting all of us, because she winks at me and says, "Just play along, honey. It's probably some cuckoo bird, but the listeners love this shit."

There's a click in my ear, and then a nervous voice comes over the airwaves.

"Hi."

My heart leaps into my throat.

That is…not a cuckoo bird.

"How's it going?"

A smile tickles my lips. *Hi, how's it going?* She's calling into a live radio show, and *that's* her opening line?

"And to *whom* are we speaking?" Hughie inquires in a jovial voice.

"Um. I'm sorry. I didn't plan this ahead of time. I just saw on your social media that you were doing this show, and I couldn't not call." She pauses. "I'm talking to Wyatt, by the way, not you, Hughie."

I choke out a laugh.

Ashley looks at me. "You two know each other?"

When I nod, she motions with her hand to use my words, and I remember we're on the radio. "Yes, we know each other," I say, unable to keep the smile off my face.

Hughie pipes up again. "You still haven't introduced yourself, *muse.*"

"Oh. Right. My name's Blake."

"Solid name," he tells her.

"Can I talk to Wyatt now?" she asks with a sigh.

Hughie snickers. "Permission granted, muse."

My pulse is racing as I wait for her to continue.

"So...yeah...I've spent the last few days trying to think of the perfect way to grovel, because I'm told that's how I'm going to win you back," Blake says, and every person in the booth goes wide-eyed like they just won the lottery.

I imagine this is probably the most exciting thing that's ever happened at this radio station. Even Ashley is trembling with excitement.

"Freckles," I start. "You don't have to—"

"Don't you *dare* interrupt her," Hughie chides.

"I know I messed up." Blake's voice trembles. "I pushed you away, and I said things that I wish I could take back. I'm not going to repeat them here, because I don't want the whole world knowing our business. Maybe just part of our business. I said a lot of things, but the one thing I never said is that I love you."

I grip the edge of the table, suddenly needing to steady myself. Those words in my ear—and apparently everyone else's ears—release a flood of emotion inside me.

"I love you," she repeats. "I love the way you look at me like I'm worth writing songs about. I love how you see me. Like, *really* see me. And I miss that. I miss being seen by you, and I can't go another day feeling the absence of that. The absence of *you*."

My eyes burn, and I'm worried I'm dangerously close to crying. On live fucking radio.

"You were right. I was telling myself stories too. That I'm not special compared to other people. I thought that if I hid in the background, nobody would notice how unimpressive I was. But you know what? I don't need to impress anyone but myself. And maybe you, because I want you to be proud of me."

Proud of her? Jesus Christ. I don't think I've ever been prouder in my life. The girl of my dreams is professing her love on live fucking radio. It's the kind of magic that people like me sing about.

"So if you mean it and nothing's changed, then maybe when you finish your interview, you can come down to the lobby, because that's where I am right now," Blake says. "Waiting for you."

Silence. The entire studio is still and silent. Even Hughie looks a bit misty-eyed.

Swallowing hard, I glance at the hosts. "Would you be mad if I left?"

Ashley lets out a breathless, squeaky laugh. "Oh my God, go get her already."

I rip off my headphones, and I'm out that door in a heartbeat. Down the narrow hall toward the stairwell, because the station is only two floors and I'm not waiting for a damn elevator. I hurl myself down the stairs two at a time, bursting into the lobby only seconds later.

There she is. Looking beautiful as ever in jeans and a hoodie. *My* hoodie, I realize. It's my old band sweatshirt, which she must've taken with her from Tahoe. I hadn't even noticed it was missing.

Her hair is in a braid, strands falling into her eyes, and she pushes them behind her ear before casting a smile in my direction. The smile that stops my world.

For a moment, I don't move. Eyes locked on her. Afraid that if I blink, she might vanish.

Then she says, "Hi," and the dam of emotion breaks.

I reach her in three long strides and wrap my arms around her. She hugs me back, crushing herself against me, clinging to me.

When she peers up at me, I see the sincerity shining in her eyes. "I meant everything I said. I love you, Wyatt. And I'm so sorry. After the hospital, I just… I think I lost my mind a little."

"I'm not angry, baby. I told you I was going to wait."

And I did wait, because I always knew she would come back to me. That what we had this summer wasn't just a fantasy or a beautiful dream. It was real. I felt it, and so did she.

"I'm afraid," Blake admits.

"Of what?"

"Of how much I love you. How much I want to be with you." Her voice shakes. "I'm afraid that there's someone else who can make you happier than I can."

"Jesus, freckles. That's impossible. Nobody else makes me feel the way you make me feel." I stroke her cheek. "Do you remember the night on the roof? The boathouse? You said you wanted to be someone's obsession. Their undoing. Well, you're mine, Blake Josephine Logan. You want obsession? I think about you every goddamn day. When we're in the same room together, I have to force myself not to look at you too long because I know I'll never look away."

Her eyes well up, and I run my thumbs along the bottom of them, catching the tears before they fall.

"I love you." My voice grows hoarse, and I have to stop to clear my throat. "I need you to tell me you believe me."

"I believe you—"

I crash my lips over hers before she can finish, kissing her the way I've wanted to kiss her since we left Tahoe. She rises on her tiptoes and kisses me back, hungry and desperate, as if she's missed this as much as I have, and we stand there kissing in the lobby of a radio station in Boston, the rest of the world forgotten.

My breathing is ragged by the time I pull back. "You being here..." I swallow to moisten my arid throat. "Does that mean you're coming with me on tour?" I hastily add, "It's okay if the answer is no—"

"Yes," she interrupts, her eyes shining. "The answer is obviously yes, Wyatt."

"What about school?"

"I'm graduating early."

"And the podcast?"

"We're recording it over video call until I get back."

My heartbeat refuses to regulate, hammering wildly against my ribs. "You're really doing this? You're coming with me?"

"Yes." Her eyes, those gorgeous blue eyes, gleam with reassurance. "There's nowhere else I'd rather be."

# Epilogue

**DEAN'S FRIENDS**

ALLIE HAYES

Sorry to create yet another group chat, but I'm getting worried and I think we need a parents' meeting.

ALLIE HAYES

The boys still aren't speaking.

JAKE CONNELLY

Give em time.

DEAN DI LAURENTIS

They'll settle it on their own.

ALLIE HAYES

It's been almost a year! Brenna, back me up.

BRENNA CONNELLY

I refuse to participate until you change the name of the group chat back to what it was.

DEAN DI LAURENTIS

It didn't have a name before!

BRENNA CONNELLY

Exactly.

*ALLIE HAYES CHANGED THE NAME OF THE GROUP CHAT TO GROUP CHAT.*

DEAN DI LAURENTIS

Get your generic bullshit out of here, Allie-Cat.

*DEAN DI LAURENTIS CHANGED THE NAME OF THE GROUP CHAT TO HOT PEOPLE ONLY.*

BRENNA CONNELLY

I'll accept that one.

## GOLDEN BOYS

WYATT GRAHAM

AJ, just heard you're not coming to Tahoe this summer? Wtf? I haven't seen you in ages.

AJ CONNELLY

You were on tour.

WYATT GRAHAM

Tour ended two months ago...

GRAY DAVENPORT

Dude, you're fucking coming to Tahoe.

AJ CONNELLY

I'm working.

And I already told you to quit asking me shit in this chat. Family emergencies only, otherwise I'm out. Message me solo next time.

GRAY DAVENPORT

So fucking dramatic.

GARRETT GRAHAM

Bro, if they actually get married, we'll finally be related.

JOHN LOGAN

Do you think Dean and Tuck are jealous of us?

GARRETT GRAHAM

Obviously.

Content warning: This book contains sensitive material, including discussions of pregnancy loss. Please consider before reading.

# Acknowledgments

This book was a joy to write. Not only because I adore these two characters, but because it allowed me to revisit the Off-Campus world and see our OGs as parents. Getting to experience John Logan as a dad was honestly so much fun. I can't remember the last time I laughed that hard while writing a book.

A quick note: Although *Love Song* takes place in a real location, I took a lot of liberties, and what you're reading is a fictionalized version of Lake Tahoe. For example, while some of the ghost stories I mention are indeed real legends, the major one is entirely a figment of my imagination. And while there is a real lighthouse in Tahoe, I created a fictional one on the island to suit the plot. I also fudged a few locations/neighborhoods. So, if you're a resident of Tahoe, please rest assured that any errors were most likely intentional.

While the writing process itself is a solitary one, getting this book into your hands couldn't happen without the help and support of some pretty amazing people:

My editor, Christa Désir, who helped me shape the story into its best version and really helped me understand these characters. Thank you for being you.

Everyone at Bloom Books for their hard work on not just this release, but all my releases, with a huge shout-out to Madison Nankervis, who tirelessly works to market my books and makes everything sparkle (and for whom I will purchase a black market Labubu and have it shipped across an ocean because I love her THAT MUCH).

The team at Raincoast who champion my books in Canada—Jamie and Christina, I adore you!

My agent, Celeste Fine, and the rest of the Park, Fine & Brower team—Haley, Charlotte, Andrea, John, Emily, Stephanie, Angela, Abby, and Kat. You are a well-oiled machine, and I am eternally grateful to have you on my team.

Eagle/Aquila Editing for always dropping everything to proofread for me.

Team Elle Kennedy: Natasha, Nicole, Erica, and Lindsey and Shaye from Good Girl PR. I would wither away without you. And I'd laugh a lot less. You guys make my day, every day.

And as always—you. The readers. The reviewers. The bloggers. The influencers. Book-lovers. You are my greatest support, and the reason I'm able to do what I do. I appreciate you, forever.

Love,

Elle

# About the Author

John Russo

A *New York Times*, *USA Today*, and *Wall Street Journal* bestselling author, Elle Kennedy grew up in the suburbs of Toronto, Ontario, and holds a BA in English from York University. From an early age, she knew she wanted to be a writer and actively began pursuing that dream when she was a teenager.

Elle is the author of more than fifty contemporary fiction and romance novels, published by a variety of major houses. Her work includes the Off-Campus series, the global phenomenon that has captivated millions of readers around the world.

Website: ellekennedy.com
Facebook: AuthorElleKennedy
Instagram: @ElleKennedyAuthor
TikTok: @ElleKennedyAuthor

www.ingramcontent.com/pod-product-compliance
Lightning Source LLC
LaVergne TN
LVHW100500110826
845146LV00002B/462

* 9 7 8 1 4 6 4 2 4 7 0 3 3 *